CONTEMPORARY AMERICAN FICTION

THE BURNING WOMEN OF FAR CRY

Rick DeMarinis is the author of four previous books. His stories have recently appeared in *Harper's, Antaeus, Cutbank, The Quarterly,* and *The Antioch Review.* His collection *Under the Wheat* won the prestigious Drue Heinz Prize in 1986; his latest collection, *The Coming Triumph of the Free World,* is being published by Viking. DeMarinis lives in Missoula, Montana.

W9-DAG-587

THE
BURNING WOMEN
· OF FAR CRY ·

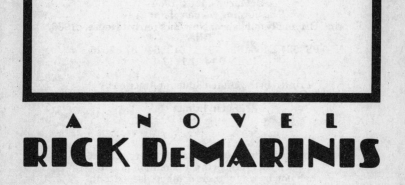

A NOVEL
RICK DeMARINIS

PENGUIN BOOKS

PENGUIN BOOKS
Published by the Penguin Group
Viking Penguin Inc., 40 West 23rd Street,
New York, New York 10010, U.S.A.
Penguin Books Ltd, 27 Wrights Lane,
London W8 5TZ, England
Penguin Books Australia Ltd, Ringwood,
Victoria, Australia
Penguin Books Canada Ltd, 2801 John Street,
Markham, Ontario, Canada L3R 1B4
Penguin Books (N.Z.) Ltd, 182–190 Wairau Road,
Auckland 10, New Zealand

Penguin Books Ltd, Registered Offices:
Harmondsworth, Middlesex, England

First published in the United States of America by
Arbor House Publishing Company 1986
Published in Penguin Books 1988

The first chapter of this book originally appeared
as the short story "Gent" in the collection
The Best American Short Stories 1984,
edited by John Updike.

LIBRARY OF CONGRESS CATALOGING IN PUBLICATION DATA
DeMarinis, Rick, 1934–
The burning women of Far Cry.
Reprint. Originally published: New York : Arbor House, c1986.
I. Title.
PS3554.E4554B8   1988   813'.54   87-32826
ISBN 0 14 01.1117 4

Printed in the United States of America by
R. R. Donnelley & Sons Company, Harrisonburg, Virginia
Set in Primer

—PART 1—

A YEAR after my father shot himself my mother married a two-faced hardware salesman named Roger Trewly. In public, Roger Trewly smiled as if someone holding a gun on him had said, "Look natural, Roger." At home, though, he was usually cross and sullen and would rarely answer civilly if spoken to. He was a crack salesman and was once awarded a plaque engraved with the words: *Ace of Hand Held Tools.* There is a photograph that records the event. He is standing with the owner of the store, Mr. Fenwick, in front of a display of braces-and-bits, hammers, rip saws, and planes. Both men are smiling, but the difference in their smiles has stuck in my mind through the years. Mr. Fenwick is smiling like a man who has just been found naked in the girl's gym and isn't at all humiliated by it. There's a ferocious gleam in his eyes challenging anyone to file a complaint. He looks like a well-to-do madman, capable of anything, absolutely sure of everything. Roger Trewly is smiling as though he's just spilled boiling coffee in his lap at the church social. His face shines with desperate sweat and his begging eyes are fixed on Mr. Fenwick. If you cover the lower half of Roger Trewly's face with your thumb, you will see that his small, pale eyes have no smile in them at all. They have a puzzled, frightened cast, wide with adrenaline. They are the eyes of a man who has understood nothing of the world in his thirty-five years.

Rick DeMarinis

That anxious, kowtowing smile tries to hide this terrifying vertigo, but I don't think Roger Trewly fooled very many people. When my father, who was a war hero, braced his deer rifle against his heart and pressed the trigger with a forked twig, everyone was shocked. But when Roger Trewly jumped off the Mill Avenue bridge into the heavy rapids of the Far Cry River, no one in town was surprised, least of all my mother. "I saw it," she said. "I saw it coming."

MOTHER was only thirty-two years old the spring that Roger Trewly drowned himself, but four years of living with a terror-struck two-faced man had taken the bloom off her spirit. She didn't have gray hair yet, she didn't have wrinkled skin, she had not become bent or shaky or forgetful, but she acted like an older woman with not a whole lot left to live for. If you weren't a child, and could see things for what they were, you would have called her beautiful in spite of the lines and hollows of weariness that masked her true face. She was petite, almost tiny, with high, youthful breasts, and her hair was the color of polished mahogany. She kept it long and she brushed it until it crackled with a suggestion of dark fire. She had large, widely spaced eyes, the gray-specked green of imperfect emeralds, and a smile that made you want to jump up and do chores. My father, who was a large, powerful man, called her "doll." He loved to pick her up in his strong arms and whirl her through the house whistling or singing, like a happy giant whose dreams had come true at last.

"MA, you're so pretty!" my sister, LaDonna, said one bright summer afternoon in 1952, a little over a year after Roger Trewly killed himself. Mother was dressed up for the first time since the funeral. "Look, Jack!"

4

LaDonna said, pulling me into mother's bedroom. "She looks like a princess!"

It was true. She was beautiful in her dark blue dress and white, high-heeled shoes and little "pillbox" hat. Her face had recovered its sharp-edged prettiness. She looked young and exotic. Her perfume struck me like a shocking announcement. We both put our arms around her and hugged her tight. "Princess! Princess!" we yelled, imprisoning her in our linked arms. I'd turned twelve years old that spring and shouldn't have been carrying on like that, but I was as overwhelmed by her as LaDonna was. She had come out of herself at last, like a butterfly out of its winter cocoon, and we clung to her as if we knew there was a real danger of her flying away from us. But she pried off our greedy arms and said, "Don't! You'll wrinkle me! I'm only going out on a date!"

She went out into the living room where the man was waiting. I hadn't realized that a stranger had entered the house. His name was Gent Mundy, the owner of Mundy's Old Times Creamery. LaDonna and I stood in front of mother like a double shield between her and this man, but we were only a nuisance and she sent us outside to play. And when Gent Mundy asked her to marry him several weeks later, we accepted the news like the condemned victims of a rigged jury.

GENT lived in a large, slate-gray house next to his creamery on the main east-west street of Far Cry. We were all invited there to have dinner with him. After cookies and coffee in the living room, he gave us a tour.

"This would be your room, Jackie," he said to me. "My" room was on the second floor. It had a large dormer window that looked out on the parking lot of the creamery where all the milk trucks were kept when they were not making deliveries. The room was about twice as big as the one I had at home, and the walls had been freshly painted light blue. There was a "new" smell in the room, and I realized then that all the furniture still had price tags on it.

Next he showed us the room he and mother would have. It was half again as big as my room, and the bed in it had a bright pink canopy. Mother sat on the bed and bounced lightly up and down twice. "This *is* something," she said, the thin light of greed sharpening her eyes. Gent sat next to her and the bed wheezed. The depression he made in the bed forced her to sag against him. She looked like a child next to his bulk.

"I think she's warming up to the idea, kids," he said, winking nervously. He was bald, and the top of his head was turning pink in mottled patches. It looked like a map of Mars, the rosy, unknown continents floating in a white, fleshy sea. Gent Mundy was a tall man. He had a heavy torso, but his legs were painfully thin, almost spindly. His chest sloped out into a full, belt-straining stomach. His large head made his shoulders seem abnormally narrow. He had alert, pale blue eyes and a wide, friendly mouth that was fixed in a permanent half smile, a smile warned off suddenly, as though by a cautionary second thought. He was an odd-looking man, but he was friendly and alive and open to everything that was going on around him. He wasn't powerful and wild like my father, but he wasn't two-faced and careful like Roger Trewly, either.

He was especially attentive to Mother. If she sighed, he would put his arm around her small waist as if to boost her morale. If she touched her nose before sneezing, he would quickly have his handkerchief ready. If she looked bored or disinterested, he would smoothly change to a livelier subject of conversation. If she began to rant at length about some ordinary injustice, he'd listen carefully to every word, and then, to prove he shared her concern, he'd repeat verbatim certain things she had said.

Some deep and fragile longing made him fall colossally in love with her. I almost winced to see it, even though I didn't understand what I was seeing or why it moved me to wince.

He made something of her name, Jade, and of her size. "Tiny perfect jewel," he once called her. "Jade, Jade, how I'd like to set you in gold and wear you on my finger!" When he said things like this, his eyes would get vague with tears.

LaDonna's prospective room was next to mine. Instead of fresh paint on the walls, it had new wallpaper —fields of miniature daisies against a light green background. "I had this done especially for you, honey," he told her, his voice low and secretive, as if it were a private matter between just the two of them.

Gent was forty-eight years old and had never been married. "I think I have a lot to offer you," he said, after the tour. We returned to the living room and sat down uneasily in the large, overstuffed chairs. Gent made some fresh coffee and poured each of us a cup. I picked up a *National Geographic* and thumbed through it. LaDonna picked up the silver cream pitcher. She brought it close to her face to study it. Mother held her steaming cup of coffee several inches from her lips, blowing thoughtfully. Careful lines appeared on her forehead. A tall clock ticked patiently in the polished hallway. A black woman with low-slung breasts and dusty feet was talking to a white man in a sun helmet. I turned the page to an article about funeral customs in Sumatra. Gent was sweating now, and he mopped his head with his napkin. "Well, no," he said, as if agreeing to some unspoken criticism. "I'm no Casanova, I grant you that. I'm no Tyrone Power, that's for sure! But I am moderately well off. I can provide handsomely for all three of you. The milk business . . . " And here he seemed to be stumped for the precise words. A dreamy look came over his face and he smiled at the perplexity of the thing in his mind. " . . . is, is a *good* business." His face reddened, and his forehead was lacquered again with sweat.

Mother put the cup to her lips and drew a little hissing sound from it that made all three of us lean toward her. We were poor. Mother had a little pension, but it barely put food on the table and paid the rent. My father was out of work when he shot himself, and Roger Trewly, even though he was the "Ace of Hand-Held Tools," never made enough to keep up with the bills.

Mother set the cup down and said something. Her back was straight and some untamable pride made the small muscles around her mouth rigid.

"What was that, Jade?" Gent said, leaning closer to her. "What was that your wonderful mother said, kids?"

LaDonna stood up. "It was yes," she said sternly. "Our wonderful mother said yes, she will be happy to marry you, Mr. Mundy."

LaDonna was like that. She saw the truth of a situation and spoke her mind easily, and often with a sharp tongue. Though she was only eleven years old at the time, she had her future planned. She was going to be a scientist. She had no doubts about this. Her hero was Albert Einstein. A picture of the long-hair genius hung on her bedroom wall. She claimed to understand the general drift of his writings, if not all the math involved. She said that Einstein knew everything he would ever know when he was sixteen, he just hadn't found the words to put it in. She had an aggressive curiosity about nearly everything, and an ice-cold, relentless intelligence to back it up. I always knew she was something special, though her detached brilliance sometimes worried me.

When she was seven she made a jigsaw puzzle out of a frog, a salamander, and a cat-killed flicker. She spread out their innards on the backyard picnic table, trying to match them, organ for organ. The big and small differences fascinated her. Mother threw a fit when she saw the slimy, sun-pungent mess and called her Little Miss Frankenstein. But LaDonna was also affectionate and full of ordinary eleven-year-old ideas.

So, when LaDonna said yes for mother, it was with such crisp authority that Gent clapped his hands together and said, "Oh, Jade, you don't know how happy you've made me! You'll never regret this, I promise!"

LaDonna and I liked Gent, though he was overly neat and too concerned with cleanliness. One day, while visiting our house, he began to fidget. We were all sitting at the kitchen table waiting for mother to take a box cake out of the oven. Finally Gent pushed away from the table and found himself an apron. "I'll clean up a little while we're waiting," he said. He began to sponge-clean the sink and the counter next to it. Then he went after the greasy stove top with Ajax and a hard-bristle brush. When he finished that, he knelt down and searched the floor for dust balls. There were no dust balls. Dust that found its way into the kitchen got mixed almost instantly with the haze of grease that covered everything. Mother wasn't a very good cook and preferred to fry most of our food. When she cooked for us, grease hung in the air like fog. Gent ran a finger along the base of the counter. He stood up then, a gummy gray wad stuck to his uplifted finger, his half smile bravely in place.

"Christ on a crutch, Gent," Mother said. "You don't have to do that." She stood up and tried to yank loose his apron ties. But Gent danced nimbly out of reach.

"No, no, Jade," he said. "Honestly, I don't mind at all. In fact, I like to tidy up. I've been a bachelor for nearly half a century!" He scraped and scrubbed until the whole kitchen gleamed. Mother watched him from her place at the table. She lit a cigarette and blew smoke noisily through her teeth. After Gent finished mopping the kitchen floor, he found the vacuum cleaner and went to work on the living room carpet.

"No, no!" he yelled over the sucking roar, as if someone was trying to change his mind. "Let me do it! I don't mind a bit!"

He was wearing a suit. The apron had pink and white checks, with a ruffled trim. He had thrown his green, hand-painted tie over his left shoulder as if to keep it out of the way of the machine.

Mother got up and went outside. I watched her through the kitchen window. She crossed the backyard slowly and sat down at the picnic table. She lit another cigarette and stared into the hedge at the end of our property. A neighborhood cat jumped up on the table next to her, its vertical tail quivering, but Mother swept it away with a quick flash of her arm.

THE night before Gent and Mother were to be married, Gent gave me a present. It was a dark blue suit with powerful gray stripes running through it. He also gave me a stiff, blue-white shirt and a shiny red tie with a picture of a trout painted on it. The trout had a red-and-white lure in its mouth. Big drops of water flew off its head like sweat.

"Christ God!" Mother said when she saw me in my new outfit. "Look at you, Jackie! It's the president of the First National Bank himself!" She was honestly taken by my appearance. She pressed both hands flat against her stomach and laughed nervously. I went into her bedroom and looked at myself in the full-length mirror. I raised an eyebrow and frowned and curled my lips, one side of my mouth up, the other side down. I didn't look bad. I felt I looked handsome in that ugly gangster way. "Say your prayers, sucker," I snarled, imitating Edward G. Robinson.

Gent fixed us dinner that day. Mother had allowed the kitchen to get grimy again, but Gent cleaned it before he started cooking. He was a good cook. He made a standing rib roast, scalloped potatoes, and three kinds of vegetables blanketed in a rich yellow sauce. I wore my blue suit to the table. LaDonna had received a new dress for the occasion. Gent was very generous to us. I had found a ten-dollar bill in the inside coat pocket of the suit, and LaDonna had found a five pinned to her skirts. I ate dinner like a steel robot, but still managed to get salad dressing on my tie and yellow sauce on my coat sleeve.

The wedding took place in a minister's back office. It was stuffy and hot in there, and my blue suit made me feel sick, so I slipped out the door just as the minister was getting up a head of steam on the subject of the good marriage and how easily it can jump the tracks and wreck itself in the rocky ravine of neglect. Good grooming, for instance, said the minister. Married folks tend to let themselves go as they gradually become familiar with one another. I saw Gent wink at mother when the minister said this, for Gent was nothing if not neat. And then, said the minister, there are the cat-footed evils of spite, inattention, and the always misguided sense of independence. Amen, Doc, said Gent, under his breath.

I felt better out in the street. It was a cool day in early autumn. I walked to the closest drug store and bought a pack of cigarettes. The clerk didn't blink an eye. I guess I looked smoking age in my blue suit, shirt, and tie. I also bought a cigarette lighter that had the shape of a leaping fish. It looked pretty much like the trout that was jumping on my tie. The idea of my tie and cigarette lighter matching each other appealed to me.

I walked back to the church learning how to inhale.

Rick DeMarinis

The smoke made me dizzy in an agreeable way. I knocked the ash off my cigarette several times so that I could use my fish-shaped lighter to light up again. Lighting up needed a style, and I studied myself in store windows trying to perfect one. When I reached the church, I sat down on the front steps and lit up again. Some kids ran by pointing at me and yelling, "I'm gonna te-ell, I'm gonna te-ell," but I blew some smoke at them and laughed suavely at their childishness.

After the wedding we went for a drive in the country in Gent's Buick Roadmaster, a black four-door sedan the size of a hearse. Gent parked next to an abandoned railroad depot. Mother and Gent walked down the old weedy railbed, and LaDonna and I explored the decaying brick depot. I found a set of ancient water-stained tickets that would have taken someone all the way to Chicago.

The windows of the depot were broken out and the floor was littered with a dank mulch of shattered glass and slimy leaves. I lit up a cigarette. LaDonna watched me with slowly widening eyes. I acted as though smoking was a trifle boring, as though smoking for us veterans was something to be endured fatalistically, like old wounds that would never quite heal.

I gave LaDonna a drag. Her brave curiosity wouldn't let her refuse. She drew a lungful of smoke. I could see that she wanted to choke it out, but she wouldn't let herself. "Give me one," she said, the words grating on her parched vocal cords. I gave her one and lit it for her. She inhaled again and blew smoke furiously out her nose, her teeth grinding together in a tough smile.

"L.S./M.F.T.," I said, imitating the radio commercial.
"What?"
"Lucky Strike means fine tobacco," I said. "So round, so firm, so fully packed, so free and easy on the draw."
She looked at the white cylinder in her hand. "Tastes like burning crap," she said.

We walked out onto the crumbling platform where people from another generation caught trains for Chicago. We could see Mother and Gent hugging down the railbed in the shade of an old rusted-out water tower. They kissed. Gent in his dark brown suit looked like a top-heavy bear. He was so much taller than Mother that he had to lean down and hunch his back as he gathered her in his arms. The kiss was long and awkward and Mother dropped her purse into the weeds. She tried to lean away from him to retrieve it, but Gent held her fast in his desperate arms, his legs spread for power. It looked like a bear had caught up with a Sunday picnicker. I took out my fish lighter and watched them through a curtain of orange flame.

My suit and tie made me look older, and smoking made me feel older. Feeling older widened my interests. I took a bunch of Gent's magazines up to my room once. I got them out of his office, which was a large paneled room next to the kitchen. Some of the magazines had full-color pictures of women wearing skimpy bathing suits. Others were of a more general interest. I read a *National Geographic* article about the home life of Stone Age people. There were some drawings to go along with the article. The drawings showed short stubby women with furry tits tending a fire. They had faces only a zoo keeper could love. In the hazy distance, a group of short men without foreheads were carrying a huge woolly carcass of some kind. The caption under this drawing said: "THE BACKBONE OF DOMESTIC HARMONY IS THE SUCCESS-FUL HUNT."

I set the magazine aside and looked at the pictures of the women in bathing suits. These were modern women —long-legged, smooth, with faces that were angelic and yet available. They seemed to radiate heat. The Stone Age men in the *National Geographic* would have murdered entire forests full of woolly animals for a smile from one of those faces.

I'd been lying on top of my bed in my pajamas, but now I felt too restless and warm to go to sleep. I got up and put on my suit. I watched myself smoke cigarettes for a while in the mirror above my dresser. I looked good, I was developing style. I wished my neck wasn't so skinny. I cinched my red tie, drawing the loose shirt collar tighter around my throat.

It was late, but I went into their room anyway. I guess I wanted some adult company. I snapped on the overhead light. There was a great rolling commotion in the canopied bed. I sat down in the chair next to Mother's vanity and lit a cigarette.

"Say, listen to this," I said, flipping open the magazine I had brought with me. "This story is about a day in the life of a linoleum cutter. It tells about this Stanley Wallach. He cuts linoleum twelve hours a day in Perth, Australia, and hopes to save enough money in twenty years to buy his own island. He's going to call it New Perth and crown himself king. King Stanley the First."

"Jackie," Mother said, sitting up in bed. "You shouldn't come barging into a bedroom like that. You're old enough to know better."

I felt suave in my suit. I put out my cigarette just so I could light another one. I wanted them to see my style. Gent was sitting on the edge of the bed, his back to me, his large pale head in his hands. He was in his shorts. I blew a recently perfected smoke ring toward them, winking.

"When did you start smoking?" Mother asked.

But I only crossed my legs and laughed in a sophisticated way, sort of tossing my head back and winking again, this time at the ceiling. I felt clever. I felt that I more or less had an adult's grasp of things.

"And there's this family," I continued, "who talk backasswards to each other, if you can swallow it. No one but themselves can get what they're saying. It's like a foreign country right in the middle of the neighborhood."

"Jack, old boy," said Gent, getting heavily to his feet. The lump in his long shorts swung as he stepped around the big bed. His bulky stomach rolled above his thin white legs. "Jack, you really ought to tap on a door before storming in like that."

I thought for a few seconds, then said, "Sklof, taht tuoba yrros."

"What?" Gent said.

"That's how they must do it," I said. "Talking backasswards."

Mother took a deep breath. It looked like she was about to smile. "Jackie . . . ," she said.

I blew a fat doughnut straight up into the ceiling. "Okay, okay," I chuckled. "I can take a hint." I winked at them. Smoking had also given me a stylish chuckle, a husky little bark that trailed off into a world-weary wheeze. I stood up and yawned. I stubbed out my cigarette in their ashtray. "Guess I'll hit the old sackeroo," I said. "See you people in the morning."

I strolled slowly out of their room, as if the reluctance was theirs, not mine.

MONEY and a nice big house made all the difference to Mother. She now looked young and happy again. She had a lively bounce to her walk and she wore makeup every day. She bought herself a new dress on the first of every month and her collection of shoes outgrew her closet. She looked beautiful in the morning in her red silk duster and lavender mules, and she looked beautiful in the afternoon in her expensive dresses.

Gent was proud to have such a good-looking young woman for his wife and he made no secret of it. Her small size thrilled him, just as it had my father. But where my father would pick her up and dance her through the house, Gent seemed almost afraid to touch her, as if she were made of rare porcelain.

He would take us for Sunday car rides in the Roadmaster just to show her off to the town. Mother would sit in the front seat next to Gent with her skirts hiked up for comfort, and LaDonna and I would sit in the back, reading the comic section. The Roadmaster had a radio, and Mother would search the dial for music as we idled in second gear through the streets of Far Cry.

The town on the north side of the river was usually smoky because of the tepee-shaped chip burners the lumber mills used to get rid of waste. On the south side, the air had a sulfurous sting to it because of the paper mill. On Sundays, though, the air on both sides of the river was not so bad. We'd drive down the tree-lined streets of the north side, and then, if we felt like it, we'd cross the Mill Avenue bridge and cruise the wider, treeless streets of the south side. Sometimes Gent would pull over and park and we'd listen to the radio for a while. People on the sidewalks, looking into the car, would smile and nod as if to approve our way of killing Sunday.

MOTHER had a baby by Gent Mundy. It was a big baby and the delivery was an ordeal. It gave her milk leg and she had to stay in bed for nearly a month after she got home from the hospital. The head of the baby was so large that for a time the doctor thought it would not be able to pass through the birth canal. And when it did pass, it tore her badly. Gent felt terrible about this. I saw him once kneeling at her bedside, crying loudly, his face in his hands. But Mother healed quickly and soon the big, happy-dispositioned baby became the central attraction at our house.

They named him Spencer Ted. Spencer Ted looked

like Gent, and Gent couldn't get over it. "The Mundy heir," he'd say, amazed. If I was in earshot, he'd get flustered and add, "No offense to you, Jack." But it didn't matter to me since no boy of thirteen cares much about inheriting a creamery. "My precious strapping fellow," Gent would coo to the big, round-headed baby, and if either LaDonna or I were nearby, he'd insist, "But, say, I love you kids too, just as if you were my own!"

All this didn't matter to LaDonna or me. We liked Gent because he was easygoing and generous. He gave us practically anything we wanted. LaDonna hinted for a microscope of her own, and Gent went right down to the Sears outlet and ordered an expensive binocular microscope complete with lab kit. I barely complained one day about having to ride my old, rusty Iver-Johnson bike, and the next afternoon after school I found a beautiful new Schwinn on the front porch, complete with basket, headlight, foxtails, and horn.

It didn't matter to me or LaDonna that Gent loved Spencer Ted best because we loved the new baby, too. He was happy as a cabbage and cute in an odd sort of way. All babies are more or less cute, but Spencer Ted's cuteness wasn't baby cuteness. It was the cuteness of joke postcards, where unlikely combinations are relied on to produce a humorous effect. Like a fish wearing a saddle and a cowboy in the saddle twirling a rope, or a poodle smoking a pipe and reading the newspaper. With Spencer Ted, it was a fringe of red hair around his ears, which made him look like an old scholar, and a round, tomato-red nose, which made him look like a seasoned drinker. He had deep-set, coal-black eyes that missed nothing, and radiantly pink ears that bloomed under his fringe of hair like roses.

Spencer Ted seemed as pleased with the brand-new world as Gent was with his brand-new heir. Often LaDonna and I would take Spencer Ted out for a walk in his stroller, and when we did this, LaDonna liked to pretend that we were his parents. It was a game that tickled her, and she would say things such as, "We must find a suitable nurse for our darling little man, dear." She would speak in a stagy voice and people near us would wink and chuckle, for we were only children ourselves.

Sometimes we would sit down on a park bench and LaDonna would hold Spencer Ted in her lap. Being held in a lap was a signal for him and he would begin turning his big round head impatiently, looking for a full breast. This made LaDonna nervous and she would give him his pacifier, which only gentled him for a few seconds. He would spit the pacifier out, arch his back angrily, and then grind his soft, drunkard's face into LaDonna's milkless ribs.

"Mama spank!" LaDonna once said, embarrassed by Spencer Ted's aggressive search for satisfaction, and Spencer Ted, arrested by her sharp, scolding voice, looked at her like an old scholar stumped by an obscure text, his eyes wide with dismay. LaDonna immediately regretted her tone. "Oh, no, Spencey," she said. "Mama would never spank *you.*"

W E always went to Grassy Lake on the Fourth of July. Grassy Lake was a recreational area for the people of Far Cry. Spencer Ted was almost one year old by then, and we took him up to the lake thinking that he'd be thrilled with the fast boats, the long expanse of deep blue water, and the evening fireworks. But he was cranky and balked at everything we tried to interest him in. He sat under the beach umbrella with Gent, fussy and critical, while LaDonna and I made sand castles and Mother swam.

I didn't know Mother could swim, but she swam like a young girl out to the diving platform, which was about fifty yards from shore. LaDonna and I watched her, amazed. When she reached the platform, she pulled herself easily out of the water and stood on the planks, shimmering with wet light. She took off her bathing cap, releasing her long, shining hair. Then she found a sunny spot and lay down on her back.

The arch of her ribs, her nicely muscled legs, the graceful reach of her relaxed arms, and the mass of dark, glossy hair pillowing her head and shoulders made all of us gaze out across the water like the stranded victims of a shipwreck afflicted with thirst-caused visions. It was like a spell. Finally Gent said, in dreamy baby-talk, "Thaz you booly-full Mama, Spencey," and Spencer Ted, recognizing at last the impassable gulf between him and Mother, released a ragged forlorn sob.

LaDonna and I turned our attention back to our sand castles. They weren't very elaborate and we didn't mind wrecking them as soon as we got them built. We erected a city full of sloppy skyscrapers. "Let's A-bomb it," LaDonna said.

I was the B-29, arms out, rumbling through the hot sky, radio chatter of the crewmen alive in my head, sighting in on the muddy skyline of our city. Then, as I approached it, I picked up speed, bomb bay doors open, crew tense, and I released the bomb, Fat Boy. I had to be Fat Boy then, and I fell on the city, back first, squashing it flat and LaDonna made the A-bomb noise, the rolling boom and bleak sigh of the high sweeping wind.

We did this several times, and then I dove into the lake to wash off the mud. I swam out toward the diving platform, thinking to join Mother, but when I looked up I saw that there was a man standing behind her. He was big and heavily muscled. He had black hair, bright as freshly laid tar. He lifted his arms and flexed. The biceps jumped impossibly tall with cords of angry veins, violet under the oiled skin. Then he put his hands on his hips and drew in his stomach until his rib cage arched over the unnatural hollow like an amphitheater. His thighs from his kneecaps to hips were thick with bands of visible muscle. He moved from one pose to another, finally relaxing, hands on hips at a cocky angle, a swashbuckler's smile on his tanned face. Mother glittered like booty at his feet. But she acted as though she didn't see him, or even know he was there.

I swam back to shore, and joined Gent and Spencer Ted under the umbrella. LaDonna was building another city. This one was futuristic, with tall spires and cylinders and oddly concave walls. I got a half-dollar from Gent and bought a package of firecrackers—"ladyfingers"—and a package of "whistlers." I thought we could blow this city up with ordinary explosives, one building at a time. Gent and Spencer Ted took a nap. Gent was lying flat on his back with a towel over his face and Spencer Ted was tucked in the crook of his arm. I was afraid the "whistlers" might wake them, but they didn't.

After the city was wrecked, I watched Mother swim. She stroked the water like a professional channel swimmer, but she wasn't swimming back to us. She was swimming parallel to shore, away from the platform. The muscle man with the black hair was in the water too. He didn't swim as gracefully as Mother. The water churned around him and his black hair whipped from side to side. Even so, he swam much faster than Mother and was soon even with her. They treaded water for a while, about one yard apart. I thought I could hear them talking. Then they swam back to the platform, side by side. He tried to match his stroke to hers, but it wasn't easy for him. While she looked smooth and natural, he looked drugged.

He climbed out of the water first, then helped Mother. He pretended that she was too heavy for him and that she was pulling him off balance. He somersaulted over her into the water with a gigantic splash. Mother climbed up onto the platform, laughing. He joined her and then did a handstand. He began to walk around the perimeter of the platform on his hands while Mother shook out her hair. Mother leaned sharply to one side and then to the other, combing her hair with her fingers, while the muscle man walked on his hands. It looked like some kind of crazy dance.

Gent and Spencer Ted were awake now and looking out across the water at Mother. Spencer Ted's bald head looked like a smaller version of Gent's. Spencer Ted lifted his fat white arm and pointed toward the diving platform. He moaned crankily and blew a fat spit bubble.

It was nearly evening. Soon the fireworks would begin.

GENT'S hobby was the baritone sax. He had played it more or less professionally for two years when he was a young man. The band he'd played for was called Professor Lindstrom's Waltzmasters, a seven-piece outfit that toured the small towns around Far Cry. Gent played his sax now just for the relaxation it gave him. He would sit in the basement playing tunes under a bare bulb next to the oil furnace. The sound traveled through the heat ducts and you could hear him no matter what room of the house you were in. He played almost every evening after supper. LaDonna and I liked to hear him play, and Spencer Ted never failed to get drowsy, as if the music was a lullaby just for him, but Mother didn't enjoy it at all. She would sit in the front room with a magazine spread in her lap and grit her teeth against the sound, which, coming through the heat ducts, sounded more like a murmuring human voice than an instrument.

"Suffering Jesus," she'd say, whipping through the magazine with page-tearing fury.

Sometimes I'd lay in bed and smoke cigarettes while

he played. The songs rattled in my heat register. It seemed like the house was humming absentmindedly to itself.

I dozed once, letting the cigarette fall onto the bedspread. The stink of hot fabric gave me a disturbing dream. I'd been reading one of Gent's nudist magazines, and in my dream I was watching Far Cry burn. There were several women trapped in the upper floors of one building, screaming for help. "I'll get help," I told them, but as I ran through the streets of the town I realized that I didn't know where help was. To make things worse, I was naked among the well-dressed citizens. I got lost and the farther I ran the more unrecognizable things became. But I could still hear the women screaming.

A noise in the hall woke me up. It was Mother, outside my door, cursing. She stomped down the hall and went into her bedroom, slamming the door. I got up and saw what I had done to the bedspread. There was a scorched spot on it the size of a dime.

I went out into the hall and tiptoed toward Mother's bedroom. The door was ajar and I peeked inside. She was lying on the bed, crying.

"What's wrong, Ma?" I asked, unable to check the alarmed waver in my voice.

She'd been lying on her back and now she raised herself on her elbows. Her hair was wild and the look in her eyes made me take a step backward. She had a look on her face that I had seen before, but had forgotten.

"I can't stand it," she said. "I'm going crazy, Jackie."

I entered the room then and said, "What can't you stand?"

She pointed at the heat register. "Among other things," she said, "that god-awful noise."

I closed the heat register and threw a rug over it. Even so, the nasal honk of the big sax murmured in the room. I offered her a cigarette from my pack. My hand, I noticed, was shaking. She looked at me for a long moment. And then I remembered where I'd seen that expression before and why it made me nervous. It was a look she often wore when married to Roger Trewly. Sad and bitter and something worse, something dangerous, like despair. She swung her legs off the bed and accepted my cigarette. The small bones of her hands moved me, the narrow wrists, the incredibly fine hair of her forearms, the delicate upper arms, the neck . . . It took me half a dozen flicks to get my lighter to work and the orange flame it gave illuminated her wet face. She took a deep drag and blew smoke down between her knees. I went back to the doorway and leaned on the jamb.

"What's so bad about it?" I said. "It's just music."

But she only shrugged slightly.

I saw in her dresser mirror that my cigarette was hanging at a perfect angle from my lip. This was something I'd been practicing. The actors Bogart and Ladd were the experts, and I'd been trying to match their style. The rising smoke made me squint. It was the Bogart squint, the Ladd squint. I noticed that the cigarette barely bounced when I talked. I was learning to talk without moving my lips, like Bogart, like Ladd. If the cigarette bounced or jumped around, it made you look foolish and unworldly.

"Music is music," I said, the Lucky Strike rock steady.

"People make mistakes, Jackie," she said. She looked at me, her eyes big and luminous with tears, and I knew then the value of the Bogart-and-Ladd squint.

"Mistakes," I said, my eyes narrow.

"They think they're doing the right thing, but they're only doing the *next* thing, if you follow me."

"Right," I said.

She sobbed loudly then and cupped her hand over her eyes. I wanted to run to her, to kneel before her on the floor and put my head in her lap. But when she took her

hand away from her eyes she seemed like a child herself. She was smiling.

"You'll make your share of mistakes, Jackie," she
said. "Believe me."

I shrugged, raised an eyebrow. "Maybe so, then again,
maybe no."

"Oh, yes, don't worry, you'll put your foot in it a few
times before you're through."

I grinned sagely. "You could be right," I said, "and
then, you could be wrong."

A tender scornfulness lifted the corners of her mouth.
"You'll understand what I'm telling you someday."

I blew a hard jet of smoke across the room. "Hell, Ma,
I *get* the point."

Suddenly she was next to me. Her electrified hair
grazed my cheek and the smell of her—perfume, smoke,
and the thin acidity of sex—backed me through the door
and out into the hallway.

"He's finished playing that goddamned thing," she
said. I noticed for the first time that the music had
stopped. "I'll get dessert on the table."

"Great, Ma!" I said, losing the cigarette. I picked it up
quickly and cupped it in my hand. "Are we having
peach cobbler and whipped cream again?" Cobbler
loaded with big freestone peaches smothered in
whipped cream was my all-time favorite, with a little
cinnamon sprinkled on top.

She touched my cheek with her red-nailed fingertips
and smiled. "I have to pee," she said. "Why don't you run
out to the creamery and get a half-pint of whipping
cream, and then I'll fix some cobbler for you. Okay?"

She kissed me lightly on the cheek. I went down the
stairs, three at a time, whistling.

GENT bought me a secondhand snare drum along with
brushes and sticks. He wanted me to learn a few

rhythms so that I could accompany him now and then. "Some tunes need to have the rhythm laid down before they can be played properly," he said.

"I don't know how to play the drums," I said.

"Don't worry, I'll teach you. There's nothing to it. Sometimes the sax can't stand alone, Jack. The drum gives it a kind of spine."

I'd seen drummers on television and I knew he was wrong about it being easy to do. Watching Gene Krupa could make you dizzy.

Gent saw my dubious frown. "I'm just going to have you learn a few basic rhythms, no fancy stuff, Jack. I want to do some sambas and jump tunes, and maybe a waltz now and then for old time's sake."

He was right. The rhythms he wanted me to play were easy to learn, though it took a while to manage the sticks and brushes. *Thump* boomachick chick-chick-chick-chick-chick, for the samba, Kitty-*cat* kitty-*cat* kitty-*cat,* for jump. The waltz was a dimwit, *run* dog run, *run* dog run.

We would go down into the basement and under the bare bulb hanging from the joists, we would play our tunes. The drum sat on a chrome stand and I sat behind it on an old piano stool. I didn't mind doing this for Gent. In fact, I came to enjoy our little sessions. He was a good teacher and I was a fast learner, and the dreamy sound of the old brass baritone sax was easy to listen to.

Something other than music, though, came out of his horn. Something in it resonated with an inexpressible feeling locked deep inside. Maybe it was loneliness, maybe it was rage, there was no way to know, but it was there, alive and breathing, a third presence in the basement and sometimes it sent a shiver through me. I saw the sax not so much as a musical instrument than as a mechanical device, a syphon that drew feelings out of him that were dangerous to keep.

I saw evidence of it in his face, too. As he played, his

face changed. He would close his eyes and his forehead would crease into a fierce, gull-wing frown. His lips would lock over the mouthpiece in a bloodless snarl, and his nostrils would flare with the effort of pulling air into his struggling lungs. He often looked like he was fighting for his life as the gentle, civilized music rolled from the horn. His ears would get red, his neck would bulge, and his fingers, working the mother-of-pearl valve buttons, would curl into hooks. Sweat poured off his head and his armpits became swampy, even though the songs were mild, old-time favorites, such as "The Anniversary Waltz," "Embraceable You," "Time on My Hands," "Slow Boat to China," "Amor," and "Brazil."

Mother wasn't too happy about my playing the snare drum for him, but she never came out and said so. She might look up from a magazine or television show as Gent and I headed for the basement, glancing sharply at the sticks in my hand as I tapped them together in some rhythm I was working on, but she never said anything more than, "Try not to make too much noise, Jackie," or, "I'm putting dessert on the table in half an hour."

Once when Gent and I were getting worked up over a jump tune called "I'm a Ding Dong Daddy from Dumas," I thought I heard somebody banging the floor above us with something heavy, like a cast-iron skillet. It broke my rhythm for a second, but Gent never lost his fierce determination. He rammed each note home as if everything depended on its perfect expression. If the world was scheduled to end in the middle of a riff, it would have to end without Gent. Gent would keep playing while the continents fell into the oceans and the earth fell into the sun. Time was a tool to give the music a backbone, not the ordinary thing whose passage you either dreaded or prayed for.

* * *

THE disasters that were coming to our household seemed to be linked to our gradual realization that Spencer Ted was not going to be a normal child. By the time he was two years old he stood just three inches short of four feet and weighed over sixty pounds. His fringe of red hair coarsened and grew down the back of his neck and then spread out in fuzzy wisps toward his broad shoulders. He had big bony knees and hard red elbows. His feet were long and wide, the toes fat. His bawl was grand and tireless, a solid tenor wail that could make you want to cover your ears. He called Mother "Marmy" and Gent "Parpy." He called LaDonna "Sissa," and he called me "Burr." When he was hungry it was, "Titta, Marmy! Pencey want titta now!" And when Mother lifted him to her lap he'd make great smacking sounds and reach for her high, full blouse. Mother had tried to wean him, but Spencer Ted would have nothing to do with glass bottles or mashed food on a spoon, and his baleful, ear-splitting bawl made Mother relent.

All this didn't help her moods. LaDonna and I liked Gent a lot and it worried us that Mother was taking everything out on him. And in trying to make things better, Gent only aggravated her further. He started doing most of the cooking and all of the house cleaning. He'd vacuum and scrub, dust and polish, wearing Mother's aprons. He'd set out sumptuous meals for us and garnish the table with a new centerpiece every week. But Mother was cold and indifferent to his efforts. In fact, she seemed to resent his thoughtfulness. Once at dinner, she began to pick on him with a calculated meanness.

"Eat your food like a man," she said, each word delivered like a slap.

LaDonna and I looked at her, shocked.

"Pick, pick," she said.

27

Gent looked up quickly at her, his half smile faltering.

"I said, why don't you at least fill your face like a *man?*"

I saw LaDonna's nostrils turn white as she drew in a deep breath of air. I cleared my throat, as if to speak. I had nothing to say.

"You eat enough to keep two boar hogs alive," said Mother, "but you pretend to nibble, dainty as any girl."

Gent lowered his fork. He stared at his plate, unable to look at her. Though her own plate was nearly full, she lit a cigarette.

Gent had made stuffed porkchops, lyonnaise potatoes, string beans with almonds, Jell-O salad, and a beautiful custard pie was waiting on the sideboard.

"I'm getting old," Mother said. "I'm losing my figure."

"No, no," Gent crooned to his plate.

"Shut up! Look at yourself! Look at me!" She jammed her cigarette into the Jell-O salad and stood up. We all looked at her and she looked at us. There was an empty moment, tense with possibility. I felt anything could happen then, anything at all. The ceiling might have caved in, the table might have burst into flames, the lights might have gone out or gotten a thousand times brighter. I cleared my throat, my mouth opened.

"*You* shut up too!" she said, and stomped away from the table and up the stairs.

Spencer Ted, already too big for his high chair, cut loose with an ear-ringing lament. Gent looked at us, an apologetic grin on his face. You could see his big soft body absorbing blame.

"It's not your fault, Gent," LaDonna said.

My face was hot. I was proud of LaDonna for speaking up. I wanted to say something to Gent, too, but I couldn't think of anything that wasn't outright stupid.

LaDonna tried to give Spencer Ted some Jell-O, but he moved his red face right and left, avoiding the spoon.

"Marmy, Marmy, Marmy, Marmy," he wailed, a dreamy pessimistic chant.

I left the table and went upstairs. I didn't like the way things were going. Things had gone badly before, but I didn't want to believe it was an unavoidable pattern. Life was correctable. That's what I believed in those days.

She was in the bathroom, but the door was wide open. She was sitting on the lid of the john with an unlit cigarette held loosely between her lips. Her legs were crossed. The knee of the top leg was uncovered and the full calf below it bulged. I stepped forward, offering the flame from my trout lighter.

"Isn't life a joke, honey?" she said after she'd taken a few quick puffs to get the tobacco roasting. Tears were streaming down her face and into the corners of her brilliant smile.

The dazzling light of her smile burned my little speech to the ground. I wanted to remind her of our good fortune, of Gent's kindness and generosity, of how good the future of the milk business looked. But now I could only light my own cigarette and squint at her through the smoke.

"You've gone and grown up on me, Jackie," she said, and in spite of myself, I grinned with helpless pleasure. Her tears had damaged her makeup a little, but most of it was still rigidly in place. She looked like a hardened queen, forced to rule over a bitter and useless country.

"Why, just *look* at you, Jack," she said.

New tears fell down her face, but these tears, I believed, were tears of pride.

ONCE a man came to visit while Gent was in the basement by himself playing the sax. Mother brought this man into the front room and served him coffee and doughnuts. I was watching the "Texaco Star Theater" on the Philco, but she snapped the set off and shooed me upstairs to my room. The man, his jaws packed with doughnuts, winked at me as I got up to leave. It was one of those private winks between conspirators. My face got hot and I decided then and there that I didn't like him.

He wore white pants and a black T-shirt with the sleeves rolled up to the shoulders. He had big, fleshy arms, but they didn't give the impression of strength. It was clear that he was proud of his arms because of the elaborate tattoos emblazoned on each bicep. The tattoos were identical: grass-skirted women surrounded by blue bolts of lightning. He wore his hair, which was the color of damp straw, in a rolling pompadour. I guess he was handsome, in a flat-face, broken-nose way, but he had small, shifty eyes. You could tell by looking at him that he thought his best feature was his smile. His teeth were always showing, in a kind of superior leer.

There was a louvered grate in the upstairs hallway that let heat circulate through the house freely, and I used it to spy down on them. I opened the louvers and looked through the grate at the front room. I could see most of it. They were sitting on the couch, laughing and talking. Music from Gent's sax hummed through the house. Mother brought the man a bottle of beer. The man put his hand on her knee. He flexed his fleshy arms and the grass-skirted women threw their hips from side to side in the blue rings of lightning. Mother touched the tattoo on his right arm gingerly, as if the lightning bolts had the power to electrocute. I closed the louvers hard, filling the upstairs hallway with a boom like thunder.

I became a desperate spy in my own house. I hid myself in closets, behind sofas, under the staircase. I found warps and cracks in door frames that could be used as spy holes, and I learned how to use the duct system of the furnace as a kind of listening device. I'd crawl into the big coal furnace, careful not to raise a choking ash dust, and squat down in the middle of it and listen to the ghostly whispers that funneled down the ducts. This, of course, could only be used in the hot summer months.

I learned to identify footsteps, breathing, throat clearing, nose blowing, coughing, and even the length of the silences between the page-turning rattle made by someone reading a newspaper. I went through the mail, checked the grocery lists, inspected the laundry, sifted through garbage. I checked the house for places where incriminating things might have been hidden. I was charged with frantic energy. Outrage and titillation battered my confused heart.

In one of my searches I found some pictures and books in Gent's dresser under his socks. I took them to my room and locked my door. The pictures were of men and women and animals doing things to each other. My throat got dry as I sorted through them. They were very old pictures. They could have been taken in the ancient days of the Roman Empire, if cameras had existed then. The men were stoop-shouldered and skinny and had long beards. The women were hefty and stern and had long, braided hair. They were in a field among the ruins of ancient buildings. Old stone fountains, fragments of statues, and broken columns littered the background. The photographs were tinted yellow, and the once-glossy finishes were webbed with cracks. But they were clear enough. I broke out into a clammy sweat and shoved the pictures under my pillow. I went to the bathroom, my heart fast, my urgent crotch bulging.

When I finished, I went back into my room for a smoke. LaDonna was sitting on my bed thumbing through a book that I'd left out in the open. She was absorbed in it. I sat down next to her and read a sentence over her shoulder: "His pink-helmeted cavalier parted the tender gates of paradise and lingered there momen-

tarily to savor the anticipated delight of his long-
awaited conquest."

"Where in the heck did you *get* this junk?" LaDonna
demanded.

"Gent's dresser," I mumbled.

I felt ashamed, of course, but I was clammy again,
thinking of that pink-helmeted cavalier lingering at the
tender gates of paradise. I took the pictures out from
under my pillow. LaDonna snatched them out of my
hand.

"A *horse!*" she said, her voice husky and unfamiliar.
"She's doing it with a *horse!* That's disgusting!" But I
could see that her moral anger was quickly yielding to
curiosity.

The photograph was titled "Old Bucephalus and
Friend." Old Bucephalus was eating at a tuft of pale
grass. His friend was fixed to his underside by means of
a leather harness. Her large yellow breasts had rolled
nearly into her armpits.

"What they're doing . . . is that scientifically possible?"
LaDonna asked.

"Better check it out with Mr. Einstein," I said, thinking of his picture on her wall. In that picture, Einstein's
sad, watery eyes seemed to be looking out at a hopeless
world.

She picked up the stack of photographs and studied
them one by one. Her eyes were wide and she was biting
her lip. The bridge of her small, well-shaped nose was
white with intensity. Her sharp, scientist's mind absorbed every detail.

When she finished with the stack of pictures she
looked at me. It was a sidelong look, pert with the hun-
ger for knowledge. "Jackie," she said. "Can I ask you
something?"

"Shoot," I said, finally lighting up the cigarette I'd
been holding in my fist. It was slightly bent, the tobacco
falling out of the ends.

"Is yours . . . your *thing,* I mean . . . like that?" She pointed to a picture of a man wearing nothing but gartered socks. He was displaying himself for all to see. He was silly looking, but he had what looked like the top third of a major-league baseball bat to show off.

I squinted at the photograph, cigarette hanging perfectly from my lip. "Nope," I said. "He's circumsized."

"That's not what I meant and you know it," she said primly. "I meant is yours that big when it gets big? I didn't know they could get that big."

I studied the photograph, tilting it one way, then another, squinting through smoke and glare. "He's just an old freak," I said, flipping the picture aside.

"Then you're *not* that big," she said. I didn't especially care for her tone.

I let some smoke trickle out the corners of my worldly grin.

LaDonna went to my desk and rummaged through it until she found a ruler. She picked up the photograph of the old freak and held the ruler against it. "He's about three inches tall," she said. "Now, let's suppose he's about your height, Jack. About five feet seven. That gives us a scale of about twenty-two to one." She moved the ruler on the photograph and brought it close to her face. She looked like a scientist doing serious work in a lab. "His thing is about nine-sixteenths of an inch long." She looked up at the ceiling, eyes shut tight, doing the arithmetic mentally. "Jeepers," she said. "That means in real life it's in the neighborhood of twelve inches!"

I tapped the ash from my cigarette into my pants cuff.

"Maybe in the olden days men were more like horses than they are today," she said. "Maybe things like fallout and DDT made men shrink up."

LaDonna, always the scientist. "Could be," I said. I offered her a cigarette and we both lit up. Then we went through the pictures again.

* * *

I wasn't a happy spy, but I was thorough. I found a Kleenex with lipstick on it under a sofa cushion. The lipstick matched Mother's favorite shade, Fire Engine Red. The impression on the Kleenex wasn't of lips, so it wasn't as if Mother had used it to blot her lipstick dry. It was a crude smear, a wide red scar, as if someone had wiped lipstick off his neck.

I had the uneasy conviction that something large and ominous was happening in our home. It was happening all around me, practically in front of my eyes, but I couldn't see it. It was like being in a movie theater. Your eyes are glued to the screen where all the real interest is supposed to be, but out of the corner of your eye you see something moving. It's the couple next to you. You can hear them breathing, you can hear the wet slide of tongues, you can hear fabric stretching, and you can almost make out the muted words and hot whispers, but if you turn to look at them, they quit.

And that's how it was at home. All I had were suspicious but nonincriminating glimpses: stained Kleenex, hairpins on the carpet, a dollar bill with a word (GAR) printed on it in blue crayon, an empty package of Old Gold cigarettes crumpled in the downstairs bathroom's shower stall, the recurring smell of Vitalis hair oil greasing the air, a green convertible parked now and then among the milk trucks, wild and sudden laughter violating a quiet afternoon.

Mostly I saw the ordinary doings of the household. But sometimes these ordinary doings seemed far-fetched and charged with a strangeness all their own. Once I saw Gent saluting himself over and over in the vanity mirror. Spencer Ted was in the bedroom with him, sitting in the middle of the bed. Gent had dressed Spencer Ted in a little soldier's uniform. He watched Gent snap salutes, turn smartly on his heel, report for duty, stand at attention, move to parade rest, and double-time march in place. Spencer Ted stared at him with slack-jawed fascination.

Gent used a dust mop for a rifle and he gave himself marching orders, imitating the gruff voice of a drill sergeant. Spencer Ted clapped his big red hands together, thrilled, great salvos of drool falling from his mouth.

Then war broke out. Gent dropped into a crouch and fired his dust mop at the enemy. He stood up as if grievously wounded and fell across the bed, causing Spencer Ted to teeter.

"Parpy! Parpy!" Spencer Ted shrieked.

Recovered from his wounds, Gent got up and made savage bayonet stabs into the dresser. He brought the mop end into the window drapes hard, as if clouting an enemy soldier in the face with his rifle butt. Then he sat down on the bed, tired.

"Moe, Parpy! Do moe!" Spencer Ted pleaded.

"No, Spencey. Your pop's winded."

But Spencer Ted always got his way. I think it was his voice that did it. He let out a chuckling howl that made Gent wince. The chuckling tightened into a choking, and his face got purple, and green snot plugged his nostrils.

"Okay, okay, Spencey," Gent said. "A little bit more, and that's all. The trucks are going to come in any minute now."

Gent looked out the window at the street. Then he hid himself behind a drape. When he emerged, he had a sly, wily look on his face. Slowly he bent down and picked up one of Mother's lavender mules. His face was now perilous looking. Then, in a movement too quick for Spencer Ted to follow, Gent bit the toe of the slipper and lobbed it into the closet.

Gent made a big spitty hand-grenade explosion in front of Spencer Ted's face and waved his arms wildly to describe the terrible spray of shrapnel. This so sur-

prised Spencer Ted that he turned bright red and could
not get his breath. When he recovered, he began to sob.
Gent picked him up, grunting with effort. Spencer Ted
was now almost eighty pounds.

Gent sat down on the bed and rocked Spencer Ted in
his lap. The roar of the first milk truck returning from
its route rattled the window. "Daddy's got to go to work
now, Spencey," Gent said, trying to get up. But Spencer
Ted wouldn't slide off Gent's lap. He held on to Gent's
shirt, his white-knuckled fists defiant.

MOTHER'S visitor found Gent's saxophone upsetting.
"That so-called *mu*sic is ruining my mood," he said. He
said it as a kind of warning. They left the house and
went out into the parking lot. I closed the upstairs hallway grate and went into my room. From the window, I
saw Mother and the man climb into a milk truck. The
man took the driver's seat and Mother crouched next to
him in the seatless well. The man put his hands on the
steering wheel and belched so loudly that I could hear
it, even though my window was closed. The parking lot
was lit by a mercury-vapor lamp fixed to a telephone
pole. The man's constant leering smile was a blue glow
under his nose. Mother handed him a quart bottle of
beer and he uncapped it with an elegant gesture that
made you think of champagne. He raised the bottle
high, as if offering a toast, then put it to his lips. As he
drank his long neck worked like a pump. I could see the
muscles of his throat rise and fall, rise and fall. Mother
threw her head back and laughed. I couldn't hear her,
but I could imagine it. She had a wonderful laugh, full
and careless and delicate. She could not stop laughing
at his working neck. She covered her mouth with both
hands and rocked back and forth in the well. Even when
he had finished and had set the bottle down, she kept
laughing. I found myself grinning. He laughed a little

too, but the humor of the situation was less obvious to him than to us. To stop her from laughing, he picked up the bottle and handed it to her as if to say, If you think I'm so funny chugging my beer then let's see you try it. But she only took a little sip and handed the bottle back. He drank some more, tilting the bottle high. As she watched his neck drawing beer into itself, she lost control again. I knew her laugh was infectious, and as I heard it in my mind, I began to laugh too. I laughed until tears rolled down my face. Mother and I were laughing together like crazy at the man's stupid neck. When the man finished off the bottle, he released another explosive belch.

Eventually Mother and I calmed down. The man yawned. Mother touched one of his tattoos and he made the girl jump. I pulled down my shade.

THE man's name was Guy Rampling. He worked for Gent, it turned out, as a milkman. Sometimes Guy would stay for dinner. Gent seemed to like Guy well enough, and Guy conducted himself like a faithful employee in Gent's presence. Gent acted as though he didn't know otherwise. They told each other jokes and off-color stories about adventures in the milk business, and they sometimes tried to discuss politics.

"These bleeding hearts, these eastern egghead pinkos," Guy Rampling said one evening at the dinner table. "My man's McCarthy. He'll put those fruits where they belong."

"McCarthy?" Gent said. "He looks like a gangster to me."

"He's just tough. We need ten more like him in Washington."

"Maybe you should run for office, Guy."

Rampling gave Gent his leering grin, as if the suggestion had already crossed his mind. "I'll tell you true, boss

37

man. This boy would not be afraid to kick some pinko ass."

Guy glared at each of us, as if to make the impression of his toughness stick. "This Stevenson dipshit," he said, pointing a dripping fork at Gent. "Here is your pure example of the Communist front man. I believe he was Moscow-trained, correct me if I'm wrong."

"But he's from an old Illinois family," Gent said.

Guy's eyes bulged, amazed at Gent's gullibility. "There you *go,*" he said. "That's how they *do.* If they *elect* him you can schedule services for the free enterprise system. Those Russkies will have their plumbing up his chute before he takes the oath of office. He'll go to bed that night in the White House and he'll say to the missus, Say Mother, what is that cold hard thing in my chute?" Guy laughed at his own joke.

"Jesus!" said Mother, banging her plate with her fork. "Is politics all you can talk about?" She picked up her steak knife and sawed her baked potato in half.

LaDonna, who had recently become a woman, stood up in a snit. "Excuse me," she said. "I think I've got my monthly." It was an announcement. LaDonna seemed ennobled with a new sense of dignity. Her small breasts knuckled her sweatshirt.

Guy laughed again. His laugh was thin, without much humor in it. "Got a visit from your red-haired aunt?" he said, his easy smile wide and dirty.

"Oh, Christ, Guy!" Mother said. "You're horrible!"

Guy turned his attention to his food. He cut himself a large square of steak. He chewed it slowly, watching Mother with amused eyes as his big jaw labored. But Mother wouldn't meet his gaze, and he fell to serious eating, swarming on his food.

After dinner Gent set up the movie projector. He wanted to show us a film called *The World of Milk.* He had sent away to Portland, Oregon, for it. He set up some chairs in the front room. We sat and waited while he got the screen and projector set up. Then he turned out the lights and started the film. A herd of dairy cows stared out of the screen at us, chewing stupidly. The narrator said, "This is where the miracle we call *milk* begins. On the dairy farm."

"Well kiss my ass and call me cheeky," said Guy. "So that's where it comes from."

I laughed, in spite of myself.

Suddenly there was a diagram of a cow on the screen. The cow was divided up into square rooms connected by ramps. The double stomachs were the biggest rooms. All this was supposed to show how the cow converted hay into milk.

"That's stupid," LaDonna said. She had come back downstairs.

We all turned to look at her. She had changed clothes and had made up her face. The glaze of makeup made her look hot. She was wearing a sweater with a V-neck. There was a little gold chain around her throat. A sweet, nose-tickling perfume radiated from her. Guy held his arms up and made the grass-skirted girls swing their hips. "Hubba, hubba," he said.

A gray-haired, wise-looking man filled the movie screen. "Think about it," he said. "The ancients worshipped the milk-producing cow. For milk was, and is, man's first food. What is more perfect on earth than this bountiful, mother-white ocean? It is the succor of all warm-blooded animals. It is the nectar that swells from the fountain of mother love. It is love-made, love-given, and it is always taken with love. It is the abundant miracle of life we call . . . *milk.*"

A garbled din of violins creaked in the loudspeaker and then the screen went white. We stared at it until the reel began to flap. Guy lit a cigarette and frowned. He looked as if he had been driven into a deep reverie by the film. Then he belched loudly, and as if that was the signal we'd been waiting for, we all stood up and stretched.

L a D o n n a became moody and hard to get along with at times. Maybe it was because she was now a woman. She carried herself differently. Where once she would slouch through the house distracted by some important idea, she now moved with a dignified presence of mind. Shoulders back, head high, eyes cool and serious, she seemed unapproachable and remote. Not that she was actually stuck-up or bad-tempered—it was just the impression she gave. She was still herself, but now she was wrapped in a chilly aura.

Sometimes she could be touchy about minor things she once would have ignored, such as my farting in the bathroom before she got to use it, or the way I combed my hair—slicked back on the sides with pomade, ending in a perfect duck's ass, the top short and pulled forward into leathery curls that clung to my forehead. "It makes you look like one of those greaseballs who talk about hubcaps and hood ornaments all day," she said.

She began to read things that weren't scientific. She bought magazines that had articles with titles such as, "Short Cuts to Glamour" or "Sex Appeal—That Old Chameleon." She kept the picture of Einstein on her bedroom wall, but next to it there was now a larger picture of the squinty-eyed actor James Dean.

Boys began to come by the house, looking for her. They would arrive in clusters on their bikes. They turned in circles in our driveway or out in the street, yelping like spaniels. LaDonna would look down on them from the screened-in porch, as if judging the contest they had invented for themselves. It was either a yelping contest or a trick bike-riding contest. Those who fell off their bikes received a scornful laugh from LaDonna. She would point a severe finger at the fallen rider and shame him to the far side of the street. The others were driven to new heights of daredeviltry by her gestures. Sooner or later she would settle on a favorite. Wallace Porter was the first of these, a tall, turkey-necked boy of fourteen.

LaDonna invited Wallace into the screened porch and the other boys, after yelping at them for a while, took their daredevil bikes elsewhere. LaDonna then treated Wallace like company. It made him jittery and dry-mouthed. Without a gang of other boys around it was useless to bark and howl. He had to fall back on the human voice in all its cautious and well-planned modu-lations, and this made him mumble and stutter. It sounded like his tongue was sticking to the top of his mouth, and from my angle—I was slumped in a corner, pretending to read a *National Geographic*—it looked like he was shaking.

LaDonna brought him lemonade and cookies. I could tell that her formal, courteous tone was making him freeze up. He sat straight and rigid on the porch swing and ate his cookie in small, careful bites.

"Do you wish more lemonade, Wallace?" she said, full of airs. And Wallace, forced to fall back on the human voice, mumbled, "Fill 'er up," his crumb-filled mouth loose in a desperate smile.

After a while they kissed. LaDonna put her glass of lemonade down and clasped her hands behind Wal-lace's neck, forcing his face into hers. Wallace, taken by surprise, flexed against it, but even so, the kiss was loud as a slap.

Another time, up in LaDonna's room, they played dou-ble-solitaire. I was at the keyhole this time. Suddenly, at the height of the action, LaDonna scooped all the cards in a jumbled pile and pushed Wallace down to the floor. Wallace, caught off guard, tried to roll away from her but soon found himself wedged inside the vise of her thin legs. LaDonna wrestled him over on top of her and then she began to buck against him like a stung pony. Wallace hung on for dear life. It was a frantic imitation of coupling, a fully clothed dress rehearsal. When it was over they collected the scattered cards and went back to their game, subdued and tender.

Once LaDonna selected a moody boy named Preston Fixx. Preston strolled by the house one afternoon after school and watched the other boys spinning on their bikes and barking. Preston was wearing gray slacks and a clean white shirt. He was carrying a bag of groceries. Wallace Porter slammed by him broadside on his bike, causing Preston to drop the bag of groceries. The bag split open and a large economy-size box of Kotex fell out. This made the other boys hoot and cackle with murderous glee. All the boys skidded to quick, intimidating stops in front of Preston, then looked up to the screened porch, hoping for LaDonna's scornful smile and severe finger. But the humiliating gestures did not come. Just the opposite happened. Instead of being exiled, Preston Fixx was her choice for that evening.

Wallace Porter's face hung slack with disbelief. Then he collected himself and laughed like an embittered lunatic, lipping huge farts against his arm as he rode swiftly away in dangerous zigzags. He looked back over his shoulder now and then to see if LaDonna had only been kidding, but she hadn't. It was Preston Fixx in tidy clothes, and all the other grubby boys dispersed.

LaDonna served Preston lemonade on the porch, but she didn't force a kiss on him. Later, up in her room, she did kiss him, but it was a tender, appreciative peck that only brushed his lips. Appreciative, because when LaDonna talked about something called the "Lorentz Transformation," Preston seemed to be able to follow her. LaDonna scribbled an equation on a piece of paper and showed it to him. "See how it works?" she said. He frowned for a long time and then finally nodded enthusiastically. "It's really simple. Time is relative, depending on how you measure it. So is space."

"That's really something," said Preston.

"It's everything," LaDonna said, kissing him again, this time with more heat. "That equation," she said, her voice husky and low, "cuts through all the crap."

They were sitting on her bed. She pressured him down until they were lying flat, LaDonna on top. Preston squirmed free. His boner lifted his gray slacks. He staggered away from her. LaDonna was too much for him. He was a smart kid, but he wasn't in LaDonna's league. There was no one in school like her. There was no one in Far Cry like her. She was beautiful, though not in the way Mother was beautiful. Her beauty came from what was in her. She was vibrant with intelligence and passion. She was intense. She was compelling. When you were with her you found yourself waiting for her to speak. Preston, his heart enslaved, practically fell down the stairs trying to get away from a vision he could not understand. He didn't even see me, crouched in the hall.

I liked to sit in Gent's office. It was paneled in rich dark wood; there were big, important-looking file cabinets against one wall; the desk was mahogany and at least six feet wide; and the floor was covered with a thick pile carpet the color of salmon eggs. He caught me one day rummaging through his desk, but he didn't say anything. Some men were with him. The men were carrying something heavy. They set it down in an empty corner of the office. It took me by surprise. My hand was still shoved into the back of the drawer I was searching when they came in. A pamphlet I'd found earlier was still lying, opened, on top of the desk. It was titled "Sexual Vigor in Middle Age." The author was Rolphe Sydney Greenwood, M.S. It was opened to a glossy photograph of a man and a woman lying together on what looked like a bearskin rug. The man had blue-black hair thick with tight curls. He was smiling like he was posing for a toothpaste ad. The woman lying under him had her head thrown back. Her eyes were rolled up under their lids and her open mouth was twisted. She looked as if she had been electrocuted. The caption under the picture said, "Have you smiled like this lucky fellow lately?"

"Jack," said Gent. "I'd appreciate it if you didn't fool around in here, okay? This is where I run the company." He said it apologetically, as if somehow he had been the intruder, not me. I slid the pamphlet off the desk and put it back in the drawer. I closed the desk and lit a cigarette.

"Sure, Gent," I said. "I didn't think you minded."

The thing the men had brought into the office was a large concrete flywheel. It was set in a steel frame. Gent went over to it and set the flywheel turning with a little kick. "It's a circular treadmill, Jack," he said. "I had it built to my specifications. I've talked myself into doing a few exercises." He slapped his belly with both hands. "I'm getting a little on the paunchy side, don't you think? Your poor Ma thinks I'm going to keel over with a coronary any day now."

He stepped on the flywheel, put one hand on the unmoving center post, and began walking, in a kind of limping gate—the right foot having to cover less ground than the left. It looked more like handicapped walking than exercise. He walked toward me, but, of course, only the flywheel moved. It took quite a bit of effort to get the heavy wheel moving and his face soon turned red. He began to wheeze. He stepped off the wheel and took several small, staggering steps to one side, like a man who had been a long time at sea. His knees buckled. I stubbed out my cigarette and jumped up to help him. I grabbed his arm. "You okay, Gent?" I asked.

He grunted. "This just goes to prove how out of shape I am," he said.

The next day I saw Gent walking through the house wearing shorts and tennis shoes. The shorts were big and flashy, printed with pink flamingos. The flamingos were rising off a cattail marsh. There was enough material in those shorts to make a shower curtain. The tennis shoes were white high-tops. Gent's stomach fell over the top of his flamingo shorts in quivering rolls.

He went into his office. I pushed the door open a crack and watched him. He stepped onto the treadmill and began walking. He had a determined look on his face. He picked up his pace, the big white tennis shoes slapping the concrete wheel like flippers, left foot leading the right, the right mincing along behind. Soon he broke into a lumbering trot. His color went from whitish gray to fluorescent pink. His face looked like it was reflecting the hue of the salmon-egg carpet. All at once he made a braying sound and stopped dead in his tracks. The wheel, though, kept moving. It carried him around and around. It was like a small carousel, without horses or corny music.

Mother was in the front room, getting ready to go shopping. It was Saturday morning. She was wearing the prettiest dress I'd ever seen. It was dusty pink in color and flimsy. So flimsy that you could see through it. Except that you couldn't actually see through it. You just believed you could. The front room smelled like a flower bed in bloom. Mother was looking at herself in the big wall mirror and Spencer Ted was holding on to her.

Spencer Ted nearly came up to her shoulder. He had his big arms wrapped around her hips, and he was whining, "Titta, Marmy! Pencey want titta!" Mother ignored him, even though his cranky arms made her wobble off-balance on her high heels.

"Stop that, Spencey," she said. "You just *had* your

breakfast." Her voice was musical, but it was also abstract and distant. It made Spencer Ted sob. She pried his long chubby arms off her hips and pushed him away. He fell to his hands and knees and bellowed. Mother smoothed her dress and patted her hair. Outside in the street a car was idling. Its horn blared.

"Gent will fix you kids your supper," she said to me. "I might not be back by then, so you go ahead and eat without me."

The car out in the street roared. It was Guy Rampling, driving a green convertible. I went out to the porch and looked at it. It was a 1942 Mercury convertible, metallic green, customized white leather upholstery, and twin pipes with chrome echo-cans sticking half a foot beyond the rear bumper. Mother sidestepped Spencer Ted's lurching pursuit and went out the door. She got into the convertible and Guy popped the clutch, making the tires smoke. The twin pipes tromboned and the windows of the front room rattled.

I went back to Gent's office. He was still on the treadmill. He looked like a statue. His face had cooled to its normal gray-white. The still-turning wheel took him in slow circles. I watched him for a while. He seemed to be lost in thought. I went into the office, feeling invisible. I sat at the desk and lit a cigarette. When the flywheel had turned so that his face was to the wall, I slid open the right-hand top desk drawer. Then he was wheeling toward me and I put my hands in clear view on top of the desk. Then, when he was facing the wall again, I quickly slid out the book I wanted. *The Horrible Huns Sack Rome.* When I had the opportunity, I slid the crudely bound paperback book into my pants. Then I left.

AFTER supper, Gent and I went down to the basement. Gent wanted to play some waltzes. We played "Memories," "Tears on My Pillow," and "It's a Sin to Tell a Lie." Then we played, "Are You Lonesome Tonight," "Moonlight on the Manitoulin," and "The Tennessee Waltz." My hands were stiff with those slow rhythms and I asked Gent if we could switch to some jump tunes or the samba. We tried "Chinatown," but Gent's heart wasn't in it and so we went back to the waltzes. Halfway through "Springtime in the Rockies," I heard the front door open and close and the floorboards above us creak. Gent, his cheeks ballooning, his forehead deep in frown, sweat dripping from his chin, didn't seem to notice that they'd come home. It was almost nine o'clock. We went on playing our list of waltzes. I kept one ear tuned to the floorboards. They were creaking again. Creaking in a kind of rhythm. I imagined them dancing, dancing to our music. *Run* dog run. *Run* dog run. My hands on the brushes felt like blocks of ice. There was a crash and a tinkle. A floor lamp toppling? And then laughter. That wild uncheckable laughter I often heard exploding from secret rooms. *Run* dog run. *Run* dog run. *Run* dog run. The floorboards creaked. We played.

THOUGH it was August, it rained three weeks. There was nothing to do. LaDonna was so bored she slept in every morning until eleven o'clock. She ate lunch, then went back to bed to read.

One day during this gloomy weather, she asked me if I'd like to write a book with her.

"What kind of book?" I asked.

"You know," she said. She was wearing her pajamas, even though it was four in the afternoon. She had an odd look on her face. "A book like *The Horrible Huns Sack Rome* or *Handyman.* You *know.*"

I shrugged. "Sure," I said. "Fine by me."

We spent the rest of the afternoon trying to decide what our book would be about. We couldn't agree on

anything, so LaDonna said, "Let's just start it and we'll
find out later what it will be about."

She had already written a few pages, it turned out,
and she showed them to me. Her handwriting was
strange, as though she had purposely tried to disguise it.
I read:

Ina Stein was hot, tired, and in trouble again. She
was walking by herself on the boiling hot streets of
Tangier, which is in Morocco, which is in North
Africa. Her plane had been grounded because of
weak propellers. The pilot, the handsome Lance
Cravings, was sick with malaria. Ina had tried to
nurse him back to health, but Lance needed medicine. Ina hoped to find the proper medical supplies
in Tangier. Ina was close to tears, as we might well
imagine. Then she heard a friendly voice call out to
her. "Missy, Missy, you come up here." Ina looked
up and saw a man in a red flowerpot hat waving to
her out of a small window. Ina climbed the stairs to
his apartment. The man met her at the door. There
was a foreign smell in the room like a burlapy perfume that made her dizzy. She started to fall down,
but the friendly man caught her just in time. "I need
medicine for Lance Cra——" she started to say, but
she suddenly found herself gagged! Soon she found
herself not only gagged but tied naked to a pole in
the middle of the room! A dark giant with a foot-
long thing ran toward her with knives in his hands.
"Help me!" Ina screamed. "Help me, Lance!" But
she was still gagged and the words came out blurry.
"Missy, you are mine!" said the dark giant as he ran
himself into her just about as far as humanly possible! Ina tried to think about something more uplift-
ing. She applied her disciplined mind to the rigors
of Quantum Theory. She recalled how she had tried
so hard to talk about it with Mr. Howe, the science

teacher at Far Cry Junior High School, but Mr. Howe did not believe her. "Bull pucky," he said when exposed to the ideas of Planck, Bohrs, and Einstein. Mr. Howe believed with all his simple heart that the world was just as Isaac Newton said it was. "No, no, *no*," Ina scolded. "Newton is out of date. The world isn't like he said it was." Mr. Howe got sore and made her stay after school. But when Ina continued to aggravate him by arguing further, he said, "Ina, I am going to have to discipline you!" He made her stand in the coat closet where he made her repeat a thousand times "It is evil to tell lies about science." She had tried her best to tell him how the world is more or less a trick the mind plays on itself, because, at the subatomic level nothing predictable ever happens, and that the harder you try to observe something, the more unsure you are of what you have observed, and time sometimes stands still or runs backward and that everything seems to be bundles of energy, even we are bundles of energy standing upon bundles of energy, and there's nothing to say the whole works couldn't collapse in an instant like a sneeze, because there was nothing here to begin with, nothing here now, and nothing at the end of time. This made Mr. Howe so mad he began to beat her with a yardstick, lifting her skirt and pulling down her panties, oh, how it stung, and, unfortunately, that reminded her of where she was, and another dark giant with an even bigger thing fell upon her and she felt like an atom being split. This man jumped back and forth like crazy making his thing go up and in and down and out until Ina thought that she would die! Then, just as everything started to go black, Ina entered the Fourth Dimension. The room, the pole she was tied to, and the dark jumping man all froze, then gradually became ghostlike, then they were gone. She found herself back home looking for a drugstore so that she could find the medicines that Lance Cravings needed so desperately. She was in New York City, which is where she lived when not traveling the globe. When she got the medicines, she visited her mother. "Where in the world have you been, Ina?" her mother queried. But at that very moment, three men kidnapped them and took them away to a dark basement somewhere in the city! They were tied to posts and stripped naked! The kidnappers took off their clothes and each one of them had things over a yard long! "Spare my mom!" Ina yelled in desperation. But her pleas fell upon deaf ears. The kidnappers came at them with their ever so huge things and it was all Ina could do to stop herself from screaming. Back and forth the kidnappers jumped! The only thing Ina could do was to think of her personal hero, Albert Einstein. She thought of him scolding Neils Bohr by saying, "God does not play dice with the Universe, Neils," and Bohr answering back, "Oh, yes he does, Albert," and how Mr. Howe didn't understand either one of them and could only say, "Bull pucky." Ina liked Einstein ever so much better than Neils Bohr, but Bohr seemed very smart to her, too. "It is *you* who are playing dice, Mr. Neils Bohr!" she shouted. "It's only humans who are uncertain, not God!" They both looked at her, wondering how she had entered the seminar room of the Science Building at Göttingen University. Albert took his pipe out of his mouth in order to say, "Bravo, Ina. Bravo." Ina blushed shyly. "It's the Fourth Dimension," she said, "that's how I got here." And that's how she got back to Lance Cravings with the proper medicines. "Thank God you made it back," Lance said, showering her with hot kisses.

"This isn't very sexy, LaDonna," I said, handing the paper back to her.

"You try it then," she said, testy.

"Okay, I will."

But the rain was falling again and I felt gloomy and cold and uninterested in writing fake stories about girls tied to poles in Morocco getting ploughed by men with superhumanly large sex organs.

SPENCER Ted rode in the back seat with LaDonna and I sat up front with Gent. Gent was wearing a dark gray suit with a blue shirt and maroon tie. He looked like he was on his way to a convention, but we were only going up to Grassy Lake for the weekend.

Gent was in a quiet mood. He appeared to have something on his mind that required serious thought. And though we were only going fishing, he drove the car as if we were late for some important event. We sailed over the Mill Avenue bridge, weightless as a gliding bird. I felt the car lighten at the crest of the bridge and my stomach sank as we topped it.

We stopped halfway to the lake for hamburgers. It was a cold, grim little café with no customers. "We're very hungry," Gent said to the waitress, who was also the cook. He said this as if confiding a family secret, but the waitress-cook wasn't impressed. She gave Gent an irritated look.

"You're probably hard up, too," she said, and walked away.

"What did she say, kids?" Gent asked. "Did she say what I think she said?"

I shrugged. LaDonna studied her fingernails. I noticed then, for the first time, that she had become a nail biter. Her fingertips were nubs, nailless and sore.

Then the waitress-cook came back. "With or without, or what?" she said.

"The works," Gent said, still trying to be agreeable. But when the woman went into the kitchen to fry the meat, he said, "We can't eat in here, kids. Too poisonous, if you get what I mean. We'll take the stuff out to the car."

I got the crazy idea then that Gent and the waitress-cook knew each other, and for some reason the woman had come to despise Gent for something he had done. There was no reason to think this, it was just a feeling.

Outside, I said, "What did you mean by 'too poisonous,' Gent?"

Gent laughed. "Don't pin me to the wall, Jack! I only meant that the woman in there took an instant dislike to me—you saw it, didn't you? It happens sometimes, just as if you'd done something terrible. It would have been way too tense in there with her. And tension can screw up the old digestive process."

Still, I couldn't shed the idea that Gent knew the woman, that she hated him, and that our food had been literally poisoned by her in an act of revenge. What *if* she had sprinkled the meat with roach powder? What *if* she had laced the ketchup with Antrol? What *if* she had sprayed the lettuce with Flit? A woman with a grudge like hers was probably capable of anything.

I eyed my burger deluxe suspiciously. I held the first bite in my mouth a long moment before I began to chew, hoping to detect the poison's bittersweet tang. And after chewing carefully—the idea of ground glass in the meat occurred to me—I swallowed, half strangling on the mass of meat, bread, lettuce, pickles, cheese, and onions.

In fact, we all got mildly sick, except for Spencer Ted, who had eaten out of a jar of mashed bananas LaDonna had brought. There were only a few store-bought foods Spencer Ted would eat, and mashed bananas was number one on the small list. He would even take milk now from a bottle, provided it was flavored with mashed bananas, though he still insisted on Mother and only Mother when she was near.

There were some well-maintained outhouses at Grassy Lake. We'd fish for a while, then trot to the outhouses, then fish some more, then back to the outhouses, and so on, all afternoon.

By evening the sickness had passed. We were all bushed. Gent had rented a tourist cabin. It was a nice place with its own dock. We sat on the porch in a big creaky swing and watched the sun go down. The blackening water was unrippled by wind. Gent took out a little harmonica and played some tunes. He had a fifth of bourbon with him that I hadn't noticed in the car. He kept the bottle between his feet while he played the harmonica. He'd now and then bang the spit out of the harmonica and lift the bottle to his lips. After a while he began to sing. He had a crooner's voice, like Dick Haymes or Crosby. We were astonished, LaDonna and I. It was beautiful, full of tone and well-controlled vibrato, and so odd, coming from an old, top-heavy, bald-headed man with a big stomach.

> Lord knows I am a jolly fellow,
> and if I get a little bit mellow,
> it's only among my good old friends,

he sang.

He laughed and blew a few chords on his harmonica, then sang again:

> To laugh and get as fat as I intend,
> I live when I can upon clover,
> and when I die, my good friends,
> it's only all over
> and there my little comedy ends.

He tooted a harsh fanfare and then laughed again. "It's an old song I once heard when I was a kid," he said. "It's stuck with me all these years."

Bouncing Spencer Ted on his knee, he crooned:

> Go away, naughty baby!
> What's over is only over.
> Thy daddy's a rum-dumb "maybe,"
> Thy mommy a goddamned rover.

Spencer Ted, though he couldn't possibly understand these rhymes, began to fuss nervously. He rocked back and forth, swiveling his big head, muttering, "Marmy, Marmy, Marmy." LaDonna took him inside to change his diapers and heat a bottle of banana-flavored milk.

A boat out on the dark water cut a long, thin wake. The solitary rower shipped his oars and waved shyly, as if he would have enjoyed getting to know us.

Gent sipped his bourbon, eyeing the man noncommittally. Then he raised his hand and turned the palm first out and then in, suggesting a door being decisively closed, as though to throw the rower's idea of fellowship in doubt.

"Row row row your goddamned crappy little boat," Gent said under his breath. He raised his harmonica to his mouth and blew a harsh discordant pack of notes, as if to urge the lonely rower on his way.

GENT finished his bottle in the cabin and when he went to bed, he fell asleep instantly. His snores sawed through the cabin. Spencer Ted snored too, a tinier version of Gent's.

LaDonna and I were in bunk beds; I was in the lower, she was in the upper. It was hot and sticky in the cabin. Neither one of us could sleep. I got up and tiptoed out to the porch. LaDonna followed a few minutes later. We sat on the swing, being careful to not let it creak. Lightning flashed in the distance and the smell of warm, fishy rain was heavy in the unmoving air.

"What's wrong with Gent?" LaDonna asked.

"Wrong? How do you mean?"

"I've never seen him drunk like that before."

"Maybe he's not feeling very good."

LaDonna sighed. "Of course he's not *feeling* good. What I want to know is why. What's wrong with him?"

I shrugged. I had a good idea what was wrong, but it wasn't something I felt like talking about. The soft mumble of distant thunder reached us. I left the porch and walked to the Roadmaster. I got in and searched the glove compartment. I felt around under the seat. My hand touched something cool and hard. I pulled out a half-pint of bourbon. I broke the seal and unscrewed the cap and held it to my lips. The first sip shocked me. I couldn't believe that people actually drank such horrible-tasting stuff. But the first swallow had an instantaneous effect. Heat pounded up from my stomach into my head. I took another swallow. It went straight to my brain and blazed. "Hey, look *out!*" I said, grinning into the narrow-necked bottle.

LaDonna got into the car and sat next to me. She took the bottle out of my hand. She held the bottle up to the dark sky as if she could somehow determine its contents that way.

"Bourbon Deluxe," I said. "Pride of Kentucky." I took the bottle back and squinted at the label. A lightning flash let me read the fine print. "Made in Los Angeles," I said.

"What's it like?" she asked.

"Try it and see."

LaDonna, the brave researcher, raised the bottle to her lips and took a full swallow. She gagged but held it down. "Yuck!" she said.

She drank again. She took three full swallows before

lowering the bottle. I was impressed. I took the bottle and swallowed three times myself. It made me gag, but I didn't lose it. The fire in my brain crept into my blood.

"Cripes!" LaDonna said.

"Die Yankee dogs!" I said in my World War II Japanese accent.

LaDonna made the sound of a bomb falling, then the boom.

I gargled another mouthful of Bourbon Deluxe, then chugged like a steam engine pulling eighty lumber cars up a 6 percent grade.

LaDonna tried to whistle "Mares Eat Oats," but her tongue was too thick for it. She fell down across the seat giggling. She righted herself, sipped from the bottle again, and propped her bare feet on the dashboard.

We passed the bottle back and forth until it was empty, as the storm moved across the lake toward us. Long forks of lightning gave the shoreline and the pine-covered hills on either side of the lake an eerie presence. Those split-second illuminations seemed to catch the world naked and ugly. It gave away the world's awful secret: Its ugliness was hidden by sunlight. The counterfeit light of the moon falsified it.

The tall ponderosas looked alien. The pebbly beaches looked alien. Alien black clouds were gnarled with raging, half-human faces.

"Let's drive it, Jack," LaDonna said. Her wild, chalky face made me lean away from her. In the charged air, her face was unfamiliar. She wasn't my sister. *Sister* was just a word. Like *stone,* or *water.* It was LaDonna, LaDonna's nose, LaDonna's mouth, her chin, her hair, her honest eyes, but the ratchety, violet light revealed what ordinary daylight missed. A wild, unchecked spirit so completely itself that no human name could ever come close to identifying more than a fraction of it. LaDonna, yes, but so much more than LaDonna.

The keys were in the ignition. I started the Buick and

let it idle down the road in first gear. The road away from the cabin led into the woods. The woods were black and deep and the headlights only served to prove the bottomless black depth behind them. I stopped the car about a hundred yards from the cabin, but it might as well have been a thousand miles.

LaDonna slid close to me. "Let's see what it's all about," she said, her breath hot with whisky steam.

"What *what* is all about?" I said.

"You know," she said. Then the rain on the steel roof made such a din I couldn't hear what else she said. She put her hands on me, frantic and rough, and uncompromising. She pulled my shirt, popped buttons, unbuckled my belt, yanked at the zipper, dug past denim and cotton, until she found it. I said something like "whoa," but I couldn't hear myself in the drumming rain.

She turned on the cab light. She bent down and traced her nubby fingers along the hot network of veins. "It's so cute!" she shouted from below, like a diver gone down three hundred feet to inspect an unknown species of fish. "It's not at all like those awful big things in the pictures!" she reported. "It's kind of pretty, in an odd, prehistoric way."

She straddled me, knees on either side of my tense hips. I felt the scrub of her small hair.

"We better not," I offered.

"I want it," she said, between her teeth.

The rain stopped suddenly and every small sound we made was enlarged by the huge silence around us. It was as if the woods and every creature in them were holding their breath.

"Shit," she said. "It won't go in."

She pressed down with blind energy, but it wouldn't go. I yelped in pain. My teeth were grinding, my eyes were shut tight.

Something all at once broke loose in me.

"What in the world is it *do*ing?" she asked, alarmed.

A hot river roared through me, brain to foot, and spilled out into her hand, leaving me for dead.

"My God, have I hurt you, Jackie?" she asked.

I shrank away from her in fatigue and embarrassment.

"Oh," she said. "I think I get it. You've done it by yourself, haven't you?"

I shrugged.

"So *that's* what the big fuss is all about," she said, examining her scientific fingers.

The rain was slow and dreary now, and the thunder sounded like a room full of old men coughing.

I T took forever to get home. I couldn't look at LaDonna and LaDonna couldn't look at me. For one thing, we were both sick. My skull felt cracked and my stomach was filled with broken glass. And to make things worse, Gent stopped at every truck stop and café he saw. He couldn't get enough to eat. He had a cheeseburger, chicken-fried steak, ham and eggs, a hot roast beef sandwich, turkey pot pie, along with sweet rolls and tarts. We'd drive five miles then stop. Ten miles, stop. Eight miles, six, twelve.

"I could eat an entire steer, kids," he said. "Tail feathers to snout. It must be all the fresh air and exercise."

In a restaurant that was only a few miles from Far Cry, he ordered Dutch apple crunch with lumps of soft ice cream on it. "I don't want to come home banging the tables for food, do I?" he chuckled. "Your poor Ma won't want to have to feed the old man after an outing, will she?" He went on like this, talking about her as if she was fretting about our meals, as if she cared one way or the other if he ate or didn't. The sight of his big bowl of Dutch apple crunch with gobs of melting ice cream on it was too much for me. I felt as if I'd been punched in the stomach. I excused myself and went into the bathroom. I puked in a stall, hitting the seat and splashing my shoes. A man in the next stall was making a horrible stink and it made me puke again.

"Go easy, there, bud," the man said. "Life is short enough."

Back at the table, Gent was still eating. LaDonna looked thin and sickly. Spencer Ted sat in her lap banging silverware together.

"Where's your appetite, Jack?" Gent asked. "You kids still sick?"

An enormously fat waitress poured Gent more coffee. "Grand," Gent said. "Just grand."

"Food is love," said the big waitress.

We didn't go directly home. We drove around the south side of Far Cry for a while. I got the idea that Gent was stalling. It was as if he didn't want to get home too early. He was uncomfortable behind the wheel, having eaten enough food that day for three or four men, but still he drove the streets of Far Cry as if pleasure driving was his favorite activity. Then we stopped at a sporting goods store. Gent got out of the car, wheezing heavily. "You kids wait here," he said. "I'll be right back."

When he came back, he was nervous. He had a brown package with him. He tried to hide it from us by holding it down low on his leg, and when he got into the car, he slid it under the front seat. He had a funny look on his face, and I thought: *Here is where he buys his dirty books.* Why a sporting goods store would sell books like that didn't occur to me. It was the look on Gent's face that convinced me. Shame and guilt, mixed with nervousness. LaDonna didn't notice any of this. She was rocking Spencer Ted in her arms and whispering baby talk into his big red ear.

When we got home Mother wasn't in. The house was dark and had a damp, stale smell. "I guess she went out to the movies," Gent said, but the damp, stale smell of the house meant more than a few hours at the movies.

Mother had been gone as long as we had been gone. I felt sure of it.

She came back the next afternoon, explaining that her aunt Billie, who lived in Smelter City, about a hundred miles to the east, had taken sick. Mother had to go look after her for a couple of days. Guy Rampling was with Mother. They both smelled of some kind of sweet liquor. Guy carried her suitcase into the house. We all sat in the front room while Mother got cold beer for the men.

"Shit oh dear," said Guy, after chugging down half a can of beer. "That old babe sure looked bad." He wiped his mouth on his arm, then flattened his lips into a grim-humored smile. He flexed his arms indolently, making the grass-skirted girls stagger. Softhearted concern for the well-being of others was an expression foreign to his face. He looked comical. He looked like a pale chimp imitating serious thought.

Gent raised his eyebrows. "Oh?" he said. "You went with Jade?" I don't think Gent was really surprised at this. He had suffered during the night and had played his sax until well after midnight, alone. There were dark bags under his eyes.

Mother hissed and Guy blushed. "Well, she didn't have the *car*, see?" Guy said. "You had the car up to the lake, with the kids. So I says, Jade, you can use *my* car. Then she goes and tells me, Shit fire, I can*not* drive that hot-rod Merc. So I says, Hell, don't get your tit in the wringer, Jade. *I'll* drive you over to your poor aunt Billie's. So I drove her." He dug a square of yellow paper out of his watch pocket. He unfolded it carefully and held it up for all to see. "I stayed at the Cat Nap Motel, clear across town from where Jade's aunt Billie lives. This here is my receipt. I just watched the television or took walks up to the smelter. Say, that smelter sure is one hell of an operation."

"I understand," Gent said, his half smile falling.

Mother stood up. "Believe it or don't," she said. "Jesus God but you make me sick!"

Guy waved the little piece of paper over his head. "Hey, here's the damn receipt itself," he said. The smile on his face could have given a maggot the dry heaves.

ALL the eating Gent did on the way home from Grassy Lake was the beginning of a binge. He kept eating. Almost anything would do. He'd sit alone at the kitchen table eating plain bread with left-over gravy. Sometimes he bought cans of ready-made gravy, heated it in a saucepan, then poured it over the bread. Mother would slap his wrists when he did this, but she did it so softly it seemed more like encouragement than a reprimand. "Look at Mister Blimp!" she would say, but her tone was light and careless.

Guy Rampling came over often for dinner. He lived alone in an aluminum trailer house and Mother said that she felt sorry for him. She felt more than sorry for him, but that was the story she told. She felt so sorry for him that she even began to cook meals again. Usually it was fried steak, fried potatoes, canned peas or lima beans, and her one homemade specialty, peach cobbler.

Gent would cook the Sunday dinner, but he let Mother take over during the week. He smelled of bourbon most of the time and he began to let the house get dirty. He let himself get dirty, too. It was a shock to see him unshaven for two to three days at a time, his fingernails dark and ragged, his shirt stained. Still, he ran the creamery's business well and he played his sax religiously every evening.

He still treated Guy like a faithful employee and not like the low rat he was. Once I saw them sitting together at the kitchen table going over Guy's books. Guy was in his milkman's uniform, the billed cap back on his head at a jaunty angle.

"I signed up five more ladies today, Gent," he said, patting his leather-bound route book.

"You have built up that route from second-to-last to third-from-top. And all in one year's time," Gent said. He picked up the route book and hefted it admiringly.

Guy dropped his fat wallet on the table and emptied it. "And these ladies pay me on time, too, boss," he said, winking. He spread the money out on the table. I noticed that the bills were marked with crayon, the same letters I had seen printed on the dollar bill I'd found. GAR. His initials. Guy A. Rampling. Gent picked up a twenty and held it up to the light.

"Looks good to me," he said.

"You get a half a dozen more route men like me and you'll be a rich man, Gent."

Gent stared at Guy for a long moment, his half smile weak in his grizzly face. "I already am a rich man, Guy," he said.

Guy busied himself with his pile of money. "Oh, looky here," he said. "I forgot to mark one." He showed Gent a ten-dollar bill with no crayon printing on it. "Looks like I'm not such a damn hotshot after all." He took a blue crayon out of his shirt pocket and applied the blunt tip carefully to the bill. "Guy. Allan. Rampling," he said, pronouncing his own name lovingly. "I'm a careful man," he said to Gent, winking again.

"I see that," Gent said.

"When you mark your collections, what you have is a double set of books."

"Good thinking, Guy."

Guy tapped his forehead and winked. "Of course," he said quickly, "*you* keep such good records there's no need for me to do it. You're right on top of things, Mr. Boss."

Mother walked in then. "I hate to interfere with this mutual admiration society, but I'm going to cook some steaks in here."

"I like mine done, Jade," Guy said. "I don't like red meat. I like it dark and juicy, I like it smothered in onions." He said this as if he'd said something witty. He had a little self-approving smile on his face and his wink was going berserk.

"I know how you like it, Guy," Mother said, her hands on her hips, her lips tight with mock exasperation.

After dinner, Gent and I went into the basement to play some music. Gent wanted to play some fast tunes, some sambas and some jump. We played "Brazil" half a dozen times, each time in a faster tempo than the last. The sixth time we played it, I could barely keep up with him. Then it was "Amor," also in an up-tempo, followed by a half dozen jump tunes including the nearly impossible "Dizzy Spells." We were both sweating by the end of the session.

I went outside to cool off. I walked around the front of the house and then entered the parking lot by the side entrance. I heard Mother giggling.

I ducked behind a truck and listened. They were in Guy's truck, several trucks away. "You son of a bitch," I said out loud, but a burst of laughter drowned me out. I went back into the house and found a bottle of Gent's liquor. He kept it hidden under the sink, behind some bottles of bleach. It had been easy to find. It was mostly bourbon, but he also had some gin and scotch hidden there. I hated the taste of them all, but I liked the effect two or three swallows had on me.

I took a bottle of scotch, a pint, and went back out into the parking lot. I walked straight to the back of Guy's truck, knowing that they'd be too busy to notice me. The doors were not latched. I pulled one open and slipped inside.

It seems that I'd had something in mind. Something like reaching past the stacks of empty milk crates and taking his throat in my hands, my hands invincible with hate. But I only crouched behind the wooden crates, sipping scotch and listening.

I heard Guy say, "Marry me, Jade."

There was some roughhousing then, some laughing and some mild cursing, and the light slap of flesh on flesh. They pushed and giggled, shoved and gasped, and then there was a minute-long hush that was finally snapped by a wet, suctioning sound. "I am already married you dumb jerk," Mother said.

Guy's voice was low and mean. "You know what I'm *talking* about, goddammit, Jade."

There was another long hush filled with the rasping slide of fabric on fabric. I took a long drink of scotch and then had to cover my mouth with both hands against the great heaving cough that tried to escape my lungs.

It got so quiet in the milk truck that I was afraid that they'd left, or if they hadn't, that my thudding heart could be heard. I tried to make my heart slow down but it was charged with whisky and speeded up instead.

Then the long hush was broken by another wet sound. "Don't bite my lips, you hoodlum," Mother said.

I'd been leaning forward on a crate. It teetered and I slipped off, my elbows gonging on the steel floor of the truck. But they didn't hear me. A runaway commotion had begun up front that was so violent that I thought the truck had been started and set in gear in a field strewn with railroad ties. Pain from my crazy bones flooded up my arms and the wretched sob that was lumping up in my throat broke free in spite of my best effort to swallow it, but they didn't hear that, either. I rearranged myself in my hiding place, and the commotion up front settled down into an easy rocking that made the milk crates knock and rattle. Some of the crates had empty bottles in them. The bottles clinked together. It sounded like a laboring drummer, trying to get his snare drum and cowbell in synch.

I sipped my scotch, lulled by the ham-handed drummer. My eyelids drooped. Then a lively chuffing noise snapped me out of my doldrum. It was Mother, catching her breath, sobbing on the intake of air, over and over, faster and faster. Then Guy began to murmur tender *goddamns.* Through all this, I noticed that Gent was playing the sax again. Only a note came through now and then, so I couldn't make out the tune. Maybe it was "Stardust." But then I could only hear Mother. She was whining like a child, saying, "Oh *no* my God *no* oh *no.*" Guy was panting like a dog. I took a long, mind-blotting pull of whisky, but it wasn't enough to shut out Mother's terrible, muttering scream of joy.

"DON'T pick your nose, Jackie," Mother said.

I dropped my hand. We were in the front room, having coffee after dinner. I took out my cigarettes and lit up. Gent lifted a cheek and farted softly. Guy cut loose with a snappy belch. Mother jumped up.

"Jesus God!" she said. "You'd think this was feeding time at the zoo!" She went, huffy, into the kitchen. LaDonna put down her book with an exasperated plop. She got up off the couch and came over to me.

"Let me have one of those," she said. I gave her one and lit it for her.

"You too, sweetheart?" Gent said, lifting a cheek to blow another sighing fart. "Those things will rot holes into your lungs, honey."

"I *like* it," LaDonna said crabbily.

"Uh-huh," said Guy. "I'll just bet you do, brat." He winked at her and tried to give her a pinch on the thigh as she walked by him, but she dodged past his outstretched hand.

Mother came in with the cake. It was a ready-mix, chocolate, cut in thick, fudge-oozing slices. She served Guy and then Gent. Gent took two slices.

"You kids put out those filthy cigarettes first," Mother said.

LaDonna walked out to the front porch to finish smoking. It was almost dark, but a half-dozen boys were out in the street on their daredevil bikes. I heard a sharp rise in their yodeling, but LaDonna wasn't in a mood to pick and choose. She finished her cigarette, then came back into the front room.

Guy ate his piece of cake in four bites. Gent, nibbling speedily, was almost through with his second piece. Mother blew on her coffee and sipped it. I'd gone to bed drunk the night before and the strange dreams I'd had were still on my mind. They were more vivid than ordinary dreams. They were like garbled movies.

"That was one hell of a meal, Jade," Guy said. He stretched his legs out in front of him, raised his meaty arms high, and yawned.

"Very, *very* good," Gent added.

Mother gave Guy a long, steady look over her steaming cup. It made him scratch his ribs furiously. Gent chuckled nervously. LaDonna flipped her book open and bent over it, absorbed. I looked at Mother and imagined her growing smaller. Squeezing down to the size of a pea. In one dream she was smaller than a pea and made of rare stone. Not jade, because she was red in color, more like a ruby. Someone had set her in gold and I wore her on my finger. When I buffed the stone against my shirt, the ring glowed. That glowing ring had magical powers. I did something with it, while there was still time. I understood that its magic was strictly temporary. I said, "Ring, answer this question. Will the drowned man's shoes fit the running boy?" The drowned man walked out of the river singing, I can't give you anything but love, baby. He was decked out, as if for an occasion. He was me, years later. He took a piece of paper and thumbtacked it to a tree. I ran to the tree and looked at it. It was a note. It said, *Wake up, lamebrain.* And I woke, I woke up laughing.

"Suppose you let us in on the joke," Guy said to me.

"What joke?"

"Hell, *you're* the one who's laughing," he said.

I guess there was a grin on my face. I wiped it off. "Just thinking," I said. I'd been hung over, but now that I'd eaten dinner and dessert I felt a lot better. A little fuzzy at the edges, a little burned out. A little drunk. Things tended to amuse me.

"Well, think with a straight face," Guy said. "I don't like to see someone grinning to themselves unless they tell you what's so damn funny."

I thought, Who the hell are you to tell me what to do in my house? Instead of saying it, I grinned again.

Spencer Ted came waddling in. He picked up speed when he saw Mother. "Marmy, Marmy, Marmy," he chanted as he rolled headlong toward her knees. Mother put her coffee down and braced herself for his charge. He hit her knees with his stomach and toppled over onto her lap. He began to climb, his strong hands gripping her clothes, loosening them. Mother sagged in the big easy chair as he clambered up onto her lap. Spencer Ted weighed almost as much as Mother. "Titta, Marmy!" he howled, yanking at her flimsy blouse.

"Wait, Spencey!" Mother said, trying to right herself, but Spencer Ted used his weight to keep her off-balance. She sank into the softness of the chair as Spencer Ted pinned her. She tried to get traction, but she was wearing high heels and they twisted sideways on her. "Goddammit, *wait!*" she whined, but Spencer Ted was already drooling with anticipation. Her dress started to hike up on her thighs and one shoe slipped off as Spencer Ted plowed ahead, his goal in sight. His big round head butted her chest and I heard puffs of air slam out of her lungs. She grabbed feebly at his shirt. Spencer

Ted worked inefficiently at her blouse, trying to loosen a breast, his relentless hands ripping at the thin fabric, muttering, "Titta titta titta titta," in a heartbroken, self-righteous singsong. And then a breast broke free of the tangled snare of blouse and brassiere, and Spencer Ted groaned with toe-curling pleasure, as he took it in his wide jaws. Mother relaxed under him, defeated.

"Christ," she said.

"When are you going to wean that kid, Jade?" Guy asked, peevish.

"I'll need a club to do it," she said.

LaDonna snorted, but did not look up from her book.

"Excuse me," I said.

I went upstairs. I'd already searched their room, but I thought I'd go through it again. This time I began with the closet. But it wasn't there. Then Gent's dresser. No luck. One new nudist magazine with a lot of full-color pictures of flabby men with little dicks holding hands with flabbier women with saggy tits, all of them trying to look as if all this was the perfectly natural thing to do. I looked under the bed, thinking, What is so damn special about this one? Why had he hidden it so carefully?

After a few minutes I heard Gent's sax rattling the heat register. It brought back to mind another dream. Gent and I playing a misery-choked tango at the edge of the Far Cry River as a man was sucked under the rapids, the standing white waves tall and roaring throatily like the voice of a giant bent on vengeance. Behind us Mother was singing. "I'm sorry, Gent," I said. "I didn't mean to mess things up." I meant the rhythm, but he looked at me funny. The sticks were heavy as stone and I kept dropping the beat, slower and slower until I cried in frustration. Gent played on, frowning deeper into his song, ignoring me and my problems. I turned and walked back to the picnic. Mother was sunning herself on the blanket. "Come on, honey," she said, impatiently. "There isn't much time." Her eyes weren't right. They were too small and the wrong color. Black. Wind lifted her skirt. Her white legs blared.

I went out into the hallway and opened the grate. The front room was empty. I went back into my room and looked down into the parking lot, but it was empty too.

I went downstairs and slipped into Gent's office. I searched the desk. Nothing. Then the file cabinets, but there was nothing in them but business records. I tried the bookshelves, feeling behind the books. Most of the books were about creameries, dairies, and farms. Big, heavy books with photographs of stainless steel vats, men in white aprons and hats hosing them out, herds of dopey cows, clean farmers and their clean wives, prime pasture land, and so on. Some books were about famous men. Like Douglas MacArthur and Thomas Dewey. There was a fat, one-volume encyclopedia. I pulled it out. It weighed at least thirty pounds. Behind it was the brown package he'd bought at the sporting goods store. It was heavier than I'd expected. I had figured on it being a book, or several books, but it's weight ruled that out.

What then? Maybe a clay or cast-iron statue of a woman. Or of a man and a woman. Or a horse and a woman. I gave it a shake, but nothing rattled. I stood there, hefting it, listening to "Oh, Mein Papa." Gent was playing it in the lowest register of the big sax, very slowly. It sounded like a funeral dirge. The man in the river, I remembered, lifted his face up out of the water once, but I didn't recognize him, and my weakening arms were helpless.

I opened the package, careful not to tear the brown paper. There was a cardboard box inside. I opened the box. It wasn't a statue. It was a pistol. A large-caliber blue-black revolver. It was loaded. I wrapped it up again and put it back on the shelf behind the encyclopedia. When I got outside the office and back into the kitchen, my knees were shaking. Guy was in the kitchen, drinking a glass of milk. He had a sneer on his face. "Snooping, huh?" he said. I ran past him and up the stairs to LaDonna's room.

She was with a skinny red-haired boy. They were both in their underwear, sitting knee to knee on the bed, touching tongues. "Get out," I said.

The boy looked at me. "Fuck you," he said.

I grabbed his skinny white arm and dragged him off the bed and across the floor. He was taller than me but lighter by ten pounds. Even so, he broke free of my grip and threw a punch at me. It landed on my shoulder, but I was too caught up in the serious business at hand to be much impressed.

"We need to talk, LaDonna," I said.

"Why don't you ever *knock?*" she complained.

"Look, this is serious."

The red-haired boy was throwing punches at my back. It felt like someone was lobbing a tennis ball off me. I turned to tell him to beat it again and he mashed my nose. I tackled him and drove him face-first into the floor. I bent his twiglike arm back behind him and raised it until he screeched. Blood from my nose freckled his white back. The sight of my leaking blood made me mad and I lifted his arm until his hand touched the back of his head. He screeched again and cursed and finally agreed to leave.

"Why are you acting so crazy?" LaDonna said when we were alone.

"That brown package. The one Gent got at the sporting goods store on the way home from the lake? It's a *gun.*"

She looked bewildered. "A gun? So *what*? What's so special about a gun?"

"Jesus Christ, LaDonna, don't you know what's going on?" I couldn't believe she was that blind.

She sat on her bed and pulled the top blanket around her shoulders. Her grown-up face in the dark blue of her wool blanket was hard and bony and beautiful in an austere way. "Everybody and his dog's got a gun in this dumb town, Jack," she said.

"Goddammit! He's going to *kill* somebody." That didn't ring true at all and I thought about it for a minute. "No, he's going to kill him*self,*" I said.

The austere, grown-up beauty of her hard, angular face was unmoved, and I thought for a second that I understood what her intelligence really consisted of and why it would someday matter. "It's his privilege, Jack," she said softly.

My nose had stopped bleeding, but I felt my pulse ticking in it. I looked up at the picture of James Dean. He appeared to be smirking now. But Einstein, his big, sad, dark eyes wide and honest, seemed to be fully aware of the misfortune that had visited us.

GENT'S brother, Orlando Mundy, came to town. Orlando was big, like Gent, but he wasn't fat or soft. While Gent had small, plumpish hands, Orlando's hands were huge and powerful, with a fur of black hair on the backs. He had a heavy black beard and his shrewd black eyes sat on either side of his thick, triangular nose. The only family resemblance was size, but even that was deceptive since Orlando's size was of a different order than Gent's. He was from Irontree, a small mining town about two hundred miles southwest of Far Cry. He taught metal shop in Irontree High School and he also ran a mail-order inspirational literature business.

He had one suitcase with him, and a rifle case. "I've come to do a little hunting," he said. But he put his rifle and elk tags away in the coat closet as if he didn't expect to take them out again. Mother wasn't too happy to see him, but she made a place for him at the dinner table that evening and gave him the biggest steak.

Guy, who usually kept a lively conversation going at

the table, wasn't there that night. Orlando was an eater, not a talker, and the table was unnaturally quiet. Mother tried to make small talk once or twice, but Orlando only nodded or grunted. So Mother finally made a sour face that all of us saw and gave up on trying to draw Orlando out.

Later that night, I heard Orlando talking. I was upstairs, at the grate, and they were in the front room, drinking coffee. Orlando lit a cigar. "You've always had this streak," he said. Gent looked at his hands. Mother was in the kitchen, banging dishes together.

"It isn't a streak, 'Lando," Gent said. "It's just the way things develop."

"Crap," Orlando said, spitting the word. "You *say* that, but that's just your streak talking."

Orlando took my room and I slept on a cot in the basement. LaDonna helped me set up the cot and put bedding on it.

"What's he here for?" she asked me.

"Uncle Orlando? Hunting, I guess. Why?"

"He seems mad."

"He brought his rifle. He's got elk tags. He's dressed for hunting."

"Did you notice how he looked at them? Especially at Ma? Did you see his eyes?"

I shrugged. His eyes were deep-set and fierce. They were hard to look at. They were judging eyes, eyes that burned past your little pretenses. They seemed to see things in you that you didn't know existed. Such eyes could make you sweat.

"He looks crazy, Jack," LaDonna said, her voice sober with caution.

I went over to my snare drum and sat on the stool. I picked up the brushes and started a little boomachick samba beat, to impress her. I had gotten fairly good at it.

"I think he's going to do something," LaDonna said.

I wanted to say, *Maybe somebody ought to,* but I couldn't drum and talk at the same time.

THE next day Orlando raised his voice to Gent after dinner. They were outside, on the sidewalk in front of the house. A dog was barking at the ruckus Orlando was making. I was in the hedge, between the front lawn and the sidewalk. Guy Rampling had eaten dinner with us that evening. He was in the front room with Mother.

"At your own table!" Orlando said, his voice rumbling through the empty street like the wheels of a heavy truck. "That man is barely a cut above slime! And here's my question: What does that make *you?*"

Gent sat on the curb and stared at his hands.

"I see that you don't care about such things," Orlando said.

Gent shook his head mournfully. "I care," he said.

"Then what's holding you back? Do you want me to do it for you?"

"No. I want you to go hunting. That's why you're here, isn't it?"

"I'm *here,* that's the point. I smelled this bad wind all the way over in Irontree. Hells bells, I can go hunting any time."

"I can take care of my own affairs, Orlando."

"That I sincerely doubt, Gent. Nothing less than a horsewhip will do now."

I crawled back toward the house and went in by the back door. I climbed the stairs on all fours, like a cat, so as to not make them squeak. I opened the hallway grate. Mother and Guy were on the sofa. Guy had his hand under Mother's sweater and Mother was turning her head this way and that for she knew that Gent and Orlando were close by.

"Cut it out, you damn hoodlum!" she snapped, but Guy only covered her mouth with his.

* * *

ORLANDO finally did go hunting. I went with him. He drove his car as far as he could up some unused logging roads in the hills north of Far Cry, and then we started walking. I had my father's old .30-.30 carbine with me. There was a much better .308 Winchester complete with scope, but it was the deer gun he'd shot himself with and I couldn't bring myself to use it.

As we walked, and as the terrain got steep, the .30-.30 got heavy. By the time we had gone up and down half a dozen hills, the carbine felt like an armload of bricks. It didn't make sense since I was reasonably strong and had often hiked in these hills.

When we stopped for lunch, I didn't have an appetite. Orlando had packed us a sack lunch of cheese-and-baloney sandwiches along with cookies and apples, but I couldn't eat any of it.

"What's wrong with you, Jack?" Orlando said, squinting at me curiously.

"Nothing, Uncle Orlando," I said, avoiding his eyes.

We were in a thin stand of young jack pine. Chains of quilted light from the noon sun dropped through the web of sparse branches. The .30-.30 was leaning on a mossy rock about ten feet away from me. I couldn't get my mind off it. It felt like it weighed sixty pounds instead of the six or seven it actually did. That was ridiculous. I told myself it was crazy to think that. But the last few miles we walked I could barely get my breath and the muscles of my arms were quivering with fatigue. I was sick to my stomach with the effort of lugging that gun through the hills, but how could I tell Orlando that?

Orlando put a sandwich into his mouth and unscrewed the cap of his thermos. "I know about your father," he said, the sandwich in his teeth. A gray leaf of baloney, half out of the sandwich, trembled as he spoke. "And I know about your first stepfather too."

The .30-.30 glinted in the moving sunlight. "Oh," I said, my voice feeble. Then the shade of a heavy cloud covered us and the world suddenly seemed like an omen. The trees loomed darkly ominous, danger crouched behind the rocks, gliding birds fell silently to their perches. A gust of wind from nowhere made the scene jerk, and the .30-.30 slid off the mossy rock and clattered against some small stones. It picked up speed and skittered down the hill twenty or thirty feet, like a rigid but playful snake.

Orlando heaved himself to his feet. "Your sister tells me you're doing very poorly in school, Jack."

"I guess," I said, indifferently. School was a place I went because everyone else did. It was unreal, like a dream, a false world that was hard to focus on, meaningless.

"One's attitude toward life must be salutory, otherwise one shall end up adrift in a sea of self-pity, vulnerable to all manner of perversity."

"Okay," I said. I felt giddy and scornful. I bit my tongue.

His dark eyes were on me full. My throat felt dry.

"One must always make the effort," he said.

"Sometimes one must not," I said, grinning at my own choice of words.

"How's that, boy?"

"I'm thinking of quitting school. I'm old enough to work."

It was my tone of voice, not my words, that bothered him. "That's fine, Jack. But listen, whatever you do, don't get to thinking you're pulling someone else's chain when you do it. That is not the way to make a life for yourself. Do you understand me? There is nothing at the end of that chain but your failed dreams."

I turned my head to one side and spit. A word came out with it.

"How's that? What did you say?"

I looked at him then. "Shit," I said. "Just shit."

He eyed me for a long moment. "That's right," he said at last, the words lofted into the air in a sigh. "Shit is right, Jack. You are mired in it, boy. Neck deep and sinking, I'd say. And yet you are grinning." He drank from his thermos cup. He sharpened a wood match with his knife and picked his teeth thoughtfully. "I won't preach at you, Jack. I sell inspirational literature on the side, but I am not a Bible thumper. I get these ideas. They address certain difficult situations, such as yours, perhaps. They come on me, like a voice in my head. Margery, my wife, writes them down. That sound crazy to you?"

He sat down again and dug into his sack of cookies. "Go ahead and quit school," he said, his voice friendly but abstract. "You'll be all right."

"Okay," I said.

He pointed at me with a cookie. "Listen to me, Jack. Don't be afraid of taking on what lies ahead, but at the same time don't take on difficulties you don't need. Do you understand what I am telling you? Don't do harm to yourself while telling yourself it's just what you've always wanted. This is the way people delude themselves into tragedy."

A spasm lifted the corners of my mouth. I bit my tongue.

"What the hell are you grinning at, boy?"

"I'm not grinning," I said.

He stood up again and retrieved the .30-.30. He handed it to me.

"Listen," he said, "I know what's going on back at your house. Dirty news travels fast in this neck of the woods. But I mean to put a stop to it, Jack, if your daddy will not." His big face was dark against the tossing trees, and I believed him.

I looked at the .30-.30. I looked at my hands. I sighted on a squirrel, a bird, a horsefly.

"I can see that you're a bothered young man," he said. "There are things on your mind. You're mad and you're sad, and the world looks like a patch of stinging nettles to you. You're beginning to think that happiness is something you'll have to steal."

"No," I said.

"Yes. It's true. You're beginning to think like a thief. Anything worthwhile is going to have to be filched, that's what you're telling yourself, isn't it?"

"It isn't," I said.

"It's easier to tell lies to yourself than to others."

"I'm not lying."

"When you lie to yourself you never think of it as lying."

I'd taken the shells out of the carbine thinking to lighten it, and now I slipped them back into the magazine. I jacked one into the chamber and stood up. "Let's hunt," I said.

He put his big face in front of mine. "Listen to the voice in your head, Jack."

"There isn't any damn voice in my head."

"I'm telling you these things for your own good."

"Sure," I said.

"Pray with me, Jack."

"No."

"Then I'll pray for both of us."

He knelt on the ground before me and closed his eyes. "Merciful father and principal director of our fates," he said, his words rolling through the trees like stones. "Look down benevolently on us in this beautiful spot. Sharpen our senses so that we can really see it. Bust up the logjam of confusion that snarls the mind's pure river. Lighten this boy's load, put him in tune with your superior harmonies so that he will latch on to the true direction of his heart. Make him a good hunter, get him onto the narrow track that runs down the center of your unfaltering will. Amen."

He kept kneeling for a full minute, his head bowed, his eyes closed, then he stood up and grabbed his rifle. His eyes were glittering, like he was drunk. "That was the voice, Jack. That was the voice that comes to me. All at once there it is." He waited for this to sink in, but I acted deaf to it all. "Okay, hardnose," he said. "Let's go get us an elk."

We set off down the hill. There was a dry creek bed at the bottom of it. We crossed that and headed up the next hill. The brush was thicker on this slope and the going was hard. The carbine, though, didn't feel like a load of bricks anymore. It was light. Lighter than it should have been. It felt like a stick of kindling. I laughed at the idea. I felt good, and that was a puzzle to me too.

Orlando moved up the hill ahead of me. He didn't slow down or get tired or stop for rests. He might have been taking a stroll down a garden path to judge by the effort he was putting out. But it was the same for me. And it was in my mind, too. My mind was light. The only things that were in it were Uncle Orlando moving through the brush ahead of me, and a picture of some elk, standing still and alert, as in a painting of elk. When we reached the spine of the ridge, Orlando held up his hand. "There they are," he whispered. He pointed down into the gulch. A herd five strong sipped at a thin creek that glinted like a silver seam in the earth. There was one young bull with a beautiful five-point rack and his harem of four cows. One of the cows looked up as if she had heard us, but we were upwind from them and the sun was at our backs. She put her head back down to the water, the fleeting notion of danger having passed through it. They were not more than seventy yards away, an easy shot.

"Go ahead, Jack," Orlando whispered.

The downslope angle called for a cross-legged, sitting shot. I rested my elbows on my knees and brought the carbine up to my cheek. I drew the front sight down until it rested on a spot just above the shoulder of the bull. I fired. Nothing happened. The cows raised their heads from the water and moved off a few yards. The bull looked right at me, then lowered his head to the water again.

"You're low," Orlando whispered. "Your sights are off."

I levered another shell into the chamber. My first shot was still echoing in my head. The gun, for no reason, had become heavy again. My arms were too tense, holding it. I let the sight rest on the bull's shoulder, then raised it to a point several feet in the air above it. I felt that I was overcorrecting, and dropped the sight closer to the bull. I squeezed the trigger, which had become stiff with a new resistance.

My second shot was off the mark, too, and this time the elk bolted. I got up and ran down the hill after them, tripped, dug a furrow in the hillside with the gun barrel, got up, tripped again, got up, dirt caking the gun barrel and dirt in my mouth, my eyes blind with dirt, but I levered another shell into the chamber and fired wildly into the brush at the bottom of the hill.

There was a barking flash of light. My ears rang. Orlando, somewhere behind me, roared. I couldn't see anything. I was on my back, on my stomach, on my back, rolling downhill, my head full of hornets.

"Jack! Jack!" Orlando yelled. "What happened, Jack!"

The old carbine, its barrel stuffed with dirt, had blown up.

It had blown up in my face. My right cheek was cut and there was a cluster of beestings swarming up the side of my neck. Orlando was worried about my eyes. We went the rest of the way down the hill to the creek where the elk had been and he washed out my small wounds, tender as any mother.

"No real damage, Jack," he said. "You're lucky. You'll have red eyes for a few days, but it doesn't look like anything got into them."

We walked back up the hill, all our lightness gone. Orlando was spent. His breathing sounded like a blacksmith's bellows. He took short, slow steps. I didn't feel any more energetic than he did. I found the wrecked .30-.30 and slung it into the trees.

THEY talked about me as I sat between them, unseen. What will we do with Jack? Mother said.

Guy kissed the palm of his hand and then blew the kiss into Mother's hair. Cut him off, that's what, he said, drawing his steak knife across his throat to illustrate his meaning. That's what you do with snoops.

LaDonna came in. She didn't see me either. Jack's in the tree again, she said, peevish.

This made Guy laugh. He slapped the table, making the plates jump. There, just like I told you, he said.

He can't help it, Mother said. He feels bad.

And he tells lies to himself, Orlando said, buttering an ear of corn.

My face was hot and though a nice cool breeze was lifting the curtains of the kitchen window, I couldn't feel it. I am my own ghost, I said out loud. I touched my face to make sure. Gent was sitting on the floor, under the sink, rummaging through the cupboard. He drew out a bottle of bourbon and cut the seal with his thumbnail. Mercy, he said.

I pulled my half-pint of gin out from under my pillow, thinking, These damn dreams are nuts, and yet at the same time I would *add* to them, as if trying to complete something, after I had wakened. Half drunk, I was able to visualize the parts of the dream in the way you visualize them when you are asleep. My face hurt and the salve the doctor gave me to put on it didn't seem to help much. I took several quick sips, recapped the bottle, and slipped it under my pillow.

LaDonna, full-blown in my mind, said, Jack's in the tree again. Then I dozed off.

I went outside for a smoke. And then I saw him running toward the moonlit tree. The tree was in the backyard, huge, like a redwood, only branchy, like an oak. He was sprinting toward it as though being chased by something vicious, and when he reached the tree he began to climb. It was important for him to get up in the high branches because there was something waiting for him up there. The ground below him fell away and the air lightened and cooled. Voices from below yelled at him. Then he wasn't climbing any longer but walking. Walking up a hard path that led into an open field. It was a long field, blond in the bright sunlight. It was ahead of him, the thing that they'd so carefully hidden, in a stand of dark pines. The darkness in those trees was frightening, and he ground out his cigarette under his heel and returned to the kitchen, which was now empty. Hello, he said, I know you're here, but now it was their turn to be invisible. The gin was in my hand. I uncapped it. I revisualized the tree, the sunlit land on top of it.

MOTHER and Guy were in the front room. Gent was in the basement. LaDonna was in her room with the skinny, red-haired boy. I was at my grate, watching.

Orlando came in, surprising Mother and Guy. Guy had been clowning around and was sitting on Mother's lap. He jumped to his feet, grinning.

"Thought you went home," he said.

"Evidently," Orlando said.

Mother stood up and straightened her skirt. "What do you want now?" she said.

"Why don't you go into the kitchen," Orlando said to her.

"This is my house, I'll go where I damn please."

"You do a lot of things you damn please," Orlando said. His voice was even and calm, but his eyes were hard.

"Get out of here," Mother said.

"You tell him, Jade," Guy said. He sat down on the couch and lit a cigarette as if this was going to be a civilized conversation. He leaned his head back on the sofa cushion, grinning. He had a fresh haircut and his ears stood out from his head, pink and clean.

"This is my brother's house, not yours," Orlando said, pointing his thick finger at Mother.

"All right, all right," Guy said, affecting weariness. He stubbed out his cigarette slowly and stood up. "That will be just about enough from you."

"Everything was just fine until *you* had to show up!" Mother said.

"I surely don't have any doubts about that," Orlando said, laughing a little.

Guy stepped up to Orlando. "Back off, slob," he said. He stabbed a finger into Orlando's chest. Guy was taller by an inch than Orlando, but he probably weighed fifty pounds less. Orlando didn't move back or blink. They stood staring at each other for a long moment, then Orlando reached up and grabbed Guy's left ear. His big hand closed over it. He gave the ear a hard twist. Guy yelped and jumped back, but Orlando didn't let go. Guy began to lean sideways, to escape the pain, but it didn't help. He sank, moaning, to his knees, his fingers running on the air as if on the keyboard of an invisible accordion. Orlando let him go.

"You prick!" Mother said. "You bastard prick!"

Guy stood up and flexed his arms. The grass-skirted girls jumped like scared deer in the hoops of lightning. His face was dark with rage and shame. His swollen ear was blue. Guy spit into his hands and made them slowly into fists. He rotated his fists in front of Orlando's face, to let him know what he was in for. It looked as if the fists were turning the levers of some invisible crank, a slow, powerful movement suggesting unlimited torque. Orlando didn't shrink away from them, though. Instead, he reached out and grabbed Guy's right ear and gave it a crushing twist. Guy's hands stopped turning the invisible crank. The fists unclenched and the fingers began to tremble, like the palsied fingers of a stroke victim. Guy started to lean away from the pain again, sinking to his knees. He whimpered like a kicked dog. Orlando let him go.

After he collected himself, Guy rushed Orlando. He locked his arms around Orlando's legs, as though to tackle him. He drove his shoulder into Orlando's thighs, football player style, but Orlando didn't budge. When Guy's feet began to lose traction on the carpet, Orlando brought both hands down on his ears with a resounding clop. Guy staggered back to the sofa and collapsed on it. "Get me some ice, Jade," he said, touching his ears with trembling fingertips.

"Your welcome has expired in this house," Orlando said.

"The hell it has," Mother said. "You don't have one damn bit of say-so here!"

"I think I've just proved that I have," Orlando said.

"Ice," Guy said. "Quit arguing and get me some ice."

His ears looked like small raw steaks. He was worn out and depressed. He recombed his hair, then patted his oiled pompadour into place gingerly. He looked like a daydreaming barber, stretched out in one of his own chairs on a slow day.

"Stand up," Orlando said.

"I've had it," Guy said.

"On your feet," Orlando said.

Guy stood up, obediently, like a schoolboy caught in the act of some small transgression. Orlando put his hand on the back of Guy's neck and steered him toward the still-open front door. Guy resisted for a moment, then let himself be carried along. They picked up speed. By the time they had reached the porch, they were trotting. I ran to the top of the stairs to watch the action. Orlando didn't stop at the screen door. Guy yelped when he hit it. The door flew off its hinges and Guy sailed down the front steps, rolling when he hit the walk. He sat there for a few seconds, holding his left elbow and grimacing. Then he saw Orlando coming down the steps toward him and he got up and ran. Orlando came back into the front room. He wasn't even breathing hard. "I'll fix the screen door before I leave," he said.

Gent came upstairs from the basement. He was more than half drunk, but cheerful. "What's all the hubbub?" he asked. "Storm coming?" He rubbed his hands together and turned to Mother. "How about it, honey? Shall we have a little peach cobbler now?"

Mother made a terrible face at him and went into the kitchen, where she began to bang plates and saucers together as if to communicate, in some jungle way, the murderous direction of her thoughts.

ORLANDO'S visit didn't change things between Mother and Guy. In fact, he came around more than ever, not being the kind of man who will let mistreatment go unanswered. He got bolder and bolder with Mother. He'd take her to the movies, for instance, and would not bring her back until long after the second show was over. Mother claimed that Gent was too fat to go to the movies. The chairs wouldn't hold him and he would only fidget. Gent agreed that this was probably true, and they left him behind, sitting in front of the television with a bowl of popcorn and his bottle of bourbon. Mother said that Gent could not take her dancing either, for a fat man looks foolish trying to swing his partner, two-step, or waltz. And Gent was agreeable on this point too, saying that he'd rather make music any-way than dance to it.

Guy's ears never recovered from the mauling they had received at Orlando's hands. They remained purple and had become misshapen, taking on the folded-over, mangled look of the ears of an old boxer. He became ashamed of his ears and so he let his hair grow long enough to cover the top halves of them. The bottom halves hung like raw meat out of his hair.

Gent needed help in the creamery and so he hired me to work a few hours after school. His drinking was be-ginning to interfere with his conduct of the business. Besides being the owner of the creamery, Gent's job was basically a caretaking one. The equipment had to be cleaned and checked over every day. The inventory had to be counted. The drivers had to be checked in at the end of the workday.

I liked the jobs Gent assigned to me. They were simple and he paid me too much. I hosed out the big garage where the milk wagons were loaded each morning, swept off the ramp and platform where milk from the tanker trucks was pumped into the refrigerated storage vats, mopped the tile floor inside the creamery itself, and I even checked the temperature gauges on the pas-teurizing machine. Sometimes I'd watch the bottle-filling machine chug through its rounds. I would almost fall into a trance watching the line of bottles clink down the conveyor from the sterilizer, heading toward the lazy Susan filling-and-capping machine. The capped bottles would be pulled off the line by an old man named "Swede" Swenson, who would put them into the wooden crates. Sometimes I'd give Swede a hand carrying the loaded baskets into the cold storage locker. I also set traps for the rats, who loved to collect around the cheese bins, thinking that they might be able to gnaw their way inside. I hosed off the dusty milk trucks in the evenings and sometimes I'd get up early enough to help the drivers load. It was an enjoyable job, easy enough, and Gent gave me twenty dollars every Saturday even though I kept my own time and probably didn't spend more than ten hours a week working.

I suddenly had more money in my pocket than I knew how to spend. One day, while staring at my accumulating wad of tens and twenties, I got the idea of buying presents for everybody. I bought Gent a good, multipurpose pocketknife that had a screwdriver, corkscrew, cigar cutter, and awl, as well as a good blade for cleaning fish. I bought LaDonna a book of mathematical riddles and a pair of gold sandals. I bought some cards for Spencer Ted, and I bought Mother a hat.

It was a wide-brimmed hat with a little dome on top. It was bright orange with a black silk scarf tied around the base of the dome. There was a bunch of tiny plastic roses, blue and pink, tied to the scarf. The hat came in a big box, which I'd had gift wrapped at the store.

I called the whole family into the front room on a Sunday morning after breakfast and handed out the presents. I felt a little embarrassed, since there was no special occasion or holiday to celebrate. It was a kind of peace offering, a gesture to smooth things over, an impulse. My nervousness was soon picked up by everyone else. Mother was on edge. Gent was grizzled and hung over. He looked like he had other things on his mind. LaDonna was crabby and sullen. She sipped her coffee noisily. I suddenly felt that I'd gone overboard, that the whole thing was a mistake. I lit up a cigarette. "I picked up a few things," I said, casually. "I got some good deals. Things you need."

LaDonna tore the paper off her present with such slow precision that I wanted to yell at her. Then she opened the box and took out the book and the sandals. Her eyes widened and the crabby look on her face evaporated. "Oh, Jack," she said, holding up the sandals for all to see. "These are beautiful!" She began to page through the book then, hungrily.

Gent held up his knife. "Would you look at this little gadget!" he said, obviously pleased. He opened the blade, the screwdriver, the awl, the corkscrew. "A man could set up shop with this little baby," he said.

Mother took the hat out of the box. "Oh," she said, as if someone had slapped her stomach hard. "Oh."

"Try it on, Ma," I said, my hands hot and sweating. "Go ahead, try it on."

She put it on and stood in front of the wall mirror. "Jackie, it's just lovely. Really, it's the prettiest hat I've ever seen." The broad-brimmed hat spread out around her head like a perfect cloud back-lit by the sun with a dark streak of midnight running through its middle.

Guy came whistling in. "Good morning folks!" he chortled. Then he saw the presents. "Well, what do we have here? Christmas is a few weeks off yet, isn't it?"

"It was Jack's idea," Mother said. "He bought us these nice things, out of his pay. Isn't that the sweetest boy you've ever heard of?"

Guy looked at me, a thin smile on his lips. "He's a humdinger, all right," he said, and I wanted to break a table over his head.

Spencer Ted waddled in from the kitchen. He had a big sugar cookie in his hand. His lumpy diaper hung to his knees. Though she didn't move, I could almost see Mother drawing away from him. Still unweaned, he was four feet tall and unnaturally massive. His spine was beginning to curve so that he seemed to have a small hump on his back. Mother had taken him to the doctor, but the doctor had only said to keep a close eye on him. He was three years old and getting ugly.

"Hey, Spencer Ted," I said. "I almost forgot. Here you go, big boy." I pulled a tiny deck of playing cards out of my pocket and handed them to him. Each card had a picture of a bird on it. Spencer Ted grabbed them from me, sat down on the floor with a thump, and put the deck into his mouth, growling.

Mother put her hat back into the box. "I'll have to save that for next spring," she said.

Guy sniffed the air. "Don't tell me I missed breakfast," he said, pouting.

Mother put her hands on her hips and made a face. "You sure did, mister," she said, but it was hard to believe that she was actually scolding him. "Come on," she said. "I'll throw on some eggs for you." And they went into the kitchen.

No one said anything for a while. LaDonna was reading. Then Gent said, "Jack, that was quite a thing to do." He held the knife in his palm as if weighing it. Then a sadness moved over him like the gradual shadow of a cloud.

LaDonna closed her book and came over to me. She kissed me on the forehead. "I love my book, Jack. It has a discussion of the Hindu, 'End-of-the-World' problem. It's a kind of geometrical progression. I tried to show it to Mr. Howe once, but he only got mad at me." In fact, LaDonna was doing poorly in school because too many teachers were mad at her. Notes came home from the principal, calling her a "troublemaker" and "disrupter."

We all heard the muffled laughter and the scuffling noises, but only Spencer Ted turned his head toward the kitchen. He had an astonished look on his face. "Marmy?" he asked. "That Marmy?"

"Well then," Gent said, standing up. He looked haggard and lost. "Well, then, Jack. For a moment there, Jack . . ." But he seemed to lose the thread of his idea. "Jack," he said.

"I know," I said, my neck hot. "I know."

* * *

THEN Gent had a surprise for *me*. We drove up to Grassy Lake to meet a man named Carl Bowers. Gent was excited about something, I could see that, but his excitement had a tinge of gloom to it. Now and then the gloom would show through. One moment he seemed overjoyed, the next moment clouded over with doubt.

It was a boat. Carl Bowers was selling his sixteen-foot cabin cruiser. "Damn!" Gent said as we drove down to the boat ramp where Bowers was waiting for us. "I've always wanted a boat like that!"

We got out of the car and approached Bowers. The boat was on a trailer down on the launching ramp, ready to go. Gent and Bowers shook hands. It was a solemn moment. Bowers looked as if he was about to cry. Gent took out his checkbook and wrote out a check for Bowers on the hood of the Roadmaster. Bowers squinted at the check and then stuffed it into his shirt pocket. "She's all yours," he said.

Bowers put the boat into the water for us, backing the trailer that carried it down the ramp. Some old men who had been fishing off the ramp had to move out of the way and they weren't too happy about picking up their gear and standing off to one side. Gent was at the helm and I sat on a seat in the stern of the boat as Bowers backed us into the water. When the boat was mostly in the water, Bowers set the hand brake of his truck and climbed out. He shoved us the rest of the way in, then unhooked the trailer from his truck and drove away. Gent waved at him, but Bowers never looked back. "I practically stole this little beauty from him, Jack," he said, in a guilty whisper.

Carl Bowers's wife, Gent said, had cancer, and Bowers had been forced to raise cash as quickly as possible to cover some medical expenses. He put his boat up for sale in the wrong season, and Gent's low bid proved to be the highest. "I got it for a song," Gent said, gleeful now, as we idled out toward the middle of the lake.

The light was December light—you sensed that darkness was never far away—but the warm air was June. I sat in the stern, trolling, wearing only a T-shirt and jeans, and Gent fished off the side in shirt sleeves. "You know what I'm going to call her?" he said.

"What?"

"The *Jade Marie.* How does that strike you?"

"How come you're going to call her *that*?" I said.

I saw his face then and knew I'd made a mistake. I hadn't meant to question the logic of his choice of names, I just didn't know that Mother's middle name was Marie. To make up for my mistake I said, "How come *Marie*? What's the *Marie* for, Gent?"

He brightened. "Well, that's your Ma's middle name, Jack. You didn't know that? It's a lovely middle name, don't you think?"

I nodded.

"I love how it fits her first name. Jade, then, Marie. Jade Marie. It has music to it. Jade Marie. Jade Marie. I could write a song around that name. Dum da dee, dum da dee. Jack, it's a lullaby of a name."

He smiled his long half smile and reeled in. "I'm going to take a little snooze in the cabin," he said. "You enjoy yourself."

He climbed into the small cabin and shut the weathered door, leaving me all alone on the deck. I reeled in and put my pole up. The fish weren't hitting. The unseasonal heat had sent them down to the bottom and it would have taken dynamite to bring them up. I sat on the bench seat in front of the wheel and throttle. "Jade Marie," I whispered. "Jade Marie." It was true—the sound of it could make a cobra tie itself into a granny knot and shit pretzels. "Jade Marie, Jade Marie," I said, pressing the starter button.

* * *

THE lake was glassy calm and black. I cruised to the far northern end of it where a few stony islands jutted up like the rough knees of submerged giants. There were shallow channels between the islands where the water was pale green and clear. I cut the engine back to a slow idle. Schools of dolly varden dozed on the sandy bottom.

Once through the channels, I entered a swampy bay. I switched the engine off and baited my hook. On my first cast I got a strike. It was a good-size fish, but it had practically no fight in it. I dragged it toward the boat. Even when it was right next to the boat and could see me reaching down for it, it didn't try to escape. I dipped the net down under it and scooped it in. It was a good five-pounder. Then I saw what it was. A squawfish, a dingy bottom-crawling sucker, yellow-bellied and useless. I slipped it off the hook and flipped it back into the water. The big squawfish gave one lazy shove of its tail and drifted a few yards away from the boat. It lay there, only a few inches under the water, half on its side, as if its one moment in the atmosphere had caused it to forget that it was a fish. I had the feeling that it was looking at me, mildly curious. It hung in the pale green water like a yellow stain.

The boat began to rock. I looked up, expecting weather, but there was no cloud, no wind, just the unmoving December air. I opened the cabin door and looked in. Gent, in his underwear, was sitting on a bunk, retching. He was holding a bottle of bourbon by the neck.

"You want to do that over the side, Gent?" I asked.

He looked at me, his eyes flat and fishy, no recognition in them. He stopped retching and took a long drink. Then he capped the bottle, set it down, and curled up on the bunk.

I closed the door. The squawfish was still there. I

thought maybe that it had died. Its blunt nose was facing the boat and its big transparent lips were almost out of the water. I threw the rest of my night crawlers at it and the fish, as if this was just what it had been waiting for, opened its mouth in a delicate yawn.

"NAMES," Gent said, lying across the bow. He was pasting letters to the hull. They were the peel-and-stick-on letters you can buy in any hardware store. He was naming the boat *Jade Marie*. We were near a steep, stony shore, the sun a blinding flare of light in the western hills. "Names," he repeated, grunting with discomfort. "They tell the story, Jack."

He sat up and took a deep, noisy breath. He was still in his underwear and very drunk. "Jade Marie," he sang. "Jade me, Marie, oh, she laid me, Marie, for free, for free." He rolled to his knees and crawled back toward me, dragging his bottle with him. "The job's done," he said. "The little bitch-boat is monikered."

He climbed down into the cabin and came back out carrying his revolver. My heart jumped. I'd searched again for the gun that morning, but it was gone from its usual place behind the encyclopedia. "Names," he said darkly, drawing a bead on a bleached stump on the shore. "They ... [bang!] ... tell ... [bang!] ... a [bang! bang! bang!] story," he said, shooting. He fired the last shot and then refilled the gun with bullets from a carton. He put the gun down on the seat and took a short drink of bourbon. "You take Franklin," he said. "There's a name you can trust. I never knew a goddamned Franklin I couldn't count on. A Franklin, Jack, will always give you a full dollar's worth, no matter what he's selling."

He went on for a long while about names. He said that anyone could tell an awful lot about someone just by knowing the name they had grown up under. A name is

like a severe birthmark, he said. You can't grow up ignoring it. It affects the way you think about yourself. No
"Uriah" for instance, could ever really think of himself
as a happy-go-lucky slapdash roustabout. Just to say the
name aloud sounds like wind passing through a skull. A
boy named Uriah must always think of himself as a
careful old man, beyond the toys and whims of childhood. You just never mind that old crap about what's in
a name and a rose by any other label would still knock
your eyes out. No, no, no. It just isn't so. The name itself
is the key. Call a rose a "hemorrhoid berry" and watch
if anybody sniffs it. So this Franklin fellow—forget the
slant of his jib and the cast of his eyes—this Franklin
fellow will not be satisfied until he's got the job done.

It didn't make much sense to me, this drunken theo-
rizing about names, but I had the feeling that it didn't
matter to him one way or the other. I mean, I didn't
really believe that he was talking about what he appeared to be talking about. The words were just pouring
out of him like a bright cataract from a grim hill. The
cataract and the hill had nothing to do with one another.
I was old enough at the time to understand that such a
thing might be possible and so I let him ramble on without commenting or nit-picking. I might have said, "You
mean that there was never a worthless Franklin in the
history of the world or that some Uriah didn't drink and
screw himself into an early grave?" but I didn't. But I
was also young enough to think that there might be a
grain of truth in what he was saying, even though I felt
that none of it meant very much to him.

Something moved among the large stones on the
shore, an animal of some kind. It was a bighorn sheep.
Three of them, in fact, moving slowly among a cluster
of stones. They stopped and stared at us, curious. Gent
sighted on one of them but didn't pull the trigger. Instead, he put the gun down and leaned over toward me.

He cupped his hand on the back of my neck. His hand was cold and soft. He scratched at the hair behind my ears, and the bighorn sheep trotted off into some scrub pine. Gent chuckled. "Your ma and I," he said, "we're having some troubles."

I nodded. He picked up his bottle and took a drink, then offered it to me. I took several swallows. Gent looked at me, somewhat amazed. "A seasoned tippler," he said. "You'd better watch that, Jack. It can get away from you."

He was no one to talk, but there was no point in saying this. "It tastes like gasoline anyway," I said, and it wasn't a lie. Gin, bourbon, scotch—all foul and fiery and no one, I believed, would ever touch any of them if it weren't for the splendid effect they had on the mind.

"Part of the problem," Gent continued, "between your ma and me is—"

"The saxophone."

"What? The sax? No, Jack, not the sax! Where did you get an idea like that? No, it's the fact that I'm around the house too much. My office is in my home, my business is in my home, and the nature of my work gives me a great deal of free time." He drank, passed the bottle to me, I drank. "Now the point is, a woman cannot stand to watch a man taking his ease in his own home. It makes her anxious. It isn't her fault, mind you. This is something that's been bred into the female of the species down through the ages. They can't help themselves. See, tens of thousands of years ago, the man who relaxed around the campfire was as good as dead, and so was his family. Women got to thinking of a lounging man as a direct threat to their welfare—no matter that the larder is full and the checking account is flush. We're speaking of the primitive level, here, the thing that dwells underneath good sense and obvious circumstances. I have a very good business that practically runs itself. There's nothing in Far Cry by way of competition. As far as the folks of Far Cry are concerned, I am a relatively rich man. So, much of my time is my own. Oh, I do some cooking, and some household chores, but even so, if your ma sees me lounging on the divan reading one of my magazines, that age-old primitive anxiety surges up in her and she becomes peevish and out of sorts." He took another drink, passed me the bottle. I held it for a few seconds, then took a sip. I passed it back to him and he took a sip. He gave it to me, and I gave it back, and he recapped it. I waited for him to continue, but he didn't.

That's it? I wanted to say. That's what you think is wrong with Ma?

"What are you grinning at, Jack?" he said.

I rubbed the grin off my face with both hands. "Nothing," I said.

"You think I'm off the mark, is that it?"

I shrugged, fought the stupid grin twitching in my numb face. I grabbed the bottle and took a fierce pull. The sun was gone and the air was tinged with smoky blue as the long shadows of the hills swept the lake.

"She does things, I know that," he said softly. "But it's her way of telling me that she's being let down, Jack. I suppose it's true. I've been a bachelor too long. I guess I've let her down."

"No you haven't," I said.

He looked at me sharply. "No, I guess I haven't," he said. He helped himself to a lengthy session with the bottle. He picked up the gun and sighted down the bow at nothing. He fired it and a piece of the boat flew into the lake.

"You hit the *boat!*" I said. I crawled up on the bow to see what damage had been done.

"The *Jade Marie* is nothing if not durable, Jack," he said, taking a bead at something off the stern. He fired two shots, this time missing the boat. He had an ugly look on his face. An angry sadness turned the corners of his mouth severely down. His derelict eyes saw nothing but betrayal and defeat though the darkening lake and surrounding landscape reminded me of a picture postcard I once saw that had the caption "God's Majestic Handiwork Unsullied by Man."

He climbed back down into the cabin, taking the bottle and the gun with him. "Leave the gun here, Gent," I said. He looked back at me from the doorway of the cabin. "I just want to do some shooting," I said, trying to smile. He handed me the gun, grip first, then a box of shells.

But I didn't do any shooting. I started the engine and headed back to our ramp, throttle open.

W H E N the *Jade Marie* hit the foot of the ramp, I switched the engine off. I woke Gent and pulled him out of the cabin. I climbed out of the boat and then helped Gent. Before he climbed down, he tossed two boxes of bullets up the ramp. He was as drunk as I'd ever seen him. He staggered as he stepped onto the ramp, almost pitching over into the water. He was still in his underwear, but he held the gun tightly in his right hand.

I walked up to the car, thinking to back it down to the trailer. I wondered if Gent knew how to winch the boat onto the trailer, but then realized that it didn't make any difference if he knew how to or not since the Roadmaster hadn't been equipped with a trailer hitch. There was no way to haul the *Jade Marie* home. This exasperated me and I turned to walk back down to the boat ramp, but as I turned I heard the gun go off. Gent had shoved the boat off the ramp and it was drifting about a dozen yards away. He was sitting on the wet concrete slab and firing rounds at the little cabin cruiser.

"Gent! Gent!" I yelled, running up to him. "What are you doing that for?"

"I'm sending her down, Jack," he said, reloading the cylinder. "I'm sinking the *Jade Marie.*" He was speaking calmly, in the same tone of voice he would use to explain the temperature gauges on the pasteurizer.

I stepped back and watched him raise the gun and sight down the barrel. He fired and a hole the size of a quarter appeared near the bow, on the waterline. "Ho!" he yelled, pleased with his marksmanship.

I said, a bit lamely, "What about your clothes? Your clothes are in the cabin."

But he didn't seem to hear me. He fired again.

"What about Carl Bowers then?" I said, feeling the whisky come on me strong. "What about his wife? If it wasn't for her he wouldn't have had to sell you his boat."

But he didn't hear the tortured logic of all this and continued to drill quarter-size holes into the hull of the *Jade Marie,* near and under the waterline. There was only one valid logic at work: It was his boat, and he wanted to sink it.

He opened the other box of shells. The *Jade Marie* was beginning to list slightly. The impact of the large-caliber slugs was driving it farther and farther out into the lake. The moon was up off the hills, bone white and full. "Sink, bitch," Gent said calmly.

It was the worst thing you could do to a boat like that. It was such a pretty thing, a true ornament for a majestic, unsullied lake. It had a beautiful shape, clean white and perfect blue with a snappy orange flag flying off the stern.

There was an old man fishing off the shore, about a hundred feet from the ramp. He was not looking at us. It must have taken quite an effort to do that. I walked up to the car. I sat in the front seat, behind the wheel. In the rearview mirror I could see that the bow of the *Jade Marie* was under water and the stern was in the air. I got out of the car to watch it go.

But it didn't go. It hung suspended between life and

death. Gent was standing now, watching it, the gun at his side. I walked down to him.

"I'm out of bullets," he said.

"Let's go home," I said.

"Look," he said. "She won't go down. There's enough holes in her to sink two boats, but not this *Jade Marie* of mine. What do you make of it, Jack?" He was grinning, like a man hopelessly amused at the perversity of the world.

I took the empty gun out of his hand. "Let's go," I said. He had planned the whole thing and it made me snap at him. The boat rolled over suddenly, but did not sink. Whatever had been done, it had been done to me too. "Goddammit," I said.

Gent looked at me as if for the first time ever. I looked at him in the same way. We may have been right. I threw the gun into the lake as hard as I could. It bounced off the upside-down boat.

MOTHER and I were playing checkers in the kitchen. Gent was in the creamery fixing the homogenizer, which had broken down. Supper was in the oven, meat loaf and baked potatoes, and Mother had gotten out a bottle of red wine. I sat opposite her, studying the board.

I glanced up and realized then that she had been looking at me for some time. "You're getting some size to you, Jack," she said. "How old are you now?"

"Twenty-five," I said.

"What?"

"Sixteen."

"God, time flies."

In fact, I wasn't so sizable. At five foot eight and 145 pounds, I was one of the smallest boys in the tenth grade. I'd bought myself a set of barbells and I was drinking an extra quart of milk a day, hoping for some growth, but whatever growth there was came very slow.

Still, my muscles were getting lumpy and I could hoist my body weight over my head a few times in a row. I also had a fairly heavy beard. It had come in light brown with a tinge of red in it. I had let my sideburns grow out to cover some of the black pockmarks from the blown-up .30-.30.

Mother got up and brought another glass to the table. She set it down in front of me and filled it. "I guess you're old enough to have a drink of wine with your ma," she said.

I jumped her king and moved one step closer to another jump. "You damned sneak!" she said.

I took a sip of the wine. It was a new taste for me and I liked it. It didn't swamp you like bourbon or gin, but it had a nice effect just the same. Slower, gentler, and pleasantly drinkable.

She had left herself wide open to a double jump, and beyond that I could see the vulnerability of a king, but I held off because I wanted the game to last longer. She was wearing a silky, rose-colored dress, the throat open. Her mahogany hair was pulled straight back on her head and her face was a perfect white oval. She had a straight nose and full lips, which were strong and perfectly shaped. But it was her eyes that got and held your attention, big, hazel-green eyes that made you feel you were a solid and self-justified presence in the world. They could make you feel like you were scum, too, but it was this look of complete, unqualified acceptance that men fed upon. I saw, aided now by the wine, how a man like Guy Rampling could be driven to put his hands on her as often as she would allow, how a man like Gent Mundy would be moved to hide in the basement and play love songs on his sax for her sake, or in a vengeful rage sink a lovely boat named after her, and how a man like Roger Trewly, having failed to provide her with money and love, might be tempted to step over the railing of the Mill Avenue bridge when the Far Cry River was white and roaring in the spring. I thought about my father, whose love for her was full and uncompromised, and yet found it possible to hold his hunting rifle against his heart and discharge it. They said it was the war, that many coming home from it could not forget what they had seen, but I had my doubts. Something caught in my throat and I made a noise.

"Don't drink that too fast, honey," Mother said. "It's meant for sipping, not swilling."

I set my empty glass down, and after holding back for a minute, I refilled it.

"How do you like your new daddy?" she asked.

I was about to make a move that would corner a piece that she was trying to get kinged, but I slid my checker back to its square. I looked at her. For a crazy second I thought she meant Guy Rampling. By that time she had been married to Gent for four years and had not thought to ask my opinion of him before this.

"Gent?" I asked, grinning.

"Yes, *Gent.* Jesus, Jackie." She moved her piece into my back row and I kinged it. "I'd like to know how you get along with him," she said. She said this in a distracted tone of voice, as if the game before her was far more intriguing.

"I like Gent, Ma," I said.

"Do you?" she said, in that same, offhanded tone. She lifted her glass of wine. Her eyes unfocused slightly as she sipped. When she set the glass down, she said, "And you don't think he's disgusting?"

"Disgusting? No, Ma, I don't think he's disgusting." I wondered if she knew about the *Jade Marie* and what he had done to it, or that he rode home drunk, in his underwear, sleeping in the back seat while I drove the Roadmaster, drunk as Gent but roaring. I guessed she didn't.

She smiled at me, her lips wet with wine. I sat up straighter in my chair and frowned, trying to take our discussion seriously but fighting my damned grin. I rubbed my chin, imitating thought. She laughed and double-jumped my men with the king I'd let her have.

"Well, for your information, Jack, he *is* disgusting. Very much so."

I didn't want to disagree with her. "Well, sure," I said. "He does eat too much. Gee, canned bread and gravy . . ."

"You mean canned gravy and bread. But it isn't just that, Jackie. That isn't the half of it, honey."

I thought then of his little books and photographs and my face heated up.

"I don't grudge a man his appetite, it isn't that. It's what he . . ." But she had said more than she had intended. This is the impression I got. She frowned into her glass. Maybe she was a little drunk. Maybe I was too, but I thought she was going to cry and I wanted to jump up and hold her face in my hands and tell her that nothing in the world was too overwhelming to change.

"His saxophone," I said, but I knew she meant a lot more than his saxophone.

"Oh, shit," she said, laughing now. "No, not his stupid sax, Jack. Well, maybe that's part of it. Sometimes that thing can drive me up the wall. Okay, throw in the sax. Sure, that's part of it."

I was confused. I lost another man to that free-ranging king. I searched the board desperately for a move. I was down to four pieces. She had two kings, plus three pieces that were on their way into my back row. I picked up my glass and gulped down the wine. My head was hot and there was a roar in my ears.

"He's going insane," she said.

Suddenly I didn't know how to play checkers. I got the flow of movement mixed up. Was I going toward her or away from her? Were her pieces heading for my back row or were they heading the opposite way? And were kings free to jump sideways, across the red squares? The wine had given me a boner, which added to my confusion, and I was hot with shame.

"*Who's* insane?" I asked.

"Jesus God, who are we talking about, Jack?" she said, double-jumping, leaving me stripped to only two pieces, which were both trapped into a corner of the board. "*Gent,* honey. Gent's insane. Haven't you seen it? Who did you think I was talking about? President Eisenhower? You've had enough of that wine now."

"What in the hell do you mean?" I said, trying to form the thick belligerent words carefully in my mouth, but I had more or less come to believe the same thing about Gent.

"Don't get snotty with me, Jack. I mean just what I say. It isn't his fault. It's in his brain, a sickness. He's had it all along, for years, and now it's in his brain. You've seen how blue he gets."

I thought, He might have some fairly good reasons for getting down in the mouth, and she seemed to read the thought in my eyes.

"Don't you look at *me* like that!" she said. "It's not my fault that he ate raw pork!"

I swallowed some wine. "Raw pork?" I said. I didn't have a move left on the board. I tried to cheat, to slip one of my pieces into another row, but she put her hand on my wrist.

"It's not your move," she said. I withdrew my hand. "Yes, raw pork," she continued. "We think this is the problem."

"We?" I asked, but she didn't offer to explain.

"He ate some raw pork on a bet, when he was playing for that dance band. Oh, this was a long time ago, before the war. He was just a kid. The boys had been drinking and they wanted to do some crazy things. That's how people were back then. They were in some jerkwater town across the county. Someone got the bright idea that eating raw pork would be a daring thing to do. Jesus, raw pork in some jerkwater town. Can you beat that for dumb?"

I shook my head.

"They bought a package of pork from some meat market and laid down bets over who would eat the most. Gent won. He ate a pound of that damned wormy meat. And now he's paying the price. Those pork worms—tiny soliums, I think they're called—found his brain. It happens sometimes, though it's rare."

I almost puked. The burning stomach acids were in the back of my throat. I washed them down with cool wine. She poured me another glass. My straining boner was painful. I moved a checker suicidally out of a corner and into the path of her king. I had to take a leak, but I was afraid to stand up. We both picked up our glasses at the same time and drank. Our eyes met. The light in her eyes was quick and tricky. The corners of her mouth lifted into a smirk I had never seen before. Suddenly I didn't believe her.

"So," she said. "Gent is going to have to have professional care, and that's all there is to it." The words *professional care* sounded like something she read in the "Home Doctor" column of the newspaper, and I felt all at once that I had been taking part in a serious decision and that it had just been made and that's why I was sitting here with her drinking wine, giving my approval and support.

"Are they going to operate on him and pick those goddamned worms out of his brain one by one?" I said, slurring the words together.

"Maybe you've had enough of that," she said, sliding the wine bottle out of my reach. But I leaned forward and pulled it back. I refilled my glass. "No, honey," she said, sighing, her mouth now downcast and tight. "They can't operate. It's too far gone for anything like that. He's just going to get worse and worse as time goes by."

"Then what kind of professional help will help him if they can't get the pork worms out of his brains?" I pushed my remaining checker past her king, even though it wasn't my turn, and she didn't stop me.

A door slammed in the house. Her expression changed again. She touched her breasts and smoothed her hands against them. I moved again, heading for her back row. She was distracted and nervous now, Gent's problems far behind her. "I don't know, I don't know," she sighed. "The State Hospital, I guess. Down at Willow Springs."

"Bull," I said, moving again.

"They will be able to look after him better than we can here . . ."

There was that "we" again. "King me," I said, slipping my checker into her back, undefended row.

The kitchen door flew open. "Hey!" Guy Rampling said, taking off his milkman's cap. "What in the hell's going on in here? Where's the grub?" He pulled off his white jacket and scratched his ribs.

Mother got up to check on the meat loaf. Guy sat down in her place and set up a new game. "Checkers," he said. "I'll whip you in fifteen minutes, Jack," he said.

I leaned back in my chair and lit a cigarette, squinted at him through the smoke.

"Well, go ahead, hotshot," he said. "I'll give you first move."

I pushed away from the table and stood up. "No thanks," I said. "I think I'll go upstairs."

Guy pointed his finger at me and narrowed his eyes. "That's a filthy habit for a kid to have," he said. "I've got a mind to make you eat one of those weeds, just to get you to quit."

I took a deep drag and blew a smoke ring across the kitchen.

"I don't think your ma would mind a bit if I did," he said. "Would you, Jade?"

"Eat what?" she said, closing the oven door.

"One of those coffin nails he's always sucking on. If I shoved one down his throat he might think twice about how good they are, taste-wise."

I could tell that Mother didn't like him talking like that. "Don't be such a bully," she said and laughed, nervously.

Guy jumped up and pretended to come after me, but I didn't flinch as he'd hoped I would. I blew another smoke ring and turned my back on him. He put his hand on my shoulder and turned me back around. "Tough little shit, are you?" he said. He started to spar, open-handed, grazing my chin and shoulders with his fingers. "Come on. Let's mix it up, kid."

But Mother came over with a beer in her hand. "Here," she said, handing it to him. "Why don't you sit down and take a load off your feet, you must be bushed."

He took the beer and drank, his little eyes fixed on me. He belched. Then he showed me his fist, smiling. He passed the fist under my chin.

"Come on, sit down," Mother said, pulling him away.

I went up to my room. I loaded up my barbell and hoisted it over my head. After five military presses my arms were burning. I lowered it, shakily, then dropped it the last few inches. The house shook.

I looked at myself in the mirror. My biceps and triceps looked good. They were coming along. My stomach had some ripples in it. My neck, though, was still too skinny. I put on the weighted head harness and started doing my neck exercises.

LaDonna came in, a magazine in her hand. I slipped off the head harness and lit a cigarette. She wanted to talk about an article in the magazine she was reading. It was about this muskrat who had eaten the vegetation around a pond near Oak Ridge, Tennessee. The muskrat had developed bone cancer in its right hind leg.

"A real tragedy," I said, blowing a smoke ring toward her. "Makes me want to cut my throat."

She gave me an impatient look, then said, "It's radio-strontium. It acts like calcium. I mean, the bones can't tell the difference. The bones think it's just milk. And once it gets into the bones, it causes cancer. Isn't that awful?"

"I guess so," I said, bored and a little tired.

"Radiostrontium, Jack, is a man-made isotope."

"No kidding."

"It doesn't occur in nature. It's something new. Isn't that just terrible? I'll have to ask Mr. Howe about it."

I poured her an inch of gin out of the jug I had stashed in my closet.

"Don't you ever wash these glasses?" she asked, sipping from it.

"It's just scum," I said. "Not radiostrontium muck."

"Scientists all over the world are worried sick. Mr. Howe—"

"Don't mention it to Mr. Howe," I said. "You'll just piss him off."

She looked at me, confused. Smart as she was, she could be dumb about people. She tended to give them more credit than they deserved.

"Howe is an idiot," I said. "Didn't he give you an F on your last test?"

"Oh, that," she said. "It was kind of my fault, Jackie. I changed the questions, to make them more interesting."

"Idiots don't like to have their mental drawbacks pointed out to them, LaDonna."

"Radiostrontium falls out of the sky, all over the earth. It's in the grass cows eat. It's in milk, everywhere."

"Cancer rain," I said.

She looked at me, moody and distant.

"Ma's going to put Gent away," I said.

"What?" She blinked, coming back from wherever it was she'd gone. "What about Gent?"

"They're putting him into Willow Springs. They're saying he's got pork worms in his brain. He needs professional help."

LaDonna sat down on my bed. "Are you serious?" she asked.

"I guess he's been to the doctor about it. Yes, I'm serious."

"Shit," she said.

I gave her a cigarette, took another one for myself. I poured us a second round of gin. It was sloe gin, mild and tasty. I lit her cigarette first, then lit mine. We puffed on them seriously for a while, sipped our gins. After a while she said, "Jesus," in a long, slow hiss.

After another while, I said, "I'm clearing out."

She looked at me, alarmed. "No, Jackie. Don't go."

I shrugged. I took a long, hard drag on my cigarette, making the burning end crackle.

"What will you do?" she said.

I shrugged. I didn't know. "Work," I said.

Gent's sax throbbed suddenly in the heat register. It was "Peg o' My Heart," played in the lowest register of the baritone.

Swamped by gin on top of wine, I said, "Goddammit, LaDonna," and choked.

She put her arm around me. I felt small and weak. The barbells gleamed at me like a joke. "Tell me, genius sister," I said. "Is life correctable, or not? I mean, can a person *do* something to put things right, or not?"

"I don't know," she said. "It depends on what you mean by 'life' and what you mean by 'correctable' and most of all what you mean by 'right.'"

"Christ," I said. "No wonder Mr. Howe is so pissed off at you."

"The trouble with you, Jack, is that you want simple yes or no answers to hard questions."

"Is *that* it? Damn. Glad I found out before I ran for president."

"People think they're asking simple questions, but they haven't thought very carefully about the terms they're using. The questions aren't simple. The people who *ask* them are."

"So, life isn't correctable then."

"You can't say that for sure."

"Yes I can. It's too damn complicated to be correctable."

"Maybe you're right," she said. "They never planned on radiostrontium and all the other things that's in store for us down the line, did they?"

"Muskrats with bone cancer."

"Pork worms."

The gin kicked in hard all at once, and we both fell off the bed laughing. We laughed until it hurt. I reached over and touched the tears on her face. "My old sis," I said.

"Forever," she said.

THE rat eased closer to the trap, sniffing. I was under the electric churn, watching. He hunched up, as if getting set to feed, but he didn't put his head down to the bait. He sniffed the tiles all around the trap, rising on his hind legs like a prairie dog testing the wind. Then he dropped back down to snuffle at something between his front feet. He was smart enough to know that there was danger in the neighborhood, but he wanted the lump of white cheese wedged in the trap trigger bad enough to risk anything. His long, patient nose twitched and his mean, hairless tail flexed in a thoughtful arc.

A small noise made both our heads jerk up. It was a wet, slapping sound, a *toc toc toc toc*. When I looked back at the rat, it was gone. The lump of cheese was gone too. He had studied the situation long enough to solve the problem of how to snag the cheese off the trap without releasing the trigger. The *toc toc toc toc* got louder and louder and soon another sound joined in, a gravelly curse, something like "Ah yew, yew, yew, be-damn bedamn!"

I looked around. The light in the creamery was poor, but I thought I could see two white sticks in a sack. The sack was crumpled on the floor and the white sticks were jutting out of it. The sticks bent slightly at the middle, bent and straightened, bent and straightened, and with each movement I heard the low grumbling curse, "Ah yew, yew, yew, be-damn bedamn!"

I saw then that I was looking at a pair of skinny, stem-like legs with a pair of pants gathered around the an-kles. I crawled out from under the electric churn, being careful to not make any noise. I came out on a side of the churn that put me directly behind the man with the dropped pants.

It was only old Swede, working overtime. But he wasn't exactly working. He was leaning over the tex-turator and flogging his mule. The texturator was where the churned butter was smoothed out. He had opened it up and was leaning over the blades. Now and then he would lean down to scoop up a handful of resid-ual butter to lube himself. Then he would start flogging it again, saying, "Ah yew, yew, yew, be-damn, bedamn!" to urge his ancient member toward ecstasy. He had taped a pinup girl poster on a steel pipe in front of him. From time to time, he reached out with his free hand to caress her heavy, peach-colored breasts.

"What are you up to Swede?" I asked, casually.

The *toc toc toc toc* stopped dead. Old Swede froze, mid-stroke. His bony little ass quivered a bit. I felt sorry for him, but I pretended to be as mad as the boss's son ought to have been at finding an employee pounding off into the butter machine. Without turning to face me, he slowly reached down and pulled up his pants. He zipped his fly and tugged his belt. Then he turned around slowly. "Jayzuz," he said, stricken. "I thought I lock her up for the night."

I showed him my key. "You probably oughtn't to jerk off into the butter, Swede," I said.

He stuttered, slapped at his malfunctioning mouth, then whined, "Ah be-damn, kid, I—I didn't mean to. It sure as hell wasn't in my head to do it, kid."

"That's a hot one, Swede," I said. "What you're saying is that it was an *accident*? That's a hell of an accident, Swede. You got insurance coverage for accidental jacking off into a butter texturator?"

He peeled the pinup girl off the steel pipe, a slow gesture so full of defeat that I felt like apologizing for the intrusion and telling him to go on with it, that creaking, arthritic march toward ecstasy.

"Jayzuz, kid," he said, rolling up the poster into a tight cylinder. "Don't tell your old man, hey? I need this goddamn job."

Maybe he was sixty, maybe only fifty, I don't know, but he was at the end of something I had not yet begun, and I saw that, and respected it, and felt ashamed of myself for having reduced it to a joke.

"I won't tell him," I said. Then added, "If you'll do me a favor."

"Be-damn by hell, kid! Anything you say!" His watery old eyes were submissive and quick with fear. "Just so's I don't have to kill anybody!"

"Nothing like that, Swede," I said. "I just want you to buy me some wine. A gallon of it." I handed him a five-dollar bill. He smiled, half toothless, realizing his good luck.

"What else, kid? How about some aquavit? By hell, that will put some hair on your balls, kid!"

His eyes were glittering a little strangely now. I

backed away, toward the door. "Nope," I said, grinning. "Just a gallon of red wine. Okay?"

He buckled his pants fondly, chuckling to himself.

"One other thing, Swede," I said.

He looked up from his belt buckling, which was going slowly. "Hey? What's that, kid?"

"Don't flog your mule into the butter machine anymore. It's disgusting."

Swede grabbed his crotch in a savage but jubilant gesture meant to describe the no-nonsense disciplining of an unruly but basically good-natured character. "Ah, by shit, you're a hardleg and a half, kid," he said, grinning, his bright pink gums studded here and there with a brown tooth. "You're hell on wheels, kid."

SANTA Claus sat in the kitchen eating bread and gravy. The party was roaring in the front room, out on the porch, and in the front yard. It was Christmas Eve, and there was still no snow on the ground. The warm wind blew out of the south. I was drunk in the hedge with my jug, watching.

Wine gave me a smug and cozy distance on things. I felt as if I was afloat in a liquid world, bouyant, superior. I held this attitude as a kind of secret weapon and only my betraying grin gave the telltale clue to my privileged angle on things. That was how wine worked. It was different from hard booze, which made me loud and open.

I was the moving center of the world, and the best thing about it was that no one knew it. When I moved, everyone else was dragged helplessly along, or they drifted into nothingness, or fell into languid orbits at the far edges of my vision, hoping to be summoned closer by my attractive gravitational field.

This notion was great fun, whether it made sense or not, and I often broke out laughing about it. Wine, wine, wonderful wine. When I walked among them I would be careful to take long, stiff strides, keeping my arms down and in, my head straight, my face set in a sober frown. Only my uncontrollable grin, springing into my face at the odd remark or gesture, opened the door on my exotic frame of mind.

"Merry Christmas," I would say, son of the host, greeting the newcomers, pretending to be the everyday, ordinary me.

There were about fifteen people in the house. Guy Rampling brought a woman named Sarona Harkey with him. She was tall and heavily built but very good-looking, with broad, thick shoulders, a big, straight-edged, boxy ass, and long, well-shaped legs. She had a round, cheeky face with a large, handsomely upturned nose, but there was something mean in her close-set eyes, something sharp, as though she was thinking one step ahead of everyone else and would soon spring something hard to take on some unsuspecting soul.

Everyone was drunk or nearly drunk. There was a big punch bowl on the coffee table. It was mostly rum with a few different kinds of fruit juice mixed in. Sarona Harkey went straight for it and helped herself to a beer mug full. Mother was in a corner, talking to Guy. She looked mad. Guy was wearing a green suit with a red shirt and a white knit tie. His glossy pompadour was higher than ever. Whatever Mother was saying to him, it wasn't funny, but Guy acted as though she were telling him some amusing story about the hectic life of a mother of three.

I drifted closer to them. "Go to hell," I heard Mother hiss.

"Ha ha ha," Guy said, imitating amusement.

"Why are you doing this to me?" she said.

Guy looked shiftily around. "Not to worry, Jade," he said. "Don't get your tit in the wringer."

Someone put a record on the Victrola and three or

four couples started to dance. They were drunk and the men steered the women into the furniture and into other couples, and there was a lot of squealing and laughing. It was a mambo, a tricky beat that Gent hated. I had tried to pick it up and when Gent heard me practicing it on my drum he took the sticks out of my hands. "That's terrible," he said. "It sounds like war." The people dancing it didn't know how. They labored behind the beat, lifting their knees, kicking out, elbows flying dangerously, faces red, shouting. Sarona Harkey put her arm around my shoulder and said, "Let's show these hicks how it's done."

Before I could say no or duck out, she slipped her arm around my waist and powered me out among the other dancers. I took her hand in mine and put my other hand on the fleshy area of her back, just under her brassiere, but she grabbed my wrists and put both my hands on her hips. She put both her hands on my hips, urging them to move. Her hips were rotating magnificently and I tried to do the same with mine but I didn't have the smooth, swinging flexibility she had. The firm flesh of her hips made my hands sweat and her hard, pointed breasts gouged my ribs. She kicked off her shoes and picked up the pace and I had trouble keeping off her feet as the trumpets, saxes, and bongos carried us around the room. "Mambo, *jambo,* mambo, *jambo,*" she chanted, breathlessly, her white teeth flashing, her tongue wetting her dry lips from time to time.

We gyrated past Mother and Guy. Guy had a dirty twinkle in his eye. He tugged Mother's elbow to get her to look at Sarona and me. Mother turned, but she was still too mad at Guy to let herself be amused. "Merry Christmas," I said, as we passed them. A dark little man had fallen into the Christmas tree and was staggering away from it. His blue suit was covered with tinsel. Someone lifted the tone arm of the Victrola and said, "This damn spic music is too tough for me." He put on a Wayne King record instead, a slow waltz, and Sarona stalked away from me, mad.

I went out into the kitchen, where Gent was still eating bread and gravy. He was sweating heavily in his Santa Claus suit. His white beard hung stiffly from his face. There were strings of greasy gravy hanging from it. Spencer Ted was leaning across Gent's knees, half asleep, whining a tuneless lullaby to himself.

"Merry Christmas, Gent," I said.

He raised his eyes to me but didn't say anything. He lifted his hand a few inches off the table, then let it drop.

"You want some punch, Gent?" I said. "I'll get you a mug of it."

His head moved up and down slowly and I took that to mean yes. I went back out to the front room. Guy was now sitting on the sofa with Sarona. Mother was talking to a tall gray-haired man with a big nose. I dipped out a mug of punch. Sarona said, loudly, "It's men, I'm telling you, it's *men.*"

"You're wrong," said Guy, winking.

"I'm *not* wrong," she said. "It's men. All the trouble and grief starts with them. They need to be cut while they're still in their cribs. Cut them, and the trouble and grief will be done with. It's the only humane thing to do."

"Oh?" Guy said, winking at Mother and a few others, as if he had the situation under control and was merely humoring Sarona. "What are you going to do for fun, once you do that?"

Sarona laughed harshly. "See what I mean, Jade?" she said to Mother, but you could have heard her across the street. "They think their zippers represent the gates to heaven. They want you to think that dirty little stump is Saint Peter."

Guy's superior little grin faded. "The hell," he said, witlessly.

Mother started to laugh, but then remembered that

she was mad. The tall man she was with said, "Cut who? Cut who?"

"I say cut the bastards in their cribs," Sarona said. "There'd be a whole lot more peace and quiet in this world once they did. Take my word for it. They cut horses to con*trol* them, don't they?"

Guy sat up straight and pointed a finger at her. "Okay, okay, let's say you're right. The whole human race would die out then. Is that what you want? Who is going to get the women pregnant if you cut all the boy babies in their cribs?"

Sarona flicked some dust off her skirt. "Hell, that's easy. We'll just keep one out of a hundred intact, for stud. But we'll keep that one locked up in a cage, where he can't go off starting World War III."

"Where do you sign up for that job?" Guy asked, grinning.

"Goddammit, I am serious," Sarona said, slapping his shoulder.

"Hubba hubba," said Guy.

I brought Gent his mug of punch. He picked it up and drank it all in one effort. Then he slipped a bottle of bourbon out of his Santa Claus coat and filled the mug. Spencer Ted was now snoring, his head in Gent's lap. The little man in the blue suit with tinsel hanging from it was rummaging around in the fridge. "Help yourself," I said.

I went back out to the front room. Sarona was still arguing loudly about the need to cut male babies in their cribs. Most of the people around her had lost interest. Their faces were slack with boredom. A waltz as slow as a dirge was on the Victrola. I took it off and replaced it with a jump tune, "Savoy," just to liven things up. I turned up the volume to drown out Sarona and people began dancing again. I dipped myself a mug full of punch, just to see what it was like, and carried it outside.

LaDonna and the skinny, red-haired boy were on the front porch, necking. I sipped the punch. Too sweet. I handed the mug to LaDonna and wished her Merry Christmas. Then I went outside, to the hedge, where my jug was waiting. Wine, wine, wonderful wine. I saluted the gleaming jug, patted the cap before unscrewing it.

I stayed in the hedge quite a while, drinking, listening to the ever-increasing roar of the party. A tune ran through my head. I couldn't place it. It was pretty and I could hear it plainly, just as if someone were sitting next to me, humming it. Then I realized that it was me who was doing the humming. I was humming out loud, with my mouth open. In fact, I was yelling it. The trick I had played on myself struck me as very funny and I laughed until I almost wet myself. I had to unzip quickly and stand up. I pissed long and hard into the hedge, away from my wine.

Someone was next to me then, also pissing. "Merry Christmas, junior," he said. It was the tall, gray-haired man with the big nose. "The toilet had a line waiting to get in, but I couldn't wait. Say, this is one hell of a fine party your folks are putting on."

"Thanks," I said.

He grunted as he forced a few more jets of piss into the hedge. "Who is that dumb bastard with the hairdo?" he asked.

"Just some dumb bastard with a hairdo," I said, grinning.

"It figures," he said, shaking the dribble.

The man zipped up and staggered away. "Merry Christmas," I said.

"Merry Christmas, junior," he said.

I took one more drink, then headed for the house. The house was rocking. Each step I took made it rock. Left then right, left then right. The house was on rockers. The world was on rockers. But I was the unmoving center, dragging things along. The rocking front steps were not easy to mount. I went up two steps, one down. One step sideways, one step up. Up one, two down, three to the left, and I was on my side in the grass, my lungs tingling with lost wind.

I crawled around to the back of the house. Santa Claus was in the backyard, puking. Huge liquid volumes thudded into the winter grass. I almost got sick myself, watching. But I climbed up the back steps on all fours and went inside.

Guy was in the kitchen doing a handstand. His hair fell away from his mangled ears, exposing them. He had either forgotten about how bad they looked or he was too drunk to care. Sarona and Mother were leaning against the sink, watching him. They both had their arms folded under their breasts as if they were bored with him but had nothing better to do just then. Guy had taken off his suit coat and his tie. He did ten quick push-ups from the handstand position. He barked out numbers, making sure the audience realized how many push-ups he was capable of doing. Then he dropped neatly to his feet.

Sarona had a bored, sleepy look on her big face. Mother still looked put out. "Merry Christmas one and all," I said, but the words came out garbled.

Mother looked at me, at my clothes, at my face. "Jesus God almighty," she said.

"Your little shaver is shit-faced, Jade," Guy said.

I sat down at the kitchen table and fumbled for my cigarettes. My little fish lighter was out of fluid. I put it back into my pocket and just let the unlit cigarette hang on my lip.

"I told you about that, pissant," Guy said, pointing a finger at me. He turned to Mother. "Jade, this little horse's ass of yours is drunk as a lord." Turning back to me he said, "You been into that punch bowl, right?"

I did what I'd been wanting to do for a long time. I plunked my elbow down on the table, forearm raised, and slowly extended the middle finger out of my clenched fist. In a slow, deliberate gesture, I let arm, fist, and finger stand on the table in front of him like a flesh-and-blood opinion of his worth.

I expected applause, but only Sarona snorted merrily. Mother frowned at me. Guy just sat there, undisturbed. I felt great, reading his calmness as defeat. I felt justified, sure of myself, and invincible.

I saw Guy's hand moving toward me, but it didn't mean anything. It was moving slow enough to dodge, but I didn't see the need. Mother said something, but I couldn't make out what it was because of the commotion in the front room. It sounded as if someone had danced into the Christmas tree again, this time managing to knock it over. Then Guy grabbed my wrist, and for a second I thought he wanted to arm wrestle, but he yanked me out of my chair instead, so hard that my head snapped back. The force of it took me completely out of the center of things. His hand was so strong that I thought the bones of my wrist would crack in its grip. He drew me toward him and I had no power to resist and before I understood what was happening, he had thrown me across his knees and was spanking me. I tried to kick free, but he threw his leg over the back of my knees and I was scissored in place on his lap. To hold the rest of me still, he bent my right arm behind my back and pushed it up until my hand was touching the base of my skull. I was paralyzed in this position.

His hand came down hard on the seat of my pants, but I was too drunk to really feel anything. The spanks exploded in the kitchen like firecrackers. I raised my head to see if anyone was looking. I saw Sarona. She had a strange look on her face. Her eyes were wide and excited, and her mouth was moving in an uncontrolled way. She pulled her lips back tight on her teeth, in a kind of smile, but it looked more like she was trying to control the jumping muscles around her mouth. I couldn't see Mother. Other people were drifting in to see what was going on.

Then I heard Mother say, "No more, Guy. That's enough."

"No, it isn't enough," Guy said, and I could tell from the strain in his voice that he was putting everything he had into each blow. "This little ass-wipe's been asking for a good hiding for a long time."

"Let him up, Guy," Gent said, his voice shaking.

"In a minute," Guy said. "Somebody's got to be a daddy to this brat. Somebody's got to do the dirty work."

I was beginning to feel it. A dull ache moved up my spine and into my shoulders. My teeth were clenched and I realized that I was growling like a dog.

"Let him up," Gent said again.

"Uh-uh," Guy said. "No, sir. The little twerp is going to take his medicine."

More people drifted into the kitchen. A couple of people were counting spanks out loud. Someone said, "Say, is this a birthday party? I thought it was supposed to be Christmas!" And someone else said, "Hey, let me spell you, Guy. Give me a lick or two at that cutey." It was Sarona, and Guy said, "Step right up, lady."

The spanks got lighter and quicker. Sarona had moved behind me, accepting Guy's offer. Every fourth or fifth spank she gave me was off the mark and would land high up on the small of my back or kidneys where it stung fiercely. She tugged on my back pockets, trying to pull my pants down so that she could hit bare flesh. I heard Mother yell, then, "Stop it, you goddamn bitch!" and Sarona went flying across the room, back in front of me where I could see her again, but she only laughed it off and went out of the room, saying, "Anybody want to mambo?"

"Let him up," Gent said again. "Let him up or you're fired."

Guy let me up. I was surprised to find out that my face

was wet with tears and that there was snot hanging out of my nose and that I was whimpering like an eight-year-old. Gent looked half dead. There were puke flecks in his beard and his face had a gray-blue tinge to it.

Guy tried to laugh the whole thing off. "No harm done," he said, grinning, shifting his eyes from face to face looking for support. He showed everyone the inside of his beet-red hand. "Looky here, it hurt me more than it hurt him. Besides, that kid had it coming. You saw what he did, didn't you?"

I was shaking and tears were spilling out of my eyes like water from a tap and I couldn't make them stop. Gent pulled me toward him and I hid against his chest, behind his big red arms.

"Why don't you go up to your room, honey?" Mother said, her hand stroking my hair. "You shouldn't drink like that, Jackie."

LaDonna and her red-haired boyfriend were in the kitchen and had seen everything. I pushed Gent's arm away and shoved my way through the crowd. The pain had finally arrived, hot and throbbing, and I had to walk stiff-legged. When I walked past the red-haired boy, he said, "Haw haw haw," and LaDonna would not look at me.

I followed Guy to his small, aluminum trailer. It was in the middle of the night. I had a rock in one hand and a one-gallon can of gas in the other. He went into the trailer and turned on the lights. I hid in the dead weeds until the lights went out. After another half hour or so, I crept up close to the trailer. I could hear him snoring. The rock was now a brick, a heavy firebrick. I lobbed it with both hands onto the roof of the trailer. It rumbled like thunder in the hills. I liked the sound of it and so I brought a storm in and sat it on the edge of town, throwing heavy bolts of lightning into the west hills. I ducked back into the tall weeds and waited. He came stumbling out. "Who in the hell is that?" he yelled. He was wearing only the bottom half of his long johns. He stood on the metal steps of his porch, waving his fist at the night. Then he walked around his trailer, mumbling threats and cursing. He went back inside and came out with a crowbar. I could see that he was scared. He stood on the metal steps in front of his door and pointed in my general direction with the crowbar. "You there, in those weeds!" he yelled. "Show yourself so I can get a look at what a pissant you are!" I stood up, toying with the idea of letting my storm fry him to a charred crisp with a quick bolt of lightning, but decided against it—too easy. He went back inside. The lights in the kitchen came on. I heard pots and pans clanging together. A few minutes later I smelled bacon frying. I walked up to the trailer and sat down on the porch steps, dissatisfied with myself. Dissatisfied because I liked the smell of frying bacon. It made me feel good. I didn't want to feel good. I wanted to feel mad as hell and ripe for revenge. I wanted to feel murder in my blood. So I backed everything up to where I was lobbing the brick onto his roof and tried to ignore the smell of bacon. I threw it higher this time and the thunder was better than the thunder in the west hills. He came flying out, crowbar held high. He ran right past me and began to thrash around in the brush, yelling for the pissant to show himself. He swung the crowbar at shadows. The moonlit air was filled with a haze of pulverized weed. I followed him, staying back far enough to avoid the backswing of the crowbar, and then, timing my move to his wild thrashings, I hit him in the kidney area with a baseball bat I had just found lying at my feet. He fell over, groaning. I started to stomp him, but it wasn't right. Like the lightning bolt, this was too easy. He hadn't paid the full price. There he was, lying at my feet, moaning, but it wasn't good enough. It had to be better than this. So I lobbed the brick again and watched him come roaring out of his trailer. This time he had a gun in his hand. He shot up the underbrush. One bullet carried half a mile and wound up in the brain of a kindly old man who had been walking his dog. That bullet would eventually be traced back to Guy and he would be convicted of murder and he would spend twenty years in the state prison, where his stupid tattoos would incite the other prisoners to beat on him, daily. He whirled around suddenly and put a bullet over my head, but he was shooting at phantoms. He saw something move past his front window and he fired three quick shots, shattering the glass. He ran to the other side of the trailer, shooting at shapes that crawled along the foundation. Finally, out of breath, he sat down on his porch. "Damn you, pissant!" he said, feeble and confused and close to tears. He went inside. I lobbed the brick. He came out. He ran around in the burr-filled fields, shooting his gun and cursing. A stray bullet lodged in the brain of a kindly old man who had been walking his dog. The old man was the father of the chief of police. It was almost dawn. I had to go throw up because of all the wine and the smell of bacon that was coming up from the kitchen. I guessed Mother was fixing breakfast for some of the lingering drunks. The bathroom light hurt my eyes. I looked at my sick face in the mirror, stuck out my coated tongue. I heaved and heaved until there was nothing to heave. I turned out the light and sat on the cool toilet seat. Revenge, if it's going to be sweet, can't be hasty. I watched Guy running around his trailer, shooting and cursing. I decided to let him do that while I clarified my ideas. I couldn't think very clearly, and I wanted to go to sleep. Guy was getting tired running in circles. So was I. Then he went back into the trailer. The lights went out. Soon I heard him snoring. I had the can of gas with me, only now it was a five-gallon can. It was dark in the trailer, but it was easy to find my way around. I went into his bedroom. He wasn't alone in the bed. I shook the shoulder of the woman, to wake her. It was Mother. "How did *you* get into this?" I asked, but she said nothing. She didn't have anything on but the moonlight from the small, high window and her skin was dusty gray. The black, triangular shadow between the high ridges of her hips sailed into my eyes like a kite cut loose. Her half-conscious arms came snaking up toward me and suddenly I was bending down to her and my boner craned up out of my pajamas and I woke up, startled. Jesus, don't go to sleep, I told myself, if you're going to plan this right. So I lobbed the brick onto the roof of his trailer. Thunder rolled in the hills. He came stumbling out. I went inside. I woke up Mother. "Get home," I told her. "Get home now." She got up and pulled on her robe, then slipped out of the trailer. I had a ten-gallon can of gas with me. I emptied it throughout the trailer house. Guy was half a mile away, shooting at an old man who had been innocently walking his dog. "You goddamn pissant!" Guy yelled as he shot the old man down in cold blood. The chief of police watched, horrified, from his patrol car. "That crazy bastard has just killed my daddy!" he said, unseating his riot gun. I went outside and stood on the metal steps of the porch. Cold wind from the north blew snow pellets into my face as winter arrived. I saw Mother in her robe loping home through the underbrush. "Keep going," I yelled, "I'll get a blanket and catch up with you in a little bit." I ducked back into the trailer, which smelled heavily of gasoline. I pulled a blanket off his bed, then, from the doorway of the trailer I said, "Hey, Guy Rampling! Wake up you cheese-eating son of a bitch!" The bedroom light came on. North wind bellowed through the night. I heard him stumbling around. I'd let him escape the chief of police, and here he was. Then I took out my little fish lighter and started the trailer burning. I sprinted away from it. Flames blasted out the windows like the flames of blowtorches.

I heard one long, begging scream. Mother came out of the trailer, covered with fire. "No!" I hollered. "I told you to head home!" But as she walked toward me, I saw that the fire was cold and thin, the iridescent blue of forget-me-nots. Then she was standing next to me, saying, "What have you *done,* Jackie?" her voice quivering with fear and pride. "Is he dead?" I asked. "Oh, yes, Jack," she said. "He's dead." Her robe opened. The cold blue fire was gone, but light from the burning trailer made her perfect breasts glow.

JUST before the first day of spring, winter finally arrived. It snowed for a week, tying up the town. The milk trucks couldn't make deliveries because Far Cry's single snow plow couldn't keep up with the storm. We were housebound. Gent played the sax from early afternoon to dinnertime, and again during his usual hour after we'd eaten, but he didn't ask me to accompany him on drums. The music he played wasn't recognizable. It wasn't really music at all. It was as though he was pressing his pain into ragged patterns of random notes. Luckily, he didn't have much wind and the aimless sax could barely be heard throughout the house. An occasional shiver of misery would rattle a heat register, causing a head to lift, a mouth to tighten, or an eye to roll. But none of it was sustained long enough to irritate anyone for more than a second or two.

Guy Rampling snowshoed his way to dinner every afternoon and he'd stay over until after midnight. He and Mother would sit in the front room while Gent played the sax in the basement, and when Gent came upstairs, Mother would sit him down in the kitchen in front of a big plate heaped with bread and gravy. Gent would eat slowly, sometimes sitting at the table for hours, and during this time Mother and Guy would sit in the front room, making plans.

Gent was beyond caring. Mother and Guy could do anything they wanted, and Guy was mean enough to do it under Gent's nose. Once he picked up Mother and carried her into the kitchen, where Gent was eating his bread and sipping bourbon. "We got to get her to eat more, Gent," Guy said. "She's getting to be light as a feather." He pushed her up until she was sitting on his shoulder. "She's just a pea," he said. "Just a damn sweet pea." Gent followed all this with weary eyes, his chin specked with gravy. Guy whirled around and Mother's skirts flew. Gent passed his hand in front of his face, as if bothered by a fly.

But Gent was adrift in a sad sea sharked by pork worms and he didn't care. He had become distant and hard to talk to. When he spoke, he said things that had the ring of final advice from the deathbed. "Your mother is so lovely, Jack," he once said, "but she requires constant tribute, which no man can give." And once, standing at the kitchen window, staring out into the frozen yard, he said, "Wouldn't it be nice to be young again, Jack? How about that, Jackie—wouldn't you like to be young again, your best girl sitting beside you in a fine yellow car, driving down a tree-lined highway on a lovely summer day?" I started to remind him that I *was* young and didn't need to wish for such things, but he wasn't prepared to listen to me. "Wouldn't you like to smell the delicate mix of her perfume, sweat, and minty breath again? Wouldn't you like to back up and make the right turns this time and avoid all the dead ends? Wouldn't you like to be young enough to do that again, Jack, and this time do it right?" He looked at me then, his eyes alert but blind. "Sure," I said. "Who wouldn't?"

Then one April day, after a sudden and total thaw, Gent fell down the basement steps. We gathered around him. "Are you okay, Gent?" I asked, but I knew he wasn't. He was on his back, staring at the dark ceiling. He didn't seem to have any broken bones or bad bruises, but more than the wind had been knocked out of him. Mother had been in the tub and was robed and turbaned like an Arabian queen. "My God," she said quietly.

She called Guy, then went upstairs to put her clothes on. She put on her pink dress, the one that made you think you could see through it, and a pair of new white shoes. She made a fresh pot of coffee and then put some bacon into a skillet. She cracked six eggs into a bowl.

"Shouldn't we call an ambulance?" I asked.

"What?" She looked at me, with some alarm, I thought. "Ambulance?" She pronounced the word as if it were Latin.

"We can't just leave him down there, can we?"

"Oh," she said, frowning at the bowl of eggs. "No, I guess we can't. You call, Jack."

When I got back from the telephone, she said, "Look, kids, we knew this was coming. Sooner or later, but it *was* coming."

While we waited for the ambulance, LaDonna and I watched over Gent. He looked peaceful, staring at the ceiling. Even his breathing was soundless and calm. Now and then spit foamed on his lips.

Guy Rampling arrived. Ever since he'd spanked me, he'd treated me with an almost apologetic respect. He'd make sure to say hello, how was I doing, or ask what I'd been up to, and he acted as if he really meant to listen to my answers, which were not forthcoming.

Guy paled at the sight of Gent on the basement floor. He acted as though he had walked into the biggest tragedy to mankind since the crucifixion. "Oh," he said, "what in the *world.*" He patted the top of his pompadour, thunderstruck. "Oh, my, oh, my," he said, as if trying to regain his bearings.

We went upstairs to the kitchen. "Here," Mother said, handing Guy a toasted bacon and egg sandwich. "Eat this, you'll feel better."

Guy sat down at the table and ate the sandwich in half

a dozen bites. He washed each bite down with a big slurp of coffee. While he ate, he shook his head slowly, as if to make it plain that he was still thinking about poor Gent down in the basement. Mother handed him another sandwich.

Then the ambulance arrived and the attendants strapped Gent to a stretcher and carried him up the basement stairs and then out to the ambulance.

We all sat at the kitchen table. An enormous silence filled the house. Even the tall clock in the downstairs hallway had stopped ticking. It was a silence that had thickness and weight. It made Mother nervous. She lit a cigarette, then got up and began to scrape the dishes as if to put a small, homely commotion into the overwhelming stillness.

"Well, well," Guy said, thoughtfully, his face grim with the heroic determination to carry on despite all. "I guess that's it."

But it was the wrong thing to say, because the silence, which had only been delayed by Mother's dish scraping, now loomed over our heads like a huge, precarious stone.

GUY sold his trailer and moved in with us. He'd been more or less managing the creamery since Gent had begun to fail anyway, but now it was official. He moved his stuff into Gent's office. He cleared out the bookshelves and the treadmill, and he shoved the big desk against the wall so that Mother could set up a cot for him. "You watch me," he said, to all of us, as Mother tightened sheets onto the mattress. "I am going to make a money mill out of this creamery." He sat at the big desk and rubbed his hands over it possessively. "First thing I'm going to do is repaint those damn trucks. Who'd want to buy milk off one of those dung-toned crates? And another thing. That idiot name, 'Old Times

Creamery.' That's the dumbest thing in the world to call a modern creamery. *Old* milk is *sour* milk. *Old* butter is *rancid* butter. *Old* cheese is dry and moldy. You get my drift? But we're stuck with it for the time being, at least, because everybody in this town is used to it. We'll change it little by little—sort of working our way into it. See what I'm driving at?"

"Maybe you'd better ask Gent first, before you change the name of his creamery," I said.

He frowned and held his chin in his hand. "Well, that's right, Jack. That's what I should do. And if things were normal, that's exactly what I would do. But things are far from normal, if you see what I mean. The way I understand your mother's idea, Jack, is that we have to act in Gent's best interests while he's . . . laid up."

"It only makes *sense*," Mother said.

Guy brightened. "That's right! It only makes sense! What are we supposed to do, let the business go into a tailspin just because Gent isn't here to run things? Hell no! Your mother is right—it only makes sense!"

That became the byword around the house. "It only makes sense." Anything Guy wanted to do was justified by it. And everything he did was for "Gent's benefit." So when he bought a fleet of ice cream pushcarts, he said, "This little operation is going to double our summer-time profits. It only makes sense, right?"

"It only makes *sense*," Mother echoed faithfully.

He had the pushcarts painted white. Then he had a big decal of a slinking red devil pasted to the sides of each cart. The devil was licking an orange popsickle with a pointed tongue, saying, "This is one h-ll of a treat!"

He bought some expensive ice-cream-making machinery on Mother's signature. Since Gent was hospitalized and incapable of making decisions, she received the power of attorney easily and could borrow huge sums of money on his credit. Guy convinced her that the creamery could easily double its profits and that Gent had been far too lazy to pursue new enterprises. He said that if one competitor came to town, Gent would be out of business in a month. And so he bought expensive machines that made bulk ice cream, ice cream sandwiches, push ups, popsickles, and ice cream on a stick. The new ice cream operation must have run into the tens of thousands of dollars, but it only made sense, according to Guy, Mother, and the bankers who threw money at him.

Then Guy hired two dozen vendors to sell "Red Devil" ice cream from the pushcarts, giving them a 10 percent commission. Most of these vendors were old men who could not get regular work.

"Cheap labor," Guy said, explaining his reasoning.

"Well, it only makes sense," Mother said. "You wouldn't want men who should normally be working in the sawmills for that kind of work."

"I know those old bums don't exactly look like the marines on parade," Guy said, "but we're going to put them into some catchy little costumes. Hell, they'll look like trusty old kraut mountaineers when I get them all dolled up. Young mothers will feel good about them coming around to their neighborhoods and letting their kids horse around with them—even though half of those old farts probably got the syph."

The day before the operation was to go into effect, Guy had the old vendors assemble in the creamery. Guy climbed up on a pushcart to address them. "Listen up, men," he said. He had one of the new costumes in his hand. "This little number will come out of your commissions. But I'll go light on you. A dollar per week for the next twenty weeks. Okay? You'll be responsible for keeping it clean. I do not want to see any of my vendors pushing one of these Red Devil carts with the seat torn out of his pants or mud on his shirt. I will expect each and every one of you to wash the fart burns out of your pants at least once a week. You understand what I'm saying? If not, speak up. I am going to be severely strict about this. I do not want to see stained armpits. I do not want to see piss-yellow crotches. I do not want to see scuffed shoes. Nobody in his right mind will buy a popsickle from some old crumb bum with the smell of shit and grime on him. Do I make myself clear?"

The old men, who had been only half listening, nodded and mumbled. There was the smell of rotten cork in the air. Then Guy held up the costume for all the men to see. It was a pair of short, red pants, a white shirt with ruffled sleeves, a pair of wide, red-and-black suspenders, and black, knee-high stockings. On the back of the shirt was printed "I'M JUST A LI'L DEVIL!" There was a little red cap, a beanie, with two stumpy horns sticking out of it. The horns were yellow and roughly the shape of ice cream cones.

Guy hopped off the cart and picked up a large cardboard box. "Here are your uniforms men. Come up and pick out your size. I'll see you all here seven A.M. sharp, for route assignments. Anybody comes late, he can just head back downtown to the unemployment office because he has *lost his job.* Do I make myself clear? Any questions?"

Again the old men mumbled and coughed and shuffled their feet. The smell of rotten cork was joined now by the smell of cheap wine, which perked my interest.

Later that day, in the house, Guy said, "I want to talk to you, Jack."

"Sure," I said.

I followed him into Gent's office. He was wearing a blue suit. He'd taken to wearing suits ever since he'd moved in. Once I heard him say to Mother, "If I'm expected to make this creamery profitable, then I had better look the part, right?"

"It only makes *sense,* Guy," she said.

"Time to face up to the real world," Guy said to me.

I'd been drinking wine most of the day, up in my room, and so I only nodded at him, not trusting my heavy tongue with words. I had to fight back a grin, though, because along with his new blue suit he was wearing shiny mustard-colored shoes that glistened as if they were wet. The ends of the shoelaces had tassels on them. The sight of those shoes and the tasseled laces triggered giggles that weakened me to the bone, and I could barely stand upright and sober-faced. He also smelled of peppery-sweet toilet water and he had begun to grow a little Hitler mustache that sat under his nose like a smudge.

"The real world is no picnic, Jack," he said. I watched his serious face nod in the air before me as if it had come loose, like a shucked mask, and that struck me as comical too, for it was cramped with a seriousness only a circus clown would try to portray. He cupped his left hand in his right and squeezed it tenderly, to convey the difficulty of what he was trying to put into words. The hands also seemed detached and free floating, and I saw them for what they were: greedy, impatient, ruthless hooks. I made my right hand into a fist, but kept it hidden behind my back.

He was waiting for me to say something, so I said, "No, I guess it isn't."

He grinned. "Look, you've gone and grown up on us," he said, chuckling now like a car salesman. His glad hand floated toward my shoulder. I stepped back, out of reach.

"The way I see it, Jack, you are not exactly pulling your weight around here."

I grinned shyly, as if he'd complimented me. It made him clear his throat, to try again. "We—"

"We?"

"Well, your ma and me. We talked you over. Now that you've quit school and all. You're big as a man but you just don't pull a man's weight. You just sort of lay around the house, smoking those damned cigarettes. I don't know why you went and quit high school, but now that you did, things are going to be different for you."

The fist I was hiding behind my back began to knuckle my spine. I saw what he was getting at by now —he wanted me out of the house. He didn't want me looking over his shoulder while he spent Gent's money and exhausted his credit. Not that it mattered much. I'd been planning to clear out for some time, anyway. I just hadn't worked out the details yet.

He studied his fingernails. "Anyhow, we—"

"*We?*"

"Your *ma* and me. We believe that Gent set a poor example for you. Now don't get me wrong. I have a world of respect for Gent Mundy." If he saw my sneer he didn't let it get to him. "But Gent was a lazy man. He was lazy and . . . *distracted.*"

"He liked fuck books too."

He narrowed his small eyes and pointed his finger at me. "You watch that mouth, boy."

"Maybe Gent had some good reasons to be distracted," I suggested.

He took a deep breath, to compose himself. "Look, Jack. Don't get me wrong. I'm here to do for Gent what he can't do for himself. Period. I am here to help."

"Well, it only makes sense," I said, and he looked at me, finally, with his real face, and it was not a pleasant thing to look at.

"Pushing a broom around the creamery a few hours a week doesn't pay your way, Jack. It doesn't come close. So, we—"

"*We?*"

"Your *ma* and me. We decided it's time for you to move on, Jack. Time for you to jump out of the nest and try your wings. Or . . ."

He reached down into a cardboard box that was shoved up against the wall and took something out of it.

He held it up for me to see. It was a Red Devil costume. "Or," he continued, "you go to work in a real honest-to-Jesus job and make it *pay*."

Mother came in then, and I realized that she had been listening at the door, waiting for her cue. She stood at Guy's side and slipped her arm through his. "You'll do real good, honey," she said. "You're a fine-looking boy and people just take naturally to you."

"She is *right!*" Guy said, nodding at Mother with an astonished look on his face, as if she had hit on the long-buried secret of success in life. "Your ma here is smart as a whip. You'd do well to follow her advice."

"Sales," Mother said. "The future lies with sales. Only salesmen make more than doctors and lawyers. Ask anybody."

I looked at her, somewhat amazed. She looked like some brassy stranger giving a poor but self-confident imitation of Mother.

"Well, sure, that's true!" Guy said. "I just read that in *Fortune* magazine—"

"Kiss off, Rampling," I said.

Guy dropped Mother's arm and the ugly look of his true face returned. "Say that again, boy," he said, his fist doubled.

"I said, take your Red Devil idiot costumes and cram them up your ass, Rampling."

He came for me, but Mother held him back. "That is *it*," he said, his face white, his eyes wide and crazy. "I'm not taking any more from you, you little bastard. I want you gone, boy. I want you gone before dinnertime tomorrow."

They left the office. The fist I'd been hiding behind my back finally came out. It hit the air where his stupid face had been floating. It kept going in a big, slow circle, and it took me down, corkscrewing to the floor, where I sat with a thump. I guess I'd killed half a jug of red that day.

Mother came back in. "Oh, Jackie," she said. "He

doesn't mean it. You can stay. You just got him terribly riled up."

"Tell him to go fuck himself, Ma," I said.

She stiffened. "Don't you use that filthy word around *me*," she said.

"Really," I said, leering at her.

She gave me a fairly hard slap. It rocked me a little, but it didn't sting. I grinned. She slapped me again, a bit harder this time.

"Jesus God, you're going to be a worthless bum, Jack," she said.

"It only makes sense," I said.

PART 2

I MIGHT be your *ngantja,* said the little brown man in diapers. Behind him was a shimmering desert, pink with heat. The heat came from the sun, but it also came from the town behind me, which was on fire. The fire rumbled and heavy drafts of hot wind shoved me toward the little man. Now do you remember? he asked, grinning. His long, yellow teeth were flickering. I remember, I said. Something like a memory pressed up through my mind. All your lies perish in flames, he said. I am what remains. I remember, I said. But you are so small. Yes, he said. This is your most serious problem. I could get smaller. I could vanish. Where would you be then? I don't know, I said. Find out, he said. A dog knocked over a garbage can in the alley, waking me up. I sat up in bed, unable to remember what my room looked like or what street it was on or the name of the town I lived in. My heart felt knotted in my chest. "I don't know where to begin," I said out loud, but I didn't know what I meant because I was still talking to the dream.

This *National Geographic* dream came from an article I'd read before going to sleep. It was about the Australian aborigines, who believe that the hidden self, the true self, has never left the tribe's ancestral cave. The *ngantja* is the old cave dweller, the pure, untouched, and untouchable core being.

I'd packed up a bunch of Gent's *National Geographics*

and a few of his fuck books, thinking that I'd take them to him when I got the chance to visit him in Willow Springs. I'd probably have to sneak in the fuck books, but they couldn't object to the *National Geographic.*

The grinning *ngantja* raised a dark, horny finger, as if to warn me away from such smuggling.

"Good-bye, wine midget," I said to his fading image. Drink yourself to sleep and the dreams come on like that, vivid and strange. I'd spent a long, sweaty night in my apartment, a one-room walk-up over Hud Jorgenson's feed store, drinking, sleeping off and on, and reading magazines. There were three apartments over the feed store and I had the middle one, sandwiched between the others. The only window looked out on an alley. It was grim, but it was cheap. A retired railroad conductor and a disabled war veteran lived in the other apartments.

The walls between my room and the other two rooms were cardboard thin, and I could hear every sound made by my neighbors. My bed was shoved up against the wall and the man in the room on the other side of that wall would speak to me every night in a low, conversational whisper. "You asleep yet, kid?" he'd ask, first scratching the wall a little to get my attention. "Jesus, kid, this cheap buckboard they call a bed is ruining me, or whatever's left to ruin. Christ, I can hardly make pissholes in the snow anymore, if you get what I mean. It's like squeezing red-hot chili through a cocktail straw. Drip drip. It hurts me, kid."

This was the war veteran. I pretended I couldn't hear him, since I didn't want this talking through the wall to become a cozy habit. But he acted as though I heard him plainly and he wouldn't be discouraged at my silence. My refusing to respond was just a stubborn lie, as far as he was concerned. He never came out and accused me of pretending I couldn't hear him. He just kept on talking, friendly and intimate, as though I could. Whenever something crossed his mind, he voiced it. I imagined his bed shoved up against the wall we shared, and this gave rise to the uncomfortable feeling that we were in the *same* bed. I would lie on my side, back to the wall, about to drop off, when his gravelly voice would come to me, whispering confidentially, so close that I imagined his warm, sour breath on my ear. "Christ, kid, I can't sleep tonight, how about you? That goddamned dog is out there again, knocking over the garbage. I wish to hell I still had my forty-five. I'd drill that moth-eaten son of a bitch." Sometimes his voice would get sly and he'd talk about the money he was going to inherit someday. "I haven't seen that old shit-heel for thirty years, but who else can he leave the money to? My sister was killed in a head-on back in forty-seven." The old shit-heel was the war veteran's father, a wealthy farmer in the eastern part of the state. "Ten thousand acres of red wheat, kid. His goddamned farm is as big as Rhode Island.

"Kid, you won't believe this. Here I am, a fifty-year-old gimp with shrapnel in my feet and a steel plate in my head, teeth gone, stiff knee and a resectioned bowel, but my goddamned dick is hard. That's a hot one, kid. My eyes are ruined, I had six ribs removed in an Okinawan hospital, my nose looks like chewed meat, but my dick is hard as your elbow. This one-eyed bastard partner of mine thinks we ought to go out cathousing tonight, even though I need two canes to walk with and a wristwatch without glass so I can feel the time. What do you make of it, kid? How come they left me with dick and balls? Their idea of a joke?"

I thought of shoving my bed against the opposite wall, but my neighbor in the room on the other side of it was also a talker. He didn't talk *to* me so much as *at* me. I could tell he wanted to be overheard. It was a bitter voice, pinched with self-hatred. It made me cringe to hear it. This retired railroad conductor would precede his monologues with a kind of moaning growl. He'd work himself up to a pitch, then cut loose with his pent-up self-hatred. "The *hell* with you, I say the *hell* with you, Eugene! I'm sick of hearing it, you contemptible clown! No, no, don't hand me your threadbare excuses!" He never had a kind word for himself. At first I thought he had someone named Eugene living with him, but it became clear that he was alone since no one ever answered him back. He never mentioned what he had done. "Charlotte, Charlotte," he'd sob. "You lost her, Eugene! Never mind, never mind. No, she didn't want to go. It was you. It was you. Easy as pie, you said. Oh, how the wheels turn! And then it was over. Gone, gone, gone. You said they turned her against you. You said they put words in her mouth. You claimed you couldn't have known about the hospital trips, the whereabouts of the Dodge." Sometimes he'd pause, letting these cryptic phrases hang in the silence, as if waiting for me to ask what he meant, and there were times I almost did. But these silences were too tense for him, and he'd continue his catalog of failure, mentioning in this unconnected way the loss of children, fatal errors on the job, foolish investments of money, a deviant strain in his personality, cruel chickens coming home to roost, and so on.

Sometimes he'd start sobbing as he recalled the downhill course of his life. And when he'd sobbed himself out, he'd start banging. I imagined him on his hands and knees, banging his head on the floor. But sometimes he'd bang on the wall we shared and hairline cracks would appear in the thin plaster.

I bought myself an old Emerson table model radio just to drown out my neighbors, but whenever I turned it on they'd pound on the walls, mad as hell at my inconsiderate behavior. Even when I had the Emerson turned down so low I could barely hear it myself, they would complain. "Hey, kid, crank her down a notch, will you? I can't hardly concentrate on taking a crap with that damned music." Or, from the other wall, "He's trying to drive you insane with that god-awful nigger music, Eugene, not that you don't deserve anything you get, you miserable clown."

It was clear they were complaining not because the Emerson was too loud, but because they knew I was using it to drown out their monologues. I was their only audience, after all. But I persisted, and eventually they let me have my radio in peace.

One night, after drinking a quart of vin rosé, I wrote a letter to Orlando Mundy.

Dear Uncle Orlando,
Well you probably know all about it by now anyway, but I thought I better pass it along to you just in case the news hasn't traveled that direction. Your brother, Gent, is down in Willow Springs with something they call pork worm sickness, which supposedly can affect the mind, if you can believe what they say, which I barely can. Pork worm sickness, Jesus. They might as well say liver ticks or spine spiders or nose moss. Excuse the stain. It's wine, I'll be honest with you about that, but I can't see what's wrong with it since it generally makes things so agreeable. Of course you could overdo it. And that's a big area of temptation, since you would rather feel better as the night goes on than worse and the risk of hangover doesn't seem so bad by that time. Anyway, this supreme asshole deluxe, pardon my French, I mean the dopey bastard you pounded, Mr. Guy Rampling himself, has moved into your brother's house lock stock and cock and has taken over the business and let's be honest here and say that includes Ma, too. All the while Gent twiddles his thumbs in Willow Springs not knowing about Red Devil Ice Cream or the little Kraut Mountaineer winos who sell the crap off of pushcarts. He acts like he owns the place in his slick yellow shoes, you

should see him, you'd laugh. Gent sank the wrong boat, the way I see it. Rampling has blown a lot of Gent's money on a bunch of machines that barely fit into the old creamery building, so he's planning to have an addition built. All this on Gent's money or on borrowed money made good by Ma's signature which is the same now as Gent's, as far as the banks are concerned. So anyway, the son of a bitch threw me out of the house more or less. I've got a job though and my own apartment now and I guess I'm better off that way, out of there I mean. I work for Price Billetdoux Photolabs. Commissions, etc. If Gent wasn't laid up I think he would put things right, at least the creamery, I can't say about Ma since that has been going on for some time now. Maybe you could come over here sometime soon and pound on the simple bastard a little so as to discourage him. Spencer Ted stomps around the house in his usually shitty diaper crying Where is my Parp. Guy Rampling tugs on his Hitler mustache and says I am your dada now you humpback freak. I think LaDonna takes care of Spencey most of the time while Ma and Guy tear around the countryside in his Merc rapping the pipes so people will turn in his direction and think, What a wonder. Of course, what they really think is, What a turd. Or they've got their heads together about this new item for the creamery or that new item for the house, too busy to worry about Spencer Ted or for that matter my sister who is barely sixteen years old and needs some attending to herself. I was listening to the Ma Perkins show on my Emerson table model the other day thinking is there such a place in the world where people are so calm and nice and ordinary and where time moves like a turtle and nothing ever changes and who'd want it to since nice kind ordinary people are the only people you will ever see here? I guess not. It's only a radio show. Things are so different. I am writing this letter anyway. Maybe you can turn things around at the Mundy house if you'd please come back.

Yours Truly,
Your Nephew,
Jack

But I spilled more vin rosé on it and couldn't bring myself to write the letter again.

ACTUALLY, by that time, I wasn't working for Price Billetdoux (he pronounced it "Billy Ducks") Photolabs any more since he had skipped town owing two months' rent on his house. A few people were looking for him, people he owed money to, and, of course, the sheriff.

I'd answered his ad in the *Far Cry Clarion* for a "personable young man with an interest in photography for profit—no experience necessary." His photolab was in the basement of the house he rented, a three-bedroom bungalow in one of the older areas of Far Cry.

The Billetdoux front yard should have told me right away that the job wouldn't amount to much. The lawn was overgrown with spiky weeds, what grass there was had died a number of seasons ago, deep tire ruts oozy with muck grooved the yard, and a rusty tub filled with crankcase oil sat on the warped porch. But I had not turned eighteen yet and was still untuned to the distress signals the world volunteers with unfailing reliability.

As I walked up the driveway I had the feeling that the Price Billetdoux Photolab was the dark blight of the neighborhood and deeply resented by the surrounding homeowners. A quick, grim face at a window in the house next door tipped me off, a housewife who had made it her business to check out every visitor to the Billetdoux house. From the house on the other side, a huge German shepherd barked at me. Luckily, it was chained to the porch. It strained mightily at its leash until the flimsy two-by-four railing of the porch trembled.

Billetdoux himself answered my knock. He was in pajamas and bathrobe, even though it was midafternoon. He stood before me, dark, grizzled, blinded by ordinary daylight. When he focused on me, he shoved his hand into his robe pocket as if looking for a gun.

"I'm the one who called," I explained quickly. I held up the newspaper and pointed to his ad. "I want to try it, photography."

"Amigo," he said, pulling a crumpled pack of Camels from his bathrobe. "Come in."

I followed him to the kitchen. There was a plump girl at the stove peeling an egg off a skillet. She was also in pajamas and robe. She had stringy, mud-colored hair and very small feet. She looked about twelve. I figured she was Billetdoux's daughter.

"Pour us a couple of cups of java, will you Shyanne?" he said to her.

The girl dragged two cups out of the sink, rinsed them carelessly, and filled them with inky coffee. She was listless and unresponsive, as if she had been sick and was just recovering.

Billetdoux lit his Camel, drank some coffee, made a face. He had haggard, bloodshot eyes. Dark, tender-looking pouches hung like pulpy half-moons under them. He squinted at me through the smoke, sizing me up. Then he explained the job. No salary. No insurance. No fringe benefits. No vacations. Everything I made would be a percentage of the gross. I would go from door to door, trying to get housewives to let me take pictures of them and their children. I would offer them an eight-by-ten glossy for only one dollar. That was the "bait." How could they refuse? But when I went back with the print, I would also have a portfolio of five-by-sevens, three-by-fives, plus a packet of wallet-size pictures. The complete portfolio would cost anywhere from $5.95 to $11.95, depending on how many prints it contained. Of course, if they accepted the eight-by-ten bait item only, there was no profit or commission, just loss.

"You can make a hundred or more a week if you're good," Billetdoux said. "And your hours are your own. I've got a boy over in Sulphur Springs who nets one fifty."

I admitted that I didn't know the first thing about taking pictures, but he fanned the air between us as if to clear not only the cigarette smoke but also the heavy cobwebs of confusion from my mind. "I can show you how to take pictures of prize-winning quality in ten minutes, *amigo*. The job, however, is salesmanship, not art."

He took me down to the basement, where he kept his photolab. We had to pass through a hall that led to the back of the house. Halfway down the hall he stopped next to a door and tapped on it softly. Then he pushed it open an inch. I saw a woman with wild gray hair lying in bed. She was propped up on several pillows. She also had the sickroom look, just as the girl did. Her eyes were dark and lusterless and her skin looked like damp paper. There was a guitar lying across her lap.

"I've got to break in a new boy, Lona," Billetdoux said. "I'll get you some breakfast in a little bit." Lona, who I assumed was Billetdoux's wife, let her head loll off the pillows until she was facing us. She didn't speak, but her large, drugged-looking eyes seemed to be nursing specific, long-term resentments. After Billetdoux closed the door, he whispered, "Lona is very creative, *amigo.*"

The basement was hard to navigate. There was an odd assortment of household goods stacked haphazardly in teetering piles. Toasters, TV sets, radios, space heaters, typewriters, hunting rifles, tools of all kinds. It looked like the warehouse for a hardware store. Billetdoux saw me looking at all this stuff and pulled my arm to direct my attention to the photolab, which was tucked in a corner of the basement—a long, masonite-covered bench with several porcelain sinks set into it, some big plastic jugs lined up on shelves above the bench, a pair of enlargers off to one side, at least a dozen timers. The photolab had the lethal stink of strong chemicals.

He opened a cabinet with a small brass key and took out a camera. "We'll start you on the Argus," he said. "It's simple to use and takes a passable picture. Later on, if you stick with me, I'll check you out on a Rolleiflex."

He took me step by step through the Argus—from film loading to f-stop and shutter speed. "I'll go around with you the first few days or so," he said, "to show you the ropes. Then you're on your own. You're a nice-looking boy—the hausfraus will trust you." He winked, as if to suggest that trusting the likes of me and Billetdoux would be the biggest mistake a hausfrau could make.

We went back up to the kitchen. Going up the narrow wooden stairs was tough for him. He looked like he was on his last legs.

"How about some breakfast?" he said when we reached the landing. He was breathing hard, his lungs rattling.

I looked at my watch. "It's after three," I said.

"Is it? No wonder I'm so hungry. Where the Christ does time run off to, *amigo*? Well, how about some lunch then? Could you go for a bite of lunch?"

"Sure," I said. I'd missed breakfast, too.

"Shyanne," he called. "Shyanne honey, would you come in here?"

She came in, looking slightly more haggard than when I first saw her.

"Shy, hon, fix us some lunch, will you? The boy here and I are starved."

"There's no bread," she said. "Or meat."

Billetdoux pulled open a cupboard door. "How about some Cheerios, then?" he said.

"Fine by me," I said.

He poured out three bowls of the cereal, then added milk. He handed one bowl to Shyanne. "Here, hon," he said. "Take this in to Lona, will you? She hasn't eaten since yesterday."

"No one's eaten since yesterday," she said. "Except me, if you want to count that measly egg."

Billetdoux grinned darkly at me, a philosophic chuckle raising phlegm from his lungs. "Time to make a grocery run, I guess," he rasped.

We ate in silence. The milk on my cereal was slightly sour. A big, late summer fly droned past my ear and landed upside-down on the table, where it exercised its thick, feeble legs.

A loud, nasty voice broke into the homely sound of our spoons tapping on the Melmac bowls. I heard the word *swill* hiss from the hallway, followed by a complaining wail that made the hair stand on my neck. Shyanne came in carrying the bowl of Cheerios. "Lona doesn't want any cereal," she said, dumping the milk-bloated O's into the sink. "She wants Spam and eggs."

"What about toast?" Billetdoux asked.

"Right. Toast, too. And hashbrowns."

He leaned forward, his eyes damp and harassed-looking. "Listen, kid," he said. "Can you loan me ten bucks until tomorrow? I'm a little short. I had to get a new transmission put into my car last week. Cost? Jesus, kid, those mechanics are pirates."

I took out my wallet. I still had about fifty dollars from my last job. I gave him ten.

"Thanks. *Gracias, amigo.* Splendid. I won't forget this. This is above and beyond, *amigo.*"

Shyanne plucked the ten out of his hand. "I'll go to the store," she said.

"Don't forget cigarettes," he said.

147

* * *

BILLETDOUX picked a fringe neighborhood on the far
south side of town. The homes were fairly new, but they
were small and inexpensive. The yards were grooved
with the toys of small children. The houses in this devel-
opment were painted in pastels—greens, yellows, pinks,
blues—so falsely cheerful that you tended to believe
that ax murders were commonplace events.

"Let me tell you about sales resistance, *amigo*," Billetdoux whispered, his arm around my shoulder, as we
approached a house the color of orange-flavored jelly
beans. "You've got to blow right past it. She'll shake her
head, she'll start to close the door, she might mumble
something about how the money's tight, or the old man's
run off, crap like that. And here's where you have to act
fast. You lay a smile on her—you're a nice, wholesome
boy, see, with a good smile—you lay a smile on her, then
you take a crisp new one-dollar bill out of your jacket
pocket. You snap that crisp buck under her nose. Believe
me, kid, she'll freeze. Nothing but honey is sweeter than
money. Then you pitch her. 'One dollar, ma'am, one
dollar to immortalize you and your child. A *professional*
photograph, not a mere snapshot. My company will
blow this photograph up, at no additional cost to you, to
an eight-by-ten-inch portrait in living color, just like the
movie stars send out with autographs on them.' You
keep an eye on her feet, kid. At this point they've probably moved back an inch or two. Maybe she's just transferred her weight from one foot to the other. These
small observations tell the story. If she's transferred her
weight from one foot to the other, that means she's willing to listen to your spiel a little longer. If she's moved
back a half a foot, expect the door to slam on your face.
But here's where you whip out the sample photo. She'll
goggle her eyes out at the lovely mother and child in our
sample. She may look like the bride of Frankenstein and

her kid may look like a wombat, but when she sees that sample photo of the lovely lady and her blond Jesus, her eyes will light up with rekindled hope. All is not lost, says a faint little voice in her ear. At this point, the sample photo becomes a kind of magical talisman, promising to change her prospects and the prospects of her brat from dismal to rosy. After all, the camera doesn't lie, does it? And that's when you apply the clincher, *amigo*. 'And if you are not 100 percent satisfied, ma'am,' you say, 'you pay nothing. *Nada*. Not one peso. You keep the photo—what good is a picture of you and your lovely child to us?—and you pay nothing. Not one red centavo. Tell me now, how can you lose?' Then you show up a couple of days later with the eight-by-ten. If she likes it, you sign her up for a portfolio. At this point, she's in the palm of your hand."

But it wasn't a housewife who answered the door of the jelly bean house. It was a boy of about six. His little sister, naked and grimy, stood behind him, a gray pork chop in her dark hand. Pale green bulbs of snot plugged her nostrils.

"How you doing, buster?" Billetdoux said to the boy, patting him on the head.

The boy didn't speak. He started to close the door slowly. But Billetdoux put his foot on the threshold, stopping it. "Hey, *muchacho*. Is your pretty mommy home?"

The boy shook his head. Billetdoux dug into his pocket and pulled out an ancient Tootsie Roll. He gave it to the boy. "Well, no matter," he said, pushing the door all the way open and entering the house. "In a way this makes our work, ah, more interesting." He winked at me.

I followed him in with the equipment case, a little wary.

"Set up the flood lamps, like I showed you, *amigo*. Remember, the main light sits about seven feet back, the fill light about ten feet back."

I opened the case and took out the lamps and set them up on their stands. While I did this, Billetdoux set two chairs up in the middle of the living room. I moved the two lamps so that they were the proper distances from the chairs.

"Hey, buster," Billetdoux said to the boy. "Your sis got any clothes? Why don't you be a good scout and hunt up some panties for her, okay? We don't want any what you might call filthy pictures, do we? And wipe her nose while you're at it."

I set up the tripod and attached the Argus to it. The boy pulled a pair of pink panties on his sister. I took the pork chop out of her hand and put it on the coffee table. I used my own handkerchief to clean her nose. Billetdoux sat them down in the chairs. He stepped back to look at them in the blare of the flood lamps. "Good, good," he said. "Now, *amigo,* you are going to have to work on their expressions. Right now they look like starving Lithuanian refugees about to be processed into dog food. Not a cheery sight, is it?"

"Smile, kids," I said, bending to the camera.

The kids looked at me, their faces blank, empty.

"Smile won't get it, *amigo,"* Billetdoux said. "Smile is the kiss of death in this game. You've got to bring some personality out of them, whether they've got any or not. You want to get something on their faces the old lady will be tickled pink to see. This is the *job, amigo.*" He knelt on the carpet, in front of the kids, and held his hands up like a band leader. "I want you kids to say something for me, okay? I want you to say, 'Hannah ate the whole banana, Hannah ate the whole banana,' and I want you to say it together until I tell you to stop, okay?"

He stood up and said to me, "Take ten shots. Press the shutter button between 'whole' and 'banana.' Got it? Okay kids, start saying it." He raised his hands like a band leader again and started the kids chanting the phrase. I hit the button too soon the first time, too late the second, but gradually I fell into the rhythm of their singsong chant and was able to snap their pictures on the simulated smile generated when their mouths were open wide on "whole" but starting to close for "banana."

I took ten pictures, then shut off the flood lamps. Billetdoux was nowhere around. I felt uneasy about our being in the house alone with these kids. Then Billetdoux came in. He had a pork chop in his hand. "There's some grub in the icebox, *amigo,* if you're for it," he said. "Make yourself some lunch." He bit into the pork chop hungrily. "I'll say this," he said, chewing fast. "The lady of the house knows how to fry a chop."

Billetdoux began rummaging through the drawers of a built-in cabinet that filled one wall of the small living room. "Hello there," he said, lifting a pair of candle holders out of a drawer. "Take a look, *amigo.*" He hefted the candle holders, as if weighing them. "Solid sterling," he said. He slipped them into his jacket pocket. He continued rummaging. The kids didn't pay any attention to him. They were still mumbling "Hannah ate the whole banana" as they watched me taking down the flood lamps. I was working fast, sweating not just from heat now, but from fear. "Hello, hello," Billetdoux chortled, dumping the contents of a big black purse onto the dining area table. "Coin of the old realm—silver dollars, *amigo.* Cartwheels. Eighteen eighty-seven. The real McCoy. The landowners here appear to be silver hoarders . . . shameful, no?" He picked up one of the silver dollars and bit it lightly. "My kind of cookie, *amigo,*" he said, abstractly. Then he shoveled the big coins into a pile and began to fill his pockets with them. "It's rotten to hoard money like this when there's so much real need in the world today," he said, his voice husky with moral rage.

"Let's go," I said, weakly.

"One moment, *por favor,* kid," he said. "Nature calls."

He disappeared into the rear of the house. I snapped the equipment case shut, picked it up, and headed for the door. I heard the sound of water hitting water followed by a toilet flushing. As I opened the front door I believed I could hear him brushing his teeth vigorously and humming "All of me, why not take all of me."

I waited outside, down the street. He showed up in a few minutes, his pockets bulging, another pork chop in his felonious hand. He had an electric frying pan under one arm and a desk encyclopedia under the other. "You didn't get any lunch, *amigo*," he said, his forehead creased with concern. "What's the matter, no appetite? You off your feed, kid? Maybe you got a flu bug. Here, take it, this chop is for you. You'll feel better with some food in your stomach. You need to keep up your strength in this business."

I put the equipment case down. "You're a thief!" I said. I felt stupid saying it. It was like saying, "You're wearing a blue shirt!"

He lowered the chop, astonished and hurt. "Say again, *amigo*? Billy Ducks a *thief*? You're too harsh, my friend. Consider it a matter of redistributing the wealth. It's good for a society to have its wealth redistributed occasionally. Otherwise you wind up like the Egypt of the pharaohs—a few folks eating chili and caviar in posh houseboats on the Nile, and everybody else straining their milk shoving big slabs of granite around the desert. Does that make sense to you?"

"How am I supposed to go back there with an eight-by-ten of those kids?" I asked.

He raised the pork chop and bit into it thoughtfully. "Well, you won't have to. This was just a practice run. I'll develop and print that film and see what you came up with. Consider it basic training. Boot camp, *amigo*. This is boot camp."

* * *

B o o t camp lasted a week. Billetdoux was a good salesman. He almost always got into a house. Only once was
a door slammed in his face. The woman told him that
she didn't believe in photography. She had religious
reasons for keeping the faces of her children off of film.
She was a thin, angry-looking woman dressed for winter, even though it was a 75-degree day in August.

"To each his own," Billetdoux said to the closed door.
On the way across the lawn, he scooped up a sprinkler
and dropped it into his pocket.

Billetdoux had a list of hypnotic words and phrases.
He gave them to me and asked me to memorize them.
"People are self-conscious in front of a camera," he said.
"You need to put a spell on them or else you're going to
get rotten pictures." He said a woman surrounded by
her children can look like she just crawled out of a box-
car or she can look like the Madonna. The trick is to
transform the expression on her face. "You want the
face of the Mother. Mother in the generic sense. The
Mother of God Himself. This is what we're after. Self-
consciousness makes the face muscles tighten into protective expressions, all of which are false and which are
recognizable as false in the finished photograph. So you
set her on the sofa with a baby or two under each arm.
You say, Smile ma'am! What happens? She turns into a
grinning piece of stone. Sure, there is something on her
face that might pass for a smile if you had to name it,
but it looks like it was cranked into her face with a
torque wrench. My lady's eyes—they tell the story. You
need to get the small muscles around the eyes to drop
their guard. Once that happens, it doesn't matter if she's
smiling or not. The expression you get is *pure, amigo.*
So you've got to play these tricks on them. You get them
to work on something else, besides posing for the camera. You give them something to say. They think that
what they're saying is important, but it isn't. What's
important is that they think what they're saying has

some significance. 'Say cheese' won't get it. It might have worked fifty years ago when this racket was brand new, but nowadays it's an invitation to freeze. You might as well say, 'Watch the birdie,' or some fool thing like that." He gave me a printed list of words and phrases that he found effective: Tuckahoe. Round robin. Susquehanna sundog. My wonderful life. Laundry slave. Sweet swollen soil. Purloin. Slippage. The high-flying sheldrake. Shenandoah. Pool cue. "Have them repeat the whole list, if necessary. As they form those syllables, something happens to them. I guess it's the sound, or, occasionally, the meaning. I frankly don't know or care. All I know is that it works. Make up your own list. Maybe you can find some word combos that will bring out the Madonna in a jiffy. But look, the Madonna is only one of several possible poses. You've got to size up your subject. Your young, childless divorcee or widow may not have any findable Madonna in her, you know what I mean? However, she may be a secret vamp. So your list of words and phrases should have the power to call up that sleeping bimbo. Or another woman might be a latent queen bee. Similarly, there are the earth mothers, the Cleopatras, the Marie Antoinettes. Of course you're eventually going to run across the Lizzy Borden or the Typhoid Mary or the Ma Parker. Here the verbal tricks won't work. Now and again you are going to run into the extremely young mother. Here you'll want to elicit the 'Which one is the infant' pose. Candy stocking. Must I missy. Cream vat spy. Wooly winters. Morning joy. Teasy winks. Periwinkle pie. Artful Arapahoe. This is a list they'll respond to." He winked, or tried to, but the lid stuck down and he wound up staring at me with one terrible eye.

T H E last day of boot camp, Billetdoux parked his car—a 1939 Chevy whose interior smelled of moss—at the edge of the most exclusive neighborhood in town, Bunker Hill Estates. "Top of the world, *amigo*," he said, sipping black wine from a square bottle. The neighborhood was lush and hilly, the houses sprawling and surrounded by vast, perfectly tended lawns. "The land of the pharaohs," he said. "Makes me jumpy as hell, going up against them. I need this little bracer." He offered the bottle to me and I took a sip. It was sweet, thick wine, like cough syrup.

We got out of the car and started walking up the steep street toward the looming houses. Billetdoux began laboring right away, lungs rattling, barely able to put one foot in front of the other. I was carrying all the equipment, but he acted as if he had the full load. "I don't feel so hot, *amigo*," he said, stopping next to a tall, bushy hedge. His face had gone white. His mouth was a black, kidney-shaped hole—like the mask of tragedy. There was a short picket fence on the street side of the hedge. Immediately behind the fence was a narrow flower bed, then the hedge. Billetdoux stepped over the fence and into the flowers. "I'm awful sick," he said. He unbuckled his belt. He took off his jacket, handed it to me. Then he dropped his pants and squatted into the hedge until only his pale, stricken face was showing. A dark eruption of bowel noise broke the tranquil air. Billetdoux sighed. "Lord," he said. "What a relief. Must have been that goddamned chokecherry wine." He smiled weakly. I stood there, holding his jacket, the full weight of the incredible situation beginning to impress itself on me. A small dog, alerted by the commotion, came snapping up to Billetdoux. The dog was perfectly groomed. It looked like a blond wig that had come to life. Billetdoux put a hand out to it, to appease it or to ward it off, and the dog bit his finger. Billetdoux fell backward into the hedge, disappearing. The dog went after him, lusting for the blood of this hedge-fouling trespasser. Then they both emerged, Billetdoux roaring to his feet, the dog in frenzied attack. "Son of a bitch," Billetdoux said, picking the dog up roughly by its collar, a satiny, bejeweled affair. "I hate small dogs like this, don't you, *amigo*? Probably eats anchovies and cake."

I looked up and down the street, expecting a crowd of curious Bunker Hill residents attracted by the ruckus, but the street remained empty and serene. I was in awe before that unperturbed serenity. It was the serenity of people who knew who they were, enjoyed it, and who believed in their basic indispensability in the great scheme of things. Pharaohs. Serene pharaohs untouched by the small and large calamities that nipped at the heels of people like Billetdoux and me.

I turned back to Billetdoux. He was squatting back into the hedge, the dog firmly in his hand. "I really hate these lapdogs," he said, "but sometimes they come in handy."

"What are you *doing*?" I said. But I saw what he was doing.

"It's all they're good for, dogs like this."

He was using the dog for toilet paper.

"Bite my jewels, you little pissant, and I'll feed you to the flowers."

The dog whined pitifully. Billetdoux tossed it aside and stood up. The dog burrowed into the thick hedge, making a shrill whistling noise. "I feel so much better, thanks," Billetdoux said to no one's inquiry as he buckled up. I handed him his jacket and he slipped it on, squaring his shoulders in the manner of someone who has just finished important business and is ready, at last, for the next challenge. He stepped over the picket fence. "Well, don't just stand there, *amigo*. Time, like the philosopher said, is money."

We continued up the street, stopping finally at the crest of the hill. Billetdoux leaned on a mail drop. "Look," he said, "you can see the whole town from up here. Lovely, no? See the smoke from the mills? See the pall it makes across the town's humble neighborhoods? Wouldn't it be nice to live up here where the air is pure, where all you can smell is flowers and money? What do you think, *amigo*? Think I should buy a house up here, with the pharaohs?"

The town swept down from the hill and across the valley, rising again into the hills opposite us. Afternoon sunlight blazed in the windows of the houses on those hills. The river, low in the late summer, cut the town into a two-piece jigsaw puzzle. Clean white smoke rose from the tall stacks of the lumber mills and a haze covered most of the low-lying areas, dulling sharp edges and diluting colors. It was more like a painting than a photograph, perfect in its way, an artful design that hid all the small pains and pleasures that lived inside it.

"Sure," I said, thinking now of the ten bucks I loaned him that first day, the twenty I'd loaned him since, thinking of his sick wife and child, his wrecked yard, his mildewed Chevrolet.

He laughed bitterly. "No way, *amigo*. I couldn't take it. Too stuffy, if you know what I mean. A man couldn't be himself up here. I'd wind up playing their game . . . Who's Got It Best."

We walked along a narrow, tree-lined street called Pinnacle Drive. Billetdoux pointed at the street sign. "Here we are. The top of the world. The pinnacle. Everything is downhill from here. That's the definition of pinnacle, isn't it? Isn't that what they're trying to tell us? You're damn straight it is."

It might have been true. The houses were two and three stories and wide as aircraft hangars. Giant blue-green lawns were fitted with precise landscaping. Two or more cars gleamed in every garage.

We stopped at the biggest house on Pinnacle Drive, a slate-gray, four-story saltbox affair with a seven-foot wrought-iron fence surrounding it.

"What do you see, *amigo?*" Billetdoux said, his voice cagey.

"A nice house."

"A nice house, he says. Look again, *amigo.* It's a monument, dedicated to arrogance, greed, and the status quo."

I looked again. I saw a nice house with a long, sloping lawn studded with beautiful shrubs, a piece of metal sculpture—a seal or possibly a bear—curled at the base of a fine elm.

"You're stone blind," Billetdoux said when I told him this. "You'll never be a real photographer. You've got scales on your eyes. Stick to mothers and babies—don't take up real picture taking. Promise me that, will you?"

Billetdoux stepped up onto the stone retaining wall that held the iron fence. He grabbed the bars and began to yell. "Hey, you in there! We're on to you! We smell your goddamned embalming fluid, you fat-assed Egyptian mummies!" He began to laugh, enormously entertained by his performance.

Twin Dobermans came galloping up to the fence. The drapes of the front room moved. The Dobermans leaped at the fence, going for Billetdoux's hands.

"I bet they've got us covered with tommy guns," he said, stepping off the retaining wall. "Look at those front doors, *amigo.* Eight feet tall and wide enough to run a double column of storm troopers through them. Now tell me, do you honestly feel there is warm human activity blundering around behind those dead-bolted doors? No, you don't. Tight-assed, nasty, withered old pharaoh and his pharaohette live in there, stinking the place up with embalming fluid. Christ, *amigo,* it turns my stomach."

He sat down suddenly on the retaining wall and covered his face with his hands. His shoulders heaved, as if racked with sobs, but he made no sound.

"Lona is sick," he said softly into his hands. "That's

why I steal things. You called it right. I'm a thief." He looked at me, his face fighting a severe emotional spasm that threatened to dissolve it. "These people up here get a head cold and they fly to the Mayo Clinic. I can't even buy medicine for Lona." He took out his handkerchief and mopped his face with it. "Give me the Argus, *amigo*. I'll show you how to take a picture."

I opened the equipment case and handed him the camera. He began snapping pictures of the house. The drapes of the front room moved gently as if the house was suddenly filled with soft breezes.

"I'm looking at those doors," he said, sighting through the camera. "I'm looking at the shadow that falls across them on a severe diagonal due to the overhang above the steps. The effect, *amigo,* is grim. Now I'm sliding over to the left to include a piece of that window. This is interesting. This is the geometry of fear—a speciality of the Egyptians." He snapped a few more pictures, then handed me the camera. "You see, everything makes a statement. A robin yanking a worm out of the cemetery grass makes a statement—it's up to you, as a photographer, to see it. *Seeing, amigo,* that will come with maturity."

Billetdoux was full of himself. His eyes were shining with the power and accuracy of his perceptions. He looked stronger and more self-confident, and even healthier than ever. He looked brave and intelligent and generous and sane. I raised the Argus to my learning eye and took a picture of him.

The front doors of the house opened. A tall, silver-haired man in a jumpsuit came down the steps, shading his eyes to see us better. Seeing their master approach, the Dobermans renewed their attack. They leaped at the fence, turned full circles in midair, came down stiff-legged and gargling with rage.

"Down Betsy, down Arnold," said the silver-haired man when he reached us. "Is there something I can do for you gentlemen?" he asked, a charming smile on his handsome face. He was elegant and calm and genuinely undisturbed by us.

Billetdoux shoved his hand through the bars of the fence, offering it to the old man. "We're doing some freelancing for the *Clarion,*" he said.

I waved the camera for proof.

"Ah, journalists," the man said, dignifying us.

"Right," Billetdoux said, grinning horribly.

"Well, why don't you come inside and take some pictures of our antiques. Nedda, my wife, is a collector."

Billetdoux looked at me, his face so deadpan the avarice behind it was transparent. I almost giggled. We followed the old man along the fence to the front gate. He sent the dogs away and then let us in.

The man's wife, Nedda, showed us through the house. It was tastefully furnished with antiques. The dry, musty smell of old money was everywhere. It rose up in the dust from the Oriental carpets. It fell from the handsomely papered walls. It lived in the stately light that slanted into the rooms from the tall windows. It was a friendly, bittersweet smell, like stale chocolate, or maybe like the breath of a pharaoh.

After the tour, we were given ham sandwiches, cole slaw, pickles, potato chips, and iced tea. After we ate, Nedda showed us her most prized antiques. Billetdoux, still playing the journalist, snapped a dozen flash pictures. He was working with a kind of controlled panic, on the verge of breaking a sweat. His jacket pockets clinked with dead flashbulbs.

Then we went downstairs, exchanged a few more pleasantries, and left. "Guess you were wrong about them," I said.

He brushed the air between us with his hand. "Petty bourgeois front, *amigo.* Don't kid yourself."

"What's wrong with Lona?" I asked, surprising myself. It had been in the back of my mind.

He shrugged. "The twentieth century," he said. "It depresses her. She's very sensitive."

"Oh," I said.

"You think being depressed is a picnic?" he said, annoyed at me. "It's an illness, *amigo,* serious as cancer."

"Really," I said.

He looked at me strangely, then slapped his stomach hard. He made a loud barking noise.

"What's wrong?" I asked.

"I can't eat cole slaw. The bastards put out cole slaw." We were halfway to the front gate. "I can't make it, *amigo.* Let's head back." He turned quickly and headed back toward the front doors. The Dobermans didn't come after us, though I expected them to come sailing around the house at any second. Billetdoux, doubled over and barking, ran up the steps of the front porch. He rang the bell until the door opened.

"The journalists," said the pleasant old man.

"Please," Billetdoux grunted. "Can I use your facilities?"

"Most certainly," said the old man. "Do come in."

The old man led Billetdoux away. I waited in the foyer. Nedda saw me. "Oh, you're back," she said.

"Yes, ma'am," I said. "My boss had to use your bathroom. He can't eat cole slaw."

She touched her cheek with her fingers. "Oh, dear," she said. "I'm so sorry. I hope he isn't too distressed. Would you like some candy while you're waiting?"

"Yes, ma'am," I said. So these are the pharaohs, I thought.

She went out and came back with a box of chocolates. I studied the brown shapes, then selected one I hoped was filled with cream instead of a hard nut.

"Oh, take *more,*" she said, holding the box closer to me. "Fill your pocket. I'm not allowed them anyway. Neither is Burton."

Billetdoux came in, smelling of cologne. "Let's hit the

road, *amigo,*" he said. "We've bothered these fine people long enough."

"No bother at all," said Nedda. "We don't get much company these days. I'm glad you came. Do drop in again."

Out on the street Billetdoux said, "Christ, what a pair of phonies. I thought we'd never get out of there."

"Better check your wallet," I said.

He looked at me sharply but didn't say anything. I popped a chocolate into my mouth. Mint cream. I didn't offer him one. He reached into his pocket and took out a small sculpture of a Chinese monk lifting a wineskin to his grinning lips.

"Look at this piece of junk," he said. "I thought it was some kind of special jade, white jade maybe, but it's only soapstone. Chances are all those antiques are phonies, too." He tossed the guzzling monk into a shrub as we walked downhill toward his car.

M y first customer was an eighty-six-year-old man who wanted some pictures taken of himself before he died. He wanted to send the pictures to his daughter and son-in-law, who lived in Florida. He hadn't seen his daughter in seventeen years. He wore a navy blue suit coat and khaki denim pants.

My second customer was a nervous woman who couldn't say no. She clearly didn't want me in her house taking pictures of her and her children, but my sales pitch was too good. Not that she was convinced by it. She just couldn't deny the value of the offer we were making. All she had to say was, "No, I don't want any pictures right now," and that would have been the end of it. But she wasn't capable of simple denial.

My third customer was a doctor's wife who posed for me in expensive evening gowns. She dressed her children, two boys and a girl, in cute costumes. The boys

wore sailor suits; the girl, who was only three, wore an
outfit the woman identified as "The Spirit of Nurtur-
ing." The woman changed gowns four times, never
quite finding the one she wanted. I spent three hours in
her house and she wound up buying the cheap $5.95
portfolio.

One pipe-smoking woman asked me to help her pick
corn. She was tall, maybe six feet, lanky, and deeply
tanned. "You can take some pictures if you give me a
hand in my garden," she said. I said yes because I
thought her garden would be a little square patch of dirt
in her backyard. It turned out that her garden was ten
miles away, on some property owned by her ex-hus-
band. She had a 1949 Hudson Hornet that had been converted into a pickup truck. We drove out to her garden
in it. The garden was more like a truck farm. It was two
acres of corn, squash, beans, cucumbers, and beets. I
picked corn for half a day, and when we drove back to
her house, I was too tired and crabby to set up for a
photographing session. "Well, you come back another
time," she said, patting me on the shoulder with her
hard, callused hand. "You're not used to hard work, are
you?" she added, lighting up her pipe. When she got it
going, she laughed. She had a full, throaty laugh that set
off a little alarm bell in me. I looked at her for the first
time, her eyes, her pleasant, welcoming smile. I had put
her age at about forty, but her smile convinced me she
was closer to thirty. "I'm going to give you some supper,"
she said. She sat me at her kitchen table and poured me
a big bowl of beef-and-barley soup. She cut me a large
slice of brown bread and covered it with butter and
honey. It was good food and I was hungry enough to eat
it without any self-consciousness, even though she stood
behind me the whole time, massaging my shoulders, the
sweet smell of her pipe mingling with the soup steam.
When I finished and had pushed myself away from the
table, she said, "And now you can have a bath, if you

want." She said it in a lowered voice, secretively, and the alarm went off again. I told her no, and she said, "Well, take this bag of corn anyway. You earned it." She gave me about a dozen fat ears and patted me on the back again. "Margo Kryzniak," she said, as I went out the front door. "That's my name."

A F T E R my first $100 week, Price Billetdoux invited me over to celebrate my success. "You're on your way, *amigo,*" he said, uncapping a quart of cheap vodka. He made us a pair of iceless screwdrivers and we clinked glasses before drinking. "Here's to the hotshot," he said. "Here's to the man with the charm."

We drank half a dozen screwdrivers before we ran out of frozen orange juice. Then we switched to vodka on the rocks, minus the rocks. His mood changed as we got drunk. "Here's to the hot-dog capitalist," he said, turning ugly. "Here's to J. P. Morgan Junior."

He spread the photographs of Nedda's antiques out on the table before him. "There could be some money in these items, *amigo.* Enough to finance my retirement. Enough to escape the twentieth century. Unless they're fakes." He looked at me then, severe and rock-steady. "How about it, *amigo?*"

"How about what?" I said, thick-tongued.

"How about we take it. How about we pay a midnight visit to Pinnacle Drive and get us a truckload of antiques?"

My mouth was already dry from vodka, but it went drier. "No way," I said. "I'm a photographer, not a thief."

"Photographer my suffering ass!" he said. "Face it, you just don't have the belly for it, *amigo.* Look at yourself. You're about to muddy your drawers." He laughed happily, poured more vodka. My stomach rumbled on cue, and he laughed again. "Pho*tog*rapher," he said, staring into his glass.

Dinner was a blistered pizza that was both soggy and scorched. Shyanne made it from a kit. She cut it into eight narrow slices. Billetdoux and I ate at the kitchen table. Shyanne carried a tray into Lona's bedroom, then went into the living room with her two slices of pizza to watch TV.

"I should have gotten some T-bones," Billetdoux said.

"This is fine," I said.

He squinted at me, sneering. "Don't bullshit a bull-shitter, *amigo.*"

To change the subject, I told him about some of my weirder customers. I told him about the old weight-lifting champ who posed for me in a tiger-striped jock-strap, holding a flowerpot in each hand to make his biceps bulge. I told him about the couple who took turns sitting on each other's lap. Then there was the crackpot who wore a jungle hat and spoke German at a full shout to a photograph of his dead wife.

I told him about Margo Kryzniak. I told him about her truck garden, and how I had gone back to her house three times in spite of the fact that she always wanted me to do some kind of chore for her. But I didn't tell him everything.

Billetdoux wasn't amused. "You think the human condition is a form of entertainment for us less unfortunate citizens, *amigo?*" he said. "Remember: There, but for the grace of God, go I."

I thought about that for a few seconds. "Sometimes it is," I said, refusing to knuckle under to his hypocritical self-righteousness. "Sometimes it's entertaining as hell."

He leaned across the table. "You been laid yet?" he asked.

I shrugged.

"What's that mean? You don't know or you ain't saying?"

I shrugged again.

"A door-to-door man who can't get laid at least once a week is probably a homo. The guy who said opportunity knocks was a door-to-door man, believe me. Okay, so you've been laid. Big deal. There are ladies out there, *amigo,* who *pine.* It's part and parcel of the human condition. It's a permanent feature. There are yahoos in the pulpit and elsewhere who would like to redesign the species. I've got news for them. The design is fixed."

I started to say something then about Margo Kryzniak but changed my mind. He stood up suddenly. His mood seemed to brighten for no reason I could see.

"Come on," he said. "I've got something I want to show you."

We went outside to the garage. He lifted the garage door and switched on the overhead light. "Ta da!" he said.

A long, pearl-gray car gleamed under a 200-watt bulb. "Wow," I said, impressed. "What is it?"

"That's something, right, *amigo?* It's a 1941 LaSalle. I got it for a song from an old lady who didn't know what she had. It's only got eleven thousand miles on it. Get in, we'll go for a hop."

I got in. The interior was soft plush. Even the door latch clicking shut sounded like money. Billetdoux started it and backed out into the street.

"This is true class," he said, aiming the baby Cadillac down the middle of the street.

We drove to a liquor store, where Billetdoux bought another fifth of vodka.

"You drive us home," he said, climbing into the back seat with the vodka.

I slid behind the wheel and started the engine. It hummed powerfully, vibrating in the wide, ivory steering wheel. The humming engine seemed to transfer its power to me through the steering wheel, and I let the clutch out a little too abruptly, causing the rear tires to squeal on the pavement of the liquor store parking lot.

"Easy, *amigo*," Billetdoux said from the back seat.

But I felt energized as the vibrations traveled up my arms, into my shoulders and chest, tickling a tender spot just under my throat. "Zowie," I said, as I turned into the street and headed north toward the Mill Avenue bridge.

I drove into the north side of town, thinking to show Billetdoux the house I was asked to leave, but several blocks before we got there I changed my mind. What could the big gray house mean to him? And if Mother and Guy were out on the porch what could I do but duck my head and step on the gas?

Billetdoux uncapped the fifth and took a few loud swallows of vodka. He passed the bottle up to me. I took it by the neck and sipped.

"What's the matter, *amigo*?" he said. "You look blue."

"This end of town depresses me," I said, wheeling the LaSalle around in a tire-squealing U-turn.

"Too many trees," Billetdoux said. "Reminds me of a cemetery."

Billetdoux rested his forearms on the back of the front seat, his face inches from my shoulder. "I'll tell you something, *amigo*," he said. "There are two kinds of citizens in this world. One cares if he lives or dies, and the other doesn't. I'm one of those who doesn't. To me, it's all the same. Life, death, the same."

I reached back and took the bottle from him. I knew what he was saying. It was easy to feel that way, drunk. Easy to brag. I felt like telling him that, but I suddenly felt merciful. That's how the vodka affected me. What a laugh. Merciful. Jack the Merciful. I was just as big a fool as he was.

"See these sores all over my hands?" he said, ignoring my laugh. "I've got these sores because I hardly ever wear rubber gloves when I'm handling developing fluid.

Only a citizen who didn't give a shit one way or the other if he lives or dies would do a thing like that."

"You're a hero, Price," I said, all mercy gone.

He leaned back into the seat, sighing. "Well, yes," he said. "You could be right. I never thought of myself in that light, but you could be on to something, *amigo*. I just may well be a kind of unsung hero."

I brought the vodka up to my smiling lips just as the LaSalle hit a pothole. The bottle bounced into my mouth, cracking my upper lip. I drank anyway, tasting salty blood in the vodka.

Two girls stepped out in front of the LaSalle and I had to hit the brakes hard. They were hitchhiking away from a grim little bar called Owen's Place. They opened the doors and got in, one in back, one in front. "You guys are lifesavers," said the girl in the back seat. "Jesus, those pricks in there acted like we were the door prize." The girl next to me in the front had long, unnaturally red hair and a large shining nose. A gold crucifix the size of a small-caliber handgun hung from her neck on copper wire.

I headed for what I thought was the highway out of town, but before long we were bouncing down a dirt road beside some tall warehouses. Then the road petered out and ended in a trench that was filled with rusted-out home appliances. I backed the car out, turned it around, and headed in the other direction. But the road now became a plowed field.

"What exactly are you doing, *amigo?*" Billetdoux said.

"I thought I'd head out of town, maybe go up to the lake."

"You're miles off course, I'm afraid," he said, passing the bottle to the front seat.

I tried to think, but my brain was steaming with vodka.

"The thing about this dumb town," said the girl in the

back seat. "Nobody can figure out how to get here, nobody can figure out how to leave."

"Jesus, listen to her," said Billetdoux with unnecessary sarcasm.

"What about it, honey?" said the girl next to me. Her hand was on my thigh, kneading. I saw then that she wasn't a girl. She was about fifty. The grooves that circled her neck like scars gave her away, as did her earlobes, which were stretched very long because of the weight of earrings through the years.

"We don't have to leave town anyway," said the girl in the back seat. "We can have fun right here in this old burg."

"Damn straight we can!" said Billetdoux. There was a sudden commotion in the back seat. A gold, high-heeled shoe slid down my shoulder and into the front seat.

"Jesus," I whispered.

"He's not in the mood," said the girl next to me. "He's pissed off at something."

Billetdoux was grunting. Between grunts he said, "Give him a little time. He's a little backward."

I started the car and backed up at full throttle until I came to the turn-off that had brought us there.

"Easy, for chrissakes," Billetdoux said. "This isn't a goddamned half-track."

We dropped the girls off at Owen's Place. It was where they wanted to be, whether they were treated like door prizes or not.

When we got back to the house, all the lights were on. I parked the car on the lawn, running over a long-dead sapling because I couldn't find the driveway. Billetdoux didn't seem to notice.

Even though I was in the car, I could hear the TV set, which must have been turned up full blast. Behind the noise of the TV, there was a sound that reminded me of raucous crows in flight.

Billetdoux and I managed to get into the front door and then into the kitchen.

"Time, *amigo,* for a civilized drink," he said, throwing his arm around my shoulder as if we were each other's best friend.

He made a pair of half-and-half screwdrivers and we sat at the kitchen table to drink them. The noise in the house was giving me a headache that traveled all the way down into the roots of my teeth, but Billetdoux acted as if it were nothing unusual. What had sounded like noisy crows in flight was actually Lona, singing in a language that might have been Egyptian. She could have been strumming her guitar with a trowel, for all the music that was coming out of it. Her voice, too, was grating and loud, completely toneless.

"So," Billetdoux said, as though to resume some conversation we might have been having. "You've been fucking the sweet Jesus out of this Mrs. Kryzniak, is that right?"

"Not exactly," I said. His choice of words made me smile, and blood ran down my chin.

"The man plays his cards close to the chest," Billetdoux said morosely into his drink.

I changed the subject. "Say, Price," I said. "I've worked up some new words and phrases. You know, to get them to pose."

"Shop talk," he said, gloomy.

"Eerie delights."

He jerked his head up at me. "What? What did you say?"

"Eerie delights. It's great with teen-age girls—you get this terrific shy half smile from them. You'll see it when you develop my next roll. Eerie delights, Chesapeake, Chattanooga, water wondered widely, shish kebab, artificial antelopes, seldom down the settlement pond—"

"No shop talk, *amigo,*" he said, holding up his hand.

A tremendous crash shook the house, followed by two voices harmonizing in a long, throat-tearing scream.

"Oh oh," Billetdoux said.

Oh oh seemed like a totally failed response to the ugly din. I had jumped up, knocking my drink over.

"Trouble," Billetdoux said mildly, sipping at his drink.

The screams had degenerated to chuffing growls. Now and then something fell over, shaking the house again.

Billetdoux sighed. "Well, maybe we'd better go have a look."

We went back to Lona's bedroom. The door was open. For a second or two I didn't understand what I was looking at. What I first saw was Lona and Shyanne kneeling face to face on the bed, combing each other's hair. A dresser was lying on its side and a mirror was on the floor, cracked in half.

I noticed then that neither Lona or Shyanne had combs in their hands. Just great knots of hair. Lona was growling through her clenched teeth and Shyanne was hissing, her mouth wide open and vicious, like a cheetah's. Then they fell over and rolled off the bed. It seemed the air was filled with flailing legs. Billetdoux moved toward them, wary of the pumping knees and slashing feet. "Knock it off," he said, lifting his drink to his lips. He watched them for a while longer, then set his drink down on the dresser. "Give me a hand, will you, *amigo?*" he said.

He grabbed Shyanne under the armpits and lifted her off the floor. She continued to kick out at Lona as Billetdoux pulled her out into the hall. I reached for a waving leg, then thought better of it. Lona got slowly to her feet. Her gray hair had strange shapes wrung into it. Horns and antennas. Lumps that suggested awful growths. She picked up a lamp and flung it at Shyanne, who was no longer in the room. It exploded against the wall, next to my head.

"Goddamn you to hell," she said, looking around for more things to throw.

"Fat witch! Pus hole! Slop ass!" Shyanne screamed from somewhere else in the house.

After order had been restored, Billetdoux fixed us a new round of drinks. "That was intensely embarrassing, *amigo.* I don't know what gets into them," he said.

I made some kind of gesture indicating the futility of things in general, but it lacked weight. It didn't come out right. I turned it into a coughing spasm instead.

"The television, the guitar," he said. "This house is too small. They get to annoying each other. Sometimes it comes to this. But they hardly ever draw blood."

I was drunk enough to say, "How come you let your daughter treat her mother like that?"

Billetdoux looked at me. "My daughter?" he said. "What are you saying, *amigo?*"

"Your daughter, Shyanne, she—"

"My *daughter?* You think I'm beyond insult, *amigo?* You think we've reached a point in time where anything at all can be said to Price Billetdoux?"

"She's *not* your daughter?" I said, thoroughly numb to the peculiarities of Billetdoux's life, but somewhat surprised, anyway.

"Damn," he said, glumly.

"Then Lona—"

"Lona? Lona? Jesus, *amigo.* What godawful thing are you going to say now?"

"I thought Lona was your wife."

"Lona is my mom."

Shyanne came into the kitchen then. She opened the fridge and took out a bottle of 7UP. She made a face at Billetdoux. She looked at me, as if daring me to make a comment.

"Oh, baby, baby," Billetdoux said to her. He reached out and took her hand and pulled her toward him. She resisted but let herself be pulled onto his lap. He sat, bouncing her on his knee, his arms around her. "Baby, baby," he said, his voice wounded with love.

"I think you should tell her to move out," she said.

"Oh, baby, you know I can't do that. It would kill her."

"How do you think *I* feel?" she said. "Maybe you want *me* to move out. Is that what you want?" Her red lips puckered into a hard, toy-doll pout. "I'll *go*. I'll just *go*."

"Don't say that, baby," Billetdoux said miserably.

Shyanne still looked twelve years old to me. Yet the hard, unwavering stare she had leveled at me was not something a child was capable of. I moved her age up to sixteen or seventeen. But something older by five thousand years hung stupidly in her face.

"Say the word, I'll go. I'll pack," she said. "You just say the word and I'll do it."

I went out into the front room as Billetdoux began to weep on the breast of his young wife.

I watched the entire "Perry Como Show." Then I switched to a late movie. I had ignored the sounds coming from the kitchen—soft singsong assurances, the cooing words that dissolved into groaning embraces, the serious oath making, the baby-talk threats, and, finally, the mindless chitchat. I switched on "Wagon Train" and turned up the volume.

Billetdoux came in and sat down on the couch next to me. He was eating a peanut butter and jelly sandwich and drinking beer. "What can I say, *amigo*?" he said. "Are you going to think of me now as an old cradle robber? Hell, I'm only thirty-eight. Shyanne's almost sixteen. You think that's too young?"

I shrugged. "What's a dozen years more or less," I said, my arithmetic deliberately sentimental.

He straightened up, set his sandwich and beer down on the coffee table. "My situation is not easy, *amigo*. I'm crazy about Shyanne. I can't live without her, you understand that? At the same time, I've got to think about Lona. I can't set her adrift, after all she's done for me. Can I?"

"No," I said. He was chewing his lip and absentmindedly cracking his knuckles.

"Mom thinks the world of me," he said. "She calls me honey boy."

I went out into the kitchen to get myself a beer. Shyanne was still sitting at the table. She was looking at her hands, studying first the tops, then the bottoms.

"They're red," she said to me. "I hate my hands."

I got my beer, opened it.

"I'm sick of my hands," she said, bitterly. "I'd just as soon cut them off."

She tried to show me her hands, but I walked past her and back into the front room.

Billetdoux was pacing in front of the flickering TV set. "I'm going to Simonize the LaSalle," he said, winking. "And while I'm at it, I'd better check the seats for pecker tracks." He stalked out the front door like a man with pressing business.

Shyanne came in and sat down next to me. "Are you going to take me fishing or not?" she said. Her tone of voice made me feel as though I'd broken every promise I'd ever made.

"Did I say I would?" I said.

"No one's taken me fishing since we came to this stupid town."

I noticed that she was sitting on her hands.

"I know what you're thinking," she said. "I know exactly what you're thinking."

I got up and went outside. Billetdoux was out on the front lawn, rubbing wax into the finish of the LaSalle. He was holding a flashlight in his free hand.

When I got home that night, my neighbors were delivering self-pitying monologues at such a pitch that I left again and walked the streets of Far Cry until dawn.

NEITHER condemn nor approve, said the *ngantja.* Neither walk away nor reproach. Neither fish nor cut bait. Neither sink nor swim. Neither ante nor fold. Then the war veteran's scratching on the wall woke me up. "Listen to me, kid," he said. "Life's a bad job. If I still had my forty-five I'd kiss it off." You woke me up to tell me that? I almost yelled, but got up instead and turned on the Emerson. An old band singer, long dead, was singing "Me and My Shadow." Me and my *ngantja,* I thought. All alone and feeling blue. I rapped out the hokey rhythm with a pair of spoons until my neighbors slapped the walls for mercy.

Margo Kryzniak stared at me from the wall, her face dim in the early morning light. She had a worried, uncomprehending look in her eyes, as if she were trying to read fine print. It was one of my mistakes, that photograph. Except none of them were really mistakes. I had fallen in love with *halation*—the blurring effect of backlight, caving in the edges of an image. Sometimes it cut into the image, creating gaps in the flesh. Eaten by light, I thought. What a keen idea. But Billetdoux bawled me out for it. He blew up all these mistakes and gave them to me so that I could learn from them. I didn't tell him they had been deliberately shot that way. My walls were papered with women being consumed by light. Wedges, tongues, pools, and flowers of light. I thought of them as the Burning Women. Women eaten and transformed by love-starved light into spirits. They floated on my walls, and in the early morning they loomed there, misty, like patient ghosts. All this had a touch of craziness in it, I knew, but it made me feel good.

It also made me feel bad, bad in a sentimental way,

like when you imagine a woman you are destined to
lose. The imagined woman sometimes has a face, and
when you see it your heart stutters. It is always in the
face, the eyes and the small lines around the eyes where
threads of darkness are trapped; and it is in the mouth,
the tension or the lack of tension in the lips. Sometimes
you feel so bad looking at that face your fists clench or
you go suddenly weak and drop a spoon or fork, or your
knee unlocks and you throw your arms out for balance.
Sometimes you wake up with an unremembered yell
still echoing in your room and you hear your neighbors
grumbling at a disturbance. I dreamed once that my
camera wasn't a passive recepticle of light but an arm
of my will, able to transform what had been to what
could be. The way fire turns wet clay into glass, dead
rock into bright ore, random, interstellar clouds into
stars.

I sat there, listening to the radio, Margo Kryzniak's
overwhite face looking down at me. The light had
caught her hair and melted it. It floated around her face
like running, molten iron. ("Where the Jesus was your
main light?" Billetdoux asked. "In her ear?") I caught
her on the second syllable of the triggering word and
her lips were parted on it, the teeth dull as lead in the
fainter fill light. There was no main light, it was sun, a
blazing patch of it on her kitchen floor. It ignited the
pale yellow linoleum that framed her face. My fill light
stood next to the stove, recklessly aimed. We had spent
the morning picking green beans and pulling weeds.
Then, back at her house, we had lemonade. "Are you
ready now for some pictures?" I said, a bit sarcastically.
I expected more delays—the shed needed shingling,
maybe, or would I tune up her rototiller—but she surprised me by saying, "All right." We stood up at the
same time and bumped together, one unrestrained
breast rolling across my bare arm to my chest. I backed
away, half stumbling, the alarm sounding in my head,

and clumsily set up the fill light. I got the Argus and set it down on the table while I fumbled with the main light. But then she was next to me again, those long, steamy breasts now showing erect nipples through the cotton blouse. Dark arrowheads of sweat crept from her armpits. "Do you want to change clothes first?" I said, weak in the knees. "Do you want to take a bath and change?" She shook her head no, as if not willing to trust her voice. She stepped closer. There was dust in the small wrinkles around her eyes. She put her hands on my shoulders. "Be with me," she said, her voice husky and strange. Face to face we knelt down slowly to the floor, and kneeling before each other, we kissed. Her dry lips tasted of salt and dust, her tongue of lemons. I pushed her over gently, but when she was all the way down I lost all gentleness. I pulled her blouse open, wanting to see those dark, heavy breasts. Buttons rolled across the floor, the cheap fabric ripped. "I'm sorry," I said. "Jesus will forgive you," she gasped. "Okay," I said, stupidly. "Okay." Her breasts were swollen with the heat of our morning's labor, the blue surface veins visible. I bent to their sweat-filmed slopes like a steer at a salt lick as her wild hands opened my pants. Then her skirt was gathered on her hips and I was between her brown knees, probing blindly like a convulsing epileptic. She reached down to help me and the touch of her hard, warm fingers was too much. I lost it in her hand and on her disappointed thighs. "I'm sorry," I said, humiliated. "Jesus will forgive you," she said, pulling my hair with her lips. I lay on her breast, too embarrassed to get up and face her. But then her hand was on me again, and all my urgency came back, and this time she guided me unerringly home. Her face was framed in a square of light falling from the window. Sweat beads gleamed like microscopic diamonds on her lightly mustached lip. I moved now with less frenzy, my mind in control of things and even capable of objectiv-

ity as I watched her long face contort. Her hair, usually
a rich reddish earth-tone brown, burst into filaments
coated with fire, white and yellow and even blood-red at
times when it fell into the shadow at the edge of the
square of light. The Argus, which was open and ready
on the kitchen table above us, caught my eye. I withdrew from her and set the camera on its tripod, aiming
it at her face. Her half-closed eyes seemed visionless
and she wasn't curious at all about what I was up to, just
eager to get on with it. "Mrs. Kryzniak, listen to me," I
whispered into her billowing hair. "I want you to say
'shish kebab' when I tell you to, okay?" As I rammed into
her her eyelids fluttered, registering my request. "Shish
kebab," I said. "Say it. Keep saying it." She turned her
face to one side, voiding me, as she retreated within
herself, and I held her jaw in my hand and turned her
back. "Say it," I said. The cords in her strong neck stood
out as she pulled away from my hand. I stopped moving
then. "What's the matter with you?" she said, lifting her
head a bit to see me clearly. "Say it, say shish kebab," I
said. "Say it and don't stop, okay?" She said it and I
started moving again, and she said it a second time and
a third, running it together so that it seemed like one
long, loping engine of sound, slow to start but now running on its own, gathering speed. I picked up the remote
shutter release and waited until the expression on her
face became one of abstract sweetness as the syllables
moved it, an angel contemplating the magician's hands
of God as he played out the universe from his empty coat
sleeve.

But in the blowup Billetdoux gave me the angel had
flown the coop leaving behind a waxy double puzzling
over some domestic riddle—stray cat in the basement,
screen door loose and banging because the spring had
mysteriously unhooked itself, yeasted bread refusing to
rise. The wide ellipse of her mouth wasn't expressing
angelic awe but only ordinary human disappointment.

"Amigo," Billetdoux said, "you're wasting a lot of good film."

"A R E you crazy?" she asked, as if she really wanted to know.

"I don't think so," I said.

We were drinking lemonade again, at her table. She lit her pipe. We had taken a long bath together but not before she made sure the camera was still in the kitchen.

"Well, if you are, Jack," she said, sucking thoughtfully on her pipe, "if you are, Jesus can help you."

This embarrassed me somewhat. I sipped my lemonade.

"I'm telling you the truth. I used to be crazy myself. Right after my husband, Tusco, left me. It rocked me, Jack. I thank God for my garden. Hard work and Jesus Christ pulled me through." She put her hand on my wrist and squeezed. I was impressed, as I had been from the start, with her strength. We went up to her bedroom then, but we didn't get into bed until we had knelt before it and prayed for ten minutes. I meant every word I said, but after that day I never saw Margo Kryzniak again.

T H E next time I went to Billetdoux's house it was empty. A woman was there, cleaning it. She answered the door, eyeing me suspiciously. "You have something to do with him?" she asked.

Knowing something about Billetdoux, I said, "No. He just owed me some money."

The woman snorted. "You and how many others. I own this house. That tramp owed me two months' rent."

"He only owed me ten dollars," I lied. It was closer to a hundred.

"Kiss it good-bye," said the woman. She was white-

haired and stocky, her face round and red. Her unchari-
table mouth was pinched with a lifetime of disappointment. "How come you let him have money? You a relative?"

I shrugged. "Well, it doesn't matter," I said, lamely.

"Of *course* it matters," she said. Her face had turned
redder by one shade. She didn't appreciate my offhanded treatment of the world of debt and payment.
"He was a *thief,*" she said, growing redder still.

"Thief?" I tried hard to look stunned.

"You heard me. Thief and worse. What's your name?"

"Tusco Kryzniak," I blurted.

"Hah," she said, as if she'd scored a point. "The deputy
will be here in a few minutes. You just tell him all you
know about that tramp."

"Oh, what the hell," I said, grinning in a simpleminded way. "It's only ten bucks."

My soft, suckered-once-again smile turned her purple. "Only ten dollars, is it? It's people like you who
make it easy for tramps like him to get away with it."

"He didn't owe me two months' rent," I pointed out.
"Only ten bucks."

"Ten dollars or two hundred and ten dollars—the
principle is the same," she said. "Wait for the deputy.
He'll be here any minute."

"No can do," I said, giving her the simpleminded grin
again.

"You're bound by the law!" she yelled at me as I
walked up the street. "You're a witness!"

"*Adios,*" I said, waddling a bit to make her remember
me to the deputy as heavy and older by ten years. "*Adios,
amigo!*"

J O B S in Far Cry were scarce that fall, and I had to take
work on farms, picking hay at the rate of a nickel a bale.
I worked with a crew of high school boys who thought

the pay was generous. We worked fourteen hours a day loading bales into a lowboy trailer, then hauling it to a barn, where we stacked it. The nickel-a-bale pay included loading it, hauling it, and stacking it. I averaged about ten dollars a day, and the tightwad farmer didn't even provide us with lunch.

After haying season, I held some temporary jobs—dish washing in a café, shoveling snow off the sidewalks for uptown businesses, sorting mail in the Post Office during the Christmas rush. I even parked cars for the Far Cry Regency Hotel.

In the spring, just after my eighteenth birthday, I got a good-paying job in Stottlemeyer's sawmill. They put me on the planer, first thing. All new employees were assigned to the planer as a sort of test of their grit. The planer was a huge, roaring, dangerous machine that turned rough boards and planks into bright, smooth ones. Stacks of the rough lumber were carried toward the chute of the planer on a set of big feeder chains. We would stand on a loose platform of sliding boards that rode on the chains between the moving stacks of lumber. When the stacks reached the chute they were stopped by a steel lip. That was when we would have to start shoving the rough lumber off the stack, layer by layer, until all the boards had been dumped into the chute. Then we would step onto catwalks, carefully, and reposition the boards of the sliding platform behind the next stack of lumber. The process was repeated then, a roaring cycle that demanded both nimbleness and strength. It was a tremendous amount of work, more than I'd been used to, but it paid a whole lot more than anything I'd had in the previous few months.

Here's what made it rough: Though a stack we might be working on would stop at the steel lip, other stacks coming up behind us would not stop, and we would have to speed up frantically to prevent our sliding platform from being rammed up against the stack being unloaded by the oncoming stack. If that happened, the loose boards of the sliding platform would jam together hard or even pile up on top of each other, and this was a real danger since those loose boards were the only things between us and an eight- to ten-foot drop into the machinery that drove the chains. In an emergency, we could jump off the platform onto the narrow steel catwalks that ran on either side of the chains, but you would have to be very much on the ball to do this on short notice. Or, we could hit the big red STOP button that was on the wall within reach of the man on the right side of the contraption. The STOP button turned off the entire machine, blades, chute, and chains, and Mr. Stottlemeyer hated to see that happen. He didn't want his important planer operation shut down for any reason. But it broke down for ten to twenty minutes at a time anyway, and sometimes for quite a bit longer, and we looked forward to such stoppages since they gave us a welcome break from the muscle-burning work, but Mr. Stottlemeyer would have a hollering fit whenever this happened, even though nothing could be done about it until the maintenance crew fixed the problem. And so, if Mr. Stottlemeyer saw the planer stop because the men on the feeder chains weren't working *fast* enough, he'd come tearing out of his office yelling, "Pull your thumbs out of your bungholes! Dog-fuckers to a man! You boys on the rag? Don't you pussies come to work if you are on the rag!"

The man I worked alongside of was called the Ape by everyone in the sawmill, but not to his face. His name was Jarvis Cartwright, and he was permanently assigned to the planer, because, it was generally thought, he was too dumb to do anything else. Jarvis was in charge of breaking in new men. He was called the Ape because he looked like one. He was shaped like a C. He'd spent so many years on the planer that his back muscles had thickened and forced his spine to conform to their bowstring pull. Even when he was off the planer, he did not lose his stooped-over posture. He had long, thick-muscled arms, too. His hands hung down past his knees. The knuckles of his hands did not drag in the dirt, but it seemed completely possible that they could. He had a small, round head with almost no forehead, and his eyes were close-set and watchful on either side of his flat nose. He was a short man, and his curved spine made him shorter still. Though I was only five foot nine I don't think his head came much past my shoulder. Walking, he looked clumsy, like an ape attempting to mimic a full, two-legged human stride. But up on the planer, he was graceful and sure, with all the nimbleness of a monkey in a tree.

The other mill workers teased him without mercy, but they stopped short of calling him Ape. Jarvis wasn't really stupid. Stupid people don't have any sense of their dignity, but Jarvis did and the other workers were always careful about the ways in which they teased him to his face. Behind his back they would jut out their lips, chimpanzee-fashion, or scratch their ribs, or hoot like gibbons, but face to face they were more cagey. Face to face they would say things like, "You bring any bananas in your lunch bucket today, Jarvis?" Or, "How's Jane these days Jarvis?" Once in a while, during lunch breaks, you'd hear jungle birds clacking and chattering throughout the mill. And someone knew how to imitate Tarzan's call to the animals perfectly, and he would cut loose with it at odd times just to get a laugh. He was so good at it that you could hear him above the roar of the planer. But when the planer was shut down, the Tarzan call was loud enough to make your ears ring.

Jarvis was not so dumb that he didn't know who the apeman's call was meant for. He'd take it for a while, then he'd blow up. Jarvis had a temper. He was dark-skinned and the angry blood rising into his neck and face would turn him a kind of mottled purple. When he turned purple, the teasing would slack off. No one wanted to take him on. He was small, but he was power-ful. To vent his temper, he would walk over to a stack of two-by-twelves and start to toss them around the saw mill as if they were shingles. Everyone would duck for cover when he did this. The big planks went spinning through the air, clattering against the walls, gonging off the machines. Even Mr. Stottlemeyer stayed in his office when Jarvis was venting his temper. I often wondered why Mr. Stottlemeyer didn't fire Jarvis for tossing planks around the mill. At first I thought he was afraid to fire him, afraid of what Jarvis might do. Then I real-ized that Jarvis was probably the only man who would take a permanent assignment on the planer. Jarvis was valuable to Mr. Stottlemeyer, and so he got a lot of slack.

Jarvis was a worrier. That's why he was so good at breaking in new men on the planer. "Watch the feet," he'd say. I couldn't hear him above the racket, but he spoke slow enough for me to read his lips. Also, he'd kick my foot with his and point down at the sliding platform. "You are apt to lose it," he'd say, his mouth working slowly. Then he'd bring his fists together and make a vicious twisting motion, suggesting the separation of foot from ankle.

The feeder chains looked like giant bicycle chains and they sometimes moved jerkily so that the platform of boards were slammed together under our feet like the jaws of a bear trap. Once my foot got caught between two of the boards and I lost my shoe. Jarvis, moving with the speed of a monkey on the bars of his cage, got to the red STOP button and shut down the machine. Then he looked at me with his close-set brown eyes and shook his little head as if overwhelmed by the hopelessness of breaking in a new man. No one was more intelligent up on the planer than Jarvis, and he sometimes gave in to the temptation of letting you know that.

Hearing the big absence of noise from the mill, Mr.

Stottlemeyer came charging out of his office. "All right," he said. "Who's on the rag this time?" He never meant Jarvis, of course, so it went without saying who he was referring to. Mr. Stottlemeyer picked up my shoe, which had fallen through to the machinery below. He looked inside the shoe, as if expecting to find a foot. "It's empty," he said, looking surprised and then disappointed. "I don't want that machine stopped unless there is a foot in this shoe. Anything else is dog-fucking." He handed me the shoe and stomped back to his office. Jarvis nudged me and winked. He was smiling. He had large, separated teeth. "He don't really mean that," he said. "The boss was just joking you."

Sometimes the stacks of lumber were too close together, and the space we had to work in was narrow and inconvenient. This was the fault of the forklift operator who brought the stacks of rough lumber to the feeder chains from the yard. If he came too soon, he would unload the forklift anyway, for he was always in a hurry, claiming that the racket made by the planer hurt his ears. I hollered at him more than once to leave us more space between loads, but he would just flinch up his face and point to his ears as if they were deaf with the noise. Jarvis would never bother to yell at the forklift operator. Sometimes when the stacks were so close together we couldn't even turn around, he would turn slightly purple, but he'd never lower himself to complain about it to the forklift man. To Jarvis, working on the planer was a matter of pride. He would not allow himself to ask anyone for help. The planer belonged to Jarvis, it was his territory, and it was the hardest and most dangerous job at the sawmill. And even though everyone made fun of him, and even though the Tarzan calls could be heard above the roar of the machine, Jarvis knew that his job and its severe demands gave him a dignity that no one else in the mill could disturb. He never said it in so many words. I don't think he had the words to say it with. But it was in his face. I could see it shining there as we worked.

I kept my beard. It was red and thick and made me look older by four or five years. I looked all of twenty-two with it, and could now buy liquor when I wanted it without having to prove my age. I didn't buy anything stronger than wine. The harder stuff made me a little crazy. I liked to sit in my room above the feed store and sip a nice red wine while listening to the Emerson as my cranky neighbors mumbled complaints.

Jarvis kidded me about the beard. Once he gave it a little tug and said, "That is one cute snatch-scratcher you got there, Jack." Jarvis was about twenty years older than me, but he accepted me as an equal. I think he liked me because I never gave him a hard time about him looking like something that swung out of the jungle. I liked him, too. He looked after me like a mother hen up there on that planer. The jokers at the mill made remarks about us, such as, "Here comes Tarzan and Jane. How do you expect he let Jane grow hair on her face? Hey, Jarvis, don't it scratch something awful?" But if they kept this up for very long, Jarvis would start throwing two-by-twelves through the mill and they'd quit ragging us for a few days or so, but eventually it would start up again, nasty as ever.

Once Jarvis invited me to his house. He lived about two miles from the mill and we walked there together after work. I lived about four miles from the mill and walked to and from work every day and so didn't mind the shorter stroll. I could see, though, that Jarvis was embarrassed about not having a car. He explained to me that he once owned a nice car but had to give it up because of his temper. Someone once cut him off in traffic and Jarvis had rammed the other car over and over until both cars were junk. The other driver climbed out of his wreckage, meaning to start something, but when he looked in at Jarvis he changed his mind and walked away. I can imagine why he backed off, seeing Jarvis hunched like a hairless gorilla over his bent steering wheel, his face black as a purple tulip with total rage.

Jarvis was a shy man and never had much to say, even to those he liked and felt comfortable with. And as we approached his house, he stopped talking altogether and would not respond to simple expressions such as, "I'm sure glad it's Friday, Jarvis, how about you?" I figured he was nervous about bringing home company, which was probably an unusual thing for him to do.

He lived in a white frame house about a quarter mile off the highway. A narrow dirt road led us to it. It was a neat little house sitting in a square of mowed weeds. Surrounding the mowed square was a chain-link fence, and surrounding the fence were wide, bee-filled fields, thick with flowering tansy.

We went in. The door creaked. There was a woman sleeping on the sofa in the front room. She had on a thin cotton dress printed with flowers. A live bee, which had come in through the open window, had lighted on her dress, looking for pollen. She was barefooted, and her feet were gray with dust as if she'd been walking up and down the dirt road that connected the house to the highway. Her feet were perfectly shaped. Through the dust I could see that the toenails were painted dark maroon. Her hair was a rich yellow tangle.

Jarvis gave me a quick nervous glance. He swallowed and said, "That there is Delta. My old lady."

He went to her and gave her shoulder a gentle shake. "Del? Delta honey?" he said. "I brought home that kid I told you about. The one that works on the planer."

Delta opened her eyes. They were acetylene blue, so blue that I took a step backward, as if someone had cracked open the door to a blast furnace. She was not fully awake and this gave her eyes a thought-free clarity, like the eyes of a cougar or hawk. I thought to myself, such eyes ought to come with a warning: Do not look at directly without protective goggles. I almost said this to Jarvis, by way of complimenting his wife, but I held my tongue, in case he took it the wrong way.

Delta sat up slowly, arching her back as she did, and yawning. The thought-free clarity of her eyes dimmed only a little when she looked at me.

"This here is Jack, my buddy," he said.

"How do you do, ma'am," I said, taking another step backward.

She slid her legs down off the couch and scraped her feet on the wood floor, as if itching them. Then she stood up and pushed her hands through her hair. But her hair was so tangled she only managed to rearrange the knots. She had full, round breasts that were naked under the cotton dress, and a little upturned nose that had a band of freckles running across the bridge. Her mouth, in another way, was almost as shocking as her eyes. It was tiny, no bigger than the bud of a wild rose. She didn't open it. She just nodded sleepily at me, indifferent, and went into another room.

"She'll get us some dinner in a little bit," said Jarvis, and I couldn't tell if he was getting purple with embarrassment, pride, or anger.

"No hurry," I said.

Jarvis went to a cupboard that was made out of scrap lumber. I guessed that he'd used scraps from the mill to build it. He took a bottle of bourbon out of it. "Ready for it?" he said, winking.

"Sure. You got any wine, Jarvis?"

"Wine?" he looked bewildered. "You drink wine, Jack?"

"I like a taste now and then."

Jarvis had a dejected look on his face, which made

him seem comical, for his short, sloped forehead was knuckled with thought. "Wine is for bums and bankers, Jack," he said in a hushed voice, with total seriousness. "Wine ain't for us. No, no. I sure don't have any wine, Jack."

"Bourbon's fine, Jarvis."

He grinned and the wrinkles in his forehead smoothed out. He took two double-shot glasses out of the cupboard and filled them with bourbon.

He winked at me. "You want to see something, Jack?"

I drank half my bourbon and shrugged. "Sure."

He led me into the bedroom. He opened a closet door and took something out. It was wrapped in cloth. He took the cloth off carefully. It was a model of the planer made out of toothpicks, complete with feeder chains. It was about ten inches on a side and perfect in every detail. Jarvis held it in both hands, a helplessly proud grin on his dark face.

"That is really something, Jarvis," I said, honestly impressed.

He carried it to the night table next to the narrow bed. There were two little toy men on the night table. He set the planer down and put the toy men on the feeder chains. The platform they stood on was made out of popsickle sticks. He had made a stack of rough lumber out of tongue depressors, and he leaned the toy men into the stack, as if they were in the act of unloading boards into the chute.

"You and me," he said, pointing at the toy men. He gave me a whack on the shoulder and some bourbon flew out of my glass.

"That's us, all right," I said, taking a drink.

"Nobody busts their ass like you and me," he said.

"Right," I said.

He went out to get the bottle and when he came back he refilled our glasses. We drank bourbon for a while as we gazed at the toy men busting their asses on the tooth-pick planer.

"You damn betcha," said Jarvis.

"Ain't it the truth," I said.

We drank some more bourbon.

"Those shit-suckers. Those turds. Those goddamn buggers."

"You damn betcha," I said, knowing he meant the jokers down at the mill who didn't know the first god-damned thing about busting their asses.

"Dog-fuckers to a man," I said, imitating the growls of Mr. Stottlemeyer.

Jarvis buckled over. So I did another one. "You ladies got the rag on today?" And Jarvis sank to his knees and rolled over onto his side. He didn't spill any bourbon because his glass was empty and the bottle was capped. "Don't you dog-fuckers come to work when you got the rag on," I said, and tears rolled down his cheeks. Jarvis's mouth was locked open in his helpless face and he couldn't breathe. Nothing came out of his mouth but dry little clicks as he tried to take in air.

After a while we went into the kitchen. Delta was at the stove, looking dubiously into a big, cold pot. Jarvis filled our glasses and we sat down at the kitchen table. Jarvis was rocking from side to side in his chair and clacking his teeth together. "Hey, we're getting hungry woman!" he hollered. "Hey, Delta honey, this is my good friend here, crazy Jack. He's a crazy fool. Do what you did, Jack. Do that Mr. Stottlemeyer stuff."

"Pull your thumb out of your bunghole," I growled, and Jarvis spit bourbon into his lap.

Delta turned from the stove and rolled her matchless eyes. They had lost nothing of their gas-flame brilliance. I raised my glass to those eyes, but she curled her lip and wrinkled her nose. "You stupes," she said, turning back to the big pot.

Jarvis showed me his house from the outside. We

walked around it two or three times. There wasn't much to look at. It was just a square white house with a few windows in it. Then I saw the horse for the first time. It was tied to the fence on a long tether. It was outside the fence, grazing in the tansy. It was an old red horse.

Jarvis saw me looking at it. "That's old Carl," he said.

"Old Carl?"

"He belongs to Delta. She likes to take a ride every so often."

I walked back to the fence. The yard was slanted uphill and I had to lean forward slightly. It was a hot afternoon and the bees were in the dandelions.

"How ya doing, Carl?" I said.

Carl raised his head. He had a patch of green hanging from his mouth. He stopped chewing for a second to look at me, then began chewing again.

We went back into the house. Delta had some plates on the table. I pulled out a chair and sat down. My plate was full of soft, cool lumps. Some of the lumps were meat and some were vegetables. It was hard to tell which was which. I washed down each mouthful with bourbon. Delta didn't eat with us. She stood at the sink, leaning back against it, watching us with those unbelievable eyes. When we had eaten all we could stand, she picked up the plates and put them into the sink. Then she went out into the front room.

"I'll be right back," said Jarvis, his face purple. He stood up. He was a little rocky because his chair fell over backward. He went into the front room, hitting the door with the heels of both hands.

I heard him say, "What was that about, Del?"

"What was what about?" she said.

"I busted my ass all day. So what do we get for it. Cold slop from last Sunday."

"What are you trying to say, Jarvis?"

"Goddamn you."

"Shit."

"Shit is right," said Jarvis. "Shit is the word for it."

"You want a fight? I will give you a fight, Jarvis. You want a fight in front of your friend? I will give you a fight, Jarvis."

It was the most words I'd heard her say at one time. I pictured her small lips opening, the pink tongue flashing, the teeth agleam and the mean little words sizzling in spit.

"That's right," said Jarvis. "We bust our asses all day long and you do this, in front of my friend."

She snorted. "Did I hear you say *friend,* Jarvis?"

"Don't start with me."

"I never knew you had yourself a friend, Jarvis."

"I said for you to knock it off, Del."

"That sure is a laugh. The last so-called friend you brought home sure did not act like a friend, if you care to remember it."

"Goddamn you."

"Next time you bring home a friend let me know ahead of time so that I can get myself a stick."

"Shut up, Del. I'm warning you. Just shut your mouth."

Delta slammed into the kitchen. "Brother!" she said to me. "Is he ever stinko!" She sat down at the table next to me. Jarvis slammed into the kitchen. He stood, tilting, looking at us, then sat down opposite me. I filled his glass. Jarvis drank down the double shot and shoved his glass toward the bottle. I filled it again.

"Let's get boiled, Jack," he said.

"Can I get you a glass, ma'am?" I asked Delta.

She snorted. "Listen to *him,*" she said, rolling her eyes.

"Cut it out, Del," said Jarvis, darkly. He gave her a menacing look, but she didn't take it seriously.

I sipped at my bourbon. A bare foot nudged my ankle. I thought at first it was a kitten and started to look under the table, but then I realized—with a kind of electrical tingle running over my skin—that it was her. I set down my glass very carefully. Just as carefully, Jarvis filled it to the brim. This went on for some time.

I was lying on the sofa. A chair fell over in the kitchen. A glass broke in the sink. A woman was crying. I got up and went outside to take a piss. I pissed next to the dark silent shape of Carl. When I went back into the house, Jarvis had taken my place on the sofa. He was asleep. I went into the kitchen. The bottle was almost empty. I poured the last few drops into my glass and drank them. I found another bottle in the cupboard. I turned to ask Jarvis if I could open it, but he was snoring and mumbling.

Minutes or hours later I was on the lawn, looking up into the clear night. I was thinking, Those stars. Those goddamned stars. There are probably places among them just like Far Cry with people just like us lying around drunk in the grass looking up at more goddamned stars after having busted their fool asses all day long in some kind of mill. The grass was cool and damp on my shirt. Up there somewhere in the stars there was a wild-looking girl with amazing eyes and a little mouth, rubbing some poor bastard's foot while her husband got more and more to looking like an ape as he got drunk. It was a dark, moonless night and there were ten million Far Cries hanging over my head with ten million drunks lying in the damp grass with thumping boners aching to beat hell.

We were in the kitchen playing gin rummy. Jarvis's hair was standing straight up as if he'd stepped on a high-voltage cable. His face was creased and weary-looking with bourbon and sleep. Delta snarled like a cat as she slammed down card after card. Her bare foot rode my leg, ankle to knee, making me tingle all over. Jarvis said, "I swear you are cheating to beat shit, Del." Delta laughed wildly. I got the idea then that she was mean. But she looked at me over her hand with such a welcom-

ing look in her eyes that I dropped the idea. I shucked
the Jack of Diamonds.

"Jack, my man Jack, he sheds the Jack of Diamonds,"
said Jarvis, yawning. Her foot was in my lap, moving
like a kitten at play.

Somewhere outside I told myself, "Don't get any on
the lawn." I pushed my face into the chain-link fence
and tried to puke into the weeds, but it fell into the lawn
anyway.

"Giddap, horse," said Delta. She sat astride my back.
I was on my hands and knees looking for my shoe. "Giddap, giddap," she said, her voice little and cute. Her bare
heels thudded against my thighs. "What in the name of
heaven have you been drinking, horse?" she said, her
voice moving up and down like she was singing. She
laid down on top of me, her unruly breasts heating my
shoulders. She reached a hand into my shirt and pulled
at the few strands of chest hair I had.

In the house Jarvis was snoring. He was back on the
sofa. I shook his shoulder. "Hey, Jarvis. You got any
damn wine, Jarvis?" I thought of giving the Tarzan yell,
but decided that it would not be a good thing to do.
"Jarvis, this bourbon is poisoning me," I said. But he
didn't move.

"You really want some wine, crazy man?" Delta said.

We were back out on the lawn, and then we were out
in the field. I was on my hands and knees looking for my
shoe. Thistles scratched me, my face and arms, my one
bare foot.

"Yes, oh, yes. I would like some wine," I said, and my
voice was pathetic, like a lost child's.

"Would you? Well, isn't that just rosy?" she said. She
tried to sit astride my back again, but I collapsed and
rolled over and she went head-first into the weeds and
cursed at me and slapped at my head.

Then I was all alone in the weeds, crying. The little
house was far away and dark. The stars hung over it like

teeth. I rubbed the tears out of my eyes and the stars resumed their pinpoint shape. "Son of a bitch," I said, feeling like I'd missed all my opportunities. I got up and headed toward the dirt road that connected the house to the highway.

A horse came up behind me. It was trotting. I moved toward the ditch that ran alongside the road. The horse kept coming. I turned around and it was Delta, riding high on top of Carl, bareback. As she walked the horse past me, she put her foot on my shoulder and shoved. I went into the ditch.

"Here is your dumb wine," she said, dismounting. "I hope you're satisfied. What are you, some kind of Frenchy? I had to go all the way to the All-Nite to get it."

"Thank you kindly," I said, accepting the bottle.

We sat in the ditch, side by side, next to a culvert, drinking the wine. The wine smelled like bananas and liniment.

"Well, crazy man, are you going to fuck me or not?" she said, lying down.

"Hell! You bet!" I said, eager as ever, but it was a lost cause. The bourbon had taken my raging boner and had snapped its neck. Corpselike, it was unaware of the wonderful opportunity lying before it.

"What are you, a fairy?" she said.

"Booze," I said, ashamed. I got on her anyway, but this only made things worse. She put both her hands on top of my head and shoved me down.

"Then use your smart tongue, crazy man," she said. "That's what you Frenchies like, isn't it?"

"You go to hell," I said, getting up and falling down, getting up and falling down.

DELTA was on my mind day and night. Even on the roaring planer her beautiful face would calmly drift in and out of the stacks of lumber. Jarvis had to kick my feet a number of times to keep me from stepping between the boards of the platform and he'd even had to hit the STOP button on two occasions, and this caused Mr. Stott-lemeyer to call me into his office for a little talk. He asked me if I was sick or drunk. He didn't call me names, so I knew it was serious. He spoke in a fatherly way. I told him I'd been feeling subpar lately. He told me to take a week off. "Try it again in a week, Jack. If you aren't back up to speed by then I'll just have to get myself a new man. The planer operation is the heart of this mill."

I wanted that week. I wanted it more than the pay I would lose. Fate had dropped opportunity into my lap. The first day of my week off I walked straight to Jarvis's house, my heart fast with fear and love.

Delta was in the yard, brushing Carl. "I figured you'd be by," she said.

"You did?"

"When Jarvis told me you'd been turned loose for a week, I figured you'd come sneaking around."

My mouth was dry. My hands were wet. My stomach muscles felt papery. "I am not sneaking," I said.

She looked up from her brushing. She had a smug little grin on her small red lips. "You aren't? Then I guess you told Jarvis you were coming out here, right?"

I hadn't told Jarvis a thing. I had hardly been able to talk to Jarvis for days. I shook my head. "I just came by to say hello," I mumbled.

"A sneak and a liar both," she said, dragging the hairy brush through Carl's mane. "Come inside and I'll give you a glass of Kool-Aid. I just made some."

We went into the house. She took a pitcher of Kool-Aid out of the refrigerator and poured me a tall glass of it. I took a sip, but my dry mouth stayed dry. She was wearing the same flower-printed dress she'd had on that first day. Her hair was not tangled, though. It was pulled back into a neat pony tail. She was wearing shoes, brown loafers. She looked so beautiful I got dizzy.

"Boy, you sure got stinko the other night," she said, her voice friendly now. Her wide blue eyes studied me. I tried my best to stay with them, but I finally had to look away. I looked out the kitchen window at Carl. Carl was pulling up grass at the base of the chain-link fence, where it grew to several inches. A magpie was harassing him.

"Maybe you shouldn't drink so much," she said.

"I hardly ever drink that much," I said, as if giving myself a character reference.

She laughed. Then she cut her laugh short. She slid her fingers down her glass, caressing it. "Jarvis won't mind, you know," she said.

"What?" My heart felt like it had stopped.

"He really doesn't care. Just so long as I am happy. I'm free. He wants me to be free. He calls me his angel."

"He's a great guy," I said, pouring Kool-Aid into my desperate throat.

"Your goddamned right he is!" she said. "You think I need you to tell me that?"

"No, I mean it," I said. "He *is*. He is a *great* guy."

She looked out the window, needing to focus on something far away. "You probably have wondered about us."

"Oh, no," I said, too quickly. "I mean, wondered about what?"

"You think I'm beautiful, don't you?"

"You bet."

"And Jarvis. You think Jarvis is ugly."

"Well, *no,* I wouldn't—"

"A sneak and a liar, that's what you are. All of you." She was scolding me and some unnamed others. "Just come out and say it. Jarvis is ugly as your granny's back teeth."

"Well, he's no movie idol, if that's what you mean," I said, thinking of his forehead, his long arms, his curved back.

"He is as good as twenty-four-carat gold," she said. "He is better than twenty-four-carat gold. And you are just a son of a bitch, sneaking around here behind his back."

"I guess I'll head home," I said, scraping my chair.

"Sit your touchy ass down," she said, filling my glass with Kool-Aid.

"Jarvis is my friend," I said. "He's a good man. Up there, on that planer, he—"

"Quit trying to sell me something I already bought. You're just a pissant like the rest of them. Get in the bedroom."

I drank my Kool-Aid down and went into the bedroom. She pulled the blinds to darken it. Then she stepped out of her dress. She didn't have any underwear on. I got out of my jeans fast. She didn't call me pissant anymore, the rest of that afternoon.

It was the first of five amazing days.

One day she came over to my place. "What a *shit*-hole," she said, looking wide-eyed at the mess. "I don't believe men are human, none of them."

My bed was about half as wide as hers and it sagged so much that we were almost folded in half, lying in it.

"Oh, Christ, my aching back," she complained, as the weak springs creaked.

Once she came over at night, riding Carl. She tied the old horse to a drain pipe in the alley and climbed up the fire escape and rapped on my window. I'd been lying in bed, reading *National Geographics.* I had just read the words "The tongue of the Li River licks the tight green crevices between verdant islands." The blue-green picture was lovely, and I dozed slightly, slipping into those crevices, the warm, moving water all around me, when her knocking startled me awake. Her face at the dark window made my heart stumble.

"Hurry," her small lips said. I opened it and let her in.

"He thinks I'm exercising Carl," she said. "We have less than an hour."

My old bed strained under us, the brittle slats cracking, the headboard tilting, the old weak springs whispering dry complaints.

"Hold it down in there, kid," said my neighbor, the war veteran. "Christ, kid, you don't know what that's doing to me."

But I was lunging, driving her down into the collapsing mattress, and she yelled out loud, like a drowning swimmer would yell for help.

"Tell her to hold her tongue, kid," said the war veteran. "That ain't a noise an old man ought to listen to."

As she yelled, she hit. Both hands slapping at my back and shoulders. The rough heels of her feet scraped my kidneys.

"Kid, I'm going to have to take out my old cob and stroke it to death, you keep up that hullabaloo."

And then, from the other wall, "Isn't this just wonderful, Eugene?" said the bitter railroad conductor. "Isn't this exactly what you deserve?"

The bed traveled a bit, knocking over my nightstand and with it a dozen *National Geographics*.

The war veteran, his lips against the wall, moaned.

Later, over cigarettes and wine, she cried softly. I knelt before her and kissed the tears as they hit her knees and thighs.

"I don't want you to ever forget me," she said, bringing the lit end of her cigarette an inch from my arm, her bright, watchful eyes insistent.

"I won't," I said, as if the threat to burn me had been real.

SHE was a snoop. Once she went through all the drawers of my dresser, lifting up T-shirts, socks, and shorts, looking for secrets. She inspected the closet and found my Argus. Billetdoux had left town without asking for it back and since he still owed me money, I figured the camera was mine.

"This is a pretty nice camera for a mill worker," she said, dangling it by its strap.

I told her all about my old job, taking pictures of housewives and their kids.

"I bet some of those horny mamas got more than pictures from you," she said, her sidelong glance detective-sharp.

I shrugged. I thought of pipe-smoking, Jesus-loving Margo Kryzniak and her two-acre garden.

"Don't tell me about them," she snapped. "I don't want to hear about your big conquests."

"Jealous, huh?" I said.

She gasped, offended. Her little mouth popped open into a perfect O. She looked around for something to throw at me. She picked up my alarm clock and cocked her arm. I held up my hand to ward it off. "Whoa," I said. "I was only kidding you a little." I grabbed her wrist and pulled her across the room and back again. She put her nails into my face and raked. "Goddamn you!" I said. But she didn't quit. She wanted to fight. I could see it blazing in her eyes. It was something she liked to do. It came from some gamy violence that was always close to the surface. It made me hackle a little as I realized I would have to defend myself or get hurt. I tackled her around the waist and we hit the floor. She was small-boned, but she was strong. I pinned her down by the shoulders. She bucked up against me. Her hand went down, under me. She grabbed my balls and began to yank. I slapped her face hard and then I slapped her again until she let go.

"Now," she said, her teeth clenched. "Do it now, you crazy bastard."

Later on she said, "I want you to take my picture."

"Sure," I said. In fact, I'd thought of it myself. I wanted to have some pictures of her around my place.

I got out the Argus and loaded it with a fast indoor film. I sat her down at the table by the window, where the light was maximum. I took a half a dozen pictures of her, the dull backlight from the window catching her wild hair.

She was a natural subject. Posing, her face would take on an extra loveliness, as if she could reach down inside herself for it. It was as if she knew exactly what she could look like through a lens. I didn't give her anything to say. It wasn't necessary.

I watched, amazed, as she made little adjustments in her pose. Her lips thinned or pouted, her eyes darkened or blazed, her chin became strongly determined or it became weakly vulnerable.

"Can I take off my dress?" she asked, shyly.

"Anything you say," I said, trying to sound professional.

She took off her dress. She was slow and deliberate about it, as though stripping for a doctor. It made me grin. This had nothing to do with sex. This was something called "the art of photography."

I sat her on the table, legs drawn up beside her. I shot her from the left, from the right, and from the full front. She posed for every shot as if it would be a poster for a movie billboard.

"This is *fun*," she said. "When do I get to see the pictures?"

"I'll have to get some dark room gear first," I said. "Pretty soon, though."

I got out a gallon of red wine. We got drunk. I took some more pictures of her. Her poses got loose. I got a little worked up. The Argus itself began to feel like part of my sexual equipment. It was a crazy notion, and I realized it was crazy, but that didn't at all lessen the feeling. I was doing something to her with the camera.

"I'm beginning to feel lewd," she said.

Rick DeMarinis

* * *

I didn't waste any time setting up a dark room. I'd watched Billetdoux work in his lab a few times, so I had an idea what was needed. A book from the library helped fill in the gaps. I even bought a secondhand enlarger so that I could make eight-by-tens.

I brought some of the better prints out to her house. She studied them for a long time. "These are really *good,* Jack," she said, finally.

I had the Argus with me. "Want to take some more?" I asked.

"Yes!" she said. "Let's!"

"Out back," I said.

"What?"

"Out back. In the yard. There's no one around, and the house will block the view from the highway."

"In the sunshine!" she said. "In the light!"

Her dress fell to her ankles and she ran out the back door. I followed, Argus up and ready.

I sat her in a buttery patch of dandelions. I sat her in the weeds. I had her press up against the chain-link fence. I had her get on Carl. She was wonderful on Carl. She straddled him, her perfect breasts shining and triumphant under the noon sun. She laid back on him, her feet in his mane, then over on her stomach, a pink-tipped breast cutting into his shoulder.

When I developed these pictures I saw that they were something special. I made blowups of the best ones and pinned them up in my room.

"Pretty damned good," I said, congratulating myself.

I saw, for the first time in my life, that it might be possible to do something besides taking the jobs no one else wanted. I surely didn't want to work at Stottlemeyer's the rest of my life and turn into an ape like Jarvis.

Maybe I could be a photographer. A real one.

I bought magazines that specialized in nudes. Most of these magazines were sold in drugstores since they were supposed to have something to do with physical health. They had titles like *Pathways to Healthful Living* and *Sun Worshippers Weekly.* One of the magazines, called *Natural Living Outdoors,* offered cash prizes for photos of "energetic youth enjoying the great outdoors naturally." The section in the magazine where previous winners had their work featured showed nothing but good-looking young women standing naked in outdoor settings. The pictures weren't very good. The women looked self-conscious, as if they'd stripped on a dare. My pictures of Delta were a hundred times better.

Without giving it a whole lot of thought, I picked half a dozen of my best prints to submit to the magazine. The top prize was $250. I knew I'd win it.

I should have asked Delta's permission to enter those pictures, but I was possessed by the idea that I was going to be a professional photographer and not a mill worker and that idea overpowered such considerations.

Thinking only of my coming success, I mailed in the pictures. A few hours later, my common sense returned and the impact of what I had done hit me. I rushed down to the Post Office to get the pictures back, but the clerk said, "Too late. The mail truck came and went ten minutes ago."

I consoled myself by deciding the pictures were probably not all that good after everything was considered. The first glow of pride had faded. Anything will grow stale the longer you study it, and the longer you study it, the little oversights also become apparent. You begin to pick out the odd pimple, the band of freckles that in real life seem so fetching but that in a photograph look more like the discolorations of a skin disease. You see the dark tufts of hair under an arm, the dirt smudge on a foot, the dimpled thigh, the slightly uneven breasts, which, under the overhead bulb of your apartment, were heart-breakingly perfect. You see the gelding's foot-long dong hanging idiotically into the tall weeds as the light-washed girl lolls on his sagging back. You see the girl, pressed into the chain-link fence like an asylum patient begging for freedom. I burned the remaining pictures.

Sometimes I thought Jarvis knew, and other times I was sure he didn't. But the times I thought he knew slowly began to outnumber the times when I was sure he didn't, until, finally, I *knew* he knew and felt fairly sure that he knew I knew he knew.

And sometimes I was able to believe her about Jarvis not minding, about his wanting her to be free. But, back on the planer with him, I felt positive that she had made it all up. Though he never had very much to say to me, he now hardly talked to me at all. He would only rarely let his eyes meet mine, and when he did I felt that there was a deep hurt in them, a hurt that I was responsible for. Of course, that could have been an effect of guilt. My guilt. Guilt, and fear.

Guilt and fear aren't easy to live with, especially when both of these feelings were driven by love. I did love her. She stayed in my thoughts night and day, and I couldn't stand the idea of her going to bed with Jarvis. All this began to make my stomach hurt. I took mint-coated stomach pills to stop the hurt, but they only worked for a while. I started to lose weight.

The state of mind I was in made me hate Jarvis. It was a way to unburden myself of some of these misery-mak-ing feelings. He *is* an ape, I told myself. Only an ape would let his wife run free like that. Only an ape would be too stupid to care. Only an ape would think so poorly of himself that he would give his wife away to the human beings.

I quit eating lunch with him. Instead, I took my bucket out into the yard and ate among the stacks of finished lumber. I made friends with a few of the other workers. Eventually, after they saw that I didn't much care for my partner anymore, they began to open up and tell Jarvis stories. I didn't know about the Jarvis stories. It was a kind of tradition at Stottlemeyer's sawmill. One story had him going to a Tarzan movie and jumping up onto the arms of his chair and thumping his chest every time Tarzan hollered at the animals in the jungle. I laughed along with the others. I saw them watching me closely, to make sure my laughter was the real thing. They were afraid of Jarvis and I'm sure they thought of me as a possible snitch. So, to prove myself to them, I once took a couple of carrot sticks out of somebody's lunch bucket and stuck them in front of my teeth on either side of my mouth to hold my lips high and out. Then I did a bow-legged hopping monkey walk, making chimp noises. It got a big laugh.

I got better and better at this monkey imitation. One day I climbed up on a lumber stack to beat my chest and clack my big monkey teeth at the human world. I got carried away with it, hopping from stack to stack, slapping my chest, my lips propped off my teeth with carrots, dancing in wild little monkey circles. About a dozen hard-hatted mill workers were gathered around, watching me. They were having a good chuckle. At the back of the group, his close-set eyes nearly black in his purple face, was Jarvis. When he was sure that I had seen him, he turned around and walked back into the mill, holding his back as straight as it could get.

He didn't say a word about the incident. We worked side by side the rest of that shift, just as if nothing had happened. I felt it though. In the air, between us, which was as tense as piano wire.

My stomach felt like it was full of broken glass. I hated Jarvis for bringing me to this. I even thought of killing him, up there on the planer that day. As we worked down toward the low boards in a stack, I could step behind him and shove him into the planer. The flying belt-drive would throw him into the spinning blades, and that would be the end of it. Then I could have Delta for my own. I had asked her if she still let him sleep with her and she had said, "Of course. He's still my husband, isn't he? He has his rights." And those words echoed in my crazed mind as we worked. It would just be the death of an ugly ape, I told myself. I slipped, I would tell Mr. Stottlemeyer. I slipped and fell into Jarvis, knocking him off-balance. He tripped over a two-by-twelve and the belt-drive got him. There was nothing I could do. I saw Jarvis looking at me for the last time as the belt sucked him into the spinning blades. *Hit the button,* he was saying, but I knew I could never get to the button fast enough. And then he was gone. Somewhere, on the other side of the machine, there was a small plank, made of meat.

I had pretty much decided to quit the mill and leave town when the new issue of *Natural Living Outdoors* came out with one of my pictures in it. They hadn't notified me that I'd won anything, so it came as a surprise. In fact, I didn't win a dime. I was an "Honorable Mention." But they printed the picture anyway, as a consolation prize. It was the one I thought least of. She was lying on Carl, her foot dangling on his ribs. Because of the foreshortening effect of the camera lens, the foot looked twice as big as it really was. And the knobby ankle was scaled with dirt. Her breasts had flattened out so that they looked like bone-white plates balanced on her chest. Each plate had a dark raisin in its center. She was squinting in the bright sun and the smile on her face made her look simpleminded. Her body had a greenish tinge to it but her grinning-moron face was bright pink. The camera had missed every single thing that was special about her. If I had tried to make her look bad, I couldn't have done as well as that photograph. The caption, I saw to my horror, named her: "Miss Delta Cartwright and Her Bosom Buddy."

Someone brought a few copies of that magazine to the mill after it had been out for a few weeks. I'd begun to think that the whole business would pass into oblivion unnoticed. But there was a sun worshipper among the mill workers who had thumbed through the health magazines and had found Delta.

Jarvis found a copy on top of a load of rough lumber that we were about to dump into the chute. The magazine was lying open to the amateur photography section. Jarvis glanced at it, then took a longer look. He punched the STOP button and hopped onto the catwalk. An eerie silence gripped the mill. Then, as Jarvis blackened, the Tarzan-call expert cut loose with the loudest apeman call I'd ever heard. It was extra loud because he hadn't bothered to hide himself behind some distant machine or lumber pile. I guess he figured that Jarvis wouldn't want to do anything. I don't know why he would figure that. Maybe he believed that this nude photograph of Jarvis's wife, appearing in a national magazine, stripped Jarvis of everything he might want to fight over. Maybe he figured that without an ounce of dignity left to him, Jarvis would just peacefully become a full-fledged ape and like an ape would not have the terrible pride that causes so much grief in the human world. Whatever he figured, he figured wrong.

He was a tall, thick-necked Norski by the name of Odegaard. Odegaard was double Jarvis's size and this probably added to his notion that Jarvis would be unlikely to climb off his planer. But all of Odegaard's notions about Jarvis were wrong. Just as he was about to cut loose with another apeman yell, Jarvis jumped off the catwalk.

It was a huge jump that amazed everybody looking on. Jarvis landed on top of Odegaard, his knees on the big man's shoulders. He wrapped his long, thick arms around the big man's head and twisted as hard as he could. The big man danced on his tiptoes in a circle in an attempt to counteract the tremendous torque Jarvis was applying to his neck. To gather strength, Jarvis started in making short, chuffing noises. It sounded like a baboon barking. Someone in the crowd cracked a two-by-four in half. I looked around to see who had done it. But no one had a two-by-four in his hands. Then I realized that the sharp crack had come from Odegaard's neck. Jarvis had broken it. Odegaard crumpled. Jarvis hopped off him and then sat down on the concrete floor, breathing very hard. Mr. Stottlemeyer stepped forward then. He leaned down to Jarvis and took him by the hand. Jarvis got up and followed Mr. Stottlemeyer into his office.

Someone knelt down next to Odegaard and put his ear to the big Norski's chest. The door to Mr. Stottlemeyer's office was open. Jarvis was in there, sitting on a stool, while Mr. Stottlemeyer dialed the telephone.

JARVIS had worked at Stottlemeyer's for over twenty years. He had become, in that time, an actual functioning part of the planer operation. He was as necessary to it as the feeder chains, the drive mechanism, the chute, and the spinning, cylindrical blades on the other end of the chute that turned rough lumber into smooth blond boards. But Jarvis was more than just a piece of a machine. He was the heart and soul of the planer, and the whole operation seemed impossible without him up there on top of it, moving around nimbly, quick to see approaching danger. But he was gone, hauled off to jail for attempted murder, and though I was indirectly to blame, Mr. Stottlemeyer kept me on because the planer had to keep running. As Jarvis had been the heart of the planer, the planer was the heart of the sawmill.

A new man was hired to be my helper, but he wasn't any good. He was afraid. "Show him the ropes, Jack," said Mr. Stottlemeyer. "But don't show him how to fuck the dog. There's been enough dog-fucking going on around here to bring organized society to its knees."

I showed the new man, Dillard Wheeler, how to stand on the sliding platform, but he danced around on it like he was barefoot in a patch of brambles. "You can't just watch your feet, Dillard," I said. "You've got to move lumber." But after a week of trying to break him in, he was still watching his feet and most of the work fell to me.

One morning I came in drunk. I'd stayed up all night drinking wine, trying to dim the memory of what I'd done. But the wine only made me dwell on it. I wanted to see Delta again, but I didn't have the nerve to go out there. "You are a goddamned slimy bastard," I told myself. And nothing in me would rise to my defense. Worst of all, I still was in love with her. The dirty thought kept occurring to me: With Jarvis in prison, I could have her all to myself. The more wine I poured down my throat, the more reasonable this thought became. I guess this is why I didn't quit and leave town.

And the thought was still humming in my head when I went to work that morning. The mill was caught in a patch of fog, and it seemed to hang in space, unsupported, like a dark gray, ugly dream. And the planer, in the wet light of morning, looked like some kind of prehistoric bug. I didn't like the looks of it and didn't want to climb up on it any more than Dillard Wheeler did. The way my head and stomach felt, I knew the noise would make me sick.

Dillard was as useless as ever, wobbling around, watching his feet, hopping off to the safety of the catwalk whenever he thought the stack of lumber coming up behind us was getting too close. Dillard wore a hard hat, safety glasses, earmuff-style noise dampers, leather gloves that nearly reached his elbows, and an expensive pair of steel-toed boots a drop hammer couldn't dent. But he still danced around on the platform as if someone was firing bullets at his feet. He was useless, and worse than useless, he was in the *way*. I thought of Jarvis, how much the planer needed him, and then I thought of his face, just before he jumped on the Norski, the look in his round eyes, thinking, if that Norski hadn't come out from his hiding place yelling like the King of the Apes, it probably would have been *my* neck, and maybe it should have been. My head and stomach were sick with the noise, and the forklift operator was stacking the loads too close together, as though he knew the trouble I was having with the new man and wanted to add to them, and my thoughts went from Jarvis, Jarvis being led away from the crippled Norski by Mr. Stottlemeyer like a trainer with his ape, to Delta, Delta alone in the little house, Delta in her flimsy dress, Delta in my arms, her tangled hair in my hands, Delta looking up at me in bed with those heart-stopping eyes, and I only partially noticed that my foot was stuck, that sort of partial noticing that you remember later, long after it is too late, and wonder why, oh, why didn't you wake up and act before it was too late, like the first smell of smoke, how it doesn't register at first, how it only dawns on you gradually that you are smelling *smoke,* but by that time the whole damn kitchen is ablaze, and in that way, slowly, I realized that my foot had been stuck for several seconds before I understood it was really *stuck,* realizing it too late of course, and I felt rather than heard the sounds inside my foot, like crisp dry leaves being crushed, but it was the crumbling of bone, and then I screamed.

Dillard was watching his feet and dancing around, even though the boards of the sliding platform were no longer sliding but had been crimped together by the load of two-by-twelves coming up behind us, and I yelled at him, *"Hit the red button, Dillard!"* But he only grinned, embarrassed, as though I was only bawling him out again for being a dancing idiot, and I screamed again. This time he bent his helmeted head closer to me and cupped a gloved hand behind his earmuff, and his lips said, "How's that? How's that, Jack?" And there was now a black border to things, and the border was moving in on all sides, and I started to puke. "What say, Jack?" said Dillard as the jammed chains groaned. "What say?" He was forming the words carefully with his grinning lips so that I could read them, and I hit him as hard as I could, which wasn't very hard, but now, at least, there was a thread of blood running across his smile, as the black border moved in and shut off Dillard and the world.

THEY took my foot off one inch above the ankle because of the way the bones had been crushed. I was in some kind of disorganized state of mind and did not argue for a second opinion. Things were explained carefully to me, but I felt uninvolved and bored, as if I was a by-stander without much at stake. There was something dreamlike about it, and in a dream you never feel that you have the right to protest on behalf of the dreamer. The pain killer they gave me probably had something to do with it.

LaDonna came to see me. "Oh, Jackie," she said, looking at the shape a single foot makes under a sheet. She tried to hold her face together bravely, but she lost it. She climbed onto the bed and cried hard into my shoulder and neck.

"It'll be okay, LaDonna," I said.

She looked at me, her wet face shining. "Look who's the philosopher now," she said. At least there was the beginning of a smile on her lips. Then I saw something else move in her face. Curiosity.

"You want to see it?" I said.

"No," she said quickly. I could see it was a lie meant to cover her embarrassment. "Yes," she said, yielding to the one thing that she could always count on.

I pulled off the sheet and held my leg up. The thick bandage was creased with red. Sympathy and horror shoved curiosity aside and she turned away from the sight of my footless leg and started crying again. I took her in my arms and petted her hair.

"Oh, Jackie!" she wailed, and there was no consoling her now.

I stayed in the hospital for a couple of weeks and then was sent home without my right foot. I had to hobble around on crutches for a while and report back to the hospital once a week for rebandaging and instructions as to how I should go about exercising my footless leg.

"That is one fine-looking stump there," said the doctor as he wound fresh bandages around it. "Excellent tapering, my friend. No sharp point, see?"

A stump of any kind is pretty terrible-looking, I thought, but then my point of view was considerably different from the doctor's.

Two months later I was fitted for a rubber foot, and a month after that they sent me home with one. They taught me how to walk again, but I had a hard time getting the hang of it. My fear of tripping was very great. This made me limp badly, since I would raise the rubber foot up high with each step I took. The therapist said, "You are hiking your right hip, Jack." But I couldn't help it. It always felt like I was walking uphill. I would labor on the flat sidewalk as if on a 10 percent grade. I got winded a lot. I believed I looked comical to others. It must have looked like I was turning a bicycle pedal with my right leg while walking in sand with my left. Also, the ankle joint of my rubber foot creaked. "That's the leather bushing, Jack," said the therapist. "It'll soften up in time." It may have softened up, but it didn't stop creaking. My rubber foot sent out a signal that announced to all that a cripple was on his way. I guess I got testy and grim-minded because of these things. I began to spend a lot of time in bars.

In a place called the Timberjack Inn I met a woman named Helen Pritchett. She was a nice-looking divorcee of about thirty. We had a drink together. We started talking about the better bars in the area, then got to more personal things. I told her I had very bad dreams. She thought that was normal. She told me some things about her ex-husbands. She had two of them. Then my rubber foot started itching. I stamped down hard on it, turning several heads, but it kept on itching. The itch ran from the ball to the heel. It drove me wild. I wanted to unbuckle the foot and throw it against the wall.

"Let's get the hell out of here," I said to Helen.

She gave me a longish look and stubbed out her cigarette. "Okay, Jack," she said, as if she was agreeing to something that required considerable thought. But that was only her mannerism, I found out later. Often, before she would reply to a suggestion, she would seem to turn it over in her mind for a while, as if there was a lot more behind what had been proposed than was apparent. And then her reply had that odd tone of a bargain having been struck. It was confusing to me at first, but after I got used to it I kind of liked it.

"What's the matter?" she asked, as we were walking away from the Timberjack Inn.

I was lifting my right leg extra high and stomping down on the rubber foot. I was hiking my hip to beat hell. It made me mad, and I was puffing.

"Rock in my shoe," I said.

After about half a minute, she said, "Oh."

We went up to my room. I made some drinks. In terms of money I was better off now with my foot gone than I had been before. I got disability pay, I got some of Stottlemeyer's insurance money, and Dillard Wheeler had felt so bad about the accident, he had given me his car. It was eight years old, but it ran just fine and looked good.

In my room the itching got worse. I couldn't sit still. The itch was bringing out a kind of panic in me. My heart was beating hard and my hands were sweating. In the first few days after the amputation I still had feeling in my lost foot. It bothered me some—pain and itching —but the doctor said that was normal. He called it my "ghost foot." I thought that my ghost foot had been laid to rest a long time ago, but here it was, back with a vengeance.

Helen must have noticed the state I was in, but she just made herself comfortable in the new easy chair I'd bought with the insurance money and waited.

I went into the bathroom and filled the tub with cold water. I stuck my rubber foot into it, as if the nerves that were harassing me were actually in it. Of course, the burning did not go away. I unbuckled the foot and set it on the back of the toilet. I rubbed a cool washcloth over the stub at the end of my leg. But the itch was not in the stub. It was in the foot.

I hopped out of the bathroom and headed for my liquor cabinet, and I poured myself a glass full of white rum, which I drank quickly. Then I refilled the glass and hopped to my chair, spilling only a little on the way.

"I see you got the rock out of your shoe," Helen said.

Even her jokes came out like gray pronouncements. It was a characteristic I would come to appreciate.

"I am going out of my mind, Helen," I said through clenched teeth.

She gave this some thought. "Yes, it seems you are," she said.

She stayed the night. The itch eased off by 3:00 A.M. I felt as though I'd been dropped into hell and redeemed in the space of hours. I prayed that the itch would not return.

Helen undressed in front of me with the lights on like the experienced wife she was. She had a nice body. Heavy in places, worn thin in others, but I got the general impression of durability. She looked like she could absorb just about any shock the surprising world could deal out. Studying her body, I thought, There are lessons here.

She sat on the edge of my new double bed and lit a cigarette. She wasn't in any special hurry. "Put your foot on, Jack," she said.

"My foot?"

She took a long drag off her cigarette and looked at me for a while through the drifting threads of smoke. "You'll want traction, Jack," she explained.

Helen and I saw each other several more times after that first night. We liked each other's company. She had two children, a girl named Regina Jean and a boy named Will. Their father was a thousand miles east, selling used cars. Both children were afraid of my rubber foot, especially when I yanked it off and cursed it a blue streak for itching.

One day Helen said in a toneless, offhanded way that she was considering getting married again. I was surprised at how this announcement made me feel. A pain twisted across my stomach. A wave of desperation weakened my knees. I thought I had lost just about all I had to lose, but I had yet to understand what an unteachable fool the heart is.

"Who's the lucky SOB?" I asked.

She thought about it for a long while, then said softly, "It's no one you'd know. A man named Harold Radamacher. He used to be in business with my last husband."

The pain in my stomach didn't go away. I went to the doctor and he said it was a peptic ulcer. He gave me a prescription for some medicine, a strict diet to follow, and a stern warning about hard booze. But if I'd have had my choice between the ulcer and the itch in my rubber foot, I would have chosen the ulcer.

The ulcer turned me into a light sleeper. Sleeping light made my dreams vivid and terrible. I once dreamt that I was fighting with Jarvis on the planer. My foot had slipped over the steel lip and onto the moving belt. I watched helplessly as my foot was mangled in the blades. I woke up screaming something about the red STOP button.

"You're one of us now, kid," said the war veteran. His voice was in my ear, sad and kind.

"I know," I said, speaking to him for the first time.

— PART 3 —

WHY did my father kill himself?" I asked.

"It was the war," Mother said. "He wasn't the same."

"He seemed happy. I remember him singing. Once he picked you up and danced from room to room."

"It wasn't happiness. He acted that way because he was afraid of something inside of himself. All that dancing and carrying on was his way of running from it. He thought that if he ran hard enough, it would eventually leave him alone. Something like that."

"What was it, this thing inside of him?"

"I don't know. I guess you have to have it before you can know what it is."

"And the only way to get rid of it . . . I mean, since you can't really run away from it . . ."

"Yes. That's right. The only way is to point a gun at it and shoot it."

We were in a café, eating club sandwiches. She'd asked to see me. She'd heard about my accident and thought it would be best if I came home. I was surprised to see that she had put on quite a bit of weight. She had the beginning of jowls, her hips had broadened, her upper arms were round and jiggly. Even so, she was still beautiful. Her new heaviness hadn't diminished her beauty. If anything, it was now more *ample*. Less fragile, less delicate.

I don't know why I brought up the subject of my father's suicide. I guess I didn't want to talk about my foot. She'd mentioned it only once, though. "I heard about your foot," she said, when we met outside the café. I shrugged, as if it were some barely remembered misfortune. *Oh that. Shook me up for a while, but it's no big deal now.* It was less pathetic to act that way. More heroic. Like the war veteran who keeps his medals in the back of his underwear drawer. *These trinkets? Kind of cute, aren't they? Forgot I had them.*

I saw her glance down. She frowned, as if getting ready to bring up a subject closer to home, so I said, "Was he a drunk?"

"Who? Your father? No, he wasn't a drunk. He had a drink now and then, but he wasn't in love with it."

"Maybe he should have been a drunk," I said.

"Don't talk foolishness. Drinking only makes things worse. You saw what Gent did to himself."

I looked at her until her eyelids fluttered.

"Drinking makes things worse only if they can get worse," I said.

"Things are never as bad as they can get. Only weak people think that way. Life is too much for them. It destroys them."

"Gent's not dead yet," I said.

"I know he's not dead," she said. She picked up one of the thick sandwiches and bit into it. Mayonnaise slipped out from between the layers of meat onto her finger. She licked the white glob off, her tongue quick and accurate.

"Well, he's not *exactly* dead," I said.

"No, not exactly," she said.

I'd been to visit him, now that I had a car. He looked pretty much the same, only much more distracted. He didn't have much to say to me. We sat out on a lawn, in a grove of quaking aspens. His fingers moved, as if they were remembering the valves of a saxophone. I showed him a fuck book. He blinked.

"He's not exactly alive, either," I said.

Mother stopped chewing. She sighed. "No, he's not exactly alive. Why aren't you eating?"

I picked up a sandwich, then put it back down. "He's not exactly alive and he's not exactly dead. He's mister-in-between."

"Jack."

"He's dead, but he's not buried."

"Jack."

"Mister-in-between, that's who he is."

"Jesus Christ."

A woman at the table next to us made a sour face at me. I stared back at her, then licked my lips slowly, like a pervert. She looked quickly away, her face whitening.

We left the café and went home. The house had been redecorated. New furniture, new carpet, new wallpaper. Where once it had been mainly brown and gray, with touches here and there of blue, it was now orange and lime-yellow with off-white trim.

"Sure is cheerful," I said.

"Do you like it, Jackie?" she asked.

"Oh, yes. It's very cheerful. I'm glad everything is so cheerful."

"Don't start up again, Jack."

"Start what, Ma? Listen, there's no point in being gloomy, is there? I mean, why be gloomy if you don't have to? I feel better already, just being in this cheerful room."

She sighed. "Listen to me, Jack."

"No, I mean it. It's really cheerful in here."

"Are you going to listen to me or not?"

"Of course I'll listen. Why wouldn't I listen?"

She pushed a nonexistent strand of hair out of her eyes, over and over. "I feel terrible about your foot, honey," she said. "But—"

"Fuck my foot, Ma. Let's leave my foot out of it, okay?"

"I won't have that. I just won't have that, Jack." Her face got red in splotches. Her neck fat quivered.

"I'm sorry, Ma," I said. I meant it. I wanted to come home. I had begun to feel very bad living above the feed store sandwiched between the two hopeless old men.

"Look, Jackie, we want you to come home. But you're going to have to behave yourself. That's all there is to it."

I stared at the carpet. It was some kind of Oriental, packed with intricate designs. "Okay, Ma," I said.

"Guy has really made something out of this creamery, Jack. He's worked himself half to death, believe me."

"Is there any buttermilk, Ma?" I said. My stomach had started its afternoon war against itself. Every afternoon, about two o'clock, the bright pains would flare up. I doused them with buttermilk, and they'd be peaceful then until about midnight.

We went into the kitchen. I sat at the table while she poured me a tall glass of buttermilk. She poured herself a glass of red wine.

"You can have your old room back. We won't expect you to work, Jackie. Of course, if you want to help out around the house now and then—you know, the dishes, the vacuuming, the lawn—no one will try to stop you."

"I'll pull my weight," I said.

She pressed her hand on mine. "Oh, Jackie, don't worry about it. If you feel up to doing something, fine. If not, then that's fine too."

"Then everything's fine," I said, feeling, suddenly, the clammy presence of a bottomless depression somewhere in the neighborhood of my heart.

Mother sighed. "Yes, everything *is* fine, Jack. Guy has made it fine. He's done wonderfully. It's his master plan." Suddenly she laughed shrilly. "Oh! Don't *you* have any doubts about it, mister! It's quite a plan!"

"Must be one ring-tailed son of a bitch," I said.

"I am trying very hard to be patient with you, Jack,"

she said. "If you really want to come home, then you'd better not antagonize him. Guy is going to make us rich. If you want any kind of life at all, you'd do best to stay on his good side. His master plan won't allow for any nonsense. He measures our work."

I sipped my buttermilk. Its thick sourness calmed my stomach. She waited for me to put the glass down. I kept drinking, and when I finally set it down I had nothing left to say. I felt like taking a nap. Outside, a car was revving.

"Well?" she said.

"Well what?"

"Don't you want to know how he does it?"

A giddy thought crossed my mind. It made me grin. "Does what?" I said.

"Measures our *work*." Her hands were busy on the table, the fingers twining and untwining.

"What do you mean, 'measures our work'?"

"Jesus! I'm trying to *tell* you! It's his master plan."

"You mean he measures *your* work? You don't work for him. He works for you."

"That's beside the point. He has this stopwatch. He made up a big chart that lists all the jobs and he figured out the exact time needed for each job to be completed. So he rides around following the milk trucks, using his stopwatch to measure the efficiency of the driver. They get points, the drivers. One hundred is best, zero the worst. Of course there are no one hundreds or zeroes. Everyone falls in between someplace. He does it for the pushcarts, too. He'll follow those old men, just idling the car, his stopwatch timing everything they do from making change to crossing a street."

"You said *our* work, Ma. How does he measure *our* work."

She laughed again, and this time it sounded a little crazy. It was high in her throat, a kind of airless tinkling. I think she was trying very hard to make her current life seem reasonable. "Well, you know," she said, coyly. "Like my cooking, or the housework, grocery trips, that type of thing." She touched her jowl tenderly, as if to see if it were still there.

"Are you kidding me, Ma?" I said. "You hate cooking and housework."

That laugh tinkled in her throat again. She looked around the kitchen nervously. "Shh!" she said, finger to her lips. "Of course I'm not kidding, Jackie," she whispered. "It's his—"

"Master plan?"

The door to the office swung open. Guy stood in the doorway, massaging his temples. He was wearing a maroon suit and slick white shoes with brass buckles. He'd let his mustache and sideburns grow out. They were connected in a kind of scrollwork of bristles. He'd put on weight, too. His stomach bulged past the long lapels of his jacket. "Well, as I live and breathe," he said, extending his hand to me. He had an expensive gold ring on his hand set with red and green jewels. "Jack, my boy! What a genuine pleasure it is to have you back!"

We shook hands. "Hello, Guy," I said.

"Hey," he said, his face twisting with compassion. "I hear old Stottlemeyer picked up your hospital bills. You were real lucky there."

"That's what they tell me," I said.

"Hell, if you're going to tear up your foot, then do it on somebody else's property, that's what I always say." He chuckled heartily. He cocked his head and appraised my right foot. "Hell, I can't tell a shade of difference between them, Jack!"

"I can," I said.

He draped his heavy arm around my shoulder. "Jack, what can I say? You're home, and that's what counts. Right Jade?"

"Oh, I'm so relieved," Mother said, looking at the pair

of us as if she'd been hoping for this reunion for a long time.

He showed me his office. I saw that the bunk bed had been taken out. It now looked like a real office, the office of a very busy executive. The desk was littered with papers, there was a big, complicated-looking chart on the wall, there were half a dozen bar graphs on another wall, there was even a map of the world pinned up, as though he was planning to expand the business across state and even international borders.

"I got myself a headache working in here today, Jack," he said, his voice hushed with self-esteem.

We went out into the living room. Mother and Guy sat together on the new sofa. "Jack, your ma here has something to tell you," Guy said.

I looked at Mother. She was flustered. She hadn't expected this. "Oh, *you* tell him, Guy," she said, the red splotches returning to her face. The car out in the street was being revved mercilessly. A V-8, throttle wide, the twin glasspacks trumpeting.

"Goddamn that kid out there!" Guy said.

"Oh, just ignore them, honey," Mother said, rubbing Guy's hand.

"What was it you wanted to tell me?" I asked. I figured I'd get the *conditions* now. You can stay home, Jack, if . . .

"It's your ma and me," Guy said. "We're getting hitched." He took her face in his hand and kissed it.

"What about Gent?" I said.

He looked confused. "What do you mean, what about Gent?" He studied Mother's face, then released it.

"He's still alive," I said. "I mean, he's still down there in Willow Springs and she's still married to him."

He slid a long cigar out of the inside pocket of his jacket. He tore off the cellophane slowly, then passed the cigar under his nose. "Alive?" he said, almost to himself. "How do you mean, *alive?*"

The car in the street howled until I thought the pistons would blow holes through the cylinder heads and launch themselves into space. The windows of the front room were singing.

"You're not making sense, Jack," Mother said, attempting sternness.

"No, he's not. That's right, Jade. He's not making sense," Guy said.

I shrugged.

"You see that, don't you, Jack?" Guy said. "You see that you're not making sense, right?"

I got up and looked out the window. It was a Ford, a '51 Victoria, lowered and leaded. The hood was up and a grease-caked boy was fooling with the engine. LaDonna was in the front seat, tall now and lovely. I wanted to go out there and see her.

"I think he realizes it, Guy," Mother said. "I think he sees that he wasn't making sense."

"He's suffered a great personal tragedy," Guy said to Mother, as though to explain my erratic thinking.

"Yes, that's true," she said. I felt, suddenly, as if I'd left the room.

"It's tough on a young kid, something like that," Guy told her, tapping her knee with the unlit cigar.

"Yes, yes," Mother said, nodding gravely.

"I mean, think about it for a minute," Guy said.

Mother turned to me. "You see, Jackie," she said, controlling her voice in the way you would when speaking to someone no longer capable of making sense. "You see, honey, Guy and I are in love."

Guy took her face in his hand again and kissed it. The pressure of his fingers made her mouth pucker abnormally. He studied her lips for a few seconds, then kissed them, over and over. I got up and went outside.

LaDonna saw me and jumped out of the car. She gave me a long hard hug. When she looked at me, her eyes were brimming. "Oh, Jackie!" she said. "I'm so sorry it happened!" She brought my hand up to her face and let her tears wet it.

The grease-caked boy cleared his throat. LaDonna stepped away from me and said, "Jack, this is Speed. Speed Torkelson. Speed, this is my brother, Jack."

Speed and I shook hands. "Howdy," he said. He nodded at my foot. "Hell of a thing, your accident."

"You get used to it," I said.

"Speed and I are engaged," LaDonna said.

I looked at Speed. He was good-looking, until he smiled. "You're kidding," I said.

Speed put his arm around LaDonna and pulled her close. They both had sappy grins on their faces.

"What about school, LaDonna?" I said.

"I'll finish," she said. "I'm a senior this coming year. Then we'll settle down."

"Settle down?" I said. "Jesus, LaDonna. What about Einstein?"

Speed leaned away from her, as if from a bad smell. "What about *who*?" he said. "Einstein? What's he talking about, LaDonna?"

"That was kid stuff, Jack," LaDonna said.

"I've got my own shop," Speed said. "Speedy's Auto Repairs."

"He doesn't look it, but Speed's twenty-five years old, Jack," LaDonna said.

"Twenty-six come October," Speed said, smiling happily. His short gray teeth looked like they belonged in the mouth of an eighty-year-old man.

"Looks like everyone's grown up around here," I said.

Speed ducked under the hood of the car again. I pulled LaDonna to one side. "He's not good enough for you, LaDonna," I said. "You're worth ten of him."

"No I'm *not*," she whispered. She looked alarmed. "Don't think that about me ever, Jack."

"Christ, LaDonna."

"No question about it," Speed said. He looked up,

grieving, from his engine. "The dag-nabbed head gasket is blown for sure." He climbed into the car and draped his hands over the wheel in a gesture of exhausted despair. LaDonna got in and slid up against him. She put her hand in his lap defiantly.

"Shoot," Speed said. Then he started the car moodily and they drove off in a blue cloud, roaring. LaDonna waved.

I went back into the house. Guy and Mother were gone, but Spencer Ted was sitting in one of the big new living room chairs, turning the pages of a comic book.

"Hey, Spencey!" I said.

He looked up, his dull eyes blank. He'd grown a lot, but not out of his early tendencies. He filled the chair, side to side. His big round head sat neckless on his thick shoulders. His drunkard's nose had gotten wider, his pink ears fleshier.

"It's me," I said. "Your brother, Jack."

He pulled himself out of the chair. "Jack?" he said. Though he was six years old now, his voice still had its babylike whine. "Jackie?"

I went over to him and took his chubby hand. He stood up and put his arms around my waist. I looked down at his hump. It was more distinct now—a pillow of flesh at the base of his neck. "You're going to do it the hard way, right Spencey?" I said.

He grinned up at me, trustfully, as though what I had said made good sense. I mussed his wiry hair a little and went into the kitchen.

Guy was sitting at the table, consulting his stopwatch. "Okay," he said. "It's set on zero. Go ahead and start that roast. You'll be pouring the wine at six-fifteen."

He pressed a button on the watch, then slipped it into his jacket pocket. "I've got to take a look at the homogenizer." He stood up and left the house.

Mother took a rib roast out of the refrigerator with a weariness that was not physical.

* * *

No one saw any trouble. The lawyer didn't, the judge
didn't, the bankers didn't, the Junior Chamber didn't,
the city, county, and state didn't, and so Mother divorced
Gent, who was declared, more or less, "Dead But Not
Buried," and after the required waiting period, married
Guy Rampling. It was winter again when we all went to
the office of the Justice of the Peace.

The office was cold and damp. A small kerosene space
heater sat in one corner but seemed to put out no heat
at all. The JP had two sweaters on and he kept rubbing
his hands together in order to generate warmth. He
raced through the civil ceremony, stumbling at every
three-syllable word. There was a radio playing loudly in
some other office, and the voice of the JP got itself tangled with that of the radio announcer. He seemed irritated and confused and eager to get the business done
with. In my half-attentive state of mind, I heard the
mingled voices of the JP and radio announcer say, "By
the powers vested in me and more than your money's
worth at Scone's Super Mart thus by the great seal of the
state of your Aunt Nell's home-baked cookies therefore
upon receiving your oaths this day rush right on down
before it's too late to Land o' Appliances for your free
toaster I now pronounce you man and wife."

"Gotcha," Guy said, taking Mother's face in both
hands and kissing her lips fiercely.

The JP slammed the book he'd been reading from
down on his desk and began to pound on the wall behind
him. "Turn the damned radio down, Cornelia! Turn it
down!" Cornelia's muffled apology made the JP sneer.
"She'll turn it down for five minutes, then she'll have it
blaring again. Cornelia's deaf, you know."

There was no honeymoon for the newlyweds because
of the "master plan," which Guy couldn't leave alone, if
only for a few days. The pushcart fleet, it turned out, had

shown a net loss for the summer and Guy felt he had to work out some new ideas in order to "stimulate the market." He read books on business practices and he began to use words and phrases from them in his everyday speech. "That blasted marginal discount factor has got a stiff one right up my chute, Jade," I heard him say once. And: "If you don't generate a quick turnover in this line, you are going to wind up with a taxable inventory worth about as much as a teaspoon of cold piss." And: "Those smart pinpricks down at the Chamber talk about *venture* capital like it was egg money, while I'm still trying to teach those old farts how to count nickels and dimes every summer."

Guy became preoccupied with ice cream. He read books about how it was first invented and marketed. Once he got excited about the famous milk dealer Jacob Fussel. We were in the front room, having peach cobbler. Guy was reading aloud about how Jacob Fussel had, over one hundred years ago, frozen his surplus milk in order to save it from turning. One thing led to another, and soon every dinner table on the eastern seaboard of the United States sported ice cream desserts. "Isn't that just a fucking wonder?" he said, his eyes misty. He got up and started pacing the floor. He cracked his knuckles. He tugged his mangled ears. He giggled. "Jacob Fussel, you wise old pinprick!" he said, his face crimped with admiration. "Jake, you money-making old ice cream genius bastard!"

Guy spent a lot of time tending his new machinery. The new equipment occupied a new wing that had been added to the old creamery building. Sometimes he would just stand in front of a machine, such as the ice cream sandwich maker, and watch it chatter through its cycles. He worried these machines through their motions, chewing on his fingernails, as if his watchdog eye would prevent them from making errors. He would check on his machines as much as ten times a day, sometimes sneaking up on them quietly, maybe expecting them to be loafing or producing a slipshod product. But they were flawless machines, quiet and efficient, and their products were uniformly perfect. He was obsessed with the temperature gauges. "One degree up or down and you are going to have yourself one dirty son of a bitch of a problem," he said once. He would oversee the fruit hopper to make sure not too much of the expensive ingredients were being added to the special-flavor ice creams. "Right here is where I could lose the major part of my ass," he said, pointing a shaking finger at the fruit hopper. "You got any idea at all what a ton of walnuts costs?" And once he sprinted through the new wing like someone was shooting at him. "Ammonia!" he screamed. "I smell ammonia! Shut the fuckers down! Shut them down, I tell you! Check the lines! God in heaven, will somebody please check those fucking *lines*?" But it was only me and old Swede cleaning out the scummy drains with an ammonia-based solvent and not a ruptured refrigeration line at all.

He would sit in his office until late at night, working out simple formulas. I watched him do this once. He scribbled the formula for ice cream on a piece of paper. "I want you to look at this, Jack," he said. He had a weird grin on his face. He looked both smugly proud of himself and frightened. It was as if he couldn't believe what was written on that piece of paper unless someone confirmed the arithmetic. Here's what the paper said:

$$
\begin{aligned}
1 \text{ gallon mixer} &= 9 \text{ pounds} \\
1 \text{ gallon cream} &= 5 \text{ pounds} \\
9-5 &= 4 \\
4/5 \times 100 &= 80\% \text{ overrun}
\end{aligned}
$$

Overrun was the amount of air that was whipped into the cream. I handed the paper back to him. I didn't exactly understand how these figures were arrived at, but I told him that the arithmetic looked okay to me.

"Christ, it's so goddamned beautiful, Jack! Don't you see it?"

I shrugged.

"You should've stayed in school, boy! See, what it means is this—we're selling the rubes eighty percent *air!*"

I frowned at the paper. It didn't make sense. "Eighty percent?" I said.

"Right! Eighty percent by volume! How the hell can I lose money doing that?"

He began to court men from the Chamber and had grand ideas about his future. "I'll be the kingpin, one of these days," he told us once at the dinner table. "How about that, Jade? Humble old boy like me from the wrong side of creation getting sucked up to by the big dogs downtown!" LaDonna and I kept our eyes down and our silverware moving. "Top dog, that's what I'll be," Guy said. For a joke he barked at us like a watchdog. Still, we didn't look up. To Mother he said, "Maybe they'll ask me to run for mayor. I'll do it, too, by Christ! I've got some ideas that'll shake up this sleepy old burg!"

Once he threw a party for the Chamber. He bought new clothes for himself and gave us a warning lecture. "Mind your P's and Q's, you hear?" he said, pointing his finger at us. "These are the local honchos coming over, not just a bunch of crummy freeloaders. I do not want to hear anything but the king's sweet English. I would appreciate it, Jack, if you kept yourself out of the booze, okay? And everybody watch their language. Reverend Elam and his wife are going to be here. Reverend Elam is not your typical stuffed-shirt Bible banger, but at the same time he won't be thrilled to hear the Lord's name taken in vain. None of you people seem to be able to express a simple thought without the help of *shit, fuck, asshole, son of a bitch,* and *bastard.* Those will be out. Those will be unheard words around here, everyone understand?" He pulled LaDonna aside. "I don't want that grease monkey around my party. He smells like gas and oil. I want you to wear a nice dress, not one of those slutty numbers you wear to the dances." Turning to Mother, he said, "Jade, you keep an eye on their drinks. I see any of those honchos standing around with a dry Dixie cup, I am going to be severely pissed off."

Guy prepared himself for the party by getting books on how to be an engaging conversationalist on all occasions. I walked past their bedroom and saw him through the slightly ajar door practicing in front of the vanity mirror. He was in his long johns, holding an imaginary drink in one hand, gesturing suavely with the other. "Well, sir," he said to his reflection. "As I was putting forth the other day, anybody can win unless there happens to be another entry in the race." He winked at himself and chuckled. He nodded to his imaginary audience of bankers and merchants, as if they were commenting favorably on his wit. He picked up a book called *Tasteful Jokes for All Occasions* and memorized another one. Then he rehearsed it in the same way he had the first joke.

The night of the party, Guy was as nervous as a boar in a cannery. He poured himself a whisky, then pushed it aside, untouched. "I've got to watch myself," he said. "It won't do for me to get myself plowed under. The minute I get plowed under I can't remember diddly shit." He took a slip of paper out of his shirt pocket. "A balanced budget," he read, "is no *summum bonum* of fiscal policy." He held it at arm's length and looked at it, squinting dubiously. "How in the hell did that one get on this list?" he asked. "What in the hell is a goddamn *summum bonum* anyhow?" He looked at us, a touch of panic in his eyes. "That sound like commie crap to you, Jade?" Mother shrugged. She was making the punch and couldn't be bothered with Guy's clever sayings. Guy looked at his list and read another one. "I am firmly opposed to the government entering into any business, the major purpose of which is competition with our own citizens." He looked at us, nervous and hopeful. "That's a good one, right? That'll make those cocksuckers sit up and clap for joy, right?" Mother made a wry face as she dumped a quart of dark rum into the punch bowl. "Jesus, Guy," she said. But Guy only consulted his list again. "According to the theory of aerodynamics," he read, laboring over the unfamiliar words, "the common bumblebee is unable to fly. But the bumblebee, being ignorant of the theory of aerodynamics, goes right ahead and flies anyway—and makes a little honey everyday to boot!" He slapped his leg. "That's flat beautiful!" he said. "You kids understand that one, don't you? Oh, that'll tickle the shit out of them, won't it, Jade?" He put the list back into his pocket. "But here is the corker," he said. "This one will have them pissing down the chair legs." He stood at attention and closed his eyes. "A *young* man who is not a socialist hasn't got a heart," he recited. "But an *old* man who *is* a socialist hasn't got a head." He retrieved the whisky he'd denied himself and drank it down. "Now, by God, if that doesn't make their day I don't know what will. Isn't that the smartest thing you've ever heard?" He slammed down the empty glass and poured himself another.

Nine o'clock chimed on the big hall clock and no one had shown up for Guy's party. "Looks like the honchos aren't coming," Mother said.

Guy slapped his stomach and flinched with pain. I recognized the gesture. "Get me some soda, Jade," he said through locked jaws.

"Don't get yourself an ulcer, Guy," I said. "They'll probably show up."

"Rich people never come to parties on time," LaDonna said.

"Just what the hell do you two know about it!" Guy thundered. "Who said these pinpricks are rich? Hell, I can buy out half of them and tell the other half to line up to kiss my rosy ass!"

LaDonna only smiled at him. A few years earlier she would have sniffed and left the room, head high. This smile was something new. She was amused, anticipating catastrophe. It was a thin, superior smile. She was lovely in her black strapless gown. She looked twenty-one at least, though she was barely eighteen. Her breasts had filled out and she was as tall as me.

Mother brought Guy his soda. He drank it down. The party had been set for eight. The cold cuts, which had been out since seven o'clock, were turning crisp at the edges. The cheese loaf was sweating. The dip was stiffening. Finally, at 9:20 the guests began to arrive. First to come was Reverend Elam and his wife. Guy rushed to greet them.

"Here's the sky pilot himself!" Guy said, a little drunk by that time. "How do, missus," he chortled to Mrs. Elam, a very large woman with strange gray eyes. "Come on in and chow down, you look like you could use a snack! Jade, show Mrs. Elam here where to sling her coat. That's Dutch cheese and Norski fish balls over there! Help yourself! Plenty more where that came from!"

"Actually," said Reverend Elam, a small, dapper man in a dark brown suit, "we can't stay very long. Hester's sister is quite ill."

Both the Reverend Elam and his huge wife, Hester, were clearly not enthralled by Guy's little welcoming speech. Hester took off her fur coat and handed it to Mother with a tentativeness that made me think she wanted to turn around and run out the door. Coat off, she was even bigger than I'd first believed. Breasts the size of ottomans loomed beside her perfectly groomed husband. She wore a black, loose-fitting dress and a little gray hat the size of a teacup. She had a strong, nice-looking face but her lipstick was smeared a bit, as if she put it on in the dark. She walked to the sideboard and picked up a fish ball. She studied it for a few seconds then pulled it daintily off the toothpick with her large red lips. She ate one more fish ball, chewing slowly, then moved on to the cheese loaf. She cut herself a wedge and tasted it, taking a small crumb carefully between her teeth.

As if there was something magnetic about her, we stood watching her sample the snacks. Guy stood with his hands in his pockets, jingling change and grinning stupidly. Reverend Elam rubbed his small, thin hands together heartily, as if proud of his wife's appetite. "She's doing well, don't you think?" he asked.

"Hey, that's what it's for," Guy said. "Eat all you want, missus!"

My foot started itching. The itch came and went. Sometimes it would be quiet for weeks at a time. When it came back, it came back with a vengeance. I put all my weight on it, letting the left foot float above the carpet.

More guests arrived: Hudson, the owner of Inland Mercantile; Everson, of Everson's Appliances and Hardware; Naismith, owner of the two radio stations in Far Cry; Big Natty Northberry, president of the Chamber; Marshall, the Cadillac agency manager; Boynston, owner of A-One Farm Implements; Marchetti, owner of the Acme Slaughterhouse; Huggins, the mayor; Arp, the jeweler; and a half a dozen others of equal importance. At first they were all carefully unimpressed as they sized up their host, his house, the furnishings. But as the rum punch began to take hold, the men loosened up, laughing and joking and then settling into serious opinionating about politics and business. The women, their smiles glazed with boredom, moved off to the kitchen and dining room. I heard Guy recite, "Never put your trust in money—put your money in *trust!*" There were a few appreciative chuckles.

Big Hester Elam stood all by herself against a wall, eating slowly and watching the festivities from a distance that was more than a matter of inches and feet. Something in her eyes, something they emitted, like long shafts of cloudy gray light, made me think of oceanwide distances.

I walked up to her, stomping my burning foot into the carpet. She was chewing a fish ball slowly.

She noticed me and almost smiled. I speared a fish ball and popped it into my mouth. Those gray eyes in that enormous face studied my working mouth and I stopped chewing and swallowed, gulping the fish down.

"Show me your house, would you?" she said.

"Sure," I said.

She caught my arm at the elbow. Her hand was surprisingly slender, the fingers long. Though I was leading the way, it felt as if I was being directed.

We left the front room. I caught Reverend Elam's eye as we moved toward the stairs. I smiled and he smiled back, but as he watched us climbing the stairs his smile faded. He looked alarmed. I winked and mouthed the words, "No problem, I don't mind."

I showed her all the bedrooms, the bathroom, the closet space in the hall, the heat registers, the nice carpeting. I felt like a real estate salesman, desperate to make a sale. But as I babbled on, the gray distance returned to her eyes.

"I guess this is kind of boring," I said.

She didn't answer. Instead, she turned her back on me and walked down the hall to my room. The party downstairs was roaring. Guy was making some kind of speech about the price of labor. Someone was clapping methodically.

Mrs. Elam walked into my room and sat down on the bed. She put her hands to her face. Her massive shoulders quaked. I remembered, then, the look of alarm on Reverend Elam's face as we moved up the stairs. My heart picked up speed. Something I didn't know about was going on here. Tears leaked out between her fingers. Small moans escaped her lips. I went over to her and cleared my throat. She looked up, her eyes so sad and so gray that my lungs tingled with the urge to whimper.

"What's wrong, Mrs. Elam?" I managed to say. "Don't you feel well?"

"Oh, lost," she said. "Lost, they're all lost."

The party below made a sound like one voice, grumbling.

"I'll get your husband," I said.

She caught my hand and pulled me down beside her. "No, it's too late," she said. "Too late, too late."

Her voice was deep and so unhappy that it broke my heart to hear it.

A woman somewhere said, "Oh, yes! We love our life here in Far Cry!"

Mrs. Elam stood up suddenly. She towered over me, like a cliff. All I could see when I looked up was the black underside of her giant breasts.

"Lost, lost," she said, pulling her dress up until it was gathered around her hips. She didn't have any underpants on. The rich, sour smell of a sun-warmed creel filled the air around me. I tried to stand up, but she put her hands on my shoulders, holding me on the bed.

"We can help them," she said.

"I don't think so," I said, squirming away from her.

Reverend Elam came in then. "Oh, Lord," he said. "I was so afraid of this."

He took her hand and pulled her away from me. She sank into a chair and covered her face with her hands again.

"I'm so sorry, Jack," Reverend Elam said. "Hester is unwell. It isn't her sister who's sick. She has no sister. It's Hester, I'm afraid. She's home from the sanitarium.

I thought a little party would be good for her. Apparently I was wrong. I'm sorry."

"It's okay," I said, shrugging.

He stepped closer to me and put his hand on my shoulder. "I'd appreciate it if you kept this to yourself," he said.

"Mum's the word," I said.

He looked at me for a long moment, then went to his wife. She was now staring blankly out the darkened window. "Come on, dear," he said. "We should get you back before they close the main gate."

She stood up slowly, docile as a zoo animal, her gray eyes showing no distance in them at all now.

After they left, I stayed in my room thinking about Hester Elam. Something that couldn't be written off as craziness gave her eyes a quality that made my stomach flare with pinpoints of pain. It was as if she had been blessed, or cursed, with perfect mote-free vision, vision that let her see us as we really were, and her mind couldn't manage the horror of it.

I went down to the kitchen to get some buttermilk. The party had thinned out to a few people, all drunk. I took my buttermilk out to the front porch. LaDonna and Speed were out in his car, necking. The thought of her wasting herself on that drip made my stomach hurt all the more and so I went back in.

"Have another one, Chester," Guy was saying to a very drunk man who was searching himself for something.

"Gin," said the man. "Make me a gimlet, will you Rampling?"

The man's wife pointed a finger at Guy. "Don't give him a goddamn thing," she said.

"Who took my cigarettes?" said the drunk. He stood on one foot. The other foot was six inches in the air, as if looking for the first step of a flight of stairs. The foot didn't come down. He was off-balance, close to falling. He had a scowl on his red face.

"Fuck her, Rampling. Give me a gimlet. You got a cigarette?"

Guy gave him a cigarette and lit it for him. *"Gim*let?" he said, losing his poise. "You sure you want a gimlet on top of all those punches? Rum and gin, Chester, I don't know about that. You might wake up hoping someone will shoot you."

"I'll shoot the shit-ass," said Chester's wife.

"Fuck her, Rampling. She's a cunt. You know what I mean?"

"Don't give him a thing," said the woman. "He's drunk."

"I am not drunk."

"You are drunk."

"I am not drunk. You're drunk. She's drunk, Guy. She's a drunk cunt and a bitch to boot."

"Sticks and stones," said the woman.

"Now how about that little ole gimlet? You gonna give me a goddamn gimlet or do I have to get ugly? I can get ugly, you know that? I can be a mean fucker when I get pissed."

"One gimlet coming up, Chester," Guy said, laughing thinly.

"That's the *only* thing that'll be coming up," said the man's wife.

The man's foot finally came down. It threw him off-balance and he staggered sideways into Guy. Guy held him up until he regained his footing. "What's that supposed to mean, you old cow?" said the man.

The woman smirked. She looked around the room. She winked at Guy. "You know what I mean. I mean a gimlet coming up is the only thing that'll be coming up."

"She's talking about my dick, Rampling," said the man.

"A crooked log always makes a straight fire," Guy said, quoting from his little list of sayings.

Both the man and the woman looked at Guy. Guy

shrugged and held his hands out, palms up. "Just an old saying," he said.

"I don't think that's very goddamn funny," said the man.

"It doesn't make sense," said the woman.

"Look, are you going to get me that drink or shall I take my business elsewhere?"

"One gimlet, coming right . . . one gimlet on the way," Guy said.

"I'm warning you," said the woman.

The man took a deep breath and hit his wife on the jaw. She fell into the snack table.

"Gimlet," said the man. "Okay, Rampling? If it isn't too much trouble?"

"Gimlet it is," said Guy, backing away from the man, one foot behind the other, as if on a tightrope.

The drunk and his wife had been last to arrive, and so they stayed past midnight. The man, Chester Simmons, owned six whole blocks of downtown Far Cry and was generally considered the wealthiest man in town. After hitting his wife, he stayed in the kitchen talking to Mother. On one of my buttermilk trips to the refrigerator, I saw him trying to lay his head on her lap. She was sitting at the kitchen table and he was crawling around under the table.

Out in the front room, the man's wife was lying on the sofa with an ice pack on her face. She was snoring. Guy sat on the end of the sofa. Her stockinged feet were in his lap. Guy's face was stiff with disappointment and self-pity. He was worn out from playing up to the honchos of Far Cry. He grabbed the foot of the wife of the richest man in Far Cry and spoke to it. "I could jam my prick up your fat ass, you old bag of guts, and nobody in this pissant town, including your limp-dick husband, would say boo."

* * *

I T was a bright, sunny day on top of the tree and the familiar meadow spread out before me like a golden carpet. I felt invited. The stand of dark pines was directly ahead and I started trotting toward it. I was afraid, but I was also thrilled about getting there. I saw a path leading through the pines and I took it. Before long, I was standing in front of our house. This amazed me. I'd left everyone asleep, I'd walked out to the tree in the backyard, climbed the tree, found the sunny meadow, crossed the meadow to the dark pines, entered the pines, found the path, and now here I was back in front of the house I'd just left. There were some significant differences, though. No street. No creamery. No neighborhood. Just the house, set in a clearing, looming. I took a deep breath and went inside. I went upstairs to my room. It was just as I'd left it. I got into bed and began to fall asleep. It was profound sleep, sleep within sleep, and I panicked, trying to stop myself from entering it. I sat up in bed, my heart pounding, wondering if I had come all the way awake. In the doorway, silhouetted by a light in the hall, was Hester Elam. I couldn't see her face clearly but her silhouette was unmistakable. She was tall as a grain elevator and as she leaned toward me the room sagged, anticipating her weight. Then she was over me, a grain elevator filled with sun-warm trout, a fishy reek, and a great steamy darkness settled on me, pinning me to the bed. My scream was weak under her full, naked weight and as I tried to roll away from her, her massive knees held me fast. "So many would come home," she said, her voice soft and sane as a lullaby. Sweat from her thighs and belly steamed the closing air. I sucked for breath, sobbing for it, as odor from a thousand rank creels filled with trout fell on me. I heard her heart's rhythmic thunder stroking creation. And then, all at once, there was no more room under her. Wiry hair and soft damp flesh pressed my face. The weight of that embrace increased until I thought I'd be crushed, and then her flesh yawned open, accepting first my face, then my head and shoulders, and I fell into her, upward through a fleshy channel. I traveled easily and without fear, breath no longer necessary, and my sense of motion gave way to a sense of absolute stillness as I entered a wide, horizonless sea. I was warm and happy and mindless, pleased with my journey, never wanting to retrace it. I thought, How stupid they are to leave, over and over, climbing out time after time into the cold light that illuminates nothing and then rising up on two legs to positions of small power and token respect, as if this perfect, unmoving sea could ever be put out of the mind and forgotten. And then I saw that I wasn't alone in the quiet, dark sea. I had a twin, a companion, and this other one was very near to me. Though there was no light, I could see him. I recognized him right away. *Ngantja,* I said. Yes, he said. So this is the cave, I said. Yes, he said. But I'm at home, in my room, asleep, I said. Yes, he said. Then my room and the cave are the same thing, I said. He opened his mouth but did not speak. I am always in the cave, but most of the time I don't know it, I said. An understatement, he said. Just answer yes or no, I said. But he only smiled. I woke up. I got out of bed and hopped to my mirror.

The dark room was illuminated by flashes of thunderless lightning. I appeared to myself in the millisecond flashes as a violet apparition. I smiled in the dark.

I T was a winter of sobering dreams. Some I remembered, most I didn't. My stomach was healed by buttermilk and I tried drinking wine again before going to bed, but as before, wine only made the dreams more vivid. I was glad when spring came. By my twentieth birthday, I was ready to change my life again. I asked Guy for a real job and he said I could start out with the Red Devil pushcart crew. To his surprise, I agreed. In fact, the idea of walking my ass off all day long through the streets of Far Cry appealed to me. The itch in my rubber foot seldom nagged at me now, but just hanging around the house doing odd jobs made me nervous and restless. I didn't get tired enough to sleep well.

In spite of my limp, I could move a cart pretty fast. "That was damn good, Jack," Guy said, having followed me on the first leg of my route. "You got from Ninth Street to Maple in four minutes flat. How's your foot feel?" I shrugged. He was driving the Roadmaster, letting it idle in first. I turned up Maple, slowed down to a stroll, and began to flap my bells. There were seven bells welded to a steel bar, and the bar was attached by wires to the pushcart's handle. While pushing the cart I flapped the hanging bells with a couple of free fingers.

Guy reset his stopwatch. The excited faces of little children appeared in the windows of houses as I called to them with my bells. Soon, they were out in the street, gathered together in ragtag clumps, holding bright coins up for me to see.

"Okay," Guy said, talking out of the side of his mouth. "There are your targets. Now, you'll want to move the stuff fast. Don't stop to talk to the little bastards. They'll kill your schedule if you let them. Hell, you'd be tying their shoelaces and wiping their snotty noses if you gave them half a chance. Just say, Sure kid. Okay kid. That's great kid. Act like you couldn't give a fat turd one way or the other and they'll eventually get the idea. Keep your cookie hooks out of the coldbox, kid—tell them that, because sure as hell they'll try to reach down inside the box. Your job is to keep those popsickles and Gopher Cones moving. Especially the Gopher Cones. Push the Gopher Cones, Jack. They're short a nickel? Send the little shits back to the house. I want those Gopher Cones to *move.*"

I pushed my cart toward the grimy mob. They shoved their eager little chests up against my cart, against my legs, pressing impatiently. A few grabbed my change apron and jingled it. "Hey," Guy said from the Road-master. "Don't let them mess with your money. They dump it and you'll kill half an hour picking up nickels and dimes." Then, as I started handing out popsickles, push ups, and Gopher Cones, Guy began to measure my work with his stopwatch. When the last kid ran off with his ice cream, Guy said, "Fine job, Jack. You scored eighty-five on that stop. Real good for your first day. This is what we call *productivity*. My master plan can't work unless we get good productivity. See, we want to make that goddamned ratio of money-over-time bulge on the top-heavy side. This is the heart of good business prac-tices."

Though I had no love for Guy Rampling, I didn't mind working the pushcart route. It was a warm spring so far, and it was good to be outside walking around town. I didn't even mind wearing the little kraut mountaineer costume and the little red beanie with the ice cream cone horns. Because of the getup, no one paid much attention to my limp. I still tended to hike my hip now and then, especially when I was behind schedule and needed to move out, but generally my limp was barely noticeable. And Guy pretty much left me alone. Once a week he might drive by, slow down, holler some advice or encouragement, but that's about the only time I saw him. He was too busy with his master plan to spend much time worrying about my progress as an ice cream vendor.

Guy's master plan involved a lot of other things to worry about. He'd decided to "diversify his assets" by investing in other businesses unrelated to the creamery. For example, he bought out one of the partners of a downtown clothing store called Kepzig's Fine Clothes for Men, and he was providing the "capitalization" for a brand-new restaurant called Mom's Kitchen. "It's ab-solutely crazy to keep your money in the bank at four percent," I heard him tell Mother one night. "Hell, the bankers take that money and invest it at eight or ten percent and maybe even twelve percent. So why can't I do what the bankers do? Answer me that, Jade?" Mother didn't answer him, but an answer to that question popped up in my mind. Maybe, I thought, the bankers know a little more about investing money than you do, Guy. "Oh, they just love to take your money and give you four percent for it," Guy said, beginning to rant. "But if you let them do it you are just asking them to put their plumbing up your chute." He stood up and bent over comically, pointing to the seat of his pants. "Here it is, boys. Take a shot at it. It's free." He laughed at his joke until tears came into his eyes.

The Gopher Cone was Guy's blockbuster surprise for the pushcart season. He'd worked on it all winter. The Gopher Cone was ice cream molded into the shape of a cute gopher. He'd paid a lot for the mold design and machinery, but he was sure it would be a huge success. As far as I could tell after a few weeks on the job, the Gopher Cone wasn't doing very well. It was hard to see the chocolate lump rising up out of a short cone as a gopher. I wasn't sure what it looked like, but it seemed that its designer had never really *seen* a gopher. It was too long in the neck and the head was too narrow. The body, in relation to the head and neck, seemed snake-like. But probably the real reason for its disappointing sales was the price. At twenty-five cents it was the highest-price item in the cart.

Aside from running around with his stopwatch, Guy didn't spend much time running the creamery's business anymore. He hired an accountant to deal with it, a man named Perry Overcast. Perry Overcast was a tall, thin man of twenty-five who looked forty-five. He was nearly bald, wore thick glasses, and was very nervous. He was also very timid and shy, and whenever he came over to the house to work, he'd come to the back door and then slip into Guy's office unnoticed. Only the whirring racket of a calculating machine announced his presence. Perry would check in the pushcarts every night, taking the money we'd made, counting it, calculating our commission, and then dumping the coins into a machine for automatic sorting and wrapping. Then he'd take the money home with him and deposit it the next day in the creamery's account at the bank. He also checked in the milk truck drivers and he handled the wholesale accounts to the grocery stores around town. All this freed Guy to meet with his new partners, work out deals, and further develop his master plan.

Perry Overcast was an accountant, and a meek one at that. He wasn't a "boss." And since the truck drivers and pushcart vendors had to deal only with him, their work habits began to get a trifle lax. I once passed a milk truck on my route. The driver was nowhere in sight. I went around the block a couple of times and each time I passed the milk truck there was no sign that the driver had come near it. I hung around the neighborhood waiting for the driver to show up. I did this out of curiosity and not from a sense of loyalty to Old Times Creamery. Finally, the driver came out of a house. He lingered on the front porch with the housewife whose favors he'd been enjoying. They kissed several times. He looked over his shoulder at his truck and said something to the woman. She nodded and he went to the truck and got out a case filled with milk, cream, cheese, and butter. He carried the gift to the woman and she accepted it with a squeal of joy.

I saw scenes similar to this a number of times. Different drivers, different housewives, different routes, but the procedure was pretty much the same in each case. Guy still made his rounds with his stopwatch, but so infrequently now that the drivers felt they were safe. "It only makes sense," I told myself.

Guy also became deeply involved with the Chamber's

autumn project, the Founder's Day Parade. The Founder's Day Parade was held every year in honor of Jules
Brightman, the pioneer who first settled in the valley of
the Far Cry River back at the turn of the century. Guy
was negotiating with the president of the Chamber for
the amount of representation Old Times Creamery
would be allowed in the parade. Guy wanted the entire
fleet of thirty-eight pushcarts marching together like an
army unit. "Can't you see it?" he said. "Thirty-eight
kraut mountaineers pushing those pretty white carts.
Four abreast and nine deep with a couple of the snappi-
est ones up front to lead! All of them in step, ringing
their bells!" But the president, Big Natty Northberry,
was not enthusiastic. We were at the dinner table and
Mother had put out seven-dollar steaks and imported
wine. "Can't see it, Guy," said Northberry, cutting himself a chunk of meat the size of a wallet. "Twenty
maybe. Twelve, fifteen, more likely. Besides, Ace Milk
Products wants to enter a fifty-foot float, a giant milk
cow they call Miss Acey Deucy. The whole damned parade will seem like a tribute to milk rather than a cele-
bration of the pioneers. No can do, Guy, I'm sorry."

The expression of high, enthusiastic excitement
faded from Guy's face. "What in the fuck is Ace Milk
Products?" he asked.

Ace Milk Products, it turned out, was a new company
in town. They had moved in practically overnight from
out of state. Guy had been too wrapped up in his pet
projects to notice. I knew that Guy had been developing
an ulcer for some time now, but when Ace Milk moved
into town, announcing itself as a "company of the jet
age," his stomach pains got so bad he went to a doctor,
who immediately diagnosed his trouble as duodenal
ulcers. The mere mention of the new company in his
presence doubled him over with pain. "Who the fuck
are those assholes, coming into *my* town?" he'd ask. To
counterattack, he changed the name of the creamery—

something he'd been wanting to do since he'd first taken over—to "Mode o' Day Dairy Products."

Once, an Ace Milk milk man came to our door, not realizing where he was. He wanted us to sign up for home delivery. Guy heard him talking to Mother. He ran out to the porch and grabbed the man by the lapels, carrying him down the steps, across the lawn, and to his truck, all the while screaming in his face. "They are crawling all over this town like ants," he said when he came back into the house. He was holding onto his stomach with both hands.

The quick, unannounced change of the company's name to Mode o' Day confused all our old customers. Many of them believed that Old Times Creamery had gone out of business and that a second new company had come to town, Mode o' Day Dairy Products. Taking advantage of this confusion, Ace Milk Products began to take milk routes away from us. Guy feverishly had some broadsides printed up, explaining the name change and assuring that the company was still the same old reliable company with the same old reliable products, but like most advertising broadsides, they went unread. I saw dozens of them clogging storm drains around town.

On top of this, the Ace Milk management didn't play fair. They used tactics that made Guy cough up blood. They cut prices so deeply that no profit could be made. They offered bonus gifts to the customers of Mode o' Day if they switched over to Ace Milk, gifts such as toasters, pepper mills, a one-month supply of laundry detergent, and so on. They took out full-page ads in the *Clarion*, which made dubious claims about the superior cleanliness of their milk plant operations—suggesting, slyly, that certain other local creameries were typhoid swamps by comparison. Some Mode o' Day drivers claimed that they were being sabotaged by Ace Milk thugs. They reported slashed tires, sugar in gas tanks, milk on the doorstep being replaced with bottles full of sour milk bearing the Mode o' Day label. These contentions were never actually proved, but Guy was ready to believe anything about his competitor. "Two can play that game," he said.

When I came home to live after my accident, I saw that Guy had changed quite a bit since his happy-go-lucky days as a wife-stealing milkman. But now he began to change radically. He became distracted and sullen. He walked oddly. He took short, careful steps, as if he was holding an egg between his knees. I couldn't figure out why he was doing this. Then I realized it was because of his stomach pain. He was trying to avoid jiggling his potbelly. I often caught him talking to himself—not just muttering a word or two but holding full-fledged arguments with invisible companions. He usually did this in the privacy of the bathroom or in his office when Perry Overcast was not there. "And then we'll see whose ass gets reamed, won't we?" I once heard him brag. "Once the shoe is on the other foot, once they get a taste of their own medicine, then we'll see who goes belly up and begs for mercy, by God. This is *my* town. I *made* it my town, you sons of bitches. Guy Allan Rampling isn't going to roll over and play dead for a bunch of slickers." And after such a talk, he'd wear a coyly sinister expression, as if nursing some hell-born secret plan soon to be loosed upon his enemies.

The old days of cozy romping around the house with Mother were long gone. They acted as though they lived on different planets. When Mother tried to draw him out, he would put her off with an impatient wave of his hand, saying, "Not now, Jade. Not now." He had to work out his *tactics,* he said, to use against Ace Milk. His mind, he said, had no room for domestic bullshit. "Our goddamned survival is at stake."

He was no longer able to sit at the table and eat a complete meal. Halfway through dinner he'd jump up and run, gagging, to the bathroom. His potbelly grew and grew. His pompadour thinned and dark half-moons appeared under his eyes.

Mother took it all in stride. She didn't seem surprised or upset by what was happening. She had the frame of mind and bearing of one who has been through the mill more than once and she was not about to let Guy's troubles weigh her down. Once, when we were having a glass of sweet wine together at the kitchen table, she said, "Jack, men are infants, did you know that?"

I shrugged. It was a new wine for me. Blackberry. Mogen David. So smooth and easy to take that I believed I could start drinking again.

"It's true, Jackie," she said. "Women like me are stuck. We've got to be their stupid mamas all our lives. Cleaning up their little messes and telling them every day that they are wonderful and that they are doing just fine in the big bad world, in spite of ample evidence to the contrary."

I saw that Mother had changed, too. Changed back to normal. Whatever spell Guy had put on her, it was pretty much dissolved.

"Some men must not be like that," I said.

"Uh-huh. One in ten thousand. And he's been neutered in the war."

She was loaded. She'd been drinking a lot of wine lately. It had added a considerable amount of loose flesh to her face and arms and midriff. Still, she was pretty. Her prettiness was stubborn, not easily rubbed out by time and luck. I imagined her at ninety. Old codgers crawling under the table to lay their dim heads in her lap.

"It's true," she said.

"By your arithmetic," I said, feeling the Mogen David, "there must be only nine-tenths of a true man in all of Far Cry."

She didn't laugh. And after another second, I didn't

understand my joke either. "I have never been satisfied, honey," she said.

She said this in a husky, salt-cut whisper. My face got hot.

"It's true," she said. "I have never been satisfied. Oh, there is always that little something extra when you first have a new man, but it doesn't last. It's the long run I'm talking about. They are too self-centered to be any good in the long run." She put her glass down and looked at me. Her eyes were hard suddenly, as if she suspected that she had been wasting her breath. "Do you have any idea what I'm talking about, honey?"

I shrugged again. "I guess," I said.

"They are wonderful in the short run! Romance! Oh, give me *romance!* What a feast! But it's only a piece of trickery. Rooster cock-a-doodle-do trickery. It's the trick that pulls us in so that we can wind up being mama. Mama, Jack, they want mama. Mama with no say-so. Mama in a cage. Mama with ass up and legs wide. I was once licked by a blubbering man. 'Mama, Mama,' he cried as he licked me. He was sixty years old. I was fourteen."

Guy was in his office talking loudly to himself. Mother nodded in the direction of the office door. "Don't you be crazy, honey. You're already headed down that road, but don't go all the way. Get off it, Jack. Be a man, not a crazy boy."

Guy shuffled into the kitchen. His face was drained and the small muscles around his mouth were twitching. He went to the sink and leaned over it, mouth yawning wide. He made a liquid grunting sound and a thin strand of dark red spit shimmered from his mouth. When he finished, he went back into his office.

"Declaration of war, is that it?" he said to his invisible companion. "Is that what this is?"

Mother lifted the bottle of Mogen David. "More wine, honey?" she said.

* * *

THE vague man with the wandering eye showed me his map. "No," I said. "You're the one that's lost." I spread the map out on my cart. "This is Alder Street. You get *to* your route on Alder, but you don't start ringing your bells until you get to Elmo Street. Alder is on my route."

"The hell," he said, scratching his dead hair. His name was Cruise and he believed that he had personal magnetism. He was only forty years old, but he looked sixty. He had a dark, heavily cratered nose that was as big as a yam. Still, there was something in the way he carried himself that made you realize he actually believed himself to be unarguably attractive to others.

"Alder is my best street," I said, eyeing his bulging change apron.

"This don't make a fucken lick of sense," he said. "This make any fucken sense to you, Spider?" Spider was his dog, a grimy little three-legged poodle that rode on top of his pushcart. Cruise tilted his head to one side and made a whiny puppy sound between his sucked-in lips and Spider whined in return and danced happily on his three trembly legs.

"Sure it makes sense, Cruise," I said. "Can't you read a map?"

Cruise took a step backward, bent a knee, and made a half pivot to the left—a move only a man with unlimited appeal would think of doing. "Read a *map?*" he said, astonished at my poor grasp of his abilities. "Course I can read a map! Where do you think I'm from, Birdshit, Utah?" Spider growled playfully. His stubby tail was a vibrating blur.

Three kids tugged at my change apron. "Gimme three Red Devil banana push ups," said the oldest, a nasty-looking twelve-year-old. I opened the coldbox and the twelve-year-old stuck his face into the opening.

"Get your ass out of there," I said.

"What's that smoke?" he asked.

"Carbon dioxide gas," I said. "You stick your head in there long enough it'll turn your hair white."

"Gas? How come you got gas in there?" he asked.

"It comes from dry ice." I reached into the box and picked up a splinter of it. I handed it to him. He held it for a few seconds then yelped and threw it down. The other two kids laughed at him.

"It's *hot!*" said the twelve-year-old.

"No," I said. "It's cold. It's so cold it *feels* hot. It's a couple of hundred below zero."

I got out the push ups and took their money.

"Jesus, sport," said Cruise. "I need a drink."

"First things first," I said. "I'm taking your change, Cruise. I'll give you push ups and Gopher Cones for it, but you've been working my best street and that's my money in your apron."

I reached into his apron and pulled out a handful of quarters. Cruise stepped away from me, but I stayed on him, taking change. He turned to one side, protecting his apron, but I kicked his feet together and grabbed him around the chest. We fell into a blazing patch of daffodils. Spider yapped and danced on Cruise's cart. We rolled out of the daffodils and into some dogshit. All of the money exploded out of our aprons. The kids, who had been watching us, went for the change. I let Cruise up and we chased off the kids.

"Okay, shit-ass," said Cruise, bitterly. "You can have the fucken money. I worked my ass off for two hours, but you just go ahead and take the fucken money."

"Cruise," I said, "you have never worked your ass off in your useless life."

"Listen to him, Spider," he said. "He thinks we're from Buttfuck, Arabia, and don't know work from jacking off. I got news for you, sport. I made a living by sheer artistry long before you knew how to piss with one hand."

Cruise started to cough. He bent over and spit. His horns were mashed and there was dogshit on his knee. "All right," I said, "let's go have a drink."

We wheeled our carts to a children's park a few blocks away. It was still morning, but it was already hot. Cruise was sour with old sweat and wet with new. I probably didn't smell very sweet either.

We sat under the low branches of a big blue spruce. Cruise also kept his wine in his coldbox, only he didn't hide it in a canteen. He kept it wrapped in newspapers.

"You ought to get a canteen, Cruise," I said, but he just shrugged, uninterested in my cleverness.

"Ten years ago I coulda beat the dust out of you, sport. But I got this fucken arthritis lately—"

"Sure you do," I said.

"He thinks I'm shittin' him, Spider."

"Everything you say, Cruise, comes from your asshole," I said.

"Laugh, Spider," he said, taking out a bent cigarette and sticking it in the corner of his mouth. He lit it and squinted over the smoke, in the style of movie stars. "This is one funny kid, Spider. See, I'm laughing—ha ha." Spider made little talkative noises in his throat.

We drank for a while without saying much. Then Cruise began to rub at his crotch. "Jesus Lord," he said. "Look at that, will you."

"Look at what?" I didn't see anything.

He pointed a rust-colored finger at a bunch of little girls on the swings. They were sailing high in a random row and their skirts were flying. "Quail," said Cruise. "Those little biscuits get to me, ace. I got a screaming boner, ace. I got a boner hard as life itself."

"Cruise, for christssake," I said.

"No, I'm not kidding! Those little cupcakes drive me wild."

"Those are *little* girls, Cruise."

"Right. Yeah, I know, kid." He massaged himself lovingly and his wandering eye began to drift. I got up and sat under another tree. My wine had warmed up to a more drinkable temperature.

We stayed in the park for another hour. We were both pretty drunk. Most likely, the other thirty-odd pushcart vendors were pretty drunk, too. Dozens of men in short pants and beanies were stumbling drunk around the streets of Far Cry, selling ice cream to children.

"I wonder what old Jules Brightman'd think of his town now," I said to Cruise, just before we went our separate ways. "I don't think he'd care much for the place."

"Jules who?" Cruise said, smiling engagingly at the little swinging girls.

"Jules Brightman," I said. "The pioneer who discovered this valley and settled it once the army threw out the Indians."

Cruise blew snot into his hand then wiped it off on the curb. "Who gives a shit, sport?" he said, still smiling wonderfully, as if he thought he was Douglas Fairbanks, Jr. "Who gives a fat fuck, ace, what some old dead duck-fucker thinks?"

"You'd have made a great pioneer, Cruise," I said.

He glanced at me, his baleful, independent eye gliding to the extreme outside corner of its socket, as if it had caught a glimpse of some indistinct but swiftly approaching threat.

"Indian," he said.

"What?"

"I wouldn't of been any fucken pioneer. I would of been an Indian."

"Some Indian."

"I'd a burned the fuckheads out, then caught up with their little girls and hauled them off to my tepee. I'd have my fucken tepee crawling with pioneer quail, sport."

* * *

I went out to the creamery. Guy had called a meeting. All the vendors were assembled. Guy was mad, but he was trying to hold it in. Holding it in made his voice shake.

"Listen up," he said. "We got trouble."

The trouble was Ace Milk Products, which was starting up its own pushcart operation. Except they weren't using pushcarts. They were using a type of motor scooter/pushcart hybrid with an electric music box instead of bells. One of those scooter carts could cover as much territory as two pushcarts in the same amount of time. Guy talked about how we were going to have to move quicker, how we were going to have to be nicer to the kids, and how we were going to have to look better. "You are not taking good care of your outfits," he said, his voice so wobbly I thought he was about to cry. "Just look at yourselves."

The old bums looked at themselves. They didn't see anything to worry about. As far as they were concerned, they looked just fine.

Guy watched them for a minute, then he exploded. He shouldered into the group and pulled one grinning old man out. He dragged him to the front of the group and made him stand on a milk box. The old bum had a hard time holding his balance. He raised his skinny arms to stabilize himself and he leaned first to one side and then the other. His costume was spotted and his horns looked like they'd been bitten off. His ruffled-sleeve shirt was dirty and ragged.

"What young mother who hasn't gone completely out of her mind is going to send her kid out to buy ice cream from *this*?" he said, gingerly picking the shirt off the man's shoulder between thumb and forefinger.

The bums shuffled their weight from foot to foot, pretty much uninterested in the lecture. A few licked their dry lips thirstily, and a few were asleep on their feet. Most of them didn't look much better than the man on the milk box. Some had bent or missing horns, and there wasn't a clean or unfrayed shirt to be seen. All the short red pants were spotted and stained. A few had large holes in them.

Guy couldn't stand it. His eyes moved across the assemblage of vendors and what he saw was the moldering remains of his carefully worked-out future. A sound began to leak out of his clamped lips. It was like a toy siren. Then it sounded like a muzzled dog begging for a bone. It deepened into a growl. It gradually forced his lips open, and they lifted off his teeth in a snarl that made the entire group of vendors stumble backward a few feet. Guy howled. All the held-back anger and murderous despair whipped out of him. It was as if a steel cable that had been under an impossible strain had suddenly snapped. The bums ducked under the lethal whip of his voice.

The vendor on the milk box started to step down, but Guy grabbed him and lifted him off his feet. He carried the old man across the creamery to some sinks. The sinks were the big washtub kind, and were used to clean mops and scrubbers. The crowd of vendors followed Guy, not knowing what else to do. Guy ripped the costume off the old vendor and then dropped him into the big sink. He turned on the water. It was hot water and the old vendor began to cry. Guy added a little cold to the hot. Steam clouds billowed from the sink. When the sink was filled, Guy picked up a hard bristle scrub brush and began to wash the old man. The old man's skin turned bright pink as the brush raked him. He tried to speak, but only a sputtering "N-n-n" came out of his chattering jaws.

"You cocksuckers are going to come to work *clean,*" said Guy, as he labored on the shivering old body in the sink. "And you are going to stay clean on the job—and you are going to keep your clothes clean—now if I catch a one of you cocksuckers who is not clean—then I will personally see to it that you are clean—for if you don't keep yourselves clean—who will do it except for me and I will do it because I have a business to protect—and I will not allow a bunch of shit-eaters like you to put me out of business—no, by God, no sir, you can count on me for that—and you are making a serious mistake if you are about to ask me if I am joking around—or am I serious."

The man in the sink was bleeding. No one asked Guy if he was joking or if he was serious.

Later, in the house, Guy was still in a frenzy. He paced back and forth in the front room, slapping at his stomach now and then as if to drive off the little animal that was nibbling at it.

"Why don't you hire nice young boys, then?" said Mother. "Get a few more like Jack here." She was doing her needlework and didn't look up from it.

Guy whipped around and sighted down his finger at her. "I know what I am doing, goddammit!" he said. "You bring in young boys and you've got to deal with their families. 'How come you only give Johnny ten percent of the take after he runs his sweet little ass off all day long selling your ice cream?' That's what you'd hear. Then they'd quit on you to go to college or get married. No, my way is right. You ask anybody down at the Chamber. They'll tell you. You've got to use old losers for this type of job. They might not look so hot, but by Christ they've got no other place to go. They will stick with you."

"Then why are you so upset?"

"I am not upset at all. I am just shaping up the crew because we've got all this goddamned competition now."

"Ace Milk has nice-looking men running their ice cream carts."

Guy spun around as though he'd been punched. "What the fuck've *you* been doing, making a god-damned inspection?"

Mother kept at her needlework, not looking up. "Oh, they pass by the house now and then," she said. "Good-looking young man, with blond hair, I think. He couldn't be more than twenty-five or so."

"Why don't you invite the fucker in for tea?" Guy said, trying to laugh at the idea, but his stomach pain and agitated mind wouldn't let even fake merriment come through. What came through was a kind of snarling whimper.

"Maybe I will," Mother said softly.

"Huh? What was that?" said Guy, cupping his hand behind his ear. "I don't think I heard that right. You want to speak up a little? You want to run that by me again?"

"You heard me," she said, packing up her needlework and leaving the room.

Guy sat down heavily on the sofa and put his head into his hands. He rocked his head back and forth and whispered to the floor, "What next? What next? What next?"

PERRY Overcast disappeared. Instead of turning the money in to the bank one morning, he took it all and left town. A bank executive went over his books and discovered that Perry had been embezzling funds ever since he began working for Guy. Counting the money he didn't turn in the day he left town, he'd managed to skim over $10,000 in six months.

Mom's Kitchen went bankrupt three months after it opened. The manager had lied about his past experience managing restaurants. Food came late and cold, portions were small, and there were three cases of food poisoning in the first week.

Guy's partner in the clothing store business, Sid Kep-zig, died suddenly. Sid ran the store himself. He kept the books, ordered new stock, made up the payroll, and was the head sales clerk. He was irreplaceable. Guy adver-tised all over the state for someone capable of managing a men's clothing store, but in the meantime, he had to run Kepzig's himself. He'd spend three hours at the store in the morning and three hours in the late after-noon. I saw him once standing next to a rack of topcoats while a customer tried them on. Guy had no patience for the job. When the customer shook his head dubiously at coat after coat, Guy blew up. "Fuckhead!" he said. I was looking in through the plate-glass window out front, but I could read his lips. The man walked away from Guy quickly, knocking clothes off racks as he went. Guy fol-lowed him, cursing. "You look like shit!" Guy yelled as the man stormed out the door. "You stink! Take a bath next time you want to try on clothes, okay! Hey, I'm talking to *you*, lard-ass! Stay the fuck out of my store! We don't sell clothes to skunky faggots!"

Business at Kepzig's fell off rapidly. When the new manager took over, he had to put everything on sale at one-half off in order to attract new customers.

Then Orlando Mundy came to town. He stopped by the house. Guy hid from him. But Orlando wasn't interested in Guy. He wanted to talk to me. He'd been down to Willow Springs to see Gent. "He doesn't talk anymore," Orlando said. "He makes noises constantly, but it isn't talking. After I left him, the voice in my head said, 'Take heed.' But how can you take heed of yawnk dun dun dunna yawnk bleeropp?"

Orlando and I drove down to Willow Springs. It was a chilly day and so we sat with Gent in his white room. He was making the sounds Orlando had described to me. Very softly, a kind of sonorous mumble. "Yawnk dun dun dunna yawnk bleeropp," he crooned, with a definite rhythm. It was kind of a refrain, and he varied it with other sounds, moving up and down the register. I listened for a few minutes, then I understood.

On the way back to Far Cry I explained to Orlando what was happening. "That's a sax you hear, Orlando," I said. "He was playing a samba—'Star Eyes,' I think."

Orlando accepted that, nodding.

"He's turned himself into a saxophone," I said.

Orlando looked at me sharply.

We drove along without speaking for a while.

I turned the radio on. Orlando turned it off.

Finally, Orlando said, "Why take *heed?*" He was talking to the voice in his head, not to me.

Gent had been sitting on the edge of his bed, wearing a hospital gown. He'd lost a lot of weight. He was clearly dying. But the music was alive and strong.

He would die as an instrument.

A saxophone.

Orlando sighed. "The soul looks to the left," he said, "but the world lies to the right."

Yawnk dun dun dunna yawnk bleeropp, I thought to myself.

"Follow your soul and you are bound to trip on something in the world," he said. "But, if you keep your sights on something in the world, watching yourself every step of the way, your soul will walk off and leave you holding the bag. You will have one hell of a time from that moment on."

It was the voice in Orlando's head talking. Orlando seemed puzzled by it. "So where does that leave Gent?" he asked.

The voice didn't have much to say on that subject.

"He's mister-in-between," I said.

Orlando looked at me sharply again. He was driving very slowly, even though we were on the highway. Traffic was piling up behind us, honking.

"Dead but not buried," I said.

"His soul," Orlando said.

"His sax," I said.

Orlando stopped the car but didn't pull off the road. His eyes were wide and bright, as if something important had just been explained to him.

"Music," he said. "It's *all* music!"

Cars roared around us, the drivers cursing.

"Yawnk dun dun dunna yawnk bleeropp," I sang. Though I hadn't had a drink all day, I felt wonderfully drunk.

LADONNA and Speed screeched up next to my cart. "Jackie!" LaDonna said.

"Hi," I said.

"Two Gopher Cones," said Speed. "We're celebrating."

"Celebrating what?" I said, pulling two Gopher Cones out of the box.

"We've set the date," LaDonna said. She was half sitting in Speed's lap.

"Congratulations," I said.

"You're invited," said Speed.

"Of course he's invited!" LaDonna said. "He's my brother!"

LaDonna showed me her ring. It was white gold and had a diamond the size of a pimple set into it. Speed gunned the engine as a kind of fanfare.

"Name the first one after me," I said.

"You got it!" Speed said, gray teeth bared.

LaDonna sat all the way in his lap and they kissed. I thought of her fine mind. China, too good to use, kept safe in the cupboard. No, that wasn't it. A fine mind is no match for loneliness. In fact, it makes loneliness a real possibility. Well. LaDonna was off on a career of husbands, and there wasn't much I could do about it.

They took off, burning rubber, yelling good-bye.

Cruise came up behind me, ringing his bells.

"Goddammit, Cruise," I said.

"I can't help it, ace," he said, his free eye orbiting. "This fucken map gets me all twisted around."

We pushed our carts to the children's park to figure out the map. Cruise had a half-gallon jug of something called Emerald Milk. My canteen was empty and I filled it from his jug.

"See, this fucken map he gives us," Cruise said, shaking his head doubtfully. "I can't tell if I start over on East Avenue or if I start on Borestone. Jesus, my dogs are barking, sport."

He took off his shoes. He didn't have any socks on. The knuckles of his toes were black with shoe polish that had soaked through the leather.

"What is this?" I said. "They put something in this?" I held up his jug to the light. Emerald Milk had iodine flavoring.

"It's fortified," he said, twinkling. "It hits real good, don't it?"

"Fortified with what? Paint remover?"

"Hey, don't drink it then, sport."

I raised my canteen and took another pull. "I guess you get used to it," I said.

"Like every fucken thing else," he said, lying back into the cool shade.

"I hope you didn't used to be a dancer," he said after a while.

I'd climbed halfway up the blue spruce. Emerald Milk made you want to climb trees. I felt pretty good. I complimented myself on my attitude and wondered why I had it. "Never was," I said.

"That's good," he said. "Dancer loses a foot like that, Jesus, that's the shits."

"It's the shits anyway," I said, cheerful.

"Oh, sure, sure! Don't get me wrong! It's just like if a priest gets his dick lopped off. No big deal! But if a cocksman stumbles dick-first into a cheese slicer—it's a true curse. That's all I meant, ace."

"No offense taken," I said, moving higher.

After a while, he said, "I used to be one hell of a dancer, sport."

"I bet you were a regular gigolo, Cruise," I said.

"Go ahead, laugh if you want to. Listen, I didn't always look like this. You think I don't know what I look like? Hey, you shoulda seen me in '45! I was a fucken bear cat out on the dance floor, kid! The quim couldn't get enough of me. Said I just floated along. Said they felt like they didn't have any fucken feet when they danced with me. No offense. But that's how I was. I cruised them, ace. That's how I got my name. Cruise."

We drank a while longer, enjoying the afternoon, then we left the park. He worked Ironwood Street with me, on his way to Poplar, where he belonged.

"Rampling'll shit, he sees us walking the same street," Cruise said.

I was too loaded on Emerald Milk to care one way or the other.

"Hey," said Cruise. "Look at *that*."

A girl of eight or nine came skipping toward us. She was wearing flimsy, high-cut shorts and a halter meant for kids but cut in a style suitable for mature women with bold ideas.

"Look at that little biscuit," said Cruise. "Don't that give you a rise, kid?"

"No," I said.

"Greetings to you, girlie," said the bearcat of the ballroom. "Want some of Uncle Cruise's ice cream?"

The girl held up a quarter. "I wanna a *green* one," she said.

Cruise bent down to her. "A green one, huh?" he chuckled. His lungs loosened with excitment and he hacked up something bright and spit it out sneakily behind his hand. "A green *what,* honey?" He put his scaly hand on her shoulder.

"A *green* one," said the girl. "The kind you hold with a stick, and it goes up to the top, *you* know, *green,* when you push it."

Cruise tossed his head back in an engaging way and chuckled. He stepped to the left, stepped to the right, dipped a little, turned on the balls of his feet, then leaned down to her again. "Dah dah, dee dum!" he said, thrilled.

"Green," said the girl.

"All business, huh?" he said, winking at me. "All right, girlie. Now, what you want is a *lime* push up, see?" He squeezed her shoulder. His hand moved to the back of her neck, as if it was the hand of a trusted uncle. He squeezed the back of her neck, and then began to stroke her long silky hair. His next move was going to get him in jail.

"Cruise," I said.

He looked at me, grinning, his gamboling eye twinkling stupidly. I took him by the arm and pulled him away from the girl. "Just give her the push up, Cruise. Keep your cruddy hands off her."

He looked deeply insulted. "I ain't hurtin' anybody!" he snarled. But I held his arm and wouldn't let him near the girl, who was stamping the asphalt impatiently.

"Give her the goddamned push up, Cruise," I said. "If you touch her again I am going to slug you."

He jerked his arm away from me and pulled a lime push up out of his coldbox. Spider, who had been sound asleep, jumped up and began to bark nervously. Then he saw the girl. He rolled over immediately, as if trained to do tricks at the sight of young girls. Then he got up and danced around in a circle on his hind legs.

"Oh, look!" said the girl, suddenly heartbroken. "His little paw is *gone!*" Spider's right front leg was a stub.

He pawed the air with it and the little girl's lower lip began to tremble.

"Oh, yes, honey," said Cruise in a voice any child would understand was tragic. "It was a terrible accident."

"Poor little puppy!" said the girl, touching Spider's quivering head.

Cruise brightened. "But he's still quite a little fellow, honey. You want me to ask him to do a trick for you?"

"Oh, yes! Please!"

Cruise bent down and pretended to whisper something into Spider's ear. Then he put his ear on Spider's nose.

"He says he'll do it, honey. But he wants to go over to the park. He'll show you his best trick ever, over there in the park."

I stepped on Cruise's foot.

He gave me a bitter look. "Maybe some other time, girlie," he said. "Spider's a little crapped out right now."

The girl sauntered off, disappointed. Cruise looked like a kid who'd slept through Christmas. He reached into his coldbox and took out his jug. He tipped it back and swallowed half a dozen times. He put the jug back and wiped off his mouth on the back of his hand. "You are one hard-leg son of a bitch, ace," he said.

"Sure I am," I said.

He grinned then. "Hey kid, she was a tight little muffin, wasn't she? Damn me if she wasn't."

"Cruise, you're crazy."

He raised his eyebrows and grinned like he was one step ahead of the world. "You think so? Well, maybe I am. I could be, I guess. I don't feel crazy, but who knows, you may be right."

"You're a fucking bedbug, Cruise."

He looked at me with both eyes. The roving one tried to glide away, but somehow he held it in place. "You're pretty fucken smug," he said. "You know that? You're smugger than shit, sport."

"And you are a bedbug who is going to get his ass handed to him by some little kid's daddy."

He let the eye go its way. It sank down to the outside corner and glared morosely at the ground ten feet to my right. "I just can't help myself, kid," he said.

I took a pull of Emerald Milk myself. "Everybody can help himself," I said, half believing it.

He picked up Spider and scratched his ears. "Uh-uh. No. You're wrong, there, kid. Everybody *can't* help themself, no matter how fucken much they want to. You'll find out. Though, by the looks of you, I'd say you already had a leg up on the situation. Stop me if I'm wrong, but you lost that foot on account of a fuck-up, right? It's a chain of fuck-ups, life."

"I'm just thinking about you, Cruise. Seems like you can put your hand on a little girl or not put your hand on a little girl."

"It ain't that easy," he said.

"Yes, it is."

"No, it ain't."

"Yes, it is."

"No, it ain't."

This intelligent argument ended in an impasse. We transferred our dialogue to the bells. We rang them hard. People stepped out onto their front porches, curious about the weird commotion.

At the intersection of Ironwood and Poplar, there was a group of people bunched together. Poplar had a grassy, parklike traffic separator that ran down the middle of it. The group of people had collected on this separator. They were gathered around a tall young man wearing a white shirt. He was preaching to them.

"Let's sell those yahoos some ice cream," Cruise said.

We pushed our carts toward the group, bells clanging. A young woman stepped out of the crowd toward us.

She had a simpleminded smile on her face. "No noise," she said, putting her hands on our bells.

The young man in the white shirt was talking about Caesar. "Give to Caesar what is Caesar's," he said.

"It's Wendell Harmon," said the woman holding our bells. "He is wielding the sword. Join us brothers!"

Cruise reached into his cart and pulled out his sack of Emerald Milk. He followed the young woman to the edge of the crowd. After a few seconds, I followed him.

"What is this sword I wield?" Wendell Harmon asked.

"The word! The word!" said the crowd.

Cruise brought his sack to his lips. The man standing next to him forgave him instantly. You could tell by the sad smile and the humble eyes. I tipped up my canteen.

Wendell wound up his street sermon and a hat was passed through the crowd. The crowd was still in a state of high rapture.

"He sweetens the air we breathe," the woman who had held our bells said.

"He is of the ages!" someone else added.

"A saint among us!"

"Son of heartbroken humanity!"

"He has come to Far Cry from the wellsprings of love!"

"Amen! Amen!"

"Christ," Cruise muttered. He spit to one side, face sour.

The crowd broke up and Cruise and I were alone again. Cruise held up his sack. "Thank God for juice," he said.

"Who's the smug shit now, Cruise?" I said.

"Don't be a sucker, ace," he said.

I laughed a little at that. "Take a look at yourself sometime."

"I know what I am, sport. Damn few people you'll meet can say that."

"You'll want the Nobel Prize, next."

"This'll do," he said, tipping the jug. When he finished, he said, "I don't see how anybody can get through life sober. I bet the human beings invented juice before they invented God and the angels." He kissed the sack, then winked at me. Spider, impatient with us, stood up on his hind legs and hooted.

G∪Y stumbled away from the dinner table making strangling noises. "What's the trouble with Guy, Mrs. Rampling?" Big Natty Northberry said. "He looked like he'd swallowed a piece of glass." Northberry stood up from the table and stretched. He was over six feet tall and probably weighed two-fifty. His shirt buttons strained at their moorings.

Mother picked up the dishes and carried them to the kitchen. I collected the glasses and salad bowls. LaDonna was gone for the weekend with Speed.

"He'll survive," Mother said from the kitchen. "He's taking medicine for it now. It's just a worry-ulcer."

Northberry followed us into the kitchen. "Ulcer?" he said. "So that's it. For a minute there I thought he was sore at me. You know what they say about ulcers, don't you? It's the business man's union card."

Mother laughed politely. She scraped the dishes into the garbage. She had to bend over to do this and Northberry looked down her low-cut dress as if he had a perfect right to the view.

"But listen, Mrs. Rampling," he said. "It's not my doing, you know. Guy's got reason to be upset, but it's not Big Natty Northberry who's slipped him the shaft. I'm just the prez and the damned chairman of the parade committee. The full committee has it's own ideas. What can I do?"

"Oh," said Mother.

"I'm telling it to you straight," Northberry said. "It was the full committee. Hell, I'm just the gavel pounder

—one vote and one vote only. The full committee decided on the Ace Milk scooter-carts instead of Guy's Red Devils. Ace Milk put on a demonstration for them that was a thing to behold. You should have been there, Mrs. Rampling, really. You'd understand why they were swayed. All those cute putt-putts zigzagging around the parking lot, cutting figure eights, playing bumper tag, the music boxes all coordinated to play the 'Waltz of the Flowers' or some such tripe. It was something to see. Hell, it'll *make* the parade."

"Then you voted for Ace Milk, too," Mother said.

Northberry shrugged. "What's one vote more or less when the tide is moving one way? Sure, I voted for Ace, but believe me, it wouldn't have mattered one way or the other. Guy should have put on his own demonstration. He should have let his vendors show their stuff."

Mother put the dishes into the hot, soapy water. I handed her the glasses and salad bowls. Guy was in his office, muttering. "Would you like a cordial, Mr. Northberry?" Mother said, wiping her soapy hands on her apron.

"Suppose we drop the Mr. Northberry," Big Natty said. "We're all friends, aren't we? Call me Big Natty. And may I call you Jade? They call me Big Natty down at the office—everyone does!" He put his hand on her arm and gave it an urgent squeeze.

"Big Natty," Mother said, and Northberry slipped his arm around her waist, drawing her to him.

"Cordial, cordial," he said, thinking it over. "Yes indeed, I think so, Jade. Yes, a cordial would set me up fine."

Mother took the peach brandy out of the cupboard and poured Big Natty a small glass of it. Then she poured herself one. "How about you, Jack?" she asked. "Would you like a cordial, honey?"

"Sure, Ma," I said.

Mother glanced at Northberry. Once again he put his

arm around her waist. "He's going on twenty-one," she said.

Northberry stepped away from her and held up his hands. "No objections from this quarter," he said. "He looks all of forty-two to me!"

Northberry slapped my shoulder and laughed. Mother laughed, too. I felt compelled to join in. "You're a hell of a brave young man," Northberry said, suddenly serious. "I'll bet your Ma and Pa are real proud of you, coming back from your mishap like that. You're all man, son."

All this made me uncomfortable. "People make too much of it," I said. "A lot of people get hurt. It's no big deal."

Northberry wagged his big head in admiration. "No big deal, he says. Listen to the boy. You must be shivering with pride, Jade."

Seeing my embarrassment, Mother said, "Let's go out to the front room. It's more comfortable, and we can wait for Guy in there."

Mother and Northberry sat down on the sofa. I sat in the easy chair. "You know, Jade," Northberry said. "I think your hubby is sore as hell at me. I don't think he'll be joining us." He grinned sheepishly and patted her knee.

"How come Ace Milk gets to have the rubber cow *plus* two dozen scooter-carts, Big Natty?" Mother said.

Big Natty turned red. "That's a tough one, Jade, I'll grant you that. But, like I said, you should have been there, at the meeting of the full committee. You should have heard Don—Don Paris, of the Paris Book Shop. He made one hell of a case. 'Ace Milk is the new kid on the block,' he said. 'And Mode o' Day has been here since the Flood. We've got to give the new outfit a break.' I know it sounds unfair to you, Jade, but you would have been swayed if you'd heard him. You know Don Paris, don't you, Jade? Real tall fella with sideburns down to here."

Northberry poked a finger into each jowl. "Good-looking fella, Don is. Full of ideas. Don says, and I quote, 'Look at what they are offering this committee. Scooter-carts doing precision maneuvers, a fifty-foot inflated cow with automatic, rotating, steam-driven tits. This hick town has never seen anything like *that.*' I mean it, Jade. Hairy Don Paris had us nailed to the floor. We were whipped before we sat down."

"And so Mode o' Day gets nothing?" Mother said, sipping her cordial carefully.

Northberry rubbed his hands together as if they were cold. "No, no, we're not *that* one-sided in this thing, Jade. Guy will get to enter two or three decorated trucks. Maybe four. He can doll them up any way he likes. He can stick bathing beauties up on top of them if he wants. His milk trucks will be a hell of a fine way to end the parade."

Mother looked directly into Northberry's quick eyes. He reddened again and pretended to yawn. "This Don Paris sounds like he runs the parade committee," she said.

"Don Paris? Hairy Don? Oh, heck *no,* Jade! Not at all. Did I make it sound like that? Whoa. Let's back it up a notch. Now—Don Paris *is* one hell of a persuasive fella. I mean, he could talk the bloomers off a suffragette. He could get Carry Nation to sit down with him and drink rye whisky. But he's a mild sort of guy in spite of that. Hairy Don Paris would never steamroll a friend. We call him the poet! That's right! The poet!"

Mother didn't care much about Guy any longer, but she cared about the creamery, which was losing business fast. The creamery was her future, too. Guy had lost most of their savings on his flopped business deals and a vision of impoverished old age was beginning to worry her. So, the next morning, she went down to the Paris Book Shop to see Don Paris. I went along, out of curiosity. It was Saturday, my day off.

The Paris Book Shop was long and narrow and dim. Violin music came out of hidden loudspeakers. When we went in, Don Paris was busy with a customer. Mother and I both pretended to be interested in books. When he finally came over to us, Mother said, "I want to talk to you, Mr. Paris." Mother was formidable in a dark blue, low-cut dress and white high-heeled shoes. Her unblinking green eyes met his with perfect self-confidence.

They went to the back of the store, where his office was. He was so tall that he had to duck to get through the door. I stayed up front looking at books. A girl about my age was working the cash register. We tried to sneak looks at each other, but we both kept getting caught. She wore glasses and had a big nose. She looked shy and lonely. I liked her eyes, though, which were sleepy blue, and her mouth, which was full and well shaped. Her neck was too long, but her breasts were huge. A shy girl will sometimes try to conceal her breasts if they are outsized. But this girl had no problems with the size of her breasts. She let them have their freedom, as if she knew that they were her glory. I liked her skin, too. It was blemish-free and the color of coffee mixed half and half with cream. Her name tag said, "Zoe Rae Blazek."

I carried a book over to the register. "What's this one about?" I asked.

"Buy it and find out," Zoe Rae said.

Mother and Don Paris came out of his office then. The top of Mother's head barely reached his shoulder. I guess he was about six feet seven or eight. He was thin, though, and his feet were long and narrow. He had an odd walking style. When he walked, he leaned backward, slightly out of plumb. It was as if the top half of him had trouble keeping up with the bottom half. If you dropped a plumb line from the back of his skull, it would have hit the ground six inches behind his heels.

He had a nice-looking face, though. Fine-featured and genteel with sandy brown hair and light gray eyes.

"I'll look forward to seeing you again, Mrs. Rampling," he said.

"I will too," Mother said.

Don Paris picked up her hand and brought it to his lips. He kissed it, looked into her eyes, kissed it again. Patches of red showed through the white powder on Mother's neck.

"I've enjoyed talking to you very much," Don Paris said.

The patches of red on her neck spread to her face, which soon became uniformly scarlet. It struck me that I hadn't seen Mother blush in years.

"Thank you," she said. "Thank you for your time, Mr. Paris."

"Mon temps est votre temps," Don Paris said.

Mother opened her mouth to say something, but nothing came out.

"À bientôt," said Paris, taking her hand again.

"Good-bye," Mother said, her voice playing tricks on her.

I sneaked one last look at Zoe Rae Blazek as we left the store. She was yawning, arms raised high. Her breasts had risen with her arms, drawing her sweater up until the smooth skin of her midriff was visible.

Outside, Mother said, "What a terribly nice man."

"He must be," I said.

Mother looked at me. "What's that supposed to mean?"

"Well, for one thing, he runs the parade committee like he owns it and everybody thinks he's peachy anyway."

Mother frowned.

I lit a cigarette. "Did you get anywhere with him?"

"What?" She looked confused.

"You remember. The parade. The pushcarts. Did you make him change his mind?"

Mother laughed at herself in disbelief. "Good God!" she said. "We didn't even talk about the stupid parade!"

I took a drag. It was a nice day. I could see Zoe Rae through the plate-glass window. She was seated at the cash register, reading a book and eating an apple.

"What did you talk about?" I asked.

"You won't believe this. We talked about . . . *poetry!*"

"Poetry."

"I mean, Don, Mr. Paris, *he* talked about poetry. He read me a poem about how the Garden of Eden is in your own backyard if you only had eyes to see it with, or something like that. I don't have any idea what he was talking about. It was a beautiful poem though. He wrote it himself. I think I cried."

"Fuck oh dear," I said.

She slapped me hard. My cigarette flew out of my mouth and landed on the arm of a woman passing by. She brushed it off as though it were a mad bee. A few people stopped to stare at us. I grinned at them.

"Don't mind her, folks," I said. "She's in heat again."

She slapped me hard again. "You're such an asshole, Jack," she said.

"I know, Ma," I said.

"Am I still dreaming?" I asked.

"Maybe you are, and maybe you're not," said the man in the big hat.

"How long have I been here making a fool out of my-self?"

"Good question, son. But I don't have a clue."

"What's going on? What are they doing back there? Who are they?"

"Ditto, ditto, ditto. I don't have the foggiest. You came in with them, so you ought to know."

"Why do they have noisemakers? Whose party is this?"

"Believe me, *compadre,* if I knew I'd tell you."

I'd been dreaming, but now I was awake. Dreaming, face-down on the bar. An icy dream, something about the polar cap, an eskimo dressed in a bearskin pretending to be the *ngantja.* The *ngantja* is from Australia, I told him. The hell, he said, pretending to be astonished. Wished someone would've told me, he said. His little Oriental eyes were twinkling black stars. I've been barking up the wrong tree all these years, he said. He was making a fool of me, and I woke up, feeling like a fool, dry saliva caked on my lips and chin. I hadn't gotten this drunk since my mill-working days.

I looked around the dim barroom. The walls had been filled with bad paintings of palm trees and girls in blazing red sarongs. The empty drink before me had a little parasol sticking out of it with a kind of fruit salad clumped among the melting ice chips.

"Maybe you've got your head screwed on backward," the man in the big hat said.

"How long have I been asleep?"

"How would I know?" he said. "Maybe you've been asleep all your life. Stranger things have happened." He chuckled at the notion. He looked like a child because his hat was at least one size too big for his head, but judging from the crinkles around his eyes, the burst veins in his nose, and the lankness of the hair that stuck out from under his hat, he had to be fifty to sixty.

"What have I been drinking?" I asked.

"You just keep asking, son, but I don't know the first thing about you. Did you think that I have made it my business to look after you these many hours?" He looked into my glass. "Write me off as a meddler, but I'd say that gooey stuff is the fermented juice of the guava berry. Very dangerous."

"It's a Singapore Sling," the bartender said.

"What's in it?" I asked.

"There he goes again," said the man in the hat. "Questions, questions."

"Alcohol," said the bartender.

I swiveled around on my stool and faced the dance floor. A crowd of dancers moved like a school of fish, pulsing first one way, then the other. The women were screaming happily and the men were strutting drunk. I didn't recognize anyone.

A heavy girl danced toward me in a slow, sultry way, rotating her shoulders and lifting her plump knees. Although she was heavy, she was sure of herself as a dancer and very graceful. "Hey, everybody!" she said in a voice too loud and coarse for the perfect grace of her big, dancing body. "Look who woke up!" She put her hands on my knees and as she leaned forward her considerable weight forced them apart. She blew warm, boozy air into my face. "You are embarrassing me, sugar nuts," she said.

"I'm sorry," I said.

"Sorry doesn't deliver the mail," she said.

"I guess I'm not awake yet," I said.

"You got an excuse for just about everything," she said, reproachful now. She slammed my knees together. She grabbed my wrists and pulled me off the stool. "There's Beano and Carla to think about, you know. Try to be reasonable."

We joined the other dancers. I couldn't remember if I'd said anything about my foot. It was tingling, as if it had fallen asleep. I stomped down on it. "Go, man, go," someone said to me, clapping his hands to my stomps.

"Are you going to dance with me or are you just going to stand there kicking the floor, because if that's the case I'd just as soon leave," the heavy girl said.

I put my arms around her solid waist and she draped her arms over my shoulders, and soon we were caught up in the clumsy, energetic pulse that moved first one way and then the other.

"I guess you know by now what a hothead Beano is," said the heavy girl into my ear.

I looked around, wondering which one was Beano and why I should know what a hothead he was.

The heavy girl put her tongue in my ear. "Oh, if he saw us now—forget about Carla, just forget about her— if he saw us now, he'd blow a fuse. He's still terribly jealous, you know. He'll do anything. It doesn't matter." Her tongue got busy again.

"Excuse me," I said. I made my way to the men's room.

There was a stall and two urinals. A man was in the stall on his hands and knees. "Hey, you!" he yelled. "What in the hell time is it, anyway?"

"I don't know," I said. I headed for a urinal and unzipped.

"All right, then," said the man. "Suppose you tell me what day it is."

"I'm not sure," I said.

"Okay, okay," he said. "Let's pretend you mean that. I'm trying to keep my head. But let's go ahead and pretend you mean that crap about not being sure what day it is."

"I do mean it," I said.

"I told you I'm trying to keep my head, all right?"

"I appreciate that," I said, drilling a cigarette butt until the paper split and the wet tobacco drifted away.

"Okay, okay, wise ass. Just tell me if the sun is shining or not."

"No can do, Beano," I said.

"Jesus jumping Christ on a raft," he said glumly. "What am I going to do? What am I going to do?" He started to cry. "Why is he calling me Beano?" he blubbered.

"Don't cry," I said. "If the sun isn't shining now it will be pretty soon."

The man banged on the stall with something. "Who the fuck are you, Norman Vincent Peale?"

I looked down and saw that I'd lost the shoe on my rubber foot. The sock was grimy. I panicked a little, thinking that I was helpless without that shoe. Then I saw it by the waste paper basket. I retrieved it and sat down on the floor to put it on.

"Will someone please help me?" said the man in the stall, but I didn't think he was talking to me. His words had the offbeat tone of prayer.

I pulled myself up. I looked into the mirror and was surprised to see the perfect imprint of a pair of lips on my cheek. Very large, very red, like a joke. Something was tingling at my waist. I pulled out my shirt and looked. There was a scratch that ran from my navel to my kidney. Riding the scratch were more imprints of the giant red lips.

"Oh, please," said the man in the stall. "I am on my knees now before you. Isn't that enough?"

"It's probably past midnight but before five A.M.," I said. "Closing time is five, I think. Or maybe it's six."

The man vomited violently. "Thanks for nothing, asshole," he said, weakly. "You're a regular National Bureau of Standards."

I went back into the barroom. It was nearly empty. The music had stopped. The heavy girl was sitting at the bar. I sat on the stool next to hers. There was a fresh Singapore Sling waiting for me. "Where have you been, sugar nuts?" she asked.

"Powder room," I said.

She put her hand on my knee and massaged. "What are we going to tell Beano?" she said, her hand moving up my thigh urgently.

"We'll tell him to change his name," I said.

"Very funny. But I am serious. He's capable of anything. I'm not thinking of myself. I'm thinking about you. Really. I still love him, and I think it's vice versa. He can be a real shit, though."

"Where is this Beano jerk?" I said.

She withdrew her hand from my crotch. "He's not a jerk. Oh, he's a lot of things, but he's not a jerk."

"Okay," I said.

"Listen, I mean it."

I put a stricken look on my face. "I can see you still love Beano," I said. "I can see that Beano is number one."

"Don't be that way," she said, her hand coming back to my upper thigh. "You're a nice guy. I like you. In some ways you're better-looking than him."

"Que sera, sera," I said, sighing.

"No, listen, I mean it. We may have a future."

"I'd better just leave now," I said. "It'll be easier that way."

I slid off my stool and headed for the stairway out.

"Your drink," she called.

"You have it," I said.

I climbed the steep stairs to the street. It was morning and the town looked clean and ready for business. The bar I'd been in was a hotel bar. I looked up at the five-story building. I saw Speed's Ford parked at the curb. It was covered with streamers. Goofy signs had been soaped on the windows. Fragments of the past twelve hours or so drifted back to me. There had been a wedding. In someone's house. There had been an old bathtub full of punch. Men poured gallons of bourbon into it, along with sacks of sugar, lemon juice, rum, and spices. We dipped our mugs directly into it. Things got wild. Someone punched someone. And now, somewhere up there in this hotel, Speed and LaDonna were in bed together, recovering. I looked up at the columns of windows. They were all catching the morning sun. I kissed the palm of my hand and blew the kiss up toward the blazing windows.

She's lost, I thought. But I was wrong. She'd only started down a road that was forked with wrong turns and cratered with pitfalls. She'd divorce Speed after a year, marry again, divorce, marry, divorce, and finally come home to herself. She would find her childhood dream again, take a degree in physics, go to graduate school, and become a successful teacher at a well-known university. James Dean would no longer hang over her bed like a small idea blown out of proportion. Einstein, Bohr, and Heisenberg would eventually hang on her wall, along with the darkly troubled visionary face of Oppenheimer. "These are the true romantic heroes of our century, Jack," she would write from a sabbatical in France. And a year later, from Italy:

They say Einstein killed himself. He had some kind of heart trouble that could have been corrected by surgery. He refused the operation. That's the rumor, anyway. I think he realized that he was the helpless instrument of Inevitability. That's my god now, Jackie—Inevitability. Albert was its angel of death, he was Shiva, come to the world to give us a way to end the intolerable pain Inevitability inflicts upon Itself by becoming conscious. His humanist longings, though, wouldn't let him accept that role. He was the kindest man in the world, Jack, but he was also the angel of death. He was Gabriel. $E = MC^2$ was the trumpet blast.

But as I looked up at the windows of that hotel, I couldn't know how LaDonna's life was going to turn out. Inevitability had put her in that unworthy bed, but I could only believe that she had made the dumbest mistake of her young life. "Everything is as surprising and

as inevitable as a Bach fugue, Jack," she would write on
the back of the card announcing her fourth marriage—
this time to an Italian heart surgeon—but I could only
ask myself, *What next? What next?* as I staggered away
from the only hotel in one of the most obscure towns in
the world.

G U Y passed out folding knives. They had short, ugly
blades. "Cut their tires," he said. He said this in an offhanded way, calmly, as though he had said, "Tuck in
your shirts." He was dressed in his best suit. His eyes
were kind of glassy, though. He looked stern and sure of
himself, but he also looked dead. Even his skin looked
waxy. I think he had put some of Mother's makeup
under his eyes to cover the dark circles. He hadn't been
sleeping well, I knew, and his stomach had gotten
worse.

"How do you mean, Mr. Rampling?" said one of the
vendors.

"How do you think, you moron? You see an empty
scooter or truck, you reach down nice and easy, like you
were stopping to tie your shoelace, and you cut the living shit out of their tires."

The old vendors looked at their knives, confused. "We
could get ourselves in a lot of trouble," one of them said.

Guy laughed at him. "You *are* in a lot of trouble, shit-
for-brains. Your job is on the block. Those Ace Milk sons
a bitches are taking over your routes. We have got to put
the screws to them a little, to let them know we are alive
and kicking. I do not intend to roll over and get fucked
by a bunch of out-of-state pisswhistles. This is war,
men. Get that through your heads."

Even though he had raised his voice to us, he remained dead calm. It was eerie and several of the vendors looked furtively around the creamery as if to pick
out escape routes. But his speech was over and he

stalked out of the creamery, leaving us to stare dumbly at the deadly looking knives he'd given us.

When I was a few blocks away from the creamery, I dropped my knife down a storm drain. Maybe it was war, but it wasn't my war.

Though it was still early in the morning, the air was heating up. The afternoon was going to be miserable. By 10:00 A.M. I had sold out my stock, even the Gopher Cones, and had to return to the creamery to reload. By noon it was 93 degrees. I sold out twice more before three.

I was an hour behind schedule when I entered my best street. An Ace Milk scooter putted by me. The driver gave a snappy salute and I waved back. His electric music box was deafening. It was playing "Lucky Old Sun." He pulled up in front of me and turned off his engine. I pushed my cart beside his scooter.

"Hot mother, ain't it?" he said.

"Good for business," I said.

He narrowed his eyes at me. "That's a fact, junior. How you been doing?"

He was about thirty years old and he had a neat white uniform complete with black plastic bow tie and hard-billed policeman's cap.

"Not too bad," I said.

"Listen, junior," he said. "I don't exactly know how to tell you this, but I'd like it a lot if you would stay off of this street, okay? It's my best street, see, and you been hitting it kind of hard lately. I don't go for that."

"Is that a fact?" I said.

"So, what you are going to do is turn that box around and cool your heels for an hour or so, okay? And in the future I'd appreciate it if you didn't come up this street until after four o'clock. Five would be hunky-dory by me."

"It would be hunky-dory by me if you would go piss up a rope," I said.

"Look, ass-wipe, you're doing this for condoms and beer. But I got three kids at home and payments to make on a four-year-old Pontiac. You understand the situation? This is my bread, motherfucker."

"Life is hard," I said.

He climbed out of his little cab. "I've had about all I want from you, junior."

He hopped toward me, knee up. I turned slightly and his knee caught me on the thigh. He took a looping swing at my face. It glanced off my cheek. He swung again, but it only hit my shoulder. He stepped on my rubber foot.

"Had enough?" he said, breathing hard.

I punched him as hard as I could on the nose. Blood splashed all the way back to his ears.

"Oh!" he said, staggering backward. He covered his nose with both hands. "Oh!" he said through his red fingers.

I walked up to him and punched his hands. Blood bounced through his fingers and spattered his white coat. He scrambled up a steep lawn on all fours. He found level ground again in a vegetable garden. He stood up, holding his face with his left hand. He held his right hand up like a cop stopping traffic. "Stay there," he said. "Stay there."

"You win," I said, and pushed my cart back up the street as he'd asked me to.

I pushed my cart over to the children's park. "Too fucken hot, sport," said a voice from under the big blue spruce.

Cruise was lying on the bed of brown needles, his head propped up on a gnarled root. His jug of Emerald Milk was at his side.

"I believe I will just stay right here in this spot all fucken day long," he drawled.

I parked my cart next to his. Spider was asleep on top of Cruise's cart, twitching his way through a dream of four-legged running. I took out my canteen and crawled under the tree. "Sounds like a good idea," I said. "We'll tell Guy that we got run off our routes by the Ace Milk goon squad."

Cruise laughed. "Goon squad," he said. "They look like they suck off schoolboys." He held up his folding knife. The short ugly blade was out. "I'll tell you this, though. I ain't about to cut nobody's fucken tires." He folded the blade and put the knife into his pocket. "But it's a pretty little sticker, ain't it? So I guess I'll keep it. Might come in handy someday."

"I threw mine away," I said.

"Oh, that was real dumb, sport," he said. "You could of sold it for two, three bucks. But like I was telling Spider, Spider I says, Can you see old Cruise carving up a fucken tire like it was a Christmas turkey? Uh-uh. That is vandalism, I says. Old Cruise ain't no fucken vandalizer, Spider, is he? Not for ten percent of a bagful of dimes and quarters." He raised himself up and uncapped his jug. "I'll tell you something, ace. I abide by the law, unless it just ain't in the cards, you know what I mean? And I sure am not about to do thug work for a stupid bastard like Rampling. Stupid, ace, I mean *stupid*. That Gopher Cone, for instance. You know why they won't sell unless the fucken temperature goes over ninety? Because they look like a dead rat. That ain't a fucken gopher, it's a dead rat. Who wants to suck on a dead rat? That's what the kids call them. Rat Cones."

He went on for a while, pausing now and then to lift his jug. The prospect of tire cutting had set him off. I sipped my Mogen David, enjoying the cool piny smell of the spruce, watching the kids run around the playground, thinking about Zoe Rae Blazek and her wonderful tits.

"Hey, sport," Cruise said, suddenly alert. "Correct me if I'm wrong, but ain't that your mama over there?"

He pointed out to the middle of the park. Mother was

walking with Spencer Ted and a tall man. She was wearing a new dress. The dress was transparent pink and strapless, and her white shoulders gleamed. The dress was cut to flatter a heavy figure, and she looked very good as she sauntered through the park.

"Who's the fucken hairy beanpole with her?" Cruise said. "He looks like he's walking downhill."

"Don Paris," I said. "He owns the Paris Book Shop."

Cruise laughed, and then began a phlegmy song:

> Jelly roll killed my daddy
> drove my mama blind
> Jelly roll killed my daddy
> drove my mama blind
> If I don't get sweet jelly roll
> I will lose my mind.

He laughed again until he had to spit.

I got up and followed them, pushing my cart across the grassy playground but not ringing my bells. They were walking hand in hand, Spencer Ted waddling behind. I followed them as they left the park, hanging back about a quarter of a mile, ignoring the kids who thumped up against my cart yelling for ice cream.

They walked toward the business section of town. I pulled a little closer to them, sure that they didn't suspect anyone was following.

They went into the Paris Book Shop. I parked my cart on the sidewalk, under the awning of the store, and walked in.

Zoe Rae was reading a magazine at the cash register. She looked up at me, looked down quickly, then looked up again, smiling. "That's a darling costume," she said.

I had gotten so used to the little kraut mountaineer costume that I'd forgotten about it. I guess I blushed. "I'm a little Red Devil," I said, trying to recoup. I gave her a who-gives-a-shit-what-the-world-thinks grin. She smiled, and it was a lovely smile that would stick in my mind for some time to come.

Mother and Don Paris were nowhere in sight. I guessed that they were back in the office. Spencer Ted was on the floor, in a corner, drooling into a stack of picture books.

"I'm on my break," I said. "You want a Gopher Cone, Zoe Rae?"

She frowned a little, at my familiarity, I guess, then said, "Sure. I'd love one."

I went out to the cart and got her one. She was pleased. I liked the way she looked when she was pleased. Something told me that pleasing her would become a major concern of mine. She tried to give me a quarter. "It's on the house," I said.

"You must have read my mind," she said. "I've been thinking about ice cream for the past half hour."

Our eyes met and held. But it wasn't just her eyes. It wasn't her face, her hair, or her lovely smile. She had nice hands, nice skin, beautiful little ears, but it was none of these, either. Tits, yes, it was her tits, but it was much more than her tits. My heart was noticeable under my mountaineer's bib, the stuttering fool, kicked by lust's adrenaline.

"Mind if I browse around?" I asked.

"Go ahead. I'll even let you buy a book if you find something you like."

I looked at her and she looked at me. We both smiled, as though we liked what we saw.

I made my way, casually, toward the back of the store, as if I was really interested in buying a book. When I got close to the office, I picked up a big book called *The Great Myths of the Past* and pretended to study it. I inched closer to the office door, which was partly open, but I heard no voices. At the front of the store, Zoe Rae was busy with two old ladies. I slipped into the office.

It was empty. At the back of the office, there was a

door. I went to it, put my ear against it. I thought I could hear a conversation, but it could have been my own blood banging past my ears. I turned the knob and opened the door a crack.

It was dark on the other side. I eased the door open slowly. It was a storeroom, filled with boxes of books. I heard Mother laughing faintly as Don Paris recited a poem in French. I slipped into the storeroom and crouched behind a stack of crated books until my eyes got used to the dim light.

Paris had quit reciting his poem. He made an urgent, muffled sound—half groan, half yelp. I peeked around the stack of books. Mother was sitting in a swivel chair, smoking a cigarette. A naked, sixty- or seventy-five-watt bulb hung over her head by its wire. Don Paris was kneeling before Mother, his head under her dress. "Oh, *lovely*," he chortled. "My little cabbage! My doll queen!"

Mother looked serene and queenly as the gleeful owner of the Paris Book Shop browsed under her dress. She gazed blandly through her cigarette smoke as if into the new possibilities her future held.

"Please, oh, please, Jade," said the muffled voice of Don Paris, and Mother leaned back to accommodate him further.

I bought myself a double cheeseburger deluxe downtown, then worked my way back toward the children's park. By the time I got there, I was sold out, and so I headed back to the creamery to reload. I sold out again, within an hour and a half, and went back once more to reload. By this time it was dinnertime, but the kids kept coming out of their houses with dimes and quarters.

When the sun was a smoky red ball in the west hills, I went back to the children's park. Cruise was still under the blue spruce. He had passed out, his jug of Emerald Milk empty beside him. His mouth was slung open so wide that I looked in it to see if some kid had propped it that way with a stick, as a joke. There was a fat blue fly on his lower lip.

The air under the tree was stuffy and hot. Cruise was sweating. I brushed the fly off his lip. "Cruise," I said. "Wake up. Let's go. It's time to check in."

He sat up straight, his wide, uncoordinated eyes taking in everything and nothing. "Huh?" he said. "What from the house they tuck it away for?" He slapped his mouth with the back of his fist to make it stop babbling. "Oh, it's you, sport. You got any juice left?"

"Let's head back," I said.

I helped him to his feet. He wobbled a bit, trying to find his equilibrium. "Woof," he said. "What a fucken dream I had. I was under the floorboards of some house, fucken bugs and shit all over me. Shouldn't a gone to sleep in the heat."

We climbed out from under the tree. His cart had been moved a few hundred feet down the street from where he'd parked it. "Looks like the kids got into your stock, Cruise," I said.

"Wait a fucken minute, ace," he said. "You seen my hat?" He was crabby and dry-mouthed and his tongue clicked when he talked.

"Looks like they stole your hat, too," I said.

We walked down the street to his cart. "Hold on a fucken minute," he said, his uncontrolled eye swiveling nervously. "Where the fuck is Spider?"

I looked around. "They're probably playing with him," I said. "Spider's probably having the time of his life."

We had an audience of snickering kids. They were all under ten years old. They had gathered about fifty feet from us, ready to run if we turned on them. They looked like they had just lit the fuse of a blasting cap. One boy had on Cruise's red beanie. Nervous giggles chirped out from the group now and then.

"What are they fucken up to?" Cruise said. He looked afraid. A grown man afraid of ten-year-old kids was a strange thing to see. He was alarmed all out of proportion to the threat, which was nonexistent as far as I could tell. "Say, just what in the fuck is going on here?" Cruise said, his voice trembling.

"They probably swiped some push ups or Gopher Cones," I said. "They're waiting for you to find out and come running." I opened the cold box and looked inside. I closed it quick. "Oh-oh," I said.

"Took it all, ace?" Cruise said in a high, anxious voice. "They fucken swipe all my stock?"

"Shit, Cruise," I said. I felt a little sick. "Goddamn it, Cruise." I gave the kids a murdering look and they backed up a few feet, snickering, legs primed for sprinting.

"Let me see, sport," Cruise said. "Let me have a look at what they little bastards took."

"Cruise, no. Don't look in there. I'll take care of it."

"What are you talking about, ace? You'll take care of what?" He stepped up to the cart and opened the lid. He bent down and peered into the cold box. He looked at me and the expression on his face was the same bewildered one he'd had when I'd first wakened him under the blue spruce. His loose eye stabilized itself, as if the muscles that controlled it had suddenly stiffened in place. Then it started to drift upward as the eyeball got glassy with tears. His lower lip quivered.

"Shit, Cruise," I said.

He leaned down close to the coldbox and reached inside. He pulled Spider out by his leash. The kids shrieked and sprinted away in six directions. Spider was frozen solid. He must have been in the coldbox, wedged in among the blocks of dry ice, for three or four hours.

Cruise laid him down on top of the cart and Spider thunked like a block of wood. "I got to get him warmed up," he said, urgent and hopeful. He hovered over the little poodle, wringing his hands, wondering what to do. Then he picked the dog up and clamped it under his armpit.

"I don't think that will do any good, Cruise," I said.

"Maybe he'll be all right once he gets warmed up," he said. "Once his circulation gets to moving again, he'll be okay."

"Cruise," I said.

After a minute, Cruise put Spider back on the cart, gently this time so that he wouldn't thunk. He sucked in his lips and made a whining puppy sound, the same sound that used to make Spider jump up and dance on his three legs for little girls. Then he sat down on the curb. He held his stomach, gripped by sudden cramps. Gray liquid fell from his mouth, Emerald Milk gone sour. He made a long sound that tightened my skin with goosebumps.

"How come?" he whispered. "How come they'd just drop him in the box like that? They must of known I couldn't hear him crying."

"Kids," I said, as if that explained something.

"Sure. Kids. But why? Why would they do a thing like that?"

The kids who'd sprinted away were now edging back, not wanting to miss a minute of the show. I picked up a rock and winged it over their heads.

Cruise stood up. He put his hand on Spider's hard belly. "Spider," he said. "Oh, Spider." He picked up the frozen dog and carried him into the black shade of the spruce tree.

I had a dream of cold and warm. Cold was one definite road, warm was another. Cold, I was in an alley, trying to scrape something off my shoe. I was old and it hurt to scrape like that. Then my shoe came off, and with it my foot. I was feeble and unable to find my lost foot. My left eye was an uncontrollable rover. When I thought I had sighted my foot, the eye traveled away from it, choosing its own scenery. I wept. My life had come down to this alley. This was the sum of it. Footless, cold, half blind, and lost. Warm, I was in bed with a sweet-smelling, big-breasted woman whose voice made me throb. Sunlight rich as butter filled the clean bedroom. "Oh, food, oh, food," she murmured hungrily. I believed I was rich, but didn't grasp how I'd come to be that way. Cold, I limped into the abandoned outskirts of poor mill towns, holding my buttonless overcoat closed against a wind that poked my chest like fingers. Warm, I was seated at a wonderful table. All around me were bright, friendly faces. These were my relatives and friends. The food before us was piled high, steaming, and beautifully garnished. "Oh, food, oh, food," said the soft-eyed woman on my right. Cold, I hurt all over and there was no comfort to be had anywhere ever again. Warm, the woman stirred in her sleep and then rolled toward me, her arms pulling me in, and I was in her and she was my happiness. But then I was running, cold and scared, my right leg stumping against the asphalt, bleeding, pain hammering up my leg. Children were chasing me armed with sticks, sweetly and viciously innocent, screaming at my back. Just before they caught up with me, I slipped into the shade of an old spruce tree where the *ngantja* said, "I don't make the fucken rules, ace."

I was nervous around Zoe Rae and had to muster my courage to ask her out. I don't know why I was short on nerve around her. Maybe it was because she had been to college. She seemed very smart to me, but more than smart, too. She seemed a step or two ahead of me on several levels. I asked her to go to the movies with me but mumbled it so badly that she had to ask me what I'd said. She was amused at my choice of movies, and afterward, at the posh Lamp Lighter Restaurant, she said, "Where on earth did you learn to eat?"

It stopped me cold. "What do you mean?" I asked.

"I mean what I said. Where did you learn to hold a knife and fork?"

I shrugged. I looked at the utensils in my hands. I always held a knife and fork like that. How else could you hold a knife and fork?

"You look like you're stabbing small animals to death," she said.

I cut another piece of steak, self-conscious now about the way I held my utensils.

"No, no, no," she scolded. "You're holding your knife and fork in your *fists*. It's very vulgar." She reached across the table and took the knife and fork away from me. "This is how it's done," she said. I watched her cut her veal. "Forefinger along the back edge of the knife, to direct it. Fork held upside down, much in the same way—the left forefinger lying just above the curve where the tines are joined to the handle. The way you're eating now makes you look like a barbarian—stab, hack, and tear."

I had trouble finishing my meal, holding the knife and fork in this unfamiliar way. The people eating at the tables near us had heard her instructing me in table etiquette and I felt their eyes on me now, watching for mistakes.

I guess I should have gotten mad at her, but I didn't. She fascinated me more than she irritated me. The irritation, what there was of it, was almost pleasurable anyway. There wasn't any nastiness or superiority in her instructions. She was seriously trying to teach me something. And she was a good teacher—her instructions were clear and easy to follow and her tone of voice suggested an untiring and kindly patience.

She worked for Don Paris in the summertime because

she loved to be around books. She asked me to name my favorite books. I pretended to think it over for a while. I couldn't dredge up a single title. She didn't let me off the hook. "What was the *last* book you read?" she asked. Again I went into my thinking-it-over act. "Can you give me any title at all?" she asked. *The Horrible Huns Sack Rome* occurred to me.

"No," I said, deciding to come clean.

"Oh, my," she said. "I'm going to have to teach you so very much."

She gave me a book called *Our Mr. Wren.* I thumbed through it, promising to read it as soon as I had time. She gave me a book on philosophy. "I adore philosophy," she said. She opened the book to a dogeared page. "How mischievously surprising the universe seems," she read. "What awesome and unlikely chain of cosmic events could account for the tent-making caterpillar?"

I took her for a car ride up to Father LaPorte Dam south of Grassy Lake. We took Spencer Ted along with us. When Zoe Rae saw Spencer Ted she paled.

"What's wrong with him, Jack?" she whispered to me.

"Body outgrew his brain," I said.

"Oh, Jack!" she said, turning away, fist in her cheek, her lovely eyes brimming.

I put my hand on her arm. She was quaking. "It's okay, Zoe Rae," I said. "He's happy, and we're all sort of used to the situation now."

She turned on me, eyes flashing now with outrage. "Don't be so quick to dismiss my feelings!" she said.

"I'm sorry, Zoe Rae," I said.

She walked around the car and sat on the rear bumper. I was alarmed by her enormous and unconsolable pity. It was something that could come between us someday.

But on the way to the dam, she brightened. "I'm sorry, Jack," she said. "I tend to go overboard sometimes."

"It's okay," I said. "I guess I should have told you about Spencey before letting you meet him."

When I parked at the dam site, I tried to kiss her. She turned her head to one side, offering me her cheek. I didn't take it. A cheek-kiss would establish a kind of heatless relationship from the outset. I didn't want any part of that.

"I already have a sister," I said.

She leaned close to me. "Spencer Ted," she whispered.

I looked in the back seat. Spencer Ted was looking at his hands, tops and bottoms, working his fingers, fascinated at how the joints moved.

"He's busy," I whispered back. "He's not interested in us."

"Even so," she said.

"Spencey," I said. "Hey, Spencey. Let's go look at the big ole dam."

He looked up from the chubby machinery of his fingers, surprised to see me. "Dam? Hi, Jack, oh, boy, water."

"Right, kid. Let's go."

We climbed out of the car and walked up a steep path to an observation kiosk that overlooked the spillway. We sat on a bench and stared out at the great expanse of vertical concrete. A strong wind whipped through the kiosk, howling slightly in the posts and rafters. The water sliding over the spillway was hypnotic.

But fascination soon slipped over into boredom. "You stay here for a while, Spencey," I said. "Zoe Rae and I are going down to the car for a few minutes."

In the car we got right to it. Her lips were warm and her tongue was active. I put my hand on her breast and she made a small sound into my mouth. I unbuttoned her blouse, searched the back of her brassiere for the clasp, unclasped it after a few tries, raised the brassiere up and over her huge tits. I broke off the kiss to look at them.

They shimmered in the afternoon sunlight, the perfect nipples rosy and tight. "God," I said, kissing them over and over, mad with extreme lust. *What awesome and unlikely chain of cosmic events could account for these magnificent, rose-tipped beauties?* I thought, the thought making me smile.

"I don't know why I'm letting you do this," she said. But she didn't push me off.

"Philosophy," I said.

"Not there," she said, as I slipped a hand into her panties. "No. I mean it."

"I love you," I said.

She stiffened and pushed me away. I'd made a mistake, I realized. "I'm serious," I said. "I love you, I love *all* of you."

"Christ," she said, disgusted. "How many times have I heard that whopper before?"

She pulled her brassiere down, clasped it, buttoned her blouse.

"I meant what I said, Zoe Rae," I said. "I wasn't just bullshitting you. I've never met a girl like you in my life."

She looked at me for a long moment, trying to make up her mind. "First of all, you don't know me well enough to say something like that. Second of all, I've heard it a hundred times from the frat rats down at State College. I liked you a lot—I still do like you—but when you said that, I was right back down there in some passion pit fighting for my life. I'm so sick of it I could throw up."

"Damn," I said. "I'm sorry."

"Me too, Jack. It's just that I'm kind of emotional. I get carried away sometimes, and you get a reputation for it and they take advantage of you."

"I feel like Jack the Ripper," I said.

She laughed and picked up my hand. She scooted close to me. She put my hand back on her breast and

soon we were back where we were a few minutes earlier.

"Say it, say it," she gasped.

"I love you, I love you," I said.

But then she backed away again.

"What's wrong now?" I said, unable to keep the complaint out of my voice.

"Spencer Ted," she said. "I don't see him."

I looked up the hill at the kiosk. It was vacant. I looked
left and right, along the steep, sloping fields on either
side of the kiosk, but he was gone. I got out of the car and
headed up the steep path toward the kiosk.

I was walking too fast for the slope and began hiking
my hip. I hadn't told Zoe Rae about my foot yet, and I
didn't want to tell her now, so I slowed down to a stroll.
She came running up behind me.

"Hurry!" she said, passing me. She hadn't bothered to
button up her blouse and her brassiere was back in the
car, dangling from the rearview mirror. She reached
the kiosk well ahead of me. When I got there she was
already standing on the precipice overlooking the spillway. "Oh, *Jesus,* Jack!" she said. "He's down *there!*"

She was pointing down a steep trail that had been cut
into the side of the gorge. The trail had gone down to the
riverbed at one time, but work on the dam had shaved
it away so that only about a hundred feet of it was left.
Spencer Ted had gone down the trail to where it suddenly dropped away into nothingness. He was frozen
there, back against the cliffside, looking into the white
roar of falling water.

"Spencey!" I yelled. "Come back! Get on your hands
and knees and crawl! You can make it!"

Spencer Ted didn't move.

"You've got to go down there and get him, Jack!" Zoe
Rae said.

But the old trail was narrow and steep, too steep for
me and my rubber foot. It was also crumbling. Both feet

would have to be sensitive for slight shifts of the under-footing.

"I can't," I said. "My foot."

"What?" Zoe Rae said, confused. "You *can't?* But you have to! He might fall!"

"Traction," I said. "Toes. The muscles. The bushing . . . you can't feel the bushing move and so you can't tell what the ground is doing . . ."

She gave me a look that made pockmarks on my soul. Then she took off her shoes and started down the horrible trail, her fierce breasts glistening with the fine spray that rose up from the gorge to make multiple rainbows ornament the clear blue sky downriver. I reached out halfheartedly to stop her, but she jerked her arm away from me. I went down to all fours and followed her.

I felt my way along, the sucking pull of the tons of white falling water urging me over the edge. I put my head down and concentrated on the few square inches of earth under my eyes. I wondered what had made Spencer Ted do it. Dim as he was, he had good judgment in all the important things. He came in out of the rain. He didn't eat too much at dinnertime so that he'd have room for two helpings of dessert. Anxious about bed-wetting, he went to the bathroom several times every night before turning in. He was polite and sociable and gentle and pleasant. He was no reckless adventurer. The most daring thing I'd ever seen him do was walk down the basement stairs backward to see what it felt like. What he was doing now made no sense to me at all. And we could all be killed trying to get him off the face of that cliff.

Zoe Rae was already trying to talk him back up the trail when I got there. She was kneeling before him, coaxing him to follow her back to the kiosk. But Spencer Ted was blubbering and wouldn't be consoled. The trail ended two or three feet on the other side of Spencer Ted. Beyond that there was nothing. Just a long, clean drop into the torrent. Zoe Rae sensed me behind her. She looked at me, terror widening her eyes, determination tightening her lips. "I love you," I said, meaning it, knowing that I meant it.

"I don't know what to *do!*" she said. "He won't move!"

The wind was trying to peel us off the face of the cliff. The path was so steep at this point that it took something like willpower to stop it from becoming a frictionless slide into empty air. This was more of a mental problem than a physical one, I realized, but it was hard to make such fine distinctions at the moment.

Then Zoe Rae did something that made me think she had become hysterical. She knelt down before Spencer Ted and began to play with her tits. She held a tit in each hand and animated it. Spencer Ted stared at the display, captivated. I heard Zoe Rae yell, "This is Mr. Red Nose, Spencer Ted, and this one is Miss Chubbers. Mr. Red Nose and Miss Chubbers want you to follow them, Spencer Ted. Isn't that right, Miss Chubbers?" She lifted her right tit and made it talk. "Oh, yes, Spencer Ted. Please come with me, honey." Miss Chubbers sounded something like Charlie McCarthy. Then she lifted her left tit and made it talk. "Come on, Spencer Ted, let's go up the hill so we can play." Mr. Red Nose sounded like Mortimer Snerd. Spencer Ted, in spite of his fear, grinned a little. Zoe Rae began to move backward on her knees, holding her tits, which continued to chatter encouragement to Spencer Ted. "Come on, honey," said Miss Chubbers. "You don't want to stay here all alone, do you? Come and play with us." Spencer Ted gradually lowered himself to all fours and began to crawl after Zoe Rae. Inch by inch, we all climbed back up toward the kiosk on our knees.

Later on, in the car, with Spencer Ted asleep in the back seat, I said, "What made you think of doing that, Zoe Rae?"

"He was staring at them," she said. "He'd stare at the

water and then he'd stare at my breasts. I saw that he was fascinated by them. So I turned them into ventriloquist dummies. Don't ask me why I thought of that, though. It just occurred to me."

"Thank God it did," I said.

I was still shaking from the experience and didn't want to drive home yet. So we sat in the car, recuperating, not talking much. When we'd gotten back to the kiosk I saw that Spencer Ted had something gripped in his fist. I opened his fingers and a crushed butterfly fell out. He had followed a lovely, big Monarch butterfly down the trail, not realizing the danger. I understood the impulse.

I put my arm around Zoe Rae, but she was in no mood for it. "You were great," I said, removing my arm.

"Thanks," she said.

"No, I mean it. You were really something."

She looked at me. I didn't exactly care for the look in her eyes.

"What's wrong?" I said.

"I don't understand you," she said. "He's *your* brother, yet you weren't going to go down there after him."

"I was *going* to," I said, not caring especially for my tone of voice. "I was trying to think of a *way* to do it."

"Sure you were," she said.

"Goddammit," I said.

"Let's go," she said. "I want to go."

A moment of truth was headed our way like an avalanche. There was no way around it. "Goddammit," I said. I raised my right foot to the seat.

"What are you *doing?*" she said, mad and annoyed.

I unlaced the shoe and dropped it on the floorboard. I peeled off the sock. I unbuckled the rubber foot and set it on the dashboard. The bright pink stub had no traction and it slipped across the vinyl seat covers. "Meet Mr. Stump," I said. "Hi there, Miss Blazek," said the stump in the voice of Mortimer Snerd turned vicious.

Zoe Rae burst into tears and ran out of the car.

"I can't climb fucking mountains with this thing!" I yelled after her.

She stayed away for a while. When she came back, she was calm. I was calm, too. And sorry.

"I'm sorry," we said, together.

She sat down close to me and held my hand. "I couldn't have known about that, could I?" she said, meekly.

"No," I said. "And I was an asshole for keeping it a secret. Truth is, I didn't want to scare you off."

"I don't scare all that easy," she said.

"So I noticed," I said.

We leaned into each other, with heat.

"Hi, Miss Chubbers," I said, kissing her right nipple.

"Don't forget about me," said Mr. Red Nose.

And Spencer Ted snored.

BIG Natty Northberry showed up while we were eating breakfast. "Well, looks like I picked the right time," he said, pulling up a chair. He was smiling, but it was easy to see that he was impatient with the situation. "So, where is the big lug, Jade?" he said, filling a plate with eggs and smoked sausages.

Mother shrugged. She'd been reading a book of poems that Don Paris had given her as a present.

"You don't *know?*" Big Natty said, buttering toast. "This is unacceptable, Jade. I mean it. He can't be pulling stunts like this. One thing all the colleagues down at the Chamber insist on is responsibility."

Mother smiled calmly at him. "The world is too much with us, Big Natty," she said, quoting from her book.

"Huh? You want to run that by me one more time, Jade?" Northberry said.

"Getting and spending, we lay waste our powers," Mother said.

"Jade, Jade! I'm talking about the Founder's Day Parade! Now, where the heck is Guy? He's supposed to have his trucks down on Beech Street as of"—he consulted his wristwatch—"sixteen minutes ago."

"I'm sorry, Big Natty," Mother said. "I just haven't seen him." She poured Big Natty another cup of coffee.

"Whoa. The nerves. Now, you're actually telling me you don't know where he is? What am I supposed to make of that, Jade? He's your *husband*. Of course you know where he is. You must have some idea."

Mother shook her head. "I haven't seen him since last night. He left the house about eleven. He didn't come back. Not that I know of, anyway."

"Have you called the sheriff?" Northberry said, spooning sugar into his coffee.

"No," Mother said.

Northberry drummed the table with his thick fingers. "Look here," he said. "I don't want to meddle in your home life, Jade. But the parade must go on. With or without Mode o' Day Dairy Products. You can understand that, can't you?"

"Of course," Mother said, calmer than ever.

"Personally, Jade, I don't believe a word of this stuff that's been going around."

When no one asked what he meant, he said, "You know, these rumors about Mode o' Day milk—that it isn't safe. Too much strontium ninety in it. If you ask me, I say that's going too far. Of course, it's not clear that Ace Milk is responsible for spreading it, but who else would do such a thing? I must say, I find it a little on the shady side. Still, there's no proof Ace Milk is behind it. It could be anybody who thinks he's got a grudge against Guy."

"Strontium ninety?" Mother said.

"Bomb fallout. You know. They had a big stink a few years ago about it. A lot of baloney, if you ask me. That Stevenson character had a puppy over it. Some Canadian hunters were supposed to have gotten sick after eating a few radioactive ducks. What hooey. Ike said there was no danger, and that's good enough for me."

"Why would we have strontium ninety and Ace Milk not have it?" Mother asked.

"Right! That's the sixty-four-dollar question, Jade! That's exactly what my response would be if I were Guy. But where is the big dope? How can he respond if he's off somewhere goofing off?"

"I'll do it," I said.

Northberry and Mother looked at me.

"I'll do it. I'll drive a milk truck in the parade and I'll call the newspaper about this strontium ninety crap."

Northberry patted my shoulder. "That's the spirit, son. But the committee expects three decorated milk trucks from Mode o' Day to follow the Founder float. It's very important. I can't stress that enough. It's an honored position in the parade. Listen, I fought for that position on Guy's behalf. I had to tell them, hey, Guy Rampling deserves that spot, considering what Ace Milk is getting."

"I'll round up two other drivers," I said.

Northberry sipped his coffee. "I can't believe he'd go off and abandon his responsibilities like this," he said. "I had him pegged as an ambitious fellow. I'll make no secret of it, Jade. I'm disappointed. I'm upset. I feel personally let down."

Mother smiled slightly, but said nothing.

Northberry looked at his watch. "The parade is scheduled to start in . . . two hours, twelve minutes. Jack, old son, can you get a hold of those other drivers?"

"I think so," I said.

"He's all man, Jade," Northberry said. "I've know men with *two* complete feet who had a hell of a lot less going for them than your Jack, here."

"So have I," Mother said.

The way she said this made Northberry blush. He

stood up, banging the table with his thighs. The cups and plates jumped. "Onward and upward," he said, all business.

IN fact, it was not easy to find drivers. Founder's Day was on a Sunday and none of the regular milkmen wanted to work, especially since there was no extra pay involved. They all had Sunday plans. I went to the seedy roominghouse where Cruise lived and rousted him out of bed. He'd been down deep in a wine-fueled funk for days and it was like trying to drag a dying man out of a coma.

"Can you drive a milk truck, Cruise?" I asked when I was sure he was conscious.

His good eye fixed itself on me. The other one gazed out the window. "I can drive any fucken thing with air in the tires," he said.

His room was uniformly brown. Brown walls, brown linoleum floor, brown ceiling—brown from fifty years of cigarette smoke—brown dresser and night table, the bed was brown-painted iron and the sheets were brown. The light drifting into the room from the lone window was tan-colored. The room also smelled. It was a brown smell that had worked into the wood and plaster over a period of brown years, a sour wine and whisky mist beyond the powers of scrub brush or paint, the indelible brown of loneliness and failure.

Cruise sat on his bed smoking a hand-rolled cigarette, waiting for his blood to move.

"Cruise," I said.

He looked up.

"I'm in love." I don't know why I told him that. I guess maybe to see what he thought of the subject and its possibilities.

He took a long, thoughtful drag on his cigarette. "That's good," he said, neutrally.

305

"It's the real thing," I said.

"That's even better," he said.

"It's hard to tell if you mean it," I said.

"It's hard to tell if *you* mean it, ace."

"I mean it," I said.

"I got my own problems," he said.

"I'm going to ask her to marry me," I said.

"Many happy returns," he said.

"I don't know why I said anything to you about it."

"You wanted to see how it sounds. You wanted to see if it sounded true."

"Maybe," I said.

"Maybe *shit.*"

"Let's go," I said.

He got dressed and we left for the creamery. I didn't talk to him on the way down and that was fine by him. Ever since he'd lost Spider he'd been untalkative. He drank a lot more now, and instead of trying to charm little girls he acted reproachful toward them. When he made remarks about the girls swinging in the park, he was snide and full of contempt. They still attracted him, but his desire for them had a coldhearted, vengeful side to it.

The only other man I could find was old Swede, who wasn't too sure he remembered how to drive. I gave him a quick refresher course and we drove the milk trucks, single file and very slowly, toward Beech Street.

When Northberry saw us coming, he ran to meet us. "How come these trucks aren't decorated?" he said, unhappy with the way things were going. "Don't you understand what this parade means to local business? You think all this is some kind of children's hour? This is money! This is the economic health of our community!"

"I'll get some toilet paper," I said.

"You'll have to do better than toilet paper," Northberry said.

"I'll get *colored* toilet paper. I'll see if I can find some balloons."

We parked the trucks side by side behind the Founder float, which was a fifteen-foot-tall paper-mâché replica of the bronze statue on the courthouse lawn of Jules Brightman, founder of Far Cry. I got out of my truck and went to a nearby grocery store and bought several packages of pink, green, and blue toilet paper. The grocery store didn't have any balloons so I went to the drugstore next to it and bought a gross of rubbers.

"We goin' to drive trucks or fuck?" Cruise said when he saw the box of rubbers.

I handed him some rubbers. "Blow them up, Cruise. We need balloons." I handed him a roll of pink toilet paper. "When you finish with that, hang some of this on the truck. Try to be reasonably artistic."

"My artistic days are long gone, ace," he said, glum at the prospect of physical work. I handed him a half-gallon of Emerald Milk, which I'd bought along with the toilet paper. "Here," I said. "This will help you get creative."

I gave some rubbers to Swede and a roll of green toilet paper. "Blow up about a dozen of those, Swede, and hang that ass-wipe all over your truck." Swede looked at the rubbers and grinned.

"By hell," he said, a dirty twinkle in his sly old eyes.

When we finished decorating the trucks we all had a drink of Emerald Milk. We studied our work. The trucks looked like they had been wrapped in bandages by kids playing doctor. The blown-up rubbers bobbed from the big, rearview mirror posts on the fenders. Some were tied to the grilles and bumpers. Big Natty Northberry came by to inspect our work. He shook his head dubiously. "I don't know if I can allow this, Jack," he said. "Aren't those *condoms?*"

"No one will notice," I said. "Besides, they were the only things close to balloons I could find."

"It looks like those trucks have been driven through someone's toilet bowl. I just don't know if I can allow it."

"You can allow it," I said.

He looked at me. "How's that, son?" he said.

"I said you can allow it. This is Mode o' Day's spot in the parade. The committee gave it to us. We have the right, and we're going to take it."

"I don't think I like your tone, son. I think maybe I misjudged you. I'm sure I did, in fact."

"You're probably good at it," I said.

"How's that? Good at what?"

"Misjudging people."

His face got red and he took a step toward me, but, remembering his position as Parade Committee chairman, he turned abruptly and walked away.

"What a fucken bag of shit," Cruise said, tilting the bottle.

"Yah!" old Swede hissed in agreement.

Out of curiosity, I took a stroll up the length of the parade to see what the other entrants looked like. The Ace Milk Cow, Miss Acey Deucy, was an inflated monster. It was a guernsey, at least fifty feet long and twenty feet tall. An udder as big as a bomber's turret revolved in its belly on perfect bearings. The stubby, cylindrical teats shot jets of noisy steam every now and then, startling the crowd that had begun to collect along the parade's route. It was a wonderful device, those steam-driven teats, guaranteed to jerk any crowd out of the doldrums.

The parade started twenty minutes behind schedule. The Far Cry High School marching band was having trouble with its Sousaphone section. Two horns hadn't arrived and the band director was yelling at everyone.

Cruise and Swede sat in the back of Cruise's truck, passing the Emerald Milk back and forth. Swede was nervous. He'd had a hard time driving the milk truck to Beech Street, and was now afraid of driving it behind the Founder float for five miles. I kept my eye on him, worried that he might bolt.

Then the drum section of the band started a thundering roll. It was the signal for the parade to start. The drums settled into a brisk marching beat and the parade began to move out.

"Get in the trucks!" I yelled at Cruise and Swede. "They've started!"

I started my truck and waited while Cruise and Swede got theirs going. I yelled out my door at Swede. "Remember, keep it in low gear, Swede. Keep your foot off the accelerator. Use the hand throttle. And for God's sake, be ready to jump on the brakes if the float ahead of us stops. Stay on your toes, Swede."

Swede looked at me, alarmed, as if I had said these things to him in Chinese. He started his engine again, even though it was already idling, and an ear-piercing scream leaped up from under his truck. This demoralized him further, but he managed to get the truck in gear and it jerked forward. Cruise, on the other side of my truck, was driving with one hand and drinking with the other. His wandering left eye would sometimes drift to the far corner of its socket to watch me on the sly, as if it had some private life of its own and was looking to amuse itself wholly apart from the interests and concerns of its owner.

Music from the marching band—three floats, a girl scout troop, a band of businessmen dressed up as Indians, and a dump truck full of semifinalists from a beauty contest were between us—wafted back in patches that varied widely in volume. Sometimes only a flourish of trumpets would reach us, and sometimes it was flutes or trombones. Now and then the entire band would thunder for a few bars, only to fade away altogether as the parade rounded a corner or entered a dip in the road.

Swede made sure he stayed even with me by not taking his eyes off my front left wheel. He never looked ahead to see whether or not he was getting too close to the Founder float. He figured, I guess, that it was my job to keep the distance right.

My truck was lined up directly behind the papier-mâché Founding Father. The Founder loomed in front of me, deceptively massive. His shoulders were as wide as Paul Bunyan's. His bull-like neck supported a head that turned slowly left and right, as though to acknowledge the cheering crowds on the sidewalks. His arms were on swivels, too, and one raised itself in a salute while the other nudged an imaginary sidekick in the ribs.

From my vantage point, I saw that there were many gaps in the papier-mâché. In the Founder's legs, back, neck, and head, the framework of two-by-fours and chicken wire was easily visible. The gaps were there for ventilation, because there were six boys inside the Founder sitting on scaffolds. The boys were there to operate the ropes and pulleys that moved the arms and head of the Founder. Now and then I could see the expressions on the boys' faces, and they were having a great time. One boy sat in the head of the Founder, working the ropes that opened and closed the eyes and mouth. He could make the eyes pop open as if the Founder was waking up out of a bad dream, or he could make either eye wink good-naturedly. He could drop the jaw in dumbfounded astonishment, or he could make the Founder smile.

After about a half an hour, the parade came to a stop. The delay was a long one. I climbed out of my truck and walked up ahead. As I passed in front of the Founder float, he winked at me. I waved. His mouth opened to smile, revealing a row of shingle-size teeth. I smiled back. His huge arm rose up in a kind of informal salute. His other arm nudged his imaginary sidekick. It was a wonderful invention, and I laughed. The boys working the ropes and pulleys laughed, too.

I walked past several floats, past the girl scout troop, past the band of Indians, who were sitting on the curbs smoking cigarettes and looking at their wristwatches, and past the dump truck filled with the semifinalists. The kids in the high school band were restless and they were horsing around with each other. As I walked past them, a trombone player blew a flat note into my ear. I jumped sideways a foot and all the kids laughed. I gave the trombone player the finger and the kids laughed again.

The trouble was with Miss Acey Deucy. The tractor that had been pulling her had stalled. The driver was trying to restart it, but it wasn't catching and the battery was dying.

Clouds had moved in from the north. The sky darkened. Big Natty Northberry, who had been talking to the tractor driver, looked up at the darkening sky. "You dirty son of a bitch," he said to the weather front, loud enough for the spectators to hear.

I felt a little jumpy myself. A cold wind shot through my thin jacket. "Here comes fall," a man said to me. "I'm not ready for it, how about you?" I shook my head. There was a liquor store up the street and I headed for it. I bought myself a mickey of peach brandy and slipped it into my jacket.

When I got back to the trucks Cruise was leaning back in his seat, eyes closed and mouth open. Swede was holding on to his steering wheel as if he was guiding the truck through a field littered with babies. I took a few swallows of the brandy, which went down warm, sweet, and hard.

It began to sprinkle. The crowd went into stores and gathered under awnings for cover, and some went home. The band, probably at Northberry's insistence, began to play. I thought of the *Titanic* going down, the band on the deck playing bravely.

I hadn't eaten much breakfast and the brandy hit. I got happy. I sat in my truck and thought about Zoe Rae. I thought about Miss Chubbers and Mr. Red Nose. In my daydream they whispered hot suggestions and I was hog-wild in love. "Be mine, Miss Chubbers," I begged. "Be mine, Mr. Red Nose." They talked it over, nose to nose, murmuring secret opinions.

But all this only made me restless and so I climbed down out of the truck and walked the length of the parade again to the broken-down Ace Milk float. Jumper cables had been attached to the tractor's battery, but it still wouldn't start. There was a small crowd standing around the tractor, too disgusted to get out of the rain. Big Natty Northberry himself was sitting in the tractor seat, trying to start it.

I think I was the first to see the giant bride. She was over six feet tall and she was carrying a blanket. Her long white dress was muddy at the hem but she wasn't bothering to lift the skirts out of the puddles. She had a long, purposeful stride. She was the ugliest bride in the world, her face hairy and flat. Her dress was made of stitched-together bedsheets. She was coming down Yarrow Street, which intersected Beech at right angles. Her long blond hair hung like wet straw from her big head. As she walked, she held her stomach with her free hand. I thought that she must be part of the parade, part of some kind of little dramatic presentation in which she would take Jules Brightman for her husband and together they would tame the wilderness. A band of Indians would offer them pemmican and medicines made from the flowering bitterroot. I looked around for a bridegroom, some huge man in a black suit, but saw no one of that description.

The giant bride was headed for the broken-down float. Big Natty Northberry was still sitting on the tractor, but he had given up trying to start it. He was staring morosely at the rear of the next float in line, a logging truck carrying a single tree—a world-record ponderosa.

Stopping before Miss Açey Deucy, the giant bride spoke: "You low cunt-eaters. You maggot-faced cock-suckers. You scumbag shit-eaters and faggots. You . . . liars. You . . . fakers. You . . . you . . . bad *bad* people."

She spoke in a man's voice, loudly at first but then tapering off to a hoarse whisper. Everyone was looking at her. The blanket that she had been carrying fell to the curb. It had been concealing a twelve-gauge pump shot-gun. She raised the gun to her shoulder and pumped it. It was an electrifying moment. Northberry, as he clambered down off the tractor, said, "Whoa, ma'am. Whoa, now, lady."

But the giant bride paid no attention to him. She pointed the twelve-gauge at Miss Acey Deucy and fired. The inflated guernsey broke apart instantly, releasing a wallop of air that flattened everyone standing within fifty feet of it. Big slabs of Miss Acey Deucy were draped over the fallen. The big bride went down too, but she bounced right back up, swinging the shotgun around recklessly, daring anyone to object to her attack on the cow.

The steam-driven teats whistled all at once, causing the giant bride to fire again. She missed the udder, but the blast broke out the front window of a barber shop across the street. The udder of the rubber cow was a separate contraption, and it now stood alone, held in place by its own framework. The man who controlled it had ducked down into his cockpit, which was inside the udder. He'd evidently jammed himself against the buttons that worked the udder's rotating mechanism and steam-driven teats. Steady jets of ear-piercing steam blasted out from the cowless teats as the udder revolved.

The giant bride took aim at the spinning udder, but before she could fire another shot, two deputy sheriffs sneaked up behind her and hit her with their saps. She went down hard, collapsing in a heap of white gown and blond hair. The blond hair had gathered itself in a pile at the side of her head. It was a wig, of course, and the giant bride was no bride at all. It was Guy Rampling, gone over the edge from the pressures of hard-nosed free enterprise. The deputies dragged him into the back seat of a squad car and drove away.

The man who had been driving the tractor climbed back up on the seat and started it. It roared into life. The driver's face broke into a big smile.

"Fuel line," he said. "Must of been some shit in the fuel line. She'll be okay now, Mr. Northberry."

"Wonderful," Northberry said, still pale and shaken from the attack on Miss Acey Deucy. "Now why don't you just haul that load of garbage the hell out of here so we can have a goddamned parade?"

I walked back to the milk trucks. The sun had come out and felt like a warm hand on my shoulder. When I got to the Founder float, I noticed that the papier-mâché had been melted down into a kind of mush by the downpour. The skeletal framework was half exposed, huge gobs of mush hanging from the chicken wire. The boys operating the ropes were now clearly visible from all angles. They were still having a good time, unaware of the incident up ahead, and Jules Brightman continued to wave his tattered, dripping arm and swivel his lidless eyes at the thinning crowd, a maniac smile on his lipless mouth.

Cruise was asleep, face against the steering wheel. I shook him gently by the shoulder. "Crank her up, Cruise," I said. "The roadblock's gone." I went over to Swede, who was still hanging onto the steering wheel for dear life and staring at my left front hubcap. "Let's do it, Swede," I said.

"Ya, ya, you bet," he said, nervous and still unconvinced.

"You can do it," I said, giving him a swig of brandy. He coughed gratefully.

"Let's look good," I said. "Let's drive these crates in formation, like we mean business."

"Why so fucken sharp, sport?" Cruise said. "Why act like we give a fat fuck?"

I thought about that for a couple of seconds. It seemed clear enough to me. "Why *not*, Cruise?" I said. "Why fucken *not*?"